DARCY BURKE

USA TODAY BESTSELLING AUTHOR

CAPTIVATING the SCOUNDREL

❧ LEGENDARY ROGUES ❧

D1264679

Captivating the Scoundrel
Copyright © 2019 Darcy Burke
All rights reserved.

ISBN: 1939713676
ISBN-13: 9781939713674

This is a work of fiction. Names, characters, places, and incidents are the product of the author's imagination or are used fictitiously. Any resemblance to actual events, locales, or persons, living or dead, is purely coincidental.

Book design © Darcy Burke.
Cover design © Sweet 'N Spicy Designs/Jaycee DeLorenzo.
Editor: Linda Ingmanson.

All rights reserved. Except as permitted under the U.S. Copyright Act of 1976, no part of this publication may be reproduced, distributed, or transmitted in any form or by any means, or stored in a database or retrieval system, without the prior written permission of the author.

For my brother, Rich

Because this book made me think of Monty Python and the Holy Grail. And that movie makes me think of you. In hindsight, I should have created a character named Sir Robin. Any book is improved with more sneaking away and buggering off.

Chapter One

August 1819, Glastonbury

"IF YOU WEREN'T you, you'd be dead."

Gideon Kersey, tense as he faced the man who'd been his mentor and who was now, at least secretly, his foe, allowed himself to flinch. Just slightly. Just enough for his opponent to notice.

"I would expect that," Gideon said.

Timothy Foliot's once-dark hair was almost entirely the color of metal, his umber eyes glowing with malice beneath the hundreds of candles lighting his great hall. He sat on a dais, looking down at Gideon in judgment like some medieval king of old. But then that was how Foliot liked to be regarded.

"And yet you stand before me, still breathing." Foliot sounded rather disappointed.

"Only because I have a sword in my hand," Gideon said wryly. He was no fool, at least not anymore. He knew who Foliot was and what he wanted, just as he now knew how Foliot had used him. It was time, however, for Gideon to turn the tables and use him instead.

Foliot leaned forward slightly, his interest clearly piqued. "Is it…?"

Gideon grasped the sword, which was still sheathed in its scabbard, and lifted it slightly. "Dyrnwyn. White-hilt. The Sword of Rhydderch Hael." All were names by which the ancient weapon was known.

"Let me see." The command was whispered but carried a weight that ensured Gideon understood it was not a request.

It was nothing Gideon hadn't already planned to do. In fact, he would do more than show it to him. He had a much larger goal in mind. Transferring the scabbard to his left hand, he clasped the handle and pulled the blade free.

The guards stationed about the room all stepped toward him, their gazes locked on his movements, their breath ceasing at once to cloak the room in absolute silence save the sing of steel as Dyrnwyn slid from its home.

If Gideon had expected awe from Foliot, he would have been disappointed. Instead, the man frowned. "Are you certain that's the sword?"

It was purportedly one of the Thirteen Treasures of Britain—magical items found by King Arthur and his knights in the late fifth or early sixth century and supposedly gifted to one of the knights, Gareth, on the occasion of his wedding. Foliot wouldn't be able to judge its authenticity by simply looking at it.

"You expected it to flame," Gideon said. That was the magical quality. And it only lit when wielded by a descendant of one of the Knights of the Round Table.

Foliot sat back in his chair, a large polished mahogany piece that looked more like a throne, with gemstones set into the top corners and a single ruby sparkling above his head. "My men said it did—in your grasp."

"It did. And it will. I believe I have to be threatened, meaning I have to wield the sword with deadly intent."

Foliot's dark brows arched. "So you meant to kill my men." His lip curled. "Give me one reason we shouldn't relieve you of that sword and slay you where you stand."

"I should add that using it in defense also...activates it. I wasn't seeking to kill them, only protect the woman they sought to harm—that Forrest fellow is an idiot." The woman was Amelia, whom his half brother Penn was in love with, and with whom he was pursuing the Heart of Llanllwch, another of the Thirteen Treasures. They were awaiting Gideon at an inn not far from here.

"Forrest *is* an idiot, but he's been very useful to me over the years."

"As have I," Gideon said evenly. Forrest was Amelia's estranged husband, an obstacle to the future she and Penn had hoped to share—or so Gideon assumed. They were meant to be together, and he hoped there would be a way for that to happen.

But things didn't usually work out the way Gideon wanted. In fact, they'd never done so. Which was why he was so bloody committed to making this time different.

The Thirteen Treasures of Britain are mine, and I will find them.

"Yes, you were useful," Foliot said, dragging him back to this chess match they were engaged in. "Until you lost the sword and disappeared only to turn up with the damned thing and use it against me."

"Not against *you*," Gideon clarified. "Against your men. Against Forrest in particular. You sought to double-cross his wife—take the Heart of Llanllwch from her and not give her the book you promised."

It was a fake heart, a decoy created to hide the real one. And the book held information that would lead them to the real one. Penn and Amelia, with Gideon's help, had pilfered the book that afternoon from

Forrest's house, which was situated on the edge of Foliot's estate.

Foliot sneered. "The book is gone. But I suspect you know that." He angled his head. Though a slight movement, the guards standing at the base of his dais took notice and moved toward Gideon.

He gripped the sword and lifted it in a defensive posture. The blade lit with a pale blue, nearly white flame, sending a supernatural glow over the hall.

Loud gasps were followed by the clap of Foliot's hands. His dark eyes glowed, and he moved forward in his ridiculous throne. "It's magnificent! Bring it closer." When Gideon hesitated, Foliot waved his hand. "No one shall trouble you. Not yet anyway. *Bring it closer.*" It was another command.

Gideon moved slowly toward the dais and ascended half of the six steps to the small platform where Foliot sat. Two guards flanked his throne, their hands on the pistols they wore at their sides.

Foliot rose. He was not a large man but of average height and build. His men towered above him, as did Gideon. However, elevated three stairs above him, Foliot looked down at him, rather at the sword, which had his full attention.

"Do you want to hold it?" Gideon offered it to the man and was surprised when Foliot retreated to his throne.

"No."

The flame diminished and disappeared.

"You believe the threat is gone?" Foliot asked as he retook his seat.

"For the moment." Gideon would never not feel threatened in Foliot's presence again. The man was single-minded in his desire to possess the Thirteen

Treasures. And he didn't care who he hurt—or killed—in the process. Because of that constant threat, Gideon was working hard to guard his emotions. The sword was sensitive to them and would react accordingly. With fear or aggression, the blade would ignite again, signaling everyone around him of his intentions.

The sword was an amazing weapon but would also be a detriment if not wielded properly.

It was that way with all the treasures, or so Gideon had deduced from his intensive research. From the moment nearly two years ago when Foliot had approached him about recovering these treasures, Gideon had worked to learn all he could. However, he'd relied on the man, who'd tutored him in Arthurian lore the past dozen years, to educate him.

But a month ago, everything had changed. Sinking to lows he'd never imagined possible, Gideon had stolen the sword from Penn's sister. She'd spent years searching for it, and he'd tied her and her now-husband up, then ridden away with her prize. All because he'd wanted so badly to belong to something, to please the man who'd been more of a father to him than anyone. The man who was now staring at him with cold calculation. The man Gideon now needed to woo.

"Yes, I know the book is gone," Gideon said. "I helped Bowen steal it."

The only sign of Foliot's anger was the whitening of his knuckles as he gripped the arm of his chair with his right hand. "Why would you do that?"

"Because Penn Bowen is the best—and perhaps only—person who can find the real Heart of Llanllwch. Don't you want it?"

"So the one in the Ashmolean museum *was* fake." Foliot didn't seem surprised.

The fake heart had been found by Amelia's grandfather decades ago and placed in the museum by the Order of the Round Table, a secret society dedicated to protecting the Thirteen Treasures. A society in which Foliot and Gideon were members.

"Yes, but it is a necessary piece to finding the real one." Which Penn would do and ultimately give to Gideon. Because it belonged to *him*.

"If you helped Bowen steal the book, why aren't you with him?" Foliot asked. His ire had faded, but his doubt was still quite tangible.

"He needs the dagger, and I know you have it." The dagger was linked to the heart and was the key to decoding the information Penn needed to find the heart.

Foliot leaned back and steepled his fingers beneath his chin. He studied Gideon in silence, something Gideon was quite used to. Granted, in the past, he hadn't been surrounded by henchmen who would attack him as soon as Foliot gave the word.

"You expect me to give you this dagger and trust that you'll return with the real heart. After you've already deprived me of the sword and stolen the White Book of Hergest."

"Have I deprived you of the sword?" Gideon asked with a half smile. He sheathed the blade and handed it to him. "Take it. You tasked me with finding Dyrnwyn. I failed before, but I have it now. And the heart is nearly within my grasp. Then there will be only eleven more to find."

The task sounded incredibly daunting, and it might very well take Gideon his entire life to complete. But he would find them, and *he*—not the Order that prided itself on power and secrecy—would keep them safe.

"You are still committed to our quest?" The doubt was lessening in Foliot's tone.

"My commitment has never faltered." Gideon sank to his knee in obeisance and offered him the sword as he bowed his head.

"You'll bring it to my vault."

Gideon lifted his head. Foliot rose from his throne and walked past him down the dais toward an alcove set into the back corner of the hall behind a tapestry depicting one of Arthur's knights slaying a dragon. Pivoting, Gideon trailed Foliot, aware of the guards who fell into step behind him.

The door to the vault was almost indiscernible in the alcove—it was simply part of the wall. A candle flickered in a sconce, casting just enough light to illuminate the small space. A guard stood at attention in the corner of the alcove.

Gideon had been to the vault just once before. The room was roughly ten by twenty feet, without windows, and sealed by a thick, solitary door secured with several locks. A second guard was stationed within.

As he had the previous time Gideon had come, Foliot removed a ring of keys from his pocket and went about unlocking the various mechanisms lining the door. Gideon counted five locks, but Foliot applied only four keys before replacing the ring back into his pocket. He shifted then, blocking Gideon's view, but as with his last visit, Gideon suspected Foliot kept the fifth and final key apart from the others on the ring.

Foliot pushed the door open and stepped inside. He didn't turn, but Gideon followed him in. The scent of old parchment and dust permeated the room. Gideon swept his gaze over the interior, lit with a wrought iron chandelier in the center of the room as well as sconces on the walls set at five-foot intervals.

The guard inclined his head as Foliot moved past him and did nothing, not even blink, when Gideon slid him a quick glance.

"Bring the sword over here," Foliot said, moving to the farthest wall, where there sat a locked chest. He withdrew the ring of keys once more and unlocked the chest. "Can't be too careful," he said, eyeing the sword. "Will it fit in here?"

Gideon went to the chest and lowered the sword toward the interior. It fit with just a few inches to spare. The weapon seemed to vibrate, as if it were trying to speak to Gideon. He would have said that was absurd, but given what the sword had already demonstrated, Gideon wasn't sure if it meant something or not.

The vibration continued as he put the sword into the chest, then it jolted him so that he drew his hand away. The weapon seemed unhappy about being put into the chest. Gideon shared that sentiment. He didn't want to relinquish the sword, but it was a temporary concession in pursuit of a larger goal.

I'll come back for you soon, he promised.

Foliot pointed to the corner of the chest, where a partially wrapped dagger lay. "That's the dagger you want. Go ahead and pick it up."

Gideon hesitated, but only for a moment. He plucked up the old weapon and moved the soft brown leather to view the writing etched into the blade. This was what Penn needed to find the heart.

"I was prepared to execute you," Foliot said. "But you've pleased me greatly. To have the sword, one of the two greatest of the Thirteen Treasures, is incredibly gratifying. And to know the heart is also within my grasp is thrilling." His eyes glittered in the flickering light, evidencing his excitement. "You'll give the dagger to Bowen?"

Gideon wrapped the blade in the leather. "Yes, and he'll find the heart and give it to me."

Foliot's brow creased. "You're confident in this?"

"I am. There are…reasons he will want to help me." Not the least of which was the guilt Penn felt for having stolen Gideon's birthright.

Stolen wasn't accurate, of course—Penn no more wanted to be the Earl of Stratton than Gideon wanted to lose the title. However, Penn was their father's legitimate firstborn son, and the vicar who could prove it was on his way to London to provide the evidence of Penn's birth to the House of Lords. Unless Penn could stop him, which he wholly intended to do.

If he couldn't, Gideon would be plain Gideon Kersey. Who just happened to be a descendant of one of the Knights of the Round Table. There were worse things. And Gideon had survived them.

"These reasons intrigue me, but we'll save them for another time," Foliot said. "Let us return to the hall for supper and to discuss our next steps. There are eleven other treasures to hunt."

"Indeed there are." Gideon meant to find every one of them and keep them from the Order and whatever plans they had, specifically those of the Camelot group, the faction inside the organization led by Foliot. While the Order sought to keep the treasures hidden, Camelot wanted to possess them and wield them. For what precisely, no one knew. Or would reveal.

"Will you finally tell me who else is searching for these items?" Gideon asked. There were other descendants—men Foliot had recruited to obtain the treasures. Men who would do his bidding. Men like Gideon, until he'd realized the murderous lengths to which Foliot would go to achieve his ends.

Foliot closed the chest and locked it, but not before Gideon cast a lingering stare at his sword. "You're going to miss it." Foliot chuckled. "It's safe here."

"Yes." But safe for what? Gideon still didn't know what Foliot planned to do with the treasures once he had them all, and Gideon wasn't sure he was in a position just yet to inquire. He'd done so in the past and had always been told that Camelot's objective was to keep them safe from those who didn't deserve them. The treasures were special and had been found by worthy men, who in turn had gifted them to Gareth, an esteemed and honorable knight.

"You don't sound convinced." Foliot clapped Gideon on the shoulder as they returned to the door of the vault. "You're a part of something bigger than yourself, Gideon. These treasures transcend us. We are merely custodians of a history we can only begin to understand."

Gideon resisted the urge to roll his eyes. Foliot liked to make grandiose statements and speak in enigmatic circles.

They moved out of the vault, and Foliot relocked the door. Gideon thought of the poor guard trapped inside without a chamber pot—at least Gideon hadn't seen one.

"How often do the guards change?" he asked, hoping to glean valuable information he could use later. He doubted Foliot would answer.

Surprisingly, however, he did. "Every two hours. Can't have them overtired or hungry. Or pissing themselves." He laughed as he led Gideon back to the hall. The contingent of henchmen who'd followed them to the vault accompanied them.

As they entered, a pair of maids bustled around the feasting table preparing the meal. Like the dais, the dining area looked as though it had leapt from the pages of a medieval tome.

Foliot went to the tall chair set at the head of the table. "Let us drink and eat."

Gideon would much rather have left immediately to deliver the dagger, but he didn't dare press Foliot. There was too much at stake, and he needed the man to believe Gideon was a committed member of Camelot, that finding the treasures for Foliot was his primary objective.

Taking the chair to Foliot's left, Gideon set the dagger on the table next to his place setting. "Is this to be a typical meal?" If so, they'd be here until midnight probably.

Foliot barked out a laugh. "Not quite. I don't have many people in residence. But that will change in the coming days. Surely you haven't forgotten my annual festival. It starts in just under a fortnight."

Though he called it a festival, it was a regular house party. Not regular, exactly, because it consisted of medieval activities, including a bloody jousting tournament. "No, I haven't forgotten. It's a singular event."

"You always seemed to enjoy yourself. Until you stopped coming." Foliot sniffed as the footman poured wine.

That had been two years ago, and Gideon had been in no condition to celebrate anything. He picked up his wineglass and took a fortifying drink.

"My apologies," Foliot said. "I didn't mean to be

insensitive. But thinking of that time leads me to what I must say next." He looked toward the guards who'd gone to stand at the dais after returning from the vault. They strode toward the table and flanked Gideon's chair, stoking his unease to the levels he'd felt when he'd stood before Foliot's throne.

"Is there something amiss?" Perhaps Gideon *was* still a fool. So far, his plan tonight had executed perfectly. Too perfectly.

"While I appreciate you bringing the sword to demonstrate your fealty, I will require more than that."

Sweat broke out on the back of Gideon's neck. This man was known to kill to get what he wanted, and Gideon had seen the violence committed by his henchmen. He struggled to keep his voice even. "I'm happy to provide whatever you demand." Happy didn't come close to the true emotion Gideon felt, but pretending to like and admire this man was critical.

"As you know, I have a daughter, and it has always been our intention that she would wed a descendant. Not just any descendant—but one who comes directly from Gareth's line."

Bloody fucking hell. Did he want Gideon to marry his daughter? Gideon's blood ran cold. He couldn't marry her. He wouldn't marry *anyone*. Not again. "You think I come from Gareth's line? You've never said for certain."

"No, but I think it's safe to say that's true. The treasures should work for all the descendants, but they definitely work for Gareth's progeny—and more easily, I should think. You'll marry my daughter and solidify your position in Camelot." He lifted his glass in a toast. "As my most trusted aide."

Gideon forced himself to say what he must. "I don't

wish to marry again." The memory of Rose pierced his heart, and he pushed it away.

"I can understand that." He lowered the glass but didn't set it on the table. "However, I'm not asking you to. It's simply what's required. If you wish to continue the quest for the Thirteen Treasures, you must demonstrate your full commitment. If you don't... Well, I'd rather not contemplate that." He smiled briefly before lifting the glass once more. "To your marriage. You'll like Daphne very much." He looked at the guards, who moved closer to Gideon's chair, then inclined his head toward Gideon's wineglass.

Realizing this was not the time for a fight, Gideon picked up his glass and tapped it to Foliot's. "To wedded bliss."

Foliot grinned. "That's my boy." He took a hearty drink and set his glass down, then motioned for the footman to begin serving the first course.

Gideon had met his daughter at the medieval festivals, but barely remembered her. She'd been a child, if memory served. No, at his last festival three years ago, she'd been a young lady, but he couldn't bring her image to mind.

Not that it mattered. He had no intention of marrying her. He'd say what he needed to say and take one day at a time as he worked toward his goal.

Dipping his spoon into his soup, Foliot continued jovially as if he hadn't just threatened Gideon. "I daresay you'll fall quite in love with my Daphne. She's as intelligent and beautiful as they come. And well versed in Arthurian studies. She'll be a marvelous partner for you." He smiled at Gideon before sipping from his spoon.

Not only did the man expect Gideon to marry his

daughter, he expected him to fall in love with her too? Well, that was never going to happen. His capacity for love was almost nonexistent.

Itching with anticipation to leave with the dagger, Gideon suffered through the interminable dinner, followed by a medieval musical entertainment. It was well into the middle of the night before Foliot stood to retire. He'd said it wouldn't be a typical meal, but it was. The only thing missing was one of Foliot's women, who typically joined him after the meal.

Throughout the evening, he'd extolled his daughter's virtues and restated his threats in every way imaginable. Gideon would marry his daughter if he wanted a future in Camelot. Hell, if he wanted a future at all. The fact that this was a horrible basis for a marriage, let alone one that was supposed to include *love*, seemed quite lost on Foliot. The man was deranged.

And Gideon didn't trust him.

"I'll expect to see you back here for the festival. With the heart in hand. We'll announce your betrothal then."

Foliot left the hall, and Gideon didn't waste time departing. He was all too aware of the guards watching every step he took. Foliot would have him followed, of course, and probably Penn as well.

Gideon's objective had just become much more difficult. To avoid being leg-shackled to Foliot's chit, he needed to find the treasures and take down Camelot. Time was now against him, along with everything else.

He was playing a very dangerous game. And Gideon meant to win.

Chapter Two

HOLLYHAVEN WAS A charming, well-apportioned house backed by a small woodland. Green pastures rolled before it, and an inviting curl of smoke whispered from a rear chimney. It was lovely and picturesque and apparently housed one of the finest medieval libraries outside a university.

The coach stopped in the drive, and Daphne Foliot waited for her coachman to open the door. Only it wasn't him but Argus, her manservant, rather, her personal guard according to her father, who greeted her. On occasion, he beat the coachman to the step.

Daphne nodded at him as she descended, and then walked toward the house. The door opened before she reached the stoop, and a middle-aged woman wearing an apron greeted her. "Good afternoon, welcome to Hollyhaven. You must be Mrs. Guilford."

"I am indeed," Daphne said brightly, though it was a lie since she was in truth Miss Foliot. But it didn't do to gallivant around Wales and southwestern England as a miss.

The housekeeper opened the door wide in invitation. "Mr. Bowen is expecting you." Daphne had corresponded with Mr. Bowen about the manuscript she wished to view, and they'd agreed upon her visiting today.

"Thank you." Daphne walked into the reception hall, where she was greeted by gleaming dark wood and a plush red-and-moss-green patterned rug.

"This way," the housekeeper said, gesturing to the left where a door stood ajar. "Would you care for me to take your hat?"

"Oh, yes, thank you." Daphne untied the ribbons beneath her chin and handed the bonnet to the housekeeper.

She took the hat and went to the open door, pushing it wider and announcing, "Mrs. Guilford is here to see you." Stepping aside, the housekeeper smiled at Daphne and allowed her to go inside.

"Good afternoon. Welcome to Hollyhaven." The deep voice greeted her as she entered, and she offered a curtsey to her host. Tall with dark hair streaked with a bit of gray and his complexion a light olive, the scholar was far more attractive than she'd expected. What *had* she expected? A wizened old man with spectacles, probably.

"Thank you, Mr. Bowen. I'm so grateful for this opportunity to view your manuscript."

"It's always my pleasure to share my library when I am able. Come and sit. I have the text ready for you on my worktable." He indicated a small book that lay open on a long table in the center of the impressive library. Dark wood shelves lined the walls, and a bay window overlooked the drive and front lawn.

Daphne moved toward the table, feeling a bit awestruck. She'd seen copies of this story, but Mr. Bowen possessed the oldest known version. She dearly hoped she'd find what she was looking for.

"Good afternoon." A feminine voice drew Daphne's attention to the doorway. A very pretty woman with blond hair entered the library and, given the way her gaze connected with Mr. Bowen and the intimate smiles exchanged, Daphne assumed she was his wife.

"Margery, allow me to present Mrs. Guilford. Mrs. Guilford, this is Mrs. Bowen."

"How do you do?" Daphne gave another curtsey.

"Rhys said you came to look at the Arthurian story that was likely written by Elidyr. At least that's my husband's supposition, and I must confess, he is rather brilliant." Mrs. Bowen looked toward her husband in keen admiration.

"His scholarship on the subject of Welsh texts is unparalleled," Daphne said. "If he says it was written by Elidyr, who am I to dispute him?"

"Did I hear someone say Elidyr?" Another gentleman came into the library. He was tall and broad-shouldered, with the dark complexion of a Welshman like Mr. Bowen. However, where Bowen's eyes were also dark, this man's were a vivid blue. He was accompanied by a woman, blonde like Mrs. Bowen, but the similarity ended there.

"Mrs. Guilford, we have a rather full house at the moment. This is my son, Pennard Bowen, and his betrothed, Amelia. They are to be wed tomorrow."

"Pleased to meet you," the younger Mr. Bowen said.

Daphne bobbed again, thinking she would surely perfect her curtsey before the day was out. "The pleasure is mine, Mr. Bowen."

"Please call me Penn. My father is Mr. Bowen."

"Are we holding a family meeting or conducting research? Either way, you can't think to leave me out." This came from yet another woman who entered the library. She was young, also Welsh, with ebony hair and dark eyes. She had her father's coloring but her mother's chin and mouth. This was undoubtedly another child of the Bowens.

"Mrs. Guilford, this is my daughter, Cate," Mr.

Bowen said. "And her new husband, Elijah, the Earl of Norris."

Daphne dipped an even deeper curtsey since they were peerage. "It's my honor to make your acquaintance," she said.

Norris was even taller than the Bowen men, with blond hair and a rigid bearing she would swear was due to a military background. She'd grown up with plenty of army men who worked for her father after leaving their commissions. Papa liked to help former soldiers, and so there were a great many of them either employed on his estate or living there as tenants.

"Everyone, Mrs. Guilford is here to see the Elidyr text."

The countess came toward Daphne and drew her to the table. "How fascinating and wonderful to meet another female antiquary. You are an antiquary, aren't you?"

"I wouldn't say so, no. At least not in the general sense. I am a scholar of Morgan le Fay. Or Morgana. Or whatever name you'd like to give her."

The countess's dark eyes lit with appreciation. "Splendid! Any female scholar is more than welcome here. I'm an antiquary myself, as is my brother."

"I also happen to work at the Ashmolean Museum," Penn said dryly.

Daphne had heard of him, of course—both in the antiquarian community at large and specifically from her father. Just as he'd told her of the elder Mr. Bowen. The rest of the people in the library were unknown to her. Though Mr. Bowen had invited her to come, she felt like a bit of an intruder. But perhaps that was because of what she'd just learned—that there was to be a wedding tomorrow. She turned her head toward

Penn and his betrothed. "May I offer my felicitations on your marriage?"

"Thank you," Penn said. "But that's not nearly as exciting as why you're here. Are you hoping to learn something new from the text?"

His soon-to-be wife elbowed him in the ribs. "It's plenty exciting," she said softly but with heat.

"The most exciting day of my life, darling." He brushed a kiss against her temple, and for a brief moment, Daphne wondered what that might feel like. Then she reminded herself that she didn't care.

Addressing Penn's question, she said, "I am hopeful this text includes a clue about Morgan. It is a personal endeavor to read everything that may be associated with her."

"What a wonderful enterprise," the countess said. "I wager you know her rather well."

"As well as I know myself." It was perhaps the most honest thing Daphne had said that day.

"Well, don't let us keep you," Mr. Bowen said, approaching the table and holding out a chair positioned in front of the book. "Please sit. I only ask that you remove your gloves and don one of the pairs we use for handling my manuscripts. Oh, blast." He turned from the chair. "Where are the gloves?"

The air in the room seemed to compress and the temperature to rise. Someone else entered—a man. He was nearly as tall as Penn, with the same dark hair. However, his eyes were deep gray, like a storm moving over the tor.

He picked up a pair of gloves from a table near the door and brought them to where she stood between Mr. Bowen and the countess. "I believe I heard Mrs. Thomas saying she'd just laundered these."

"Yes, I thought I'd put them on the worktable already," Mr. Bowen said. "Gideon, allow me to present Mrs. Guilford. She's a scholar of Morgan le Fay and has come to read the Elidyr text. Mrs. Guilford, this is the Earl of Stratton, a cousin to us."

"It's my pleasure to make your acquaintance," Daphne said, dropping into yet another curtsey. If she had to do so again, she wondered if her knees would hold up. Or maybe her wobbly knees were due to this newest arrival. There was something darkly attractive about him, dangerous almost. Perhaps that was because he hadn't smiled at her as everyone else had done. Instead, he affected a slight bow, as if he could barely be bothered.

He murmured, "Mrs. Guilford."

She was horrified to feel a tremor in her belly at the timbre of his voice. Shaking away the sensation, she returned her attention to Mr. Bowen. "May I?"

"Of course. Would you like me to send everyone away? You needn't suffer an audience if it will distract you."

"It's quite all right." There was something…warm about the family clogging the room. And that was just it: they were a family. She'd always wanted one, but instead had only her father and the myriad hirelings he'd paid to watch over her since her mother had disappeared. Her gaze drifted briefly to Mrs. Bowen. How nice it must be to have a mother.

Banishing the maudlin thoughts, Daphne sat at the table and began to read the manuscript.

"You read Old Welsh?" the countess asked.

Daphne lifted her head and looked across the table to where the young lady had moved to stand. "Yes."

"How wonderful. I can't believe we've never met."

She sat down opposite Daphne, and color splashed across her cheeks. "Forgive me. I shan't interrupt you again."

Her excitement was contagious. Daphne hadn't ever met another young woman with interests similar to hers, and she found herself wanting to speak with her. But she didn't have much time—she had to travel to Glastonbury tomorrow. Besides, these people had celebrations to commence.

Daphne returned to reading and was soon engrossed in the tale of Arthur's battle at Badon Hill. She wasn't sure how much time had elapsed before she finished, but when she looked up, the countess was still seated across from her, and Mr. Bowen sat at the end of the table to her left.

Had everyone else gone? She turned to look about the room and saw that the others were gathered in a seating area near the large bay window, save the Earl of Stratton, who leaned against the bookshelves studying a book of his own. His head lifted, and his gaze found hers.

She looked away abruptly. There was something vaguely familiar about him, but she wasn't sure if that was true or simply her mind wanting to have a connection with him.

"Did you find what you wanted?" the countess asked eagerly. "I love that story. Elidyr was an excellent writer."

"He was indeed. I'd heard of this version of the tale, of course, but I'm quite pleased to finally read it for myself." Daphne hadn't answered her question. She hadn't found precisely what she wanted, but she also hadn't found anything she *didn't* want to find. Meaning, her theory was still possible. "I was hoping the text would name Arthur's healer."

"The man who gave him the cloak?" the countess asked.

Daphne's mouth curled into a smile. "Who says it was a man?"

The countess drew in a sharp breath. "You think it was Morgan. She is sometimes his healer, depending on what you're reading."

"Precisely. Those tales are far closer to who she really was."

"Instead of the evil, manipulative woman later texts paint her to be." The countess scoffed. "Have you written anything on the subject? I'd love to read it."

She had, in fact, not that anyone had ever read her writing. "You'd want to?"

"Absolutely. If you'd consider sharing."

Delight and pride clashed with fear and anxiety. She'd long wanted to be recognized for her intellect and to be able to contribute to Arthurian scholarship, but she was, alas, a woman. "I...would...yes." She couldn't shake the hesitation and skepticism from her voice. Her father had supported her studies but hadn't wanted her to share them—it was part of the devil's bargain she'd made with him several years ago.

"Should we have some refreshments?" Mrs. Bowen asked, rising from the settee in front of the window.

"I don't wish to keep you," Daphne said. "You've a wedding to prepare for."

"Just stay for a bit," the countess said with a smile. "I'd dearly love to hear your theories about Morgan as a healer."

Daphne glanced around at the wealth of knowledge these people represented and decided she could stay for a bit. Perhaps they would know something about the cloak. She smiled at the countess. "If you insist."

"Excellent. You must call me Cate. I feel as if we are going to be great friends." Cate looped her arm through Daphne's and led her to the settee her mother had vacated. Mrs. Bowen left the library, presumably to organize the refreshments.

Penn's betrothed, Amelia, sat on Daphne's other side, while Penn and Mr. Bowen claimed two empty chairs, and a third was occupied by Lord Norris. Stratton didn't leave his position near the bookshelf, nor did he abandon his book. She wondered what he was reading.

Daphne drew off the gloves Mr. Bowen had provided. "I think it's quite obvious that later stories featuring Morgan present an overdramatized version of her—to better serve the men's stories."

"That sounds accurate," Cate said, rolling her eyes. "You believe she was a real person, then?" Cate took the gloves from Daphne and set them on a table next to the settee.

"Of course. Don't you?" Daphne had presumed so, given the woman's interest, but that was a supposition she perhaps should not have made.

"I do, actually." She flicked a glance toward her brother and another one toward the Earl of Stratton, who didn't look up from his book.

If they believed the people in these stories and legends were real, did they also believe in the Thirteen Treasures? That was something Daphne wouldn't ask. The less attention those items received, the better.

"Have you any definitive proof?" This question came from the woman on her left, Amelia.

"Not in my possession, no." But there was a text by a contemporary of Arthur and his knights—a monk named Anarawd—and she believed there must be mention of Morgan in it. Mr. Bowen purportedly had a copy of it, but denied its existence. Daphne looked at the bookshelves and wondered if it was there. It seemed likely the people in the room knew about this text, but again, she perhaps shouldn't make assumptions. Which was why she wouldn't bring it up.

"But you still believe," Cate said with a hint of admiration. "You mustn't ever stop, even when people doubt you. I had a quest to find something once, and I persisted until I found it." The pride in her voice was unmistakable, as was the glow of love between her and her husband as they exchanged a warm glance.

Daphne was moved and inspired by the woman's confidence—and her success. "What did you find?"

"Oh, just an old sword. I gave it to Penn." Cate had hesitated just a bare moment, but enough to draw Daphne's curiosity. She suspected it was more than just an old sword, but she also suspected further queries would go unanswered. Antiquaries could be incredibly verbose but occasionally tight-lipped when it came to matters of treasure. And so much of their world involved treasure—at least to someone. What was an old sword to most could be the most fascinating thing to someone else.

Or it could possess value and import beyond anyone's imagination, like the cloak Daphne was committed to finding. A cloak she believed Morgan had made. "Fulfilling your quest must have been incredibly gratifying," she said softly.

"Yes, quite. My husband would tell you it was the happiest moment of my life, but he'd be wrong." She grinned at him.

"I wouldn't say that," the earl said. "I'm arrogant

enough to say the happiest moment is when you married me."

Cate laughed, along with most of the others in the room. "One of many happiest moments, along with you allowing me to sort through the former earl's antiquities." She leaned close to Daphne and whispered, "Elijah wanted to sell it all off."

Daphne had heard that a previous Lord Norris had possessed an astonishing collection. "What a travesty that would have been."

"Indeed, but we shall sell some of it. The estate came with a bit of debt, I'm afraid."

"If you find anything pertaining to Morgan, I do hope you'll let me know," Daphne said. She had no idea if the Norris collection included any such thing, but it was always worthwhile to ask.

"Certainly. And how shall I write to you? We must establish a correspondence, because I definitely plan to read your papers."

"You can write to me at Hawthorn Cottage in Keynsham." It had been her mother's family's home, and now it was Daphne's primary residence. She'd moved there last year from Ashridge Court with her father's permission. She had a small staff, including her personal guard, as well as her great-aunt Ellie.

"Excellent," Cate said. "And you may write to me at Cosgrove. We'll be going back there after the wedding. I do hope you'll come for a visit some time."

"I should be delighted." Especially if she found anything relating to Morgan, though Daphne thought she would enjoy just talking with Cate and sharing information.

Mrs. Bowen returned with the housekeeper. Each carried a tray laden with drinks and cakes and biscuits.

The refreshments were arranged on a table near their seating area, and soon everyone was rising to fetch something to eat or drink. Daphne took the opportunity to peruse the bookshelves in case something spectacular leapt out at her—such as the name Anarawd. As if Bowen would keep such a valuable item out in the open or that it would be so clearly labeled.

Instead, what leapt at her was the stoic Earl of Stratton. Well, not leapt, precisely, but he did approach her. "You look as though you'd like to spend the next week in here with Rhys's books."

She pivoted toward him. "I would, in fact. I see your interest is similar." She inclined her head toward the book in his hand. His forefinger was inserted between the pages to keep his place. "What are you reading?"

"Just an old poem."

"Is that like Cate's 'old sword'?" The words fell out of her mouth before she could censor herself. "Pardon me," she murmured, turning from him and edging away along the bookshelf.

"Are you suggesting this book and Cate's artifact are more than what we say?"

She shrugged. "I find with antiquarians, you can never be quite certain they speak the truth." She cast him a cautious look, thinking she should probably stop talking entirely. Better still, she should take her leave before she said something truly regretful.

He surprised her by chuckling. "You are, of course, correct. But this really is just an old poem." He opened the tome and showed it to her. It was written in Middle English.

"'Pierce the Ploughman's Crede,'" she said, recognizing the lines.

"Very good. Tell me, if I pull a random text from the shelf and read a few lines, will you be able to guess what it is?"

That sounded like a terribly fun game. And she wanted to play it—with him. Her heart picked up speed. "Probably."

"Astonishing," he whispered.

"Mrs. Guilford," Cate said, "would you care for some tea or lemonade? My mother makes the best lemonade."

"Mrs. Guilford…" the earl mused. "Why didn't Mr. Guilford accompany you today?"

"Because he's dead." Nonexistent, actually, but dead would suffice. "And you needn't apologize. We were wed briefly before he succumbed to a fever, and it was several years ago."

"So young to be widowed," he said. "I wouldn't put you at five and twenty."

"Next year," she said, wondering how their conversation had become so intimate and yet felt so…normal. Daphne preferred to keep her secrets—and her lies—very close. "Please excuse me." She turned and went to have a glass of lemonade before the astute earl learned anything else about her.

When Daphne arrived on the other side of the library, Cate asked her what she wanted, then poured the lemonade. As she sipped the tart beverage, Daphne stole a glance toward Stratton. He'd gone back to reading his book.

It was just as well. She didn't have time, patience, or interest in flirting with anyone. Pity, because it had felt divine.

It was past time to take her leave, unfortunately. Between the familial atmosphere, the tantalizing wealth of books, and the enigmatic allure of the earl, Daphne could have happily stayed until they turned her out.

"I must be going," she said. "I've intruded quite long enough." She turned to Mr. Bowen. "Thank you so very much for allowing me to read the Elidyr text. It was most enlightening."

"I hope you'll return another time—when we aren't in the midst of a wedding. You look as if you'd like to spend some time perusing the library."

"You are too kind." Indeed he was. Daphne's own father wouldn't have extended such an invitation. He guarded his books and antiquities with an almost paranoid obsession.

"I'll just fetch your bonnet from the hall," Mrs. Bowen offered.

Everyone bid Daphne farewell as she started toward the hall. Just as she crossed the threshold, a masculine voice came from behind her. "You forgot your gloves."

It was the Earl of Stratton, of course. His dark gray eyes stared down at her as if he could see well past her secrets and lies. It was rather unnerving. But also strangely intoxicating.

She took the gloves from him, and their bare fingers touched. The connection dashed through her like a hummingbird taking flight. "You seem to be the bearer of gloves today."

"However I may be of service." He offered her a slight bow. "Good day, Mrs. Guilford."

"Good day, my lord." She dipped another brief curtsey before turning to take her hat from Mrs. Bowen.

"Have a safe journey," she said with a warm smile. "You're not traveling to Keynsham tonight, I hope."

Setting the bonnet on her head, Daphne retied the

ribbons beneath her chin while holding her gloves in one hand. "No. I'll stay in Monmouth tonight and leave for Keynsham in the morning." After spending the night at home, she'd continue on to Glastonbury, to Ashridge Court for her father's medieval-themed house party.

Mr. Bowen's brow creased. "I'm sorry I can't offer you a room here."

Daphne was a bit sorry too. Though she'd spent a short amount of time with them, she liked these people, particularly Cate. "I wouldn't want to intrude on the wedding. It was kind enough of you to have me today. Thank you again." Daphne took her leave and pulled her gloves on as she strode to the coach.

"Find what you wanted?" Argus asked as he helped her into the vehicle.

"Yes." But not what she'd hoped. She was no closer to proving Morgan was Arthur's healer or finding the cloak she'd made for him.

As the coach drove away from Hollyhaven, she shook away the lingering effects of the Earl of Stratton's attentions. She'd so wanted to find the cloak before her father's party so that she could return home triumphant—and perhaps in possession of something to tempt her father to negotiate.

That was not to be, however, and she chastised herself for nursing the foolish dream. She didn't know if she'd ever find the cloak, and she was all but certain she'd never talk her father out of the marriage he intended to arrange for her. Still, meeting Cate, a woman of distinct courage and persistence, had given her a beacon of hope.

She'd cling to that until she had nothing left.

Chapter Three

GIDEON WIPED A hand over his tired eyes. He'd read the poem a dozen times now and hadn't gleaned a damned thing. There had to be something. It included one of the Thirteen Treasures—the cloak—and someone had come specifically to see it.

Someone with dark auburn hair and eyes the color of sherry ringed with moss. And a touch that had sparked something he'd long thought extinguished.

Snorting in disgust, he flipped back to the start of the poem. He hadn't meant to flirt with her that afternoon. It had been a long time since he'd flirted with anyone. But old habits were apparently very hard to break, especially when in the presence of someone who stirred the man he used to be.

The man he refused to become again.

"What the devil are you doing in here at this hour?" Penn came into the library carrying a lamp, which he set at the opposite end of the table.

Gideon sat back in his chair and blinked at his half brother. "I'm reading. The more important question is what you're doing in here. You're getting married in a matter of hours."

"Which is why I needed a drink." Penn went to the sideboard at the other end of the library in the corner. "Whisky?" He didn't turn as he asked the question.

"Please." Gideon rose, stretching his back and massaging his nape.

Penn returned and handed him a glass, then they

moved to the seating area—drinks were not allowed at the worktable. Rhys had very stringent rules about his library, which both Gideon and Penn had heard about since they were boys.

"Looks like you're reading the Elidyr text," Penn said, dropping into a chair while Gideon sprawled on the settee, crossing his feet on one end while he leaned on the other.

"I was."

"There's nothing in there," Penn said. "Since we returned with the heart a few days ago, we've scoured this library for clues about the Thirteen Treasures."

"Then why did Mrs. Guilford want to read it?" Who the hell was she anyway?

Penn sipped his whisky. "Because she's obsessed with Morgan. You know how these things work. You remember my sister's obsession with Dyrnwyn. Which made your stealing it from her especially egregious."

Gideon flinched. "I shall never live that down."

"Of course you will."

"But I shouldn't. I can never atone for what I did."

"I'd argue that risking yourself to help us find the Heart of Llanllwch was a fairly good attempt." Penn narrowed his eyes at Gideon. "It's time you told me how you got the dagger."

Since arriving the day before, Gideon had shrugged off their questions in the interest of focusing on the wedding. There was no way he was going to reveal that he'd agreed to marry some unknown chit. "I had to give him the sword." At Penn's look of fury, Gideon scowled and held up his free hand. "Save your outrage. It's a temporary loan."

Penn's dark brows pitched low over his eyes. "Does Foliot know that?"

"It doesn't matter. That's what it is. And I need the heart."

"I told you I would give it to you. But not so you could give it to him." Penn practically growled the last.

"I have to prove my loyalty," Gideon said. "You're going to have to trust me that I'll get it all back. I have a plan." If he could find the cloak, which he must since he intended to find all the treasures, he could use it to steal the items back. The cloak would make him invisible.

"I don't suppose you'd care to share that plan?"

"Not just yet." Gideon didn't want their help. Not because he didn't trust them, but because he didn't want to endanger them. "This is my responsibility, Penn. I have to find all the treasures and keep them safe from the Order and especially from Camelot."

"And yet you've delivered one right to them and plan to give them another. Damn it, Gideon, you shouldn't do this alone."

"I should involve you and Amelia?"

"Me, yes, but not Amelia."

Gideon let out a harsh laugh. "You really think she'd let you do it without her?"

It was Penn's turn to scowl as he took a drink of whisky.

"I promise I will ask for help when—and if—I need it," Gideon said. "Now tell me about how your man Egg plans to find this vicar."

Penn blew out a frustrated breath and kicked his legs out straight from the chair, crossing them at the ankles. "He's going to leave immediately after the wedding. The vicar was last seen in Gloucester."

"And you have someone stationed in London?"

Penn nodded. "Charlie—my most loyal assistant at

Oxford. He's loitering about the Lord Chancellor's office to see if the vicar shows up."

"And what if we don't find him?" It was a possibility they had to accept—and discuss.

"At all? That would remove any obstacle," Penn said with a wry stare. "If you mean what if we don't find him in time, I'll try to convince Parliament that I'm not who he says I am."

Gideon snorted. "That doesn't sound particularly effective."

"We'll find him. We *must*." Penn sounded determined, which Gideon appreciated. "Have you been to Stratton Hall?"

"No."

"You should go there now. If the writ of summons has been dispatched, you could simply go to London and claim the title. If you're the earl, it won't matter what the vicar says."

"You don't know that."

"You can't argue that it would strengthen your position." He was probably right, but Gideon didn't have time to go to Stratton Hall, which was two days in the opposite direction of Glastonbury, nor did he have time to go to London.

"Does Parliament even send writs when it's prorogued?" Gideon mused. "In any case, I need to return to Glastonbury."

"Bloody hell, Gideon, what's more important: claiming the title you deserve or endangering yourself with Foliot?"

Gideon smiled. "You put it that way and it seems silly for me to go to Glastonbury." He sipped his whisky.

"But you'll do it anyway," Penn grumbled. "Has

anyone ever told you that you're stubborn?"

"On occasion." Gideon's father had made stubborn into an art form. In fact, the more you told him not to do something, the more he did it. Which was probably how he'd ended up so far from respectability. And Gideon didn't want to repeat his father's mistakes. "Do you know anyone we can send to Stratton Hall to see if the writ has been received there?"

"I'll find someone," Penn said. "And where should I send word?"

"Ashridge Court."

Penn pushed out a frustrated breath. "Will you go to London to answer the writ?"

Despite Penn's growing irritation, Gideon kept his voice even. "Eventually."

"Dammit, Gideon, I do *not* want to be the earl."

"You'd probably be a better one than me." People would certainly like him more. Between Gideon's licentious past and the rumors surrounding his wife's death, his reputation was exceedingly poor. And most didn't know he'd added theft to his accomplishments.

Penn narrowed his eyes. "I know what you're thinking, and stop it. You aren't a bad person—you aren't your father."

"No, I'm not him, but that doesn't excuse my behavior." He took another drink. "Let's not discuss that. I'd rather talk about your wedding tomorrow."

"In a moment." Penn uncrossed his ankles and drew his legs up to sit forward in the chair, pinning Gideon with an earnest gaze. "You've more than proven yourself to me—and to my father. We want to support you in your quest, however we can. Promise me you'll ask for help if you need it. Particularly if you're in danger."

Gideon looked down at the glass in his hand, finding it easier to contemplate the amber color of the liquid than look at Penn. "I appreciate you saying that. I will ask for help—if I need it." He lifted his gaze to Penn's. "I promise." He was just going to make damned sure he *didn't* need it. He wouldn't imperil them. This was *his* quest, his responsibility. "Now tell me what you have planned after you and Amelia are wed."

"Hopefully not be an earl." Penn exhaled. "We planned on going to London. Amelia hasn't spent much time there. Then we'll return to Oxford. She has already announced her intention to completely reorganize and potentially refurbish my house." He shuddered. "Perhaps marriage wasn't the best idea."

Gideon knew he spoke in jest. "After all you've been through together, nothing will keep you from marrying her, so don't even joke about it." He laughed before taking another drink.

Penn grinned. "True." He lifted his glass in a toast and sipped the whisky before sobering. "Would you do it again?" he asked softly. "Marry, I mean."

"I have no interest in doing so." That much was true. Though he was apparently on his way to finding himself leg shackled, unless he could manage to complete his quest before that came to pass. He had no idea how quickly Foliot would push them to wed. Perhaps his daughter would refuse, particularly when she learned of Gideon's background.

He could only hope.

"You loved Rose," Penn said.

"I did." He hadn't at first. He'd admired her. Sweet and gentle, with a warm sense of humor, she'd inspired him to strive to be a better man. But when she'd fallen from her horse and died just a few months into their union, he'd realized the affection he'd begun to feel toward her was love. More than two years later, the loss pierced him still. As did the rumors that he'd killed her. He could suffer gossip and innuendo. He had for years and simply ignored it for the palaver it was. But hearing people say he'd killed the most beautiful thing that had ever happened to him cut deep, and it scarred her memory.

"What are you two still doing up?" Rhys came into the library wearing a banyan over his pantaloons. His gaze fell on the whisky in their hands. "Toasting Penn's wedding?"

Gideon pulled his feet from the settee and sat up. "Indeed we were." He raised his glass. "To Penn and Amelia—"

"Wait, I need one." Rhys rushed to the sideboard and poured himself a glass, then rejoined them, taking the end of the settee Gideon's feet had just vacated. "Continue."

"To Penn and Amelia. May their union be long and filled with love and laughter."

Rhys lifted his glass. "Hear, hear!"

They all drank, and Gideon finished his, reasoning it was time to evade further conversation. He rose and crossed the room to deposit his glass on the sideboard.

"You getting a refill?" Penn asked.

Gideon turned and came back to them. "No. I'm heading to bed."

Rhys frowned. "But I just got here."

"Gideon doesn't want us to lecture him about not returning to Foliot's estate."

"Ah." Rhys looked toward his foster son. "I trust you already took care of that?"

Penn nodded. "For all the good it did me. I also

encouraged him to see if a writ of summons had been issued, and if so, to drag his arse to London."

Rhys transferred his gaze to Gideon. "Wise, if a bit crass, advice."

"I'll let Penn fill you in on our plan—I've every intention of claiming the earldom, but I would feel much better about things if we knew that vicar would keep quiet."

"We'll find him, Gideon. I'd be a terrible earl, and I don't want it." Penn's intent to locate the vicar was as strong as Gideon's to hunt down the remaining eleven treasures.

Gideon went back to the table and the open Elidyr text. "I was in here reading when Penn found me."

Rhys joined him, having left his glass of whisky somewhere else. "You're looking for clues?"

"I need to find the cloak." Gideon pivoted toward him. "I haven't the slightest idea where to look. When I think of Penn finding the heart and Cate finding the sword, I just don't know if I have their ability."

Rhys smiled. "Of course you do. It's a family attribute." He winked, and Gideon couldn't help but smile. They were all related—Rhys was a distant cousin of Gideon and Penn as well as being Penn's foster father. That relationship was the reason Penn's mother had given him to Rhys to raise. She'd been ill and wanted to ensure Penn would be well cared for and, most importantly, kept away from his true father, the Earl of Stratton. The man had poisoned everything he touched, driving both his wives away but maintaining his grasp on Gideon. And that was how Gideon had been poisoned too.

Gideon shoved the unpleasant emotions away. "I don't know if I agree that I possess such an attribute, but I will at least try. For now, my best opportunity is to work with Foliot. He's been searching for these treasures for some time. He may have information we don't."

"I would expect that," Penn said, joining them at the table. "Father, can you think of anything we've forgotten about the cloak? Anything that may be a place to start?"

Rhys brought the book in front of him and turned the pages. "The cloak is only mentioned in a few stories, most notably *Culhwch and Olwen*. And of course it's mentioned in the Anarawd text, which most people don't know about." He looked over at Gideon. "Does Foliot know of that?"

Gideon shrugged. "I have no idea. Remind me what it says."

"It's really just a list of the Thirteen Treasures, which includes the cloak," Rhys said. He flipped to the back of the book and exhaled. "I've long wondered if there could be more texts by Anarawd out there somewhere. It was your grandfather's family who knew of it and kept it safe."

"Do you think my grandfather might have had something else buried in his library?" He'd died two years ago so they couldn't ask him.

"If there is, it's doubtful he knew of it." Rhys returned his gaze to Gideon. "It's time I share something with you. When your grandfather became ill—it was just after you wed—he sent me some things he meant for you to have. He was very specific that I not give them to you until after your father died. He worried that you might share them with him, and he didn't trust your father." Rhys winced. "I hope you understand my need to honor your grandfather's wishes."

"I do." Though it pained Gideon to acknowledge that was necessary. Whatever his father's sins, he'd always loved Gideon, and for that reason, Gideon had been vulnerable. Even after he'd realized the depths of his father's depravity.

Rhys went to the bookshelf behind his desk. Gideon's heart had picked up speed, and now he held his breath in anticipation. Rhys had his back to them so they couldn't see what he did, but the bookshelf sprang open.

Gideon sucked in a breath and looked toward Penn. "Did you know about that?"

"The room? Yes." Penn's brow furrowed. "But not that he was keeping things left to you from your grandfather."

Rhys came back to the library with a chest that was nearly three feet wide and perhaps two feet tall. He set it on the table and handed Gideon a key.

Gideon turned the implement over in his hand and thought of his grandfather—Lord Nash, his mother's father. He hadn't been allowed to see him after his mother had left, but they'd corresponded. He'd been warm and intelligent and would have been a far better father to Gideon than his own.

Without further hesitation, he unlocked the coffer and opened the lid. Lined with a thick purple fabric akin to velvet, the interior smelled of parchment and age. Inside were several items—some jewelry, a few books, and a sheaf of papers tied with twine. On top sat a folded piece of paper with his name scrawled across it in his grandfather's hand.

Gideon picked up the paper and opened it carefully.

My dear Gideon,
It is my greatest hope that you will appreciate these
items as much as I do. They are family heirlooms,
many of which have been passed through the centuries. I
trust that you will pass them on in turn.

That would require Gideon to have a child, and right
now, he had absolutely no intention to do so.

As you know, the de Valery manuscript is highly
valuable, particularly when paired with its mate, which
is in the possession of Rhys and Margery Bowen. It is
up to you if you want to keep the manuscripts together.
The other highly valuable item in this box is the
original Anarawd text, which I painstakingly bound
myself. This you must keep safe.

Gideon set the letter on the table and picked up the
book that sat on top of the others in the chest. Bound
in dark blue leather, it looked rather new, not at all like
an antiquity. He set it on the table and opened the
cover.

"That's the Anarawd text. I haven't seen that in
twenty-five years," Rhys said softly. He reached for a
pair of gloves on the end of the table handed them to
Gideon. "Be very careful with it. It's survived over a
thousand years because it's been locked away from light
and touch. I didn't realize Nash had bound the papers."

Gideon drew on the gloves as his gaze moved over
the Latin. "You're certain the poems don't contain any
information about where the treasures were hidden?"

Rhys shook his head. "No, but it's possible I missed
something. When was the last time you read it, Penn?"

"It's been a few years. Hasn't Cate started reading

it?"

"Started reading what?" As if summoned by her name, Cate stepped into the library. She set her candle down on a small table near the door as she moved inside.

"The Anarawd text," Penn said.

Cate joined them at the table, her dressing gown whispering across the floor as she moved. "In fact, I was just coming down here to read another poem. It was hidden from me for so long—forever, in fact—that I am eager to catch up." She said this with a hint of annoyance directed at her father and Penn.

Rhys winced. "I've apologized profusely. And don't blame Penn—I swore him to secrecy. I shouldn't have kept it from you."

"No, you shouldn't have." She looked over the chest and the open book beside it. "What's all this?" She inhaled sharply as she read the book. "Is that…the original?"

"It is," Gideon said. "These are things my grandfather left to me. It seems you weren't the only person who was deprived."

Rhys grunted. "When you're all parents and you have to make tough decisions, come back and we'll discuss it then."

Gideon could scarcely wait to go through the items piece by piece. But he couldn't take it with him. He didn't dare. He looked to Rhys. "Will you keep this safe for me when I leave?"

"Of course."

Penn yawned. "I'd best turn in. Can't show up to my wedding exhausted."

"We should all go up," Rhys said. "Although I daresay Gideon won't be able to sleep until he's gone through that box. Cate, leave him in peace with it tonight." Rhys looked at Gideon with regret. "I'm sorry. I would have given it to you before if I hadn't promised your grandfather."

"It's all right. I'm just glad to have it now. Thank you."

Rhys clasped his shoulder. "You're welcome. You're always welcome—in our home and in our hearts."

Gideon appreciated that more than he could say.

Rhys went to collect his and Penn's glasses and return them to the sideboard. Penn took a step toward Gideon. "Remember what I said. I'll come at a moment's notice."

"Thank you."

"I don't know what he told you," Cate said, "but I'm here for you too—and so is Elijah. I think he's warming up to you."

Gideon let out a dark laugh. "I doubt that, and I hope not. If he'd done to my wife what I did to you, I'd want to eviscerate him, and I don't think that sensation would wane."

"All right, perhaps I exaggerated, but you did save his life, so he's not really holding a grudge." She stood on her toes and kissed his cheek. "Sleep well."

They left Gideon alone with his newfound treasures, and he sat back down at the table to investigate every piece. The de Valery manuscript was there, as well as two more books. He'd never felt more certain about his objectives or the fact that he *would* achieve them.

At any cost.

Chapter Four

DAPHNE HAD ENDED up staying in Keynsham for an extra night. Great-aunt Ellie had dropped a book on her foot and was hobbling about, so Daphne had insisted on looking after her for a day. It had also delayed her return to Ashridge Court, which she wasn't entirely looking forward to.

It wasn't that she didn't want to see her father. She'd just hoped to have something to show him—if not the cloak itself, a clue at least. Or proof that Morgan was who Daphne said she was.

Instead, she returned empty-handed for her father's annual medieval festival. She'd arrived that afternoon, but her father had been too busy to see her. Instead, he'd requested she join him in his private study before the welcome banquet.

She made her way downstairs to the back corner of the house, smoothing the bright green silk of her gown. One of her father's guards stood outside the study. There was always at least one in his orbit.

"Good evening, Papa," she announced as she stepped inside.

Her father stood up from his favorite chair angled before the hearth. "Daphne! Let me see you." He grinned widely as she turned in a circle for him. "The gown fits beautifully."

"As usual. Thank you." Father always had new costumes made for her for the festival, and this year was no different. Her room was full of evening gowns, daywear, and riding costumes. "Your doublet is especially fine," she said. Gold and silver threads sparkled against the dark blue velvet.

He puffed up his chest, which was already larger due to the padding in the doublet. "Thank you. I do believe it's my favorite. Come and sit with me so we may talk for a bit before I must attend to my guests."

She sat on the small settee situated in front of the fireplace, and he retook his seat.

Papa's dark brown eyes gleamed in the sunlight streaming from the diamond-paned windows beyond the fireplace. "Tomorrow is the falconry exhibition. I do hope you plan to partake."

She'd had her own kestrel until two years ago when Millie had died. Her father had wanted to replace the bird, but since Daphne spent most of her time at Hawthorn Cottage now, she'd prevaricated. She braced herself for another assault. Father liked it when she shared his interests.

Surprisingly he didn't press the issue. "The day after will be jousting."

She smiled. "Your favorite."

"Always." He laughed. "Now, tell me what you've learned this summer. I haven't seen you since June."

She'd sent letters, but she never disclosed findings in writing—per her father's directive. "I wish I could say it has been fruitful, but alas…"

He frowned. "You have nothing to report?"

"I'm afraid not. I'm rather disappointed. But while I have no further evidence to support my Morgan theories, I also haven't found counterevidence. I am satisfied with that at least."

"As you should be. Ah well, keep at it." There was a slightly condescending tone to his words, but she was used to that. He didn't mean to denigrate her work; he just didn't find it as interesting as the Thirteen Treasures. Which was why Daphne had latched on to finding the cloak. It linked her passion—Morgan—with her father's—the treasures.

"I read Rhys Bowen's Elidyr text. I'd hoped to glean some clue as to the cloak."

Father's dark brows shot up. "You visited Bowen?"

She nodded. "He was most accommodating. His library is spectacular. Have you ever been?" It was a silly question that she already knew the answer to: no. Her father rarely went anywhere, which she found maddening considering his passion for finding artifacts. He was, however, content to allow others to do the finding for him.

Father shook his head. "Did you read anything else there?"

She wondered if he meant the Anarawd text. "No, there wasn't time. It was the eve of his son's wedding, and I didn't wish to overstay my welcome."

"Penn?" Father wrinkled his nose. "Pity you were rushed."

Daphne wondered if her father's reaction was due to Penn or the fact that she hadn't the benefit of more time in Bowen's library. "You don't care for Penn Bowen? He seemed most pleasant."

"Penn Bowen and I are often after the same antiquities, and—frustratingly—he usually gets there first. You didn't mention that you were looking for the cloak, I hope." His expression tightened as he awaited her response.

"Of course not. I'm not foolish enough to announce to the world that I'm searching for one of the Thirteen Treasures." They'd discussed the need to keep that objective secret. Too many people wanted to gain the treasures for personal gain. Plus, there was the issue of the Order of the Knights of the Round Table. They kept the treasures safe and didn't like when people went looking for them, not even members of their own order. Not that Daphne—a woman—would be allowed to be a member. "You're certain the Order doesn't know where the cloak is hidden? I find it so strange that they pledge to keep these items safe and yet claim not to know their location. How can they even be certain they exist?"

"You're aware I can't discuss the business of the Order with you to that degree."

No, he could only tell her they didn't know the location of the cloak and had been searching for it for centuries. Why she thought she could find it when a secret society dedicated to its protection couldn't was perhaps overly optimistic. And maybe a trifle arrogant.

"I can continue to hope," she said brightly. "Or maybe I'll find the cloak, and the Order will be so grateful, they'll offer me membership." Now *that* was beyond optimistic.

And apparently not the least bit amusing to her father, given his deep frown. "They'll never do that, and I pray you won't attempt to extort membership in such a devious manner."

"Of course I wouldn't." She'd never even mentioned such a thing. "You can be so paranoid sometimes."

"I have to be, Daphne. You know that. The Order is my life, and I'm dedicated to its purpose." He exhaled and flexed his hands atop the arms of his chair. "Let us move to a more important topic. I have found the perfect husband for you."

Hellfire. He'd done it. She'd no cause to doubt he

would, of course, but in the recesses of her mind, she'd hoped he wouldn't. "You have?" The question came out higher than she would have liked.

"I finally found someone worthy."

"He's a descendant, then?" Of one of King Arthur's knights. She'd known that was the expectation—and she'd exchanged the ability to choose her own husband for the freedom to pursue her research and live somewhat independently until such time as that marriage. Though she was quite old enough now to marry whomever she chose, she was a woman of her word. She would at least see if she and the man her father had chosen would suit.

"Of Gareth, I believe." Papa's gaze glinted with triumph. That had been his ultimate goal, but it was difficult to trace Gareth's line. Until now, he hadn't been able to find a male of marriageable age.

"How can you be certain?"

"He possesses certain…qualities. And his family is believed to have commissioned the de Valery manuscripts, which means they held the Anarawd text at some point."

And it was largely accepted that Anarawd had given the poems to Gareth, the last of Arthur's knights to die.

The evidence seemed circumstantial at best, but further questions were foiled by the arrival of another guest. Daphne heard the door creak as it opened, and her father leapt up from his chair with a wide grin. "Ah, here he is! And garbed in his medieval best."

"Only because you provided it," a deep *familiar* voice responded.

Rising slowly, she pivoted as her father introduced him: "Daphne, allow me to present the Earl of Stratton. Lord Stratton, my daughter, Miss Foliot."

This was the man her father intended her to marry?

He walked into the study and bowed far more elegantly than he had at Hollyhaven, presenting a muscular leg enclosed in a tight black stocking. He wore a black doublet shot with silver, and a black belt rode his hips. He was, as her father had indicated, resplendent in his attire.

"Good evening, Miss Foliot." He put just the slightest emphasis on her last name, clearly referencing the lie she'd told at Hollyhaven.

"Good evening, Lord Stratton. It's a pleasure to see you again."

"You've met?" Her father looked between them.

"Just recently," Stratton replied. "At Rhys Bowen's house. Miss Foliot came to use his library."

Father looked at her sharply, and she knew what he was thinking—that she hadn't used an alias. She turned her head to the earl and rushed to say, "I apologize for misleading you about my identity. I find it's easier to travel under the guise of widowhood." She glanced toward her father, who, by the easing of lines between his eyes, had relaxed.

The earl smiled benignly. "I can imagine."

"I shall hope your introduction went well," Daphne's father said. He looked to Stratton. "I was just going to tell Daphne about you, but I'm afraid your arrival stole my thunder."

"My apologies," Stratton said, nodding deferentially toward her father. "I was told you wished to see me as soon as I was ready for the banquet."

Her father waved his hand. "It's quite all right." He turned to the footman who stood just inside the door. "Claret for a toast."

The footman went to the sideboard where her father

kept all manner of spirits and poured three glasses of the red wine.

Daphne's father pivoted toward her as they waited. "How *did* your introduction go?"

She shot a glance toward the earl. What could they say? It hadn't been terribly remarkable. Except for the way her knees had gone soft when they'd met or the thrill that had shot through her when their fingers had touched. Fine, it had been remarkable.

Before she could speak, Stratton answered. "I must admit I was…intrigued. A woman with purpose and intellect is most alluring."

Her father grinned. "Splendid." He looked expectantly at Daphne. Was she supposed to say the same thing? And did the earl really mean that? A fluttering in her chest nearly stole her breath.

"I found him most…interesting." Was that the best she could do?

Yes. She wasn't going to pretend she'd fallen in love with him the moment they'd met, because she hadn't. To think her father expected her to marry this man she barely knew…

No, she wasn't going to make it that easy. Especially when she'd been ambushed like this. Her father may not have intended for Stratton to arrive before he'd told her about him, but he would've come shortly thereafter. In either case, Daphne had no time to formulate her reaction into a coherent and thoughtful refusal.

"This is promising," her father said as the footman delivered claret to them on a tray. The footman retreated, and her father lifted his glass. "To an auspicious beginning."

Daphne raised her glass and tapped it to the others.

She tried to avoid looking at the earl, but it was impossible. He was like a magnet, drawing her to keep glancing his way. His gaze was absolutely inscrutable, his expression impassive. He stared at her over the top of his glass as he took a drink.

"I suppose we should discuss the expectations for this union," her father said, returning to his chair. He indicated they should both sit on the settee. "We must go to the great hall shortly."

Daphne lowered herself slowly to the settee, and once she was situated, Stratton sat beside her. The seat wasn't overly large, so it was impossible for them to sit side by side without her skirt touching his leg. He was close enough that she could feel his warmth—and be drawn to it.

"I'll announce your betrothal at the closing banquet."

Before he could say anything further, Daphne cut him off. "So soon? Surely we should see if we suit."

"Of course. That will happen during the festival. Plenty of time for you to become acquainted. Rather, *better* acquainted." He winked at them, seemingly oblivious to Daphne's concern. He couldn't be, however. Though she'd agreed to wed a descendant, she'd also given him the caveat that she had to approve him. He'd understood, but had also made it clear that he'd be careful to select the perfect gentleman.

She slid a glance toward the man at her side. What made Lord Stratton that gentleman, at least in her father's eyes? "Is that acceptable to you?" she asked the earl.

He pinned her with his gray gaze. "I'm confident we can determine whether we will suit in the next five days." That told her nothing about whether he wanted to or not. Why would this man agree to wed her? She meant to find out.

"You are both dedicated to Arthur and his legacy," her father said before sipping his claret. "You're also quite clever—you'll get on very well. Furthermore, Stratton is an earl. Or at least, he's heir apparent. I suppose he hasn't officially been given the title yet."

Though they didn't quite touch, Daphne felt the earl tense. His body stiffened, and there was a slight narrowing of his eyes.

She turned toward him. "Did your father just recently pass?"

"Yes." His answer was a bit tight.

"I'm so sorry for your loss." She looked back at her father. "Given that, we should probably wait a respectable amount of time before we wed."

"I'm sure three weeks will be long enough," Papa said. "I'd thought to purchase a license so you could wed as soon as you wish, but I suppose we could wait for the banns to be read. I'll let the two of you decide."

He'd *let* them? Daphne could see that in his mind, they were already married. Well, she'd have to disabuse him of that notion later. Wait, why later?

Taking a deep breath, she smoothed her hands flat against her skirts in an effort to ease the anxiety tripping along her muscles. "Papa, let us not get ahead of ourselves. Let us determine if we will suit, and then we can begin discussing wedding plans."

Her father's eyes took on a dangerous glint that she was well used to seeing—it signaled a fit of temper was on the horizon. Would he really show it in front of the earl? "Daughter, I am merely laying out the possibilities. I have no doubt your union will come to pass." The statement wasn't so much confidence as arrogance and directive.

But would he really force her to marry Gideon if she didn't want to? He couldn't—not really. What he *could* do was turn her out and take away her allowance. She'd always have Hawthorn Cottage, but without her father's support, she'd be a pauper.

It wouldn't come to that. Her father loved her, even if he was single-minded. If she really didn't want to marry Stratton, he wouldn't demand it.

The earl looked in her direction with a half smile. "We'll take one day at a time, beginning with tonight's banquet."

"Listen to the earl," her father said. "I told you he was wise." He'd said clever, but she wouldn't quarrel with him. "Now, I need to speak with Stratton for a few minutes. We'll be down directly, my dear." He stood, punctuating that she should leave.

Stratton also stood. "I look forward to dancing with you later," he said, offering his hand to help her up.

She didn't need it but couldn't seem to stop herself from slipping her bare fingers—her costume didn't include gloves—into his. "Thank you, my lord," she murmured. She set her unfinished claret on a table near the settee, then sent her father a brief glance. "Papa."

As she made her way from the study, she wondered what her father wanted to speak with the earl alone about. Would he extract the man's promise to ensure the wedding happened no matter what? Or perhaps he had to fulfill whatever bribe he'd offered the man to marry her.

Did she really think her father was that unscrupulous? No, he was old-fashioned in his ideas about securing a marriage for her, and he could be paranoid in his obsession about Arthur and the Thirteen Treasures, but he'd been a kind and supportive father. Especially after they'd lost her mother.

Pushing away unpleasant memories of the distant past, she focused on getting to know the earl. She looked forward to determining if they would suit, plus she wanted to know what he knew about the Order and about the things that mattered most to her: Morgan and the cloak.

She also wanted to know why he'd agreed to this marriage. What could he possibly hope to gain?

But perhaps most of all, she wanted to know why her heart sped when he was close, and what would it feel like if he kissed her?

GIDEON WATCHED HIS potential bride walk from the room, the sway of her hips artfully moving the fabric of her gown as it draped her slender form. She was a beautiful woman, petite, with a delicate frame and pale skin. But her hazel eyes held a fire and her carriage a bold spirit that cautioned one not to discount her based on her size.

He had the sense she wasn't entirely committed to the marriage, which gave him hope. If she didn't particularly want the union, perhaps they could avoid it altogether. He'd cling to that thought.

"So you met my daughter already," Foliot said, retaking his seat.

Gideon sat and sipped his claret. "As Mrs. Guilford. I had no idea she was your daughter."

"Bowen didn't either?"

Which Bowen he meant wasn't clear, but Gideon

supposed it didn't matter. "No. Though they'll learn soon enough if we are to wed."

"Yes, that will be unavoidable." He twitched a shoulder. "I don't like her traveling under our name. I'm sure you can understand why."

Because a Foliot inquiring about Arthurian folklore or antiquities would raise eyebrows, particularly within the Arthurian community. He was acknowledged to be a likely member of the Order and, for those who were particularly informed, the leader of the Camelot group, whose objectives were only vaguely suspected. The consensus, however, was that they were not benevolent.

And from everything Gideon had seen, that was true. From theft to kidnapping to murder, there was nothing they wouldn't do to achieve their ends. Which was why Gideon had to stop them.

"Certainly, I can," Gideon said, answering the man's question that hadn't really been a question. "I admit I'm surprised you allow her to travel at all."

"She'd find a way to do it. She has a mind of her own, but don't let that dissuade you from taking her as a wife."

Despite what Gideon hoped, he feared he wouldn't be allowed to be dissuaded. Foliot had made it clear he expected Gideon's cooperation to demonstrate his loyalty. Failure to do so would not end well. Of that, Gideon was convinced.

"I appreciate confident women," Gideon said judiciously. And truthfully. Rose had possessed a quiet confidence in herself and in those around her. She'd believed in Gideon and his capacity for goodness when no one else had, not even himself.

"Wise man, just as I told Daphne. Her mother was

confident. Independent. Incomparably radiant." His voice trailed off, and there was a sheen to his eyes that made Gideon lower his gaze and drink his claret.

Foliot cleared his throat and sipped his wine. "Let me get to the heart of why I wanted to speak with you." He laughed. "The *heart*."

Gideon struggled not to roll his eyes. "If you're asking whether I have it, I do. In my chamber."

"You left it unguarded?" Foliot's eyes nearly popped from their sockets.

"No, I asked one of your 'footmen' to stand guard."

Sitting back in his chair with a sharp exhalation, Foliot blinked. "I should hope so. Let us fetch it before the banquet. You should have brought it with you."

Gideon looked down at his costume. "And where should I have put it? On a chain around my neck so I can advertise its presence? I didn't realize you wanted me to bring it to you before the banquet."

Foliot pursed his lips. "Very well. We'll go now, then. I'm anxious to lock it away in the vault." He finished his claret and set his empty glass on the small table beside his chair.

Gideon tossed the rest of his wine down his throat and followed his host from the room.

Ashridge Court was a stately country home dating from the late Tudor period. Though refurbished, with two wings added on in the mideighteenth century, Foliot decorated it in medieval and early Tudor fashion, making the house feel older than it really was.

Foliot's apartments, of which his study was a part, were on the first floor in the center of the house with a view over the back lawns. Gideon's chamber was located in the east wing, in a corner that afforded him a view of Glastonbury in the distance.

The footman Gideon had assigned to guard his room stood at the door and inclined his head at Foliot as they arrived. Gideon went inside and strode to the dressing area, separated by a screen from the room, where he'd left the heart wrapped in a cloth, which was how Penn had given it to him.

Holding the stone in his left hand, he unfolded the cloth and pulled it away. As soon as the tourmaline fell upon his bare flesh, he felt a strange warmth that no one else had so far detected. Like the flaming sword, the Heart of Llanllwch seemed to respond to descendants of the knights.

The power of the heart was, of course, quite different from that of the sword. It wasn't a weapon but an item to be used to gain the love of another. With it, Gideon could charm someone to fall in love with him.

Closing his fist around the stone, he stepped around the screen to face Foliot. Gideon lifted the heart and opened his hand to reveal the unassuming heart-shaped piece of tourmaline.

Foliot drew in a breath and edged closer. "It looks so…ordinary."

"Compared to the fake one that once sat in the Ashmolean, yes." Over fifty years ago, Amelia's grandfather had found a fake Heart of Llanllwch and gifted it to the museum. The Order had painted it and affixed it with jewels so that it looked like a valuable treasure to prevent people from finding the real one. It had been an effective ploy since it had taken a half century for anyone to look for the real heart—and that had been Penn, a singular hunter of antiquities. "Have you any idea why the Order didn't create imitations for the other twelve treasures?" Gideon mused aloud.

Foliot gave him a sly look. "How do you know they

haven't?"

Gideon should have expected a nonanswer. Foliot liked to keep his Order secrets close. It made Gideon wonder if he liked to demonstrate his perceived superiority or if it was possible he didn't actually know a damned thing.

"Are you going to take this to the vault?" Gideon asked.

"You bring it." He hadn't wanted to touch the sword either, which at the time had seemed odd but now seemed rather curious. Gideon knew better than to ask another question Foliot wouldn't answer, so he said nothing.

Gideon rewrapped the heart in the cloth, and they departed his room.

"I'm pleased you kept your word," Foliot said, leading Gideon to another set of stairs that didn't lead to the main hall.

"You doubted me?"

Foliot lifted a shoulder. "I doubt most people, I'm afraid." Paranoia was perhaps a better description.

"Hopefully you see that you can trust me."

Foliot paused and looked over his shoulder at Gideon. "You're marrying my daughter, so I sure as hell better. Don't disappoint me." His eyes glittered for a moment before he turned and led him down the stairs.

They made their way to the vault, which was guarded as it had been last time. Gideon waited, the stone weighing his palm, while Foliot unlocked the door. Inside, Foliot strolled to the chest and unlocked it too.

Foliot looked at him with sudden interest, his brow creasing. "It occurs to me that the heart may be of use."

Gideon gripped the stone before depositing it into the chest. "How?"

"With Daphne. You could use it to make her fall in love with you—just a little nudge, mind you. It's likely she'll develop a tendre for you on her own."

A wave of disgust washed over Gideon, and he had to work to keep the revulsion from his expression and tone. "I'd prefer to let things progress naturally." Or not. He *actually* preferred they not wed at all, and he was betting on her feeling the same—or at least hoping she might.

"You could, but the heart is meant for just this sort of endeavor."

Gideon worked to maintain an even tone. "I don't even know how it works."

"I think you just hold it and wish for the person to love you. Give it a go."

Gideon blinked at him. This was not a bloody trial run in a new phaeton. The refusal died on his tongue, however, at the dark expectation in Foliot's gaze. He was not going to accept a refusal.

Perhaps it wouldn't work. Wrapped in the cloth, the heart didn't feel warm to him. Perhaps its magic was only effective if the stone was against his bare skin. He prayed that was true.

He held up the heart and said, "I wish for Daphne to love me."

"I think you need to be more specific, lest all the Daphnes of the world begin trailing after you." He chuckled, and Gideon didn't think he could loathe the man any more than he did in that moment.

"I wish for Daphne Foliot to love me." While he said the words, he thought the opposite, *I wish for Daphne Foliot not to love me,* in the hope that such a sentiment would counteract the magic. If the magic was, in fact, working. Hell, what if he went to the banquet, and she swooned all over him?

Foliot's lips split into a wide grin, revealing a substantial gap between his two front teeth. "Well done. Into the chest it goes, then." He nodded toward the heart.

Gideon set it inside, his gaze lingering on the sword, which pulsed with energy as his hand brushed the cross guard. He straightened. Soon he would get them back, and he would hide them with the other eleven treasures. The question was where.

"We must hurry to the banquet now," Foliot said. "I don't wish to keep my guests waiting."

They left the vault and made their way to the great hall, where two long banqueting tables were set up to one side. The other was open, presumably for dancing since there were musical instruments in the corner.

The hall was full of people milling about. The butler garnered everyone's attention and announced Foliot's arrival.

Gideon picked Miss Foliot out immediately in her green dress. Her dark hair was covered with a medieval headdress and veil that trailed to midway down her back. An emerald pendant gleamed against the cream of her flesh above her fitted bodice. Like the emerald, she was a beautiful jewel.

She was also Foliot's daughter, he reminded himself, and potentially as devious and manipulative as he was. She'd already demonstrated her easy ability to lie—Mrs. Guilford indeed. And yet, he could understand the need for such a fabrication to protect herself. If, in fact, that was all it had been.

Regardless, she'd lied, and if she lied about that, what

else was she capable of? He had only a few days to find out.

She greeted him with a broad, stunning smile that startled him with its intensity. "Lord Stratton, you're seated next to me of course."

Of course.

She tucked her arm through his and guided him to the table where her father would be sitting. Naturally, their seats were next to his—Miss Foliot to his immediate right and Gideon beside her.

"We can go ahead and sit," she said. "My father will take a few minutes to greet some specific guests, and he won't want us to wait for him."

Gideon held her chair as she sat, then took his own.

She surprised him again by touching his arm. "So my father provided your costume? It's tailored remarkably well. He must have had your measurements."

"He did not, actually."

She tipped her head to the side. Her hand was still on his arm, and he could feel her heat through the linen sleeve of his tunic. "Oh. Well, his tailor is exceptional. Did he provide an entire wardrobe for the festival?"

"He did." But Gideon hadn't yet decided if he would wear it all. He didn't particularly want to stay. He wanted to go find the treasures, starting with ingratiating himself with his mother's paramour and, now that Gideon's father was dead, soon-to-be husband.

Lord Septon was one of England's leading antiquaries and a seemingly high-ranking member of the Order of the Round Table. His position was remarkable because he wasn't a descendant, but someone the Order had invited to join because of his knowledge and passion for Arthurian legend and antiquities. Septon would guard what he knew very closely, but Gideon planned to use his relationship with his mother as leverage. He'd stolen her away from Gideon over twenty years ago, leaving him to be raised by his dissolute father. Gideon hadn't forgiven Septon and never would. He would, however, pretend to in order to get what he needed.

Miss Foliot curled her fingers around Gideon's forearm, drawing his attention. "You look like you're far away. In your mind, that is."

"Just contemplating the festival." He summoned a smile as he wondered at her behavior. She was rather…focused on him.

"You've been to the festival in the past, haven't you? I wonder if we haven't met before. Not formally, of course. But perhaps we passed in a corridor or sat near each other at a banquet."

That was possible, he supposed, but he hadn't attended since before he'd married Rose, and back then, he'd kept to the rowdier contingent at the festival. He glanced toward the other table, where such a group sat at one end—they were young, already well into their cups, and would end the evening in a private salon upstairs with gaming and women. "We may have," Gideon said, addressing her musings. "But I daresay it's unlikely."

She followed his gaze, then tightened her hold on him and fluttered her eyelashes. "This festival will be different. We'll dance and attend the jousting tournament and take a ride over the estate."

Foliot arrived and looked at them approvingly before taking his seat. A footman immediately poured his wine, which he picked up and held toward Gideon and his daughter. "I knew this union was meant to be." He looked inordinately pleased with himself.

Gideon turned to look at Miss Foliot, who still clutched his arm, her eyes glazed with delight, and realized a horrifying truth: the Heart of Llanllwch had worked. She seemed to have fallen in love with him.

Chapter Five

IT WAS HOURS before the banquet drew to a close and the dancing began. Daphne danced first with her father to open things, and then she approached Stratton because he'd already said he would dance with her.

He cut a fine figure in his ebony doublet, the belt slung around his hips accentuating his trim but athletic build. Other women looked at him in open admiration, and Daphne felt a stab of jealousy.

Which was ridiculous because the only woman he'd looked at all evening was her.

Leaving the dance floor, Daphne's father led them to Stratton. "Your turn," Father said with a smile, transferring her hand to Stratton's.

He offered his arm and led her back to the dance floor. Rather stiffly.

"Do you dance?" she asked.

"Yes, but not typically this kind." He grimaced as three other couples joined them to form a circle. "I barely know what to do."

"Just watch me. I'll keep you from making a fool of yourself." She winked at him and flashed a smile, and he tried to mask a slight wince, but she caught it.

He'd been doing that all through dinner as if he were uncomfortable. Or annoyed. Or both.

"Is there something wrong?" she asked softly so the other dancers couldn't hear.

"No. Unless you count the dancing I don't know how to do."

This made her giggle. She lifted her hand to her mouth and apologized. "I don't mean to laugh at you. I just... Well, I suppose between the wine at dinner and having a reprieve from my father's eagerness regarding our courtship, I let my guard down." She exhaled and straightened her shoulders. "I'm afraid I've never been particularly adept at the duties required of a lady."

"And what are those?" he asked with genuine interest.

"Being charming. Smiling gaily. Demonstrating the right amount of wit—not too much—and engagement—more than enough."

He blinked at her. "Were you trying to do those things at dinner?"

"Yes." She frowned. "You said trying. Did I fail?"

He stared at her a moment as the music started. "No. On the contrary, you were most convincing."

This made her inordinately pleased. "Thank you. Now, do pay attention." She took his hand and led him in the dance, moving to the center of the circle and meeting the other dancers, then retreating. Then bowing and moving around each other and repeating everything in a pattern.

Stratton managed the steps well for the most part. He only ran into another dancer twice and stepped on Daphne's toe just once.

When at last the music drew to a close, she had to stifle another laugh at the look of sheer relief that flashed in his eyes. They bowed and curtsied to the other dancers, and he offered his arm, then guided her from the dance floor.

"I'm a bit overheated," she said. "Would you mind escorting me to the terrace?"

"Not at all." He skirted the dance floor and guided

her through the open doors that led to the terrace, which overlooked the dark lawn. The night air was cool, and when a breeze danced across her neck, she sighed as it soothed her heated flesh.

She took her hand from his arm and walked away to the edge of the terrace. He came up beside her, pivoting to face her. "Just to confirm the matter—your behavior at dinner was an act?"

"Not an *act*," she said, turning toward him. "An...effort."

"So you have not... You do not..." He exhaled sharply and turned toward the lawn. "Never mind."

"Whatever you meant to say, you seem relieved." She narrowed her eyes at him, trying to discern what was going on behind the dark gray of his eyes. "What aren't you telling me?"

"I'm not sure it's worth repeating."

"If we're to see if we suit, we must be honest."

He sent her a quick look that made her think he was questioning whether she would be honest, but perhaps she was reading far too much into a simple glance. Regardless of what she said, honesty was not a luxury she could always afford. It was difficult to be truthful when you were a lady forbidden from doing things such as join private men-only organizations. She'd had to develop a talent for secrecy and subterfuge.

He realigned himself back toward her. "Very well. I was fairly certain you'd fallen in love with me."

She couldn't keep from laughing again, but this time was pleased to see him smile in return. He had a stunning smile. It made her pulse speed up and her belly flutter.

When she caught her breath, she asked, "Why would you think that? We just met."

He shrugged. "Some people fall in love the moment they meet."

She narrowed her eyes at him once more. "And?"

"And before dinner, I gave your father the Heart of Lllanllwch."

She sucked in a breath. "It's here?"

He blinked at her in surprise. "You didn't know?"

"My father doesn't tell me anything like that." She tried to keep the irritation from her voice, but was fairly certain she had failed. "Where is it?"

He scrutinized her. "Am I allowed to tell you?"

Now she snorted softly. "If we wed, I'll demand it. So you'd better start practicing now."

He barked a laugh, then grinned at her. "I think I like you."

"Oh good." She didn't bother hiding her sarcasm. "Now tell me why you thought I *loved* you."

"Because of the heart. I trust you know what it does?"

She did, but she'd forgotten… Then she suddenly remembered. Her eyes flew wide open, and she gaped at him. "You used it to make me fall in love with you?"

"At your father's insistence. But it looks as though it didn't work." Once again, he seemed relieved.

"Then you aren't really a descendant." She frowned. "Father will be crushed."

"I *am* a descendant. The sword flames for me."

Her eyes widened once more, even larger than the first time, if that was possible. "The treasures are real? Rather, they're *magical*?"

He pressed his lips together and stared at her. "You didn't think they were? How is that possible for Foliot's daughter to possess such an opinion?"

"I've found no proof. I like evidence. Without it,

there is only myth and legend and conjecture. A theory, not a fact."

"You've the mind of a scientist, not a romantic. Your father is the latter."

"Yes, he is. The sword actually flames for you?"

He nodded. "And I'm not certain the heart doesn't work for me. While I verbally wished for you to love me—again, at your father's insistence—I thought the opposite. I wished for you *not* to love me."

"You think that prevented it from working?"

"That or the fact that I held it in a cloth instead of against my bare flesh. Perhaps the object needs to touch me to work."

She thought for a moment, looking out across the lawn before returning her gaze to his. "Fascinating. Can we conduct some experiments with the sword and heart to see which it is?"

"That would require your father to let me have access to them, and I'm not certain he will."

She nodded, agreeing that might be difficult given how important the treasures were to her father. That he had two of the thirteen was astonishing. But not nearly as extraordinary as the fact that they were truly supernatural.

"I do appreciate you counteracting the heart—however it happened," she said. Anger at her father crowded her fascination in the treasures, pushing them away momentarily. "He really demanded you use the heart to force my affections." It wasn't a question because she believed it.

"I'm afraid so."

She exhaled, letting a bit of her anger go. "My father is single-minded in wanting me to wed a descendant. Lest you think he's selfish, he's just as insistent that I am happy." She met his gaze. "He'd want me to marry for love."

"Even if it wasn't real?" His voice had dropped a bit, both in volume and tone.

Though she hadn't moved, she suddenly felt as if they were closer. "Why wouldn't it be real? If I felt the emotion, I would believe it."

"But it wouldn't come from you, from *us*." He gestured from her to him, touching his chest before dropping his hand to his side.

She edged toward him, wanting to actually *be* closer. "No, I suppose it wouldn't."

"Do you want me to try again without the cloth and without trying to counteract the charm?"

Whatever spell had woven between them for the last few moments split asunder. She blinked and took a step back. "No. Thank you."

She took a deep breath and pivoted toward the lawn again. "I do appreciate you not using the heart to…force things. I suppose I should pretend that it worked so as not to arouse my father's suspicions. He won't like that you didn't actually use it."

"Perhaps not, but it doesn't matter in the end. He expects us to marry."

Regardless of whether we fall in love. He hadn't said it, but they both understood that was the expectation. She peered over at him. "Why would you agree to do that?"

He'd also turned toward the lawn so they were side by side, with less than a foot between them. "I'm a member of the Order, and I support your father. That's why I've brought him two of the Thirteen Treasures."

"You brought him the sword too?" At his nod, she continued, "Then you must mean to find the other eleven."

He looked over at her, his eyes gleaming in the light from the lanterns on the terrace. "I do."

He was looking for treasure, then, just like her. Her words from earlier rose up in her mind: *We must be honest.* Could she do that? She would try—at least a little. "I am looking for the cloak."

"Are you?" For the first time that evening, she felt as though she had his complete and utter attention.

They both turned at exactly the same moment, drawing closer as they did so.

"Is that why you came to Hollyhaven?" he asked. "The Elidyr text you came to read contains mention of the cloak."

"Yes."

He arched a brow with a hint of humor. "Not for Morgan, then?"

"Not *just* for Morgan. She is entwined with the cloak. She made it for Arthur and gave it to him."

He was fully invested now, his gaze focused solely on her and his body leaning slightly forward. "How do you know she made it for him?"

A surge of pride rushed through her. "I have a fragment of a poem from purportedly the ninth century about a healer who made a garment that would protect the wearer—a man who would fight in battle."

"And then what?" he asked, rapt.

"That's it. As I said, it was only part of the tale."

"Was the wearer identified?" When she shook her head, he rushed on. "Why do you believe the healer was Morgan? Where did you find this poem?"

She held up her hand to cut him off, and just stopped herself from touching his chest. His excitement was palpable and exhilarating. A soft chuckle dashed past her lips as she lowered her hand to her side. "I will answer what I can. One question at a time."

"All right, but add who wrote this poem to the list."

"That I don't know."

"Can I see it?" He briefly closed his eyes, then pressed his lips together. "My apologies. I will contain myself."

"I like your exuberance." The night air had sufficiently cooled her, and now she was beginning to grow a bit chilled. Even so, she didn't want to go back inside where it was loud and they would likely be interrupted. She wrapped her arms around herself.

His lips curved down. "You're cold. Damn these medieval costumes. If I had a coat, I could give it to you."

Just the sentiment warmed her. "It's all right. We'll go in soon. First, let me answer your queries. I believe she was Morgan because in this fragment, the healer is clearly identified as a woman. And she sought to protect a man in battle."

"Arthur?" he asked. She nodded, and his gaze had strayed out to the lawn once more, then slammed back into her with intensity. "And where was this cloak made?"

"The poem doesn't say specifically—that would be too easy," she added wryly. "It mentions Gifl, which means forked river. I found it buried in my father's library several years ago. It's actually the piece that convinced me Morgan was a healer—and specifically, *this* healer—and gave the cloak to Arthur. I've been searching for other evidence ever since."

The edge of his mouth ticked up. "Because you love evidence."

She smiled up at him. "Yes." How nice that he

seemed to understand her. She was actually starting to consider the idea of maybe marrying him. Was he perhaps considering it too? And had he really agreed to wed her simply because he was in the Order? "Did you truly intend to marry me without having met me?" she asked. "Or did you make a promise to please my father?"

He cocked his head to the side. "Which did you do?"

She wanted to groan in frustration. He could be irritatingly enigmatic. "A bit of both. Now answer me. Please."

"Also a bit of both."

She fixed him with a direct stare. "I'd hoped we could be honest. If you are being truthful, then I shall accept it."

His eyes narrowed very briefly and glinted silver in the dim light. "The truth is I don't want to marry at all."

"Oh." What else could she say? "My father won't force us."

"I'm not sure I share that opinion," he said softly. "But *I* won't force you. You have to be absolutely willing. Are you?"

She lifted a shoulder. "I don't know yet. So far, I...like you."

"I don't know you terribly well, but from what I've observed, you don't seem the type of woman to allow her father—or anyone else—to choose her husband."

That he saw her in that light only furthered her growing admiration for him. "It must seem strange. But understand that as long as I can remember, I knew this was expected. Arranged marriages aren't popular anymore, of course, but as you know, my father is a bit rooted in another era."

He glanced toward the great hall. "Yes, but why the later medieval period instead of Arthur's time?"

"Because that's when the stories were romanticized, and, as you so aptly pointed out, my father is a romantic."

He nodded, then squared his shoulders. "Let us decide how to proceed, then. We will spend the festival deciding if we shall suit. I propose we also work to find the cloak. Perhaps if we join forces, we might be successful."

"You plan to turn it over to my father?"

"Yes. What do *you* plan to do with it?" he asked.

"Probably give it to my father. Once he sees I am an invaluable antiquary, he'll convince the Order to admit me as a member."

Stratton gaped at her. "He told you that?"

She couldn't help but feel a bit defensive. "He's hinted at it. Why, you don't think that will happen?"

"I can't imagine it, to be honest. Will you get a tattoo?" He half smiled at her, and she blinked at him.

"What?"

He bent over and pulled his boot from his foot, then rolled up the leg of his stocking. A three-inch sword was inked into the skin of his inner calf. The letters KRT wound around the guard of the handle.

She lowered herself a few inches to look at it more closely. She reached to touch it, stopping short of connecting with his bare flesh. Looking up, she found his gaze fixed on her. "Did it hurt?"

"Yes. You can touch it." Apparently he could tell she wanted to.

Her hands had grown cold in the night air, but she put her fingertips on him anyway. The slight sound of his indrawn breath floated down over her as she traced the sword. It didn't feel like anything, just him. His skin was warm, with dark hair that lightly tickled her fingers.

The spell from earlier wove around them again, and she made herself stand up. He bent to roll down his stocking and replace his boot. She took the opportunity to turn from him. Her heart beat a strong and steady, if slightly fast, rhythm.

"We should go back inside, or a marriage may not be avoidable," he said, offering her his arm.

She took it, and they walked back toward the door. "Would you like to meet in the library tomorrow morning to discuss our plan to find the cloak?"

"Yes, please," he answered. "And bring the poem, if you would."

"Of course." She was looking forward to showing it to him. "I need to attend the falconry exhibition in the afternoon, so let's meet early."

"I am at your command." He guided her into the great hall, and she immediately caught her father's eye. He looked right at them and smiled.

No, they were likely at her father's command. She just hoped she ended up wanting the same thing.

THE DREAM STAYED with Gideon long after he woke. A woman with dark auburn hair rose from the water, a diaphanous white gown plastered to the curves of her body. She came to him and knelt, bowing her head. Her hand traced along his inner calf and moved upward…

He pushed the lurid image away and made his way downstairs to the library. There was to be a meal in the great hall before the falconry exhibition, but he and Miss Foliot would have enough time to conduct their business first.

Was that what they were doing? After last night's dream, he could see doing far more than business with Daphne Foliot. A good reason to make her his wife...

But he didn't want a wife. Not after Rose. He didn't deserve a wife, and he sure as hell didn't want to suffer losing one again.

The library was situated in the west wing of the ground floor. The ceilings were high and the bookcases a dark wood that gleamed from a recent polishing. There were three different seating areas as well as a massive fireplace in which a low fire burned on this late August morning.

Aside from shelves teeming with books, there were two tapestries—of medieval age, of course—and various decorative items, some of which were certainly antiquities. Figurines, pottery, even an axe mounted on the wall.

"Oh, you're here already." Miss Foliot swept into the room wearing another medieval costume. This one was purple with a darker purple overskirt and sleeves that belled over her forearms. Her hair was completely covered with a black headdress affixed with a gauzy light purple veil that draped beneath her chin. Her gaze raked over him, and he felt a sudden jolt, due in large part to the lingering effects of that provocative dream.

"You aren't in medieval garb," she said.

"I didn't wish to bother with it today." He was far more comfortable in his regular clothing.

"Pity, I liked the stockings." Her gaze seemed to heat, but then she looked away from him and moved to a round table with four chairs.

He realized she carried a slim book, which she set on the table, and joined her there. "Is that the poem?" he asked.

"The fragment, yes." She opened the volume and pulled out a piece of parchment folded in half. Opening the paper, she withdrew a smaller piece that was torn along one side, as if it had been ripped from its binding.

"That looks incredibly fragile."

She set it atop the table in front of him. "It is."

He was afraid to touch it without gloves. Rhys would be horrified. "You should handle this with a light pair of gloves that are meant only for that task."

"That makes sense. I shall obtain a pair, thank you."

He bent to study the scrawled Latin. The lines were even and perfect and exceptionally tidy with just a single blot of ink in the lower corner. He looked over at her to see that she was watching him. "However did you find it?"

"It was tucked into a book on one of those shelves." She gestured behind him. "I've no idea how long it had been there."

"And your father doesn't insist on locking it away?" he asked.

She shrugged. "Unless he deems something valuable, he doesn't care if I take possession of it."

"Well, I daresay this is exceptionally valuable." Though the vellum was torn on one corner, in addition to the edge, it was still in remarkably good condition for a nine-hundred-year-old piece of animal skin. The inkblot drew his eye again, and he stared at it for a long moment.

"You're studying that rather intently," she said, moving closer.

He cocked his head to the side. "It's just that… It looks familiar. I want to pick this up with my bare fingers. Is that all right?" He shot a glance to gain her approval.

She nodded. "I trust you."

They were three simple words spoken in reference to him touching an ancient piece of vellum. They meant nothing, and yet for some reason they resonated inside him.

He picked the parchment up carefully, touching only as much of the edge as necessary. He held it up to allow light from the nearby window to spill through the paper.

Excitement kindled inside him. "This isn't an inkblot."

She came even closer until she stood right next to him. "It isn't?"

"No. This is a leaf. Or a rendition of a leaf. And it's precisely the mark on the Elidyr poem in Rhys Bowen's library."

She stared at the paper for another brief moment, then sucked in a breath, lifting her fingers to cover her mouth. Then she looked at him, her lips parted. "This was written by Elidyr?"

"I believe so." What an extraordinary discovery. Rhys would be beside himself.

"We should take it to Mr. Bowen. Perhaps he knows of it and what the rest of the text says."

"I've never heard of him speak of an Elidyr text other than the one he has," Gideon said.

"You're very close to him, then?"

He didn't want to reveal too much, but a bit wouldn't hurt. "He was my father's distant cousin. I spent time in the summer with the Bowens. Rhys would convey me from Stratton Hall to Westerly Cross, where my mother would meet me."

Her brow furrowed. "Your mother didn't live with you?"

"No, she abandoned me and my father to become Lord Septon's mistress." He could say the words dispassionately, but the emotions inside him still swirled like a fast-moving current that left him hollow when it passed.

"Oh my goodness, I am so sorry." She touched his arm. "I'd forgotten that she wasn't his wife, actually. And I'm not sure I ever knew she was your mother. At least, I didn't make the connection. I should have."

"Nonsense. I don't expect people to remember a scandal that happened twenty years ago, and trust me when I say I'm pleased when they don't."

"As you would be," she said softly, her gaze full of compassion that, along with her touch on his arm, gave him a sense of peace. It also stirred the desire he'd awakened with that morning.

He returned his attention to the paper, and, disappointingly, she dropped her hand from his arm. "Rather than take this to Rhys, I'd prefer to visit Septon," he said.

The thought of it curdled his stomach, but he'd learned to suffer the man because his mother apparently loved him. And while Gideon had been devastated when she'd left and would probably always carry the hurt, he'd tried to move past it.

"Are you certain?" Her empathy was foreign. Outside of the Bowen family, he hadn't been shown much of that. Unless one counted some of the staff at Stratton Hall who'd tried to mother him after she'd left.

"Yes, I'm certain. Septon is also closer than Rhys. If

he can't help us," *or won't*—but Gideon didn't say that out loud, "we can go to Rhys."

The fact was that Septon owed Gideon, and they both knew it. He'd stolen Gideon's mother away. Gideon could use that to bend the man, and he had no compunction about doing so.

She smiled up at him. "We'll leave as soon as the festival is over."

He set the poem fragment back on the table and turned to face her. "I'd prefer to leave immediately." He didn't have the patience for this bloody festival. He needed to find the treasures and secure them. Never mind whatever the hell was going on with his title and that vicar who'd gone missing.

Her smile faded. "My father won't want us to leave."

"Something tells me you don't always do what your father wants."

"Not always, no. But this festival is special to him. And there's the other matter."

He wanted to pretend he didn't know what that was, but what would be the point? "The betrothal announcement." Gideon had still been hoping that wouldn't come to pass. Perhaps if he spent the remainder of the festival partaking in drunken debauchery, Foliot would call the whole thing off.

But then he'd likely cast Gideon out or worse.

Still, leaving now for Septon's would buy them some time. Perhaps Gideon could convince her they wouldn't suit so that it became her decision. However, he wasn't entirely sure Foliot would accept her refusal either. As she'd pointed out, her father was adamant she wed a descendant. It was just the way things would be.

"Yes, the announcement. And the subsequent

wedding." She busied herself with picking up the poem and replacing it in the folded paper for protection before sliding it back into the book.

"None of which we've agreed to yet," he reminded her.

"No." She picked up the book and faced him. "But how are we to travel together to search for the cloak if we're not wed?" She raised an excellent—and infuriating—point.

He tried not to grit his teeth. "We wouldn't travel together. We would meet in various locations as necessary, and you would need a chaperone of some kind. Cate used her maid—she was a widow—when she was on the hunt for Dyrnwyn with Norris."

"Cate traveled with her husband before they were married?"

"Yes." He worked to not think about how he'd followed them every step of the way, stolen their most valuable clue, and then pilfered the sword from her the moment she'd found it.

She seemed to consider this a moment. "I doubt my father would approve."

"Why? He lets you move about parading as a widow. This isn't terribly different."

"Except rather than be alone, I'd be with you. At least some of the time," she added.

Given the things he'd done to her in his dream last night, it was perhaps best that they didn't travel together. Or even meet up as necessary. "I could go to Septon's without you."

She shook her head vehemently. "Oh no. No, no. This is our quest. You are not going to find the cloak without me." She pressed her lips together and glared at him. "I'll keep this poem to myself."

"Then we are back to the question of how to get to Septon's," he said. "I suppose kidnapping you is out of the question."

"Unless you want to invite my father's wrath, yes." She glanced toward the clock that sat atop the mantle. "Speaking of my father's wrath, we need to get to the great hall soon. First, I need to return this book to my room."

"Go on, and I'll see you in the great hall."

She turned and left, and he took a moment to organize his thoughts. They hadn't settled how they would travel to Septon's. It was only a day's ride away. He could leave on horseback after the meal in the great hall and be back tomorrow afternoon. He'd miss the falconry exhibition and most of the jousting tournament, which would likely annoy Foliot, but Gideon could make it work somehow. And he didn't need the poem—he could simply tell Septon about it. What they needed was the rest of it.

What if he found it at Septon's or learned where to go in pursuit? If he had to track down the rest of the poem, would he come back here to fetch Miss Foliot first? If so, he'd face the same issue of how to travel with a woman who wasn't his wife. Which brought him back to his primary dilemma: He liked Miss Foliot, but he didn't want to marry her.

He wanted to find the treasures and keep them away from Foliot. He'd already given the man two and didn't really want to give him any more. Better to work out how to keep them from him and get on with that. That was something else he'd have to talk with Septon about. It grated him for certain, but he'd do whatever was necessary to protect his family's legacy.

Will I marry her to do it?

The tiny voice in the back of his mind fought to be heard, but he refused to answer it. Feeling no more settled than he had when Miss Foliot had left, he stalked from the library and went to the great hall where he lingered near the fireplace, which was more than large enough for Gideon to stand inside without crouching. If he wanted to catch on fire.

Guests had gathered, and more filtered in. The banquet tables were set for a fine feast, and retainers bustled about. They too were garbed in medieval costume made from ivory and dark green linen. Gideon glanced down at himself. He was rather conspicuous, but he didn't care in the slightest.

A footman approached him and held out a letter. "This arrived for you, Lord Stratton."

"Thank you." Gideon recognized Rhys Bowen's handwriting as he opened the letter. Scanning it, he tensed. The writ of summons had arrived at Stratton Hall. He could go to London and claim his title.

Penn's argument came back to him—it would be hard for the vicar, if he ever turned up, to try to dislodge a sitting earl. Gideon *should* go. And yet he could be on the verge of finding information that would lead him to the cloak. Never mind the pressure from Foliot to marry his daughter.

Why did everything have to bloody happen at once?

Conversation diminished, and Gideon looked toward the great staircase that led into the hall. Miss Foliot and her father were descending, and they both looked quite pleased. For some reason, that alarmed Gideon.

He shook out his shoulders in an effort to relax. He was just tense with so many things crashing around in his brain.

Except looking at her didn't relax him. He was torn

between wanting to replicate last night's dream and running as far away from her as he could. He should do the latter, Foliot's anger be damned, and find the cloak. Then he could use it to sneak into the vault and take back the heart and the sword. But if anything went wrong and he needed Foliot to trust him, he'd be out of luck. Better to continue with his current plan of staying on Foliot's good side. Which likely meant marrying his daughter.

Christ, he needed an ale.

Gideon tucked Rhys's letter into his coat and made his way to a table where a footman was offering ale to the guests. Suddenly, the sound of a utensil hitting glass filled the hall, and the conversation, which had picked back up again, fell off entirely. Everyone turned toward the stairs, where Foliot stood on about the fifth step.

A footman handed him a tankard of ale as Foliot addressed the assembly. "I'm pleased to announce that the jousting tournament will have a special meaning tomorrow. It will be a celebration of my daughter's marriage to the Earl of Stratton. Please join me in congratulating them!" He lifted his tankard as Gideon's stomach fell completely through the floor.

He belatedly realized Miss Foliot had approached him. She tucked her arm through his as she pressed against his side. This was not a surprise to her as it was to him.

Gideon looked down at her. "You arranged this," he murmured.

"I did what was necessary. Just smile and look happy," she said through her wide grin.

The trap closed around him, and he wanted to lash out, to wipe the joyous, satisfied smiles from the woman beside him and her father.

He turned toward her and snaked his arm around her waist, pulling her flush against him. With his other hand, he cupped her neck and held her while he lowered his mouth to hers. If they wanted a goddamned marriage, he'd show them what it would be like for her to marry *him*.

He was Gideon Kersey, notorious rake and wastrel, wife killer, and thief.

Chapter Six

DAPHNE BARELY HAD time to understand what Stratton was about before his mouth crashed down on hers. She'd shared a kiss or two before, but never one such as this. As if a storm was unleashing upon her.

His lips moved over hers with heat and urgency, and before she could adapt, his tongue dove into her mouth, surprising her completely. She clutched at him, lest the tumult sweep her away. Which was impossible, really, because he held her close and fast. She couldn't move away from him if she wanted to.

She didn't want to.

As shocking as this was, it was also divine. The slide of his tongue against hers was an unexpected delight, sending pulses of awareness through her and settling in the region of her sex.

But it was over as abruptly as it had begun.

He pulled back and retreated to her side. He didn't smile, as she'd instructed, but he looked over the crowd with an air of arrogant superiority, as if he dared them to find fault with what he'd just done.

Instead, they all lifted their ale—those that had some—and cheered.

Heat rose up Daphne's neck as her gaze found her father on the stairs. He was not drinking. He stared at Stratton, his mouth compressed into what she recognized as an irritated line. He hadn't appreciated that public display.

Well, it didn't matter. It was done, as was their

betrothal. At least publicly, if not officially.

She could feel the tension, and likely anger, roiling through the man beside her. Hopefully, he would understand.

They took their seats, again next to her father at the head of the table. Her father clapped a hand on Stratton's shoulder before sitting. "Congratulations, my boy. You're gaining the finest wife in the realm." He bent his head between her and Stratton and whispered, "Come to my study after the feast."

She watched the muscles in Stratton's neck tighten as her father sat at the head of the table and the retainers began to serve the food.

She leaned close to him and murmured, "I had no choice."

He sent her a frosty stare that was completely at odds with the fiery kiss he'd just given her. She decided to focus on eating, which didn't sound particularly good due to the somersaults her stomach was doing.

Thankfully, this meal was not as drawn-out as the banquet the night before because of the impending falconry exhibition. As soon as her father dismissed the guests, she rose from her chair. Stratton moved to help her and then offered his arm so they could go up to her father's study.

They didn't wait for him because he was busy speaking with a few of the guests. When they reached the top of the stairs, she looked down and confirmed that her father was still engaged before saying, "You're angry."

"Yes." His dark brows crowded down over his storm-cloud eyes. "Why did you ambush me like that?"

"I had to pretend I was in love with you—because of the heart. He was so pleased that he couldn't wait to make a formal announcement. I'm sorry it happened that way. I would have told you first if I could have. Does it really matter? You knew he wanted us to marry."

"Yes, just as you knew I don't wish to." His voice was tight, strained, and he didn't look at her as they made their way to the study.

"Then perhaps you shouldn't have agreed to it," she snapped, withdrawing her hand from his arm.

"Don't pretend you weren't holding out hope that it wouldn't happen," he said with considerable heat. "You agreed to your father's matchmaking, but only if the groom met your approval."

"You meet my approval."

He stopped just before they reached the door to the study and turned to face her. "What?"

She braved the angry fire of his stare, squaring her shoulders and lifting her chin. "My father desperately wants me to marry you—a descendant of Gareth. I don't particularly care if I marry at all, and since you don't wish to marry, why not marry each other? It doesn't need to be a real marriage."

Although after that kiss, she could also see the benefits of that. But she would *not* admit that to him.

He spun on his heel and went to the study, opening the door for her to precede him. Once inside, with the door closed, he crossed his arms over his chest. She turned to face him, leery of his simmering ire.

"You're proposing a marriage in name only?" he asked.

"Yes. That allows us to travel together to find the rest of that poem and hopefully the cloak, and it appeases my father."

He was silent for a moment before muttering

something, violently uncrossing his arms and stalking across the room to look out the window.

The door opened, and her father entered.

"Let us get down to business," Papa said. "We need to change for the falconry exhibit." He looked toward Stratton, who'd pivoted to stand in profile near the window. "I expect you'll garb yourself more accordingly."

"You expect a great deal," Stratton said evenly, his tone heavy.

"Nothing you haven't already agreed to," Papa said, moving to stand beside her.

"I wasn't expecting what you just did." Stratton's voice was a low rumble. "You should have asked me first."

Her father waved his hand as if they'd only caused Stratton a minor inconvenience. She understood why he was angry—they'd agreed to spend the festival deciding if they would suit. And suddenly, they were betrothed, without telling him. Still, it shouldn't have come as a surprise.

"When do you want to have the wedding?" Papa asked. "You can procure the license this afternoon and be wed as soon as next week." He sounded hopeful.

"That's awfully fast," she said, again watching the muscles in Stratton's throat throb.

"I'll get the license this afternoon," Stratton said, surprising her. He turned his gaze to her. It had lightened to the color of ice in midwinter. "When do you wish to wed?"

"I don't know." Her answer came out as a squeak, and she coughed to clear her throat. "Next week is fine."

Her father clapped his hands together and grinned at

them. "Splendid. I am sorry you'll miss the falconry exhibition, Stratton. Daphne is quite good with the birds."

The earl didn't respond, just continued to stare at them as if they weren't really there.

"You should go prepare yourself," her father said, placing a hand on her lower back and steering her toward the door. "I'll see you on the field."

She allowed him to usher her from the room, and her last glimpse of Stratton was of him refolding his arms over his chest, a look of extreme distaste curling his lip. Then her father shut the door.

As she made her way to her chamber, her mind was a riot of emotions. She hoped Stratton would see the wisdom in their union. They would both get what they wanted—the cloak. And then what?

She recalled his kiss and shivered. She could see a future where their marriage wasn't just in name. But would he want that?

Too bad she couldn't use the heart on him.

No, she wouldn't do that. She couldn't. He'd been right when he'd said it wouldn't come from him. *From us,* he'd said. She shivered again.

She hadn't really wanted to marry, but that was because she hadn't expected to be able to do it for love. For the first time, she glimpsed the possibility, and it excited her far more than the proof she sought regarding Morgan le Fay or finding the cloak.

Entering her chamber, she grew annoyed with herself. Who was she to lose sight of her objectives because of an exceedingly handsome and riveting gentleman whose kiss set her alight and made her toes curl with desire?

She had to keep her wits about her—and her

intentions clear. She would prove Morgan was a healer who'd helped Arthur, and not the manipulative sorceress many believed her to be, whatever the price.

THE FEELING OF being trapped intensified as Miss Foliot closed the door, leaving Gideon alone with her father. How he despised this man who manipulated everyone around him. Never mind the crimes for which he was responsible, namely the murder of Cate's husband's brother, who'd been the Earl of Norris. His death had required Elijah to leave his military career and return to England to claim an earldom he'd never imagined he'd have to inherit.

Much like Penn having to be an earl when he'd never known he was the heir. But hopefully that wouldn't come to pass.

Gideon shook those thoughts away and centered his attention on Foliot. "I presume you escorted your daughter out so that you could speak with me alone?"

Foliot nodded. "You may wish to consider referring to her as your betrothed instead of my daughter. Although with the rapid advent of your nuptials, I daresay you should perhaps simply refer to her as wife." His mouth curled into a smug smile that Gideon longed to wipe away permanently.

"What do you want?"

Foliot's expression darkened to a frown. "You seem angry, and yet you agreed to this union. Have you changed your mind?" His gaze turned steely.

Gideon hadn't really ever explicitly agreed. In fact, he'd tried to say no when Foliot had first asked, and

Foliot had threatened him. "I'd hoped to have a few more days at least to get to know her—and she to know me."

"That doesn't matter since the heart seems to have worked so perfectly." Because she was pretending to love him. What a bloody mess. "Let me remind you that if you wish to remain in the Order—and in Camelot—you must display your loyalty. But, if you require more…persuasion, allow me to offer something else."

Gideon's blood ran cold as he tried to imagine what Foliot might hold over him. He said nothing, instead waiting for Foliot to play his card.

"I am aware that you are not Stratton's firstborn son." And there it was. Gideon clenched his hands into fists briefly before forcing his hands open lest he show too much of his anger.

"How? I only recently learned that."

"The vicar is here on the estate."

Gideon surged forward, eliminating half the space between them until just a few feet remained. "You kidnapped him?"

"I *invited* him," Foliot said mildly.

"How did you even know what he was about?" Gideon worked to keep his tone even, while inside, he was positively burning with rage.

"Some of my men were following Penn Bowen's assistant. That man called Egg. When they determined he was after the vicar, they wondered why he was valuable and brought him here. Unlike some people, these men are exceptionally good at doing my bidding."

Gideon tried to calm his racing heart. "Let me see if I understand—you will ensure the vicar doesn't reach London if I marry your daughter."

Foliot exhaled with exasperation. "Just call her Daphne. Yes, you have the right of it. And, I will ensure the evidence he carries, which proves Bowen's birthright, is destroyed. Then if the vicar chooses to repeat his story, he won't have any proof."

At least he wasn't threatening to kill the poor man. "I want to see the church record and watch you destroy it." That was the proof—the church's ledger recording Penn's birth and listing his true father: the Earl of Stratton.

"A reasonable request, and I will honor it as soon as the wedding is over."

Of course he would.

Foliot continued, "May I suggest you take yourself—and your new bride—to London as soon possible to claim your title? While my goal has always been for Daphne to wed a descendant, I am quite pleased for her to have an earl in the bargain." He smiled that sickly, satisfied smile again, and Gideon had to bite his cheek to keep from lunging forward. Or telling the man he was a selfish, malevolent son of a bitch.

"I'll do that," Gideon said, though he was thinking about what Foliot would do with the vicar if the wedding didn't happen... "In the meantime, I need to go to the church to obtain the license."

"Excellent. I am sorry you'll miss the falconry. Daphne has many skills. She truly will be the best wife in the realm. You're a lucky man."

He felt about as lucky as a man walking to the noose. "I'm a man who has always made the best of what life gives him. I will do that again." He bowed, then took himself from the room as quickly as possible, lest he have to listen to any more of Foliot's prattle.

He walked quickly to his bedchamber, his legs

devouring the distance in his haste. He didn't have a moment to spare. Once he reached his room, he quickly changed into riding clothes, grateful he'd given up on a valet when he'd started searching for the Thirteen Treasures on Foliot's behalf. He'd advised Gideon that it was easier to move about without one, and he'd been right.

For a moment, Gideon paused, thinking of what he'd be doing now if he hadn't succumbed to Foliot's charms at Oxford. He'd been a young man hungry for attention, especially from someone who could fill a fatherly role. He should've allowed Rhys to play that part, but at that stage of his life, Gideon had thought Rhys looked down on him because of who his father was. So he'd stayed away and been vulnerable to a man like Foliot.

Gideon finished dressing and gathered only what he needed. He couldn't look as though he were leaving permanently, but that was precisely what he was doing.

Well, permanently until he returned to fetch what was rightfully his: the heart and the sword.

He made his way to the stables, where he saddled his horse. It would be a grueling ride, and he wouldn't arrive until after dark, but Gideon had to go. He couldn't stay here and marry Miss Foliot.

Just call her Daphne.

She'd be angry. Or disappointed. Or…something. He wasn't entirely sure what she'd be. He scarcely knew her, and he didn't intend to deepen the relationship, regardless of the attraction he felt. He wasn't the man he used to be—giving in to lust and fulfilling his basest needs.

Now he had a higher purpose, and he meant to see it through.

Chapter Seven

IT WAS WELL past dinner by the time Gideon walked into the drawing room at Septon House. His body ached from the fast ride, and he'd taken time to tend his horse after he'd worked so hard to see them to their destination. The animal would need to rest for a few days, which meant Gideon would have to borrow a mount from the man he detested.

A light rain had started as Gideon had approached the manor, but his clothes were now dry as he stood near the fireplace awaiting his hosts.

"Gideon!" His mother swept into the drawing room, her dark hair lightly streaked with silver that accented the pale dove gray of her eyes. She was a handsome woman with a warm smile that he'd missed so very much when she'd left him. Even now he was torn between the lingering sadness and anger caused by her abandonment and the need to love and feel loved.

She hugged him tightly, and he allowed the gesture, reciprocating by folding his arms around her but not necessarily holding her close. When she pulled back, she searched his face. "I'm so happy to see you."

He glanced toward the doorway where she'd entered. "Where is Septon?"

"I asked him to give us a few minutes. Come, let us sit." She took his hand and pulled him to a settee, where she ushered him down and sat beside him. Her gaze was a mix of sympathy and joy. "Your father is finally gone."

"This pleases you," he said. "You can marry Septon at last," he added flatly.

Her brow creased, and her sympathy overtook the happiness. "Yes. And now you are the earl, and you can return honor and dignity to the earldom."

He squinted at her briefly as if she'd lost her mind. "Do you recall my behavior? I'm not necessarily the one to engender confidence when it comes to decency."

"That was a long time ago," she said softly. "Before Rose." She took his hand between hers. "I know her death was difficult."

It was *still* difficult. She'd been far too good for him, but her father had been thrilled to marry her to a viscount and the heir to an earldom, even one with a dreadful reputation.

"The earldom isn't mine." He hadn't decided if he would tell her, but it just fell out of his mouth.

Her eyes widened, and her jaw dropped. "What do you mean?"

"I mean I'm illegitimate. You were never married to Father. In fact, you could have married Septon years ago." Maybe that was why he'd told her, so she could feel the sting of regret that he lived with every day.

Except she already did. She'd told him countless times that leaving him had been the hardest thing she'd ever done, that she'd done it only because she truly feared her husband's temper. Gideon had never seen evidence of violence, and she'd never been explicit about what she'd meant.

His father had been a nasty drunk with a proclivity for sex. As much as he'd needed alcohol, Gideon would argue he'd needed fornication even more. Probably because he'd been proud of it. He'd encouraged Gideon to follow his guidance, to become an absolute master of the bedroom. It had been a challenge that a fifteen-year-old boy couldn't refuse.

"How is this possible?" she asked, withdrawing her hand from his to press it against her flushed cheek. "Are you saying his first wife didn't die?"

Gideon shook his head, now wishing he hadn't said anything. He didn't mean to cause her pain. They'd had enough of that. "Not when she left him. She's dead now. She left him for much the same reason as you, except she was with child, and her goal was to protect him from his father."

His mother turned her head from him and nodded. She blinked rapidly, but a tear tracked down her cheek anyway. She moved her hand to try to hide it.

Gideon touched her arm. "Don't cry, Mother."

"I should have done that for you, but I didn't have that kind of courage." She turned her head back to look at him. "You know I tried to take you with me, but he wouldn't allow it. Agreeing to let me see you at Westerly Cross for that short time each summer was all he would permit."

"I know." It had been a terrible situation, and Gideon had asked himself innumerable times if he would have done the same thing in her shoes. He wasn't sure. He thought he might sacrifice himself for his child, whatever the cost.

But he'd never know because he wouldn't ever have his own child. Rose had died with their babe growing inside her, and Gideon didn't want to suffer that kind of loss again.

She wiped the tears from her cheeks and swallowed. "How did you learn of this?"

"Penn Bowen is his heir."

"The heir to what?" Septon chose that inopportune moment to enter the drawing room. His gaze landed on Gideon's mother, and he rushed to her side. "You've been crying." He sent Gideon an angry glance.

"Don't blame him, Henry," she said, patting Septon's hand. "Sit." She gestured toward the chair angled next to her end of the settee, and he sat down, folding his long, slender legs. Septon was exceptionally tall and thin with dark gray hair and eyes to match.

Gideon looked at Septon in question and, at the man's tight nod, continued. "Penn is actually William Kersey, the rightful Earl of Stratton. His mother ran from Stratton Hall but made sure to have Penn's birth recorded in a church. The vicar promised to keep her secret until my father died. When she grew ill herself, she took Penn to live with Rhys."

Septon's gaze flickered with surprise, and he exchanged a long look with Gideon's mother. When he finally returned his gaze to Gideon, he said, "Penn won't want to be the earl."

"No, he doesn't."

Septon gave a slight shrug. "Then that's that."

"Not quite," Gideon said. "The vicar went to London to show the proof of Penn's heritage to the Lord Chancellor. However, he went missing along the way."

Septon, ever astute, narrowed his eyes at Gideon. "There's more."

"That vicar is being held captive at Ashridge Court."

Septon swore beneath his breath, and his gaze darkened. "Bloody Foliot."

Gideon delivered the final piece: "He is using the vicar—and his proof—to persuade me to wed his daughter."

With another curse, this one a bit louder, Septon stood and paced toward the fireplace. He turned toward them, his lips pale as he clenched his jaw. "Foliot needs to be stopped. The man is a menace to the Order—and everyone else."

"Yes," Gideon said evenly. "And I mean to stop him. But I need your help." The words burned his tongue.

The ire dissipated from Septon's expression, and he blinked at Gideon. "I never thought to hear you say that."

Gideon's mother reached for him again, briefly squeezing his hand. She gave him a warm smile, clearly pleased that her son had finally accepted Septon.

Except he hadn't, and he never would. Needing the man's help wasn't the same as welcoming him into his life as a member of his family. He pinned the man with a cool stare. "Don't read too much into it."

Septon nodded. "How can I be of assistance?"

"I need to find Arthur's cloak of invisibility."

A sharp laugh erupted from Septon. "Is that all?"

Gideon frowned at him. "Given that both Dyrnwyn and the Heart of Llanllwch have been found, I daresay it's not far-fetched to think the cloak could be too."

"I can tell you the Order has no idea where the cloak is." He put his hand over his heart. "And that is the truth."

"How would you know?" Gideon asked. "You aren't a descendant, and Foliot has always intimated that you don't have as much authority as you might think."

"Foliot would say that," Septon said with haughty disdain. "He never understood or appreciated the hierarchy. To him, nondescendants shouldn't even be in the Order. That's why he resurrected Camelot."

The faction within the Order sought to purge the

society of all nondescendants. Though Camelot had been quashed several hundred years ago, Foliot had brought it—and its objectives to purify the organization and collect all the treasures—back.

"That's not the only reason," Gideon said. "He wants the Thirteen Treasures, and right now, he has two of them. I must find and protect the other eleven."

Septon's eyes nearly came out of his head as his jaw dropped. "He has two?"

Gideon grimaced. "Temporarily. When I find the cloak, I will take them back."

"You *gave* them to him?" Septon shook his head in disappointment. "That was foolish."

"I wanted to regain his trust. I'd hoped to use him to find the cloak and the other treasures."

"Yet you're here," Septon said slowly. "What happened?"

"To prove my loyalty, he wants me to wed his daughter. Unfortunately, he announced our betrothal today."

"He's holding his annual festival, isn't he?" Septon asked, but seemed to already know the answer since he continued without pause. "You had to leave."

"Of course he did," Gideon's mother said. "He won't be forced into a marriage he doesn't want." She sent him a sympathetic glance.

That summed it up perfectly. "I need to find the cloak." He speared Septon with an earnest stare. "What can you tell me to at least set me in the right direction?"

Septon rubbed his palm over his forehead. "That's the problem—there is no clear direction. It's the one treasure we aren't sure actually exists."

"Why? And does that mean you know where the others are?"

"I shouldn't say. I've sworn to protect the Order's secrets."

"I *am* the Order." Gideon's voice rose.

"You're also Camelot, which means I shouldn't say. But, I will. Because of who you are and what you mean to us." He looked toward Gideon's mother, and Gideon had to stifle the urge to yell that Septon had no right to feel that way—Gideon didn't want to mean anything to him. It was a childish response, but Gideon couldn't change the way he felt.

"Where are the other treasures?"

"Together, actually. Some of them are quite large, such as the chariot and the cauldron. Because of that, they were kept with Gareth."

With Gareth? "What does that mean?"

"They are located where he is buried. And before you ask me where that is, we don't know that either. It is an island, but that is all we know."

Hell, they *lived* on an island. "It could be anywhere."

"There are clues, which I will share with you—in the morning. It's rather late."

It was, and he was tired after his journey. Still, he was eager to move forward. "You'll also share what you know of the cloak?"

"What I can, yes."

"Are you aware of a poem by Elidyr that tells the story of the cloak's creation? A healer—who is identified as a woman in this tale—sought to create a protective cloak for a warrior. It's a fragment of the entire tale, but I'm hoping you might know where I can find the rest."

As he spoke, Septon leaned forward, his mouth opening farther by the moment. "You've seen this?" At Gideon's nod, he shook his head in wonder. "That piece has been missing for years. I do know the tale, and I have a copy of it in my secret library. The original is secured with other important documents and items."

"At the Order's headquarters?" Gideon longed to know where this was. Though he was a member, the upper echelon of officials in the organization as well as their seat of operations was not disclosed to the general membership. Septon, however, was privy to all that. At least that was what he'd led Gideon to believe.

"In a way," Septon said evasively. "I can't reveal everything, and that's because I don't know. There are several locations, and I don't know what items are kept in what location."

Gideon looked at the ceiling for a moment. "So bloody secretive," he murmured.

"Do you have the poem fragment with you?" Septon asked.

"No. It is in Miss Foliot's possession, and I couldn't take the time to steal it. I had to leave Ashridge Court as soon as possible to avoid the parson's trap."

"Understandable," Septon said. "Foliot will be enraged at your betrayal."

"Yes. Another reason for me to find the cloak as soon as possible and retrieve the heart and sword."

Septon arched a dubious brow. "You really think you can do that?"

Gideon gave him a wry stare. "I'll be invisible."

His mother laughed softly, and Septon cracked a smile. "You'll still be alone. Perhaps you should enlist Penn and Norris."

He recalled the promise he'd made to Penn, but he wasn't desperate. At least not yet. "No, I won't endanger them."

"And what do you plan to do once you have those

treasures?"

"I'll reunite them with the others and protect them."

"How? Do you plan to stand sentinel over them for the rest of your life? And then what?"

"I haven't puzzled that out yet. But yes, I'll do whatever is necessary."

"What of your title?" his mother asked. "You can't stand guard over the Thirteen Treasures. You have an estate to run and responsibilities in the House of Lords."

"Not if Penn inherits," Gideon said. Even now, Foliot could already have dispatched the vicar to London. Gideon's chest pinched, not because he didn't want to lose the earldom, though that was certainly part of it, but because Penn vehemently didn't want it.

"You say the vicar is at Ashridge Court?"

"Somewhere on the estate. I had the impression he wasn't in the manor house, but I suppose he could be."

"I'll find out." Septon stood and went to a writing desk, where he sat back down and began scratching out a note.

"How?" Gideon asked, also rising and following him across the room.

Septon glanced up from his work. "Foliot isn't the only one with an army of men to do his bidding. The Order has many people who help us in our efforts."

Gideon knew that, of course. He'd heard plenty of stories from Penn and Cate and Rhys about how they stood watch over artifacts and worked—sometimes aggressively—to keep the objects safe. "What do you plan to ask them to do?"

Without pausing in his writing, Septon answered, "Find and rescue the vicar and destroy that church record."

"That would be…helpful. If you could actually do it."

Septon looked up, the edge of his mouth tilting into a half smile and his eyes glinting with mischief. "We have our ways. Trust me—it's the very least I can do." His gaze turned sincere as well as a bit sad. Yes, there was clearly regret.

Good.

Gideon turned and went back to his mother, perching on the settee beside her. He forced himself to ask the question he didn't want to care to know the answer to. "Are you going to wed now?"

"Yes. If it's all right with you."

"You don't need my permission." And yet he was strangely pleased that she'd asked.

"No, but I should like to have it. I failed you, Gideon, and I wish every day that things could have been different." She reached over and touched his face, her lips curving into a sad but somehow optimistic smile. "You seem to have turned out fine, in spite of everything. I always believed you would. You were— you *are*—such an extraordinary man."

His chest tightened. "Thank you. I want you to be happy—and for your relationship to be legitimate. Septon, you'd best marry her, or I'll have to call you out."

Septon stood from the desk with a soft laugh. "I would marry her tomorrow if I could, but I suspect you will be on the road as soon as possible, and she won't want to marry without you there." He looked toward Gideon's mother, who nodded her agreement as she beamed at Gideon.

"You're right about that," Gideon said, feeling surprisingly happy. "As soon as this is all sorted out, we'll have a wedding." He took his mother's hand and squeezed it. Then he stood and looked at Septon. "I'm still not... I'm not sure I can ever fully put the past behind me."

"I wouldn't expect you to," Septon said without flinching. "I have tried to spend my days earning the right to be with your mother, and I shall continue to do so until my dying breath."

"That is all I can hope for."

Gideon's mother rose from the settee. "Lambert had your room prepared as soon as you arrived."

Gideon turned his head to look at her. "I have a room?"

"Always. No one else sleeps there but you."

The few times he'd stayed here, he'd always had the same chamber, but he hadn't realized it was *his*. "Thank you. I'll see you in the morning." He looked back to Septon. "Early."

"Yes, early," Septon said.

Gideon went to his mother and kissed her cheek. "Good night, Mother."

She hugged him briefly. "Good night, dear."

As Gideon lay in bed staring at the ceiling, he wondered how his absence had been received at Ashridge Court. Foliot would be irate, of course. He would have dispatched his minions to Glastonbury and beyond to hunt him down. It was only a matter of time before they ended up here—if they got past the protection the Order surely kept at Septon House. On other visits, Gideon had seen men who didn't quite look like retainers. It made sense that the Order would protect one of its most important officers.

And what of Daphne? Would she be angry too? Probably. If not about the wedding, which she didn't seem to really want either, then because he'd gone to find the cloak without her. Yes, that would likely perturb her. But he didn't care. She'd tried to force him into a marriage he didn't want, even if it was in name only.

As he drifted off to sleep, he tried to maintain his anger toward her. Too bad his body remembered the soft, lush curves of her petite form when she'd pressed herself against him earlier that day and the way her sweet mouth had welcomed his.

All that was in the past. Now, she was just a dream.

BY THE TIME Daphne rode up to Septon House, she was exhausted. And it was barely midmorning. She'd left the stables at Ashridge Court just before daybreak and had stopped to change horses five times.

A groom met her and helped her dismount, then led her horse to the stables to cool him off and rub him down. Before they left, she thanked the animal for his speed.

The door to the house opened, and she was ushered inside. Daphne glanced around at the entrance hall decorated with a suit of armor, weapons, and one of the most beautiful medieval tapestries she'd ever seen.

She removed her hat and handed it to a footman before addressing the butler. "I'm here to see Lord Stratton."

"They are at breakfast... Ma'am?"

"Mrs. Guilford," she said, using her alias. She smiled for good measure.

"I'll show you to the drawing room." He started to

leave the hall, but she didn't follow him. "Would you mind taking me to the breakfast room instead? My need to speak with Lord Stratton is urgent."

The butler had turned and now clearly struggled to keep a pained look from his expression. "Of course, ma'am."

He changed direction and led her from the hall. After passing through several rooms that were even more laden with antiquities than the entrance hall—because they had more space—they arrived at the breakfast room.

"Mrs. Guilford is here to see Lord Stratton," the butler announced.

She stepped past him, pausing just inside the threshold and surveying the three people at the table. Stratton shot out of his chair.

"What are you doing here?" he asked.

She put her hands on her hips and glowered at him. "I should ask you the same thing."

"I'm visiting my mother." He glanced toward the woman seated to his right. The third person, whom she recognized as Lord Septon, was on her other side. He rose from the table. "You shouldn't have come here," Stratton said.

"You shouldn't have left me at Ashridge Court." Her lip curled as she advanced toward him. "My father was livid when you didn't return."

Stratton's eye twitched. "Did he hurt you?"

Taken aback, she scowled at him. "Of course not. He would never do that. Why did you leave?"

Lady Stratton stared up at her, her gray eyes colder than a glacier. "I should think it would be obvious, *Mrs. Guilford*. He didn't wish to be forced into marriage."

Daphne opened her mouth to refute that charge—or

at least explain it—but Stratton came forward and took her by the arm, then steered her from the room with a murmured "Excuse us."

He guided her to a small sitting room, letting her go as soon as they entered, then turning around and closing the door. "How did you know I was here?"

"You said you wanted to start searching for the cloak immediately, and when you didn't return from obtaining the license yesterday afternoon, I made my own—accurate—deduction."

"You could have been wrong and come all this way for nothing. How in the hell did you get here?" He went to the window, which faced the drive. "How many of your father's men are outside?"

"None," she said defensively. "I came alone."

He spun about, his gaze incredulous. "Are you completely without sense? Or mad? Or both?" He shook his hand. "Never mind. You're clearly your father's daughter. Which means you're mad."

She ground her teeth. "My father is *not* mad. And neither am I. You're the one who abandoned me."

"You mean I escaped your parson's trap." He pressed his lips together and moved away from the window. "Does your father know you're here?"

"No. To calm his anger, I told him that I sent you to my cottage in Keynsham to fetch my mother's pendant so I could wear it at our wedding."

"Bloody hell," he muttered.

"Then I set out this morning to meet you," she continued. "Or so I told the groom in the stable."

His eyes widened once more, and his brows dove low on his forehead. "He let you go alone? I'm tempted to go back there and ensure he's terminated from his post."

"I told him my manservant was joining me. And yes, let's go back."

He shook his head firmly. "Absolutely not."

"We *must* return. My father will—"

He quickly moved toward her, not stopping until they were scarcely a foot apart. "I don't care what your father will or won't do. *You* are definitely going back. I, however, am not."

"I'm not going without you." She lifted her chin and stared him in the eye. "Or without the cloak. We made a bargain to find it—together."

The muscles in his jaw tensed, indicating the rising level of his anger. "You violated that arrangement when you let your father announce our betrothal."

She clenched her fists as her spine stiffened like a steel rod. "That was not what we agreed to. I didn't promise *not* to marry you! And finding the cloak together certainly wasn't contingent on whether we wed." She just barely kept herself from outright shouting.

His voice had risen along with hers. "I also said I didn't want to marry, and we agreed to spend the festival deciding if we'd suit. For the love of God, woman, why do I have to keep reminding you of that?"

"And let me tell you again that I had no choice in the matter. My father saw that I was enamored of you—an act I had to put on; otherwise, my father would question why the heart didn't work—and decided we should announce the betrothal immediately. I didn't have a chance to warn you."

"It didn't occur to you to say, 'Not quite, yet, Papa'?"

She glared at him. "Your sarcasm is unnecessary. Tell me, why would I ask him to wait when I was supposed to be irrevocably in love with you because of that stupid heart?"

He groaned low in his throat, then turned from her to stalk back to the window. "We can't work together to find the cloak. We can't work together at all."

"Why not?" Some of her ire fled, to be replaced by a deep concern.

He pivoted to face her but only spared her a brief glance. "Because we don't want the same things."

"I didn't really want to marry you," she said softly— or at least softly compared to the volume at which she had been speaking. "I was just trying to find a way to help our cause."

"We have no cause. Not anymore."

"But we both want to find the cloak. We should work together. I brought the poem with me, if that helps." She patted the front of her jacket, where she had the parchment stashed against her breast.

He looked at her in horror. "You put it in your riding habit?"

"It's well protected." She narrowed her eyes at him. "Don't treat me like some imbecile who doesn't understand or value antiquities. I daresay I know more about them than you do."

He answered her with a glare. "Your father recruited me to his cause over a decade ago."

She gave him a cool, superior stare. "And he 'recruited' me at birth."

He frowned at her, and she silently celebrated her small victory. "We can't work together."

"You keep saying that, but we must," she said. "Just as we must return to Ashridge Court."

"So we can get married?"

She looked away from him, unable to bear the intensity of his stare. "Yes."

He exhaled. "I still don't want to marry you."

"I know." She returned her attention to him and saw that he'd relaxed, if only slightly. "Which is why I offered to wed in name only. Then, later, we can get an annulment."

"On what basis?" His tone was dubious.

"I haven't quite reasoned that out yet, but I'm sure we can come up with something."

He seemed to consider the notion, then abruptly shook his head. "No. I don't need to marry you. And I don't need to return to Ashridge Court. But *you* do."

"I will not. Besides, I've been riding for hours, and I am not getting back on a horse."

"I'll send you in a carriage. And I'll allow you a respite. Two hours and not a moment more. I do not need your father descending upon Septon House."

Anger and frustration churned through her. She didn't understand what had changed. They'd been keen to work together, and he'd at least seemed to accept the *possibility* of marriage. If he didn't return to Ashridge Court, he would infuriate her father, who would exact retribution. "My father will see you thrown out of the Order."

"He can try, but I'm a descendant, and I am not the one leading a shadow organization within the society."

She stared at him. "What are you talking about?"

He shook his head briskly. "Never mind. I misspoke. You're free to rest here, or I can ask the butler to show you up to a chamber. Which do you prefer?"

"A chamber." She had no intention of going quietly, but she did want to rest. She needed to think clearly in order to develop a plan. That was rather difficult to do in the presence of this aggravating man.

"Come." He led her from the sitting room back into

the entrance hall, where he asked the butler to take her a room where she could rest for a while.

Stratton pierced her with a stony glare. "Be prepared to leave at noon. Any later and you won't make it back to Ashridge Court before midnight."

She had no plans to return to Ashridge Court at all. Not without him. And she wasn't going to spend her precious time at Septon Hall closeted in a room. She was going to find that bloody cloak—with or without his help.

Chapter Eight

THE FOOD HAD long gone cold, but Gideon returned to the breakfast room after sending Daphne upstairs. His mother and Septon were eagerly awaiting him.

"Miss Foliot followed you here," Septon said.

"Yes. By herself, the fool." Gideon was angry about a vast array of things concerning her, but that was one of her worst offenses. To travel so far alone was madness. She was more like her father than Gideon had hoped.

Wait, he'd hoped for her to be...anything? Why should he care about her at all?

Because in their short acquaintance, he'd come to admire her intellect and her dedication to her work. He was also very attracted to her in a most inconvenient way. Furthermore, he just plain liked her.

Or at least he had until she'd allowed her father to send them to the altar.

Her proposition wasn't the worst idea—marrying in name and then finding a reason to annul the union. It wasn't an easy path, but it could be done. And since neither of them particularly cared to marry, they needn't worry about ruining their social standing or reputations.

He didn't have to marry her, however. He'd been a bit mad himself to think Foliot would help him without exacting a terrible price. Giving him the sword and the heart should have been enough, but Gideon had been more wrong than he could have imagined.

"So I gathered," Septon said, drawing Gideon back to the moment. "She was observed arriving alone. I was notified just before breakfast that a single female rider was approaching the estate. I had no idea it was her, of course."

Gideon now had confirmation that Septon House was protected. Not that he'd doubted it. "She concocted some tale about asking me to go to her cottage in Keynsham to fetch something for our wedding."

"So Foliot doesn't know that you left to avoid the wedding?" his mother asked.

"Apparently not."

"There may be a way to use that to your advantage," Septon said. "If you decide you need Foliot. I suppose we should repair to my private library to determine your next steps." He rose and offered his hand to Gideon's mother, guiding her to stand.

"I'll leave you to your business," she said, presenting her cheek to Septon, who kissed it. "Perhaps I'll find Miss Foliot and chastise her for trying to ensnare my son." Her eyes twinkled with mirth, and Gideon felt a pang for all the missed years, as well as a spark of affection for her eager support.

"Come," Septon said, and they followed his mother from the breakfast room. They soon parted, with Septon and Gideon going upstairs to Septon's secret library. Gideon had known of its existence, of course, but he'd never been invited to see it. Penn had, and Cate had also been inside. She'd sneaked in, however, which Gideon had only recently learned. Cate was a most intrepid woman. Like Daphne.

They were soon in a small office upstairs, and Septon went directly to a painting of an eighteenth-century gentleman surrounded by his hunters. He pushed on it, and the wall moved inward. It wasn't the entire wall, of course, but an undetectable door.

Septon preceded him inside. "Will you bring a spill from the fireplace, please?"

Gideon did as he requested, and once he stepped into the small, windowless chamber, he understood why it was necessary.

Taking the spill, Septon lit a lantern that hung from a hook on the wall. Light splashed over the room that was little more than a closet with bookshelves and a locked trunk that was tall enough to act as a table.

Septon went to one of the bookshelves and removed a dark leather tome. He set it on the trunk and opened the cover. "This is the Elidyr text. Minus the text that is on the original fragment that Miss Foliot has. I don't suppose she brought it with her?"

"She did, actually." Gideon winced inwardly. He probably should have asked to borrow it. As if she would have allowed him to take it from her sight. She would have demanded to accompany him. "I don't think she'll part from it, even for a moment," he said.

Septon pulled a small pair of spectacles from the inside of his coat and placed them on his face. "Smart woman. I don't blame her. If you can remember what it said, we may not need it." He fell quiet as his gaze dashed over the page, reading the Latin. Gideon read along with him in silence, but he wasn't as fast as Septon and had to ask him to wait to turn the page.

It was a well-written poem, though not as dramatic as the one Rhys possessed, which detailed the Battle of Badon Hill. "There's quite a bit about the healer." When Septon turned the page, Gideon gasped. "It *is* Morgan." Her name leapt from the page. Daphne was right. She should see this. Gideon knew how much it would mean to her.

"Yes, Morgan le Fay. Morgana. Morgaine. And many other derivations."

"She was not a sorceress," Gideon said.

"It depends on what you mean by that. Plenty of people think healers are sorceresses. Or witches, depending on the time period."

They read the next page and the one after that, and when Septon turned that page, he said, "This is where the page is missing—the page Miss Foliot has. I would dearly love to make this complete again."

He wanted Gideon to get it from her. "Do you want me to bring her in here?"

"Maybe not in *here*," Septon said. "I wouldn't want her to tell her father what she saw or that she knew where this library is even located." His eyes widened briefly. "I should have closed the door."

"I'll get it." Gideon went to the door and glanced out into the office. A flash of dark green skirt at the doorway from the office to the corridor caught his eye. He hurried into the office. "Daphne!"

Rushing to the door, he saw her fleeing down the corridor. "Come back here. Please."

She slowed and turned, her expression hesitant. Reluctantly, she walked toward him, her movements stiff.

He frowned at her. "What are you doing?"

"Spying."

"At least you're honest. Come on." He gestured for her to precede him and followed her into the office. "In here." He moved into the library. "She was in the office listening to us," Gideon said, turning to her. The space was quite cramped now. "How much did you hear?"

"I just arrived." She glanced toward Septon in concern. "I heard you talking about my missing page."

So she didn't know that Morgan was in the text.

Peering over the top of his glasses, Septon pinned her with a serious stare. "What is it you hoped to gain by eavesdropping, Miss Foliot? Indeed, by coming here at all."

"I want to find Arthur's cloak. And I want to prove that Morgan was his healer, and not the terrible, manipulative enchantress most believe her to be."

Septon's features softened. "I didn't realize you were a scholar."

She looked a bit surprised. "My father didn't tell you?"

"No. Should he have?"

"I thought the Order was aware of my scholarly pursuits regarding Morgan. I have...papers I've asked to share."

"Do you? Well, I'm afraid women aren't allowed to share information in the Order."

"That's why my father said that he would. But he told me no one was interested." She looked hurt, and Gideon's hatred of her father intensified.

"That may be true," Septon said kindly. "But he didn't tell me, and I would not have said that. I'm quite interested. Tell me your theories."

She hesitated, but only for a moment. "Morgan was a healer, perhaps with some mystical abilities, which I'd doubted until I met Stratton." Her gaze flicked toward Gideon. "I was so opposed to the idea of her being called a sorceress that I'd hoped there would be no magic. But given what I know now, I have to believe she had some sort of supernatural ability. Which actually makes a bit of sense when you consider her name—Morgan, which is an old word for water nymph. She is perhaps gifted with some sort of water-related ability, though I have no idea how that connects with the cloak. She first appears by name in *Vita Merlini* by Geoffrey of Monmouth, but Arthur's healer is mentioned in earlier works, such as the Elidyr text I read at Rhys Bowen's, and I am convinced that is her. There is also a Middle Welsh tale that names Arthur's physician as Morgan Tud. I believe that is further evidence of my theory." She looked between them. "Finally, I'm not entirely certain where she resided, but I like to think it was in Glastonbury—on the Isle of Avalon. And that's probably just because I used to pretend that was true when I was younger." A pretty blush stained her cheeks, and Gideon had no trouble imagining that young girl.

"Your theories are quite sound," Septon said with a twinkle in his eye. "Do you think Morgause was her sister?"

"Probably, but I admit I haven't pursued that research."

"Your father would be delighted to have proof that Morgan was aunt to several of Arthur's knights, including Gareth." Septon's gaze flicked to Gideon.

"Morgause was mother to Gareth?" Gideon vaguely recalled that.

Septon nodded. "Along with Gaheris, Gawain, and Agravain."

"So I could be related to Morgan le Fay," Gideon said, glancing toward Daphne and wondering if that had anything to do with why she was eager to let her father marry them off.

"I would say you most likely are." Septon looked

toward Daphne. "I'd like you to see something." He flipped back to the second page and moved aside so Daphne could take his place.

She perused the poem, and since she was now standing close enough to nearly touch Gideon, he knew the moment she read Morgan's name. Her body tensed, she drew in a sharp breath, and she leaned forward, her hand floating above the book so that it nearly touched the page. "She's here," she whispered in awe.

"Much earlier than Geoffrey's tale," Septon said. "This is the rest of the Elidyr poem. I believe you have the fragment?"

She withdrew the paper from her riding jacket with great care. There were several thick pieces of parchment folded around the fragment, which she gingerly revealed. She sent Gideon a glance tinged with apology. "I'm afraid I didn't bring a pair of gloves." She set the fragment next to the book on the trunk. "I had thought this was from the ninth century, but it must be earlier than that?"

Septon adjusted his spectacles and read the page. "Oh yes, it's much older than that. The sixth century, I should think. This is extraordinary. Wherever did you get it?" He looked over at her.

"I found it several years ago in my father's library. It was tucked into a book, likely forgotten. I didn't want to tell him about it for fear he'd take it from me." She looked a bit guilty.

"Don't feel bad about that," Septon said with soft encouragement. "We all do what we must to protect antiquities."

She gave him a tentative look. "May I read the entire poem?"

"I insist. Stratton and I were just reading it, but I've

read it before, and now I've seen the missing piece. You two read it together." Septon flipped the poem back to the beginning and stepped aside.

Daphne glanced up at Gideon before starting to read. Because he'd just read the start of it, Gideon spent more time looking at her than the text. Her dark auburn hair smelled of orange and spice instead of the floral fragrances most women used. It gave her an exotic air.

It was difficult to stand this close to her and not think of the kiss they'd shared the day before. Or the dream he'd had the past two nights…

He forced himself to look at the page and stop thinking of her. They were at odds. They might both want the cloak, but she would give it to her father, and Gideon would keep it from him. Furthermore, she believed her father would reward her discoveries, or at least recognize them. Gideon doubted she'd ever be allowed into the Order and didn't for a moment think Foliot would advocate for her.

When she got to the point where he'd been interrupted earlier, he focused entirely on the poem. In its completed form, it told the tale of the healer, Morgan, and how she obtained a cloak from the monks at Beckery Chapel. She "blessed it to protect the wearer." Arthur then came to the chapel where she gave it to him, and they left together. It implied he went off to fight a battle with his knights. There was also a great deal of other information woven in regarding healing and general health.

Daphne looked over at Septon. "Beckery Chapel existed during their lifetimes?"

Septon's gaze brightened with admiration. "You've heard of it? Few people know of its existence. I daresay your father must have told you. It's perhaps the earliest monastic community in Britain."

Daphne glanced back down at the text. "If Morgan associated with the monks and 'blessed' the cloak, does that mean she was Christian?"

"No, I can't imagine she was," Septon said. "Christianity was here, of course, but a woman like Morgan le Fay would have worshipped differently. And her manner of 'blessing' could be just what it means— saying a prayer over the garment. However, I believe it was more than that."

Gideon suspected he knew what Septon meant, but wanted him to elaborate. "In what way?"

"In the past—and even in some places today—there are those who associated healers, especially women, with magic or witchcraft. There is a bit of truth to the association, at least in some instances. We know it was the case with Merlin and likely with Morgan. Both were healers, and both are linked to magical items or activity.

"Merlin?" Gideon asked. "Is he somehow related to the cloak or the other treasures?"

Septon gave a slow, single nod that carried an air of skepticism. "Some think the treasures are buried with him, but as I told you before, they are not."

"Where are they?" Daphne asked.

"An island—and probably not this island," Gideon said. "Though no one can say for sure."

Daphne looked to Septon as if for confirmation. And he gave it to her, nodding.

Gideon wanted to hear more about the cloak. "So you believe Morgan enchanted the cloak so that it would make the wearer invisible?"

"That's my theory." He gave Daphne his full attention. "What do you think, Miss Foliot?"

Daphne practically bloomed in response. It seemed her ideas and expertise weren't in demand. Gideon really despised her father. He wanted to know why he hadn't enlisted her to find the cloak—or any of the other treasures.

"I think you're probably right. That makes the most sense to me. I wish we could know for sure." She briefly looked down at the text. "Where did you get this poem, Lord Septon?"

His eyes twinkled in the lamplight. "Ah, now that is an interesting tale. Lord Pritchard was my mentor, and many of the most valuable antiquities in my collection came from him. Pritch was obsessed with Arthurian lore—more than me, if you can believe that." He smiled at Gideon, who might have argued with him, but then he hadn't known Pritchard.

"I can't imagine anyone being more obsessed than you."

Daphne threw him a wry glance. "Then you don't know my father well enough."

"I do know him well enough, and you're right. He *is* more obsessed than Septon." Because he was willing to put people in danger and exact any price to get what he wanted. All in the name of Arthur. Or, perhaps more accurately, the Thirteen Treasures.

Gideon looked at her for a moment, wondering how she could be so loyal to a man capable of such malfeasance. She had to be ignorant of his crimes and transgressions.

"Back to my tale," Septon said. He directed his gaze to Daphne. "Allow me to tell you about Pritch—that's what I call him." His gaze grew a bit unfocused as he reminisced. "Pritch was a high-ranking member of the Order, a descendant, and recruited me after I demonstrated exemplary academic achievement at Oxford. He believed the Isle of Avalon was located in Glastonbury and spent a great deal of time in the area, where he came to know many people. He became rather interested in some documents the monks had at Glastonbury Abbey and which were subsequently dispersed after the abbey was stripped in 1539. Many of the manuscripts went to a local family, but not all. In fact, there was a group of documents—the Beckery Texts—that went missing for quite some time.

"They were written at Beckery Chapel?" Daphne asked.

Septon nodded. "Yes. And it is thought by some, myself included, that Elidyr was a monk there."

"So Rhys Bowen's Elidyr text came from Beckery?" Gideon asked, wondering if Rhys knew this. He planned to ask him along with how Rhys had come to have the manuscript.

"It's very likely. There is much we don't know about them. How did Elidyr come to write these tales? Did he travel with Arthur? Did someone tell him the stories?" Septon was quite passionate about this subject, but then he was about all things Arthurian. "During a trip to Glastonbury, Pritch met a woman who first told him about Beckery Chapel. He visited her several times and they grew…close. Eventually, she gave him the partial text that you just read, which he in turn gave to me. It was all she would let him have, or so he told me."

"Does that mean there are more writings by Elidyr?" Gideon asked.

"That's what Pritch said. He wanted to introduce me to the woman, but she refused. She became upset that he'd told me about her and ended the relationship soon after."

Daphne frowned. "What a shame. I would love to talk to this woman, assuming she is still alive."

Septon's expression turned grim. "I am not sure she is. I've tried to see her a few times, but have always been told she is out."

"Then you know where to go," Gideon said.

"Yes, but I'm not sure I'd advise paying a visit."

Daphne looked at him earnestly. "We have to try."

We. She meant herself and Gideon—or so Gideon believed. But they couldn't go together. If they found the cloak, he couldn't let her have it.

Septon cocked his head and nodded. "Yes. I think you must. Pritch always said she was part of a group of women—healers like Morgan—and that if he'd been a woman, they might have been more open to his interest in their history and the Beckery Texts."

"Well, I *am* a woman," Daphne said, rather unnecessarily but sparking Septon's laughter.

"Yes," he said through a wide grin.

Gideon did not laugh. He was far too aware she was a woman. One he was supposed to marry.

"All right," Septon said, still smiling at her. "I'll tell you where to go."

He would tell *her*. Not Gideon, though he'd make it clear he would be going. Apparently, he needed her to accompany him if these women would be more amenable to sharing information with a woman.

"We'll leave as soon as our horses can be prepared. If you're up to it." Gideon hoped she would say no so that he could go without her, but he knew she wouldn't.

She beamed at him. "Excellent."

It was not excellent, but it was the best he could do. As soon as he learned... What did he hope to learn?

He focused on Septon. "Do you really think it's possible any of these Beckery Texts will help us find the cloak?" Or the other treasures?

"Certainly. But you'll have to gain admittance to their library, and that will be quite a feat."

"We will," Daphne said firmly, her gaze confident.

Gideon did appreciate her optimism. It counterbalanced his pessimism. He was already thinking of how they might sneak into this library if necessary. "Where are we going?"

"To a house on the southwest edge of Glastonbury near the River Brue. In fact, it's called Brue Cottage. Though I would describe it as more than a cottage." Septon inhaled and pinned Gideon with a dubious stare. "If you could gain access to their library, that would be quite an achievement for the Order. It would do much to improve your standing." He flicked a glance toward Daphne and then shot his attention back to Gideon, who tried to silently communicate that Septon shouldn't say any more.

Thankfully, Septon understood. They couldn't discuss Camelot or the fact that they knew her father was leading it and—probably—planned to stage an internal coup. Gideon had no idea what she knew or didn't know, but he was still willing to bet she had no idea of her father's crimes.

Daphne sent Gideon an inquisitive stare but said nothing. He felt certain she would ask him about his standing later. Perhaps he would try avoiding her for the remainder of the day...

Somehow, he doubted that would be possible.

Septon opened the book to where the page was missing and looked at Daphne. "Would you mind returning your page to its home? This is a copy, of course, but I will ensure it's reunited with the original manuscript. In exchange, I would be happy to transcribe the entire text for you."

It was a more than generous offer, especially from Septon, who guarded his antiquities closely. Gideon was pleased to see the genuine appreciation light up her face.

She picked up her page and slid it into his book. "Thank you, Lord Septon. I would be delighted to return this orphan page to its parent."

"I am eternally grateful," Septon said with earnest enthusiasm. "And if I may beg another favor? This library is secret. I only share it with family and the closest of associates and friends. Stratton, of course, is family. If you two marry, you would be family too. But if you do not, I humbly ask that you not share what you've seen or that you're even aware of it. I'm sure you understand that many people would seek to gain entry and even to steal from me."

"I want to say that I can't believe someone would do such a thing, but my father keeps guards for the same reason." Was that what he'd told her? Not that in addition to stealing his antiquities—and his collection paled in comparison to Septon's—there were people who wished him harm?

"A wise choice." Septon didn't tell her that he also had guards, but they stayed hidden unless they were needed—or unless Septon was hosting a large event. Foliot had them out in the open all the time, medieval festival or not. For him, it was more to demonstrate his power and to intimidate. At least that was Gideon's perspective.

Septon picked up the book and replaced it on the shelf. He looked expectantly toward Gideon, who understood the silent communication.

Gideon turned to Daphne. "Come, let us repair to the formal library downstairs."

"Yes, we've many things to discuss." Her gaze took on a guarded quality. "Please, lead the way."

Many things to discuss, while he privately worked out how to part ways with her—for good.

DAPHNE SLID SURREPTITIOUS glances toward Stratton as they made their way downstairs. He'd offered her his arm, and she'd considered not taking it. But if he would be gracious enough to present it, she would be gracious enough to accept it.

Even while she harbored a healthy ire toward him.

When they reached the library downstairs, she took her hand from him and folded her arms over her chest. Then she fixed his back—because he'd continued into the room—with a haughty stare. "What is your plan for us to travel alone? When we were going to marry, it was not an issue. Now, it's a potential scandal."

Stratton turned, his reaction nonexistent. His gaze was as cool as ever, his features impassive. "If you've no plans to wed, does it matter? I'm fairly certain you don't spend your time in London Society."

She wrinkled her nose. "Heavens, no."

"You would have had to if you'd become my countess."

"Yes, well, that doesn't seem to be in danger of happening," she said flatly. She wasn't upset that they weren't marrying, though she had convinced herself that he would be better than most. She was upset that he'd left without a word and had planned to cut her out of finding the cloak. She suspected he still might, and was certain he'd go to Brue Cottage without her if Septon hadn't pointed out that her feminine presence might be helpful.

For the first time, being a woman was actually working in her favor.

She unfolded her arms but didn't relax her stare. "Since we aren't married, how do you propose we travel together? You'd mentioned traveling apart and meeting up. We could do that, I suppose."

His eyes blazed with indignation. "God, no. It's bad enough you rode here alone. I'm not allowing you to ride to Brue Cottage that way." He raked his gaze over her from head to toe. "We could pass for siblings."

"You don't get to allow or disallow me anything. You are not my husband." She blew out a breath and with it a measure of her frustration. "We'll use aliases, then. And if we're recognized? That's a distinct possibility in Glastonbury since I grew up there."

He frowned at her, his brow furrowing. It should have made him unattractive, but she realized— annoyingly—that was impossible. "You'd prefer we pretend to be married."

It would be less risky, but she could tell he thought she meant to trap him somehow. "We can be siblings. What are our names?"

"Mr. and Miss Morgan."

She tried not to laugh, but a small one escaped. And she was fairly certain she detected a slight flash of humor in his gaze. "What if I want to be Mrs. Merlin?"

"That's fine, but it might be a little too...strange."

She narrowed her eyes slightly. "I was joking."

His mouth barely ticked up, but she caught it. "I

know."

"There is a very real chance we'll be seen, and my father will be looking for us."

"Will he?" Gideon asked. "I thought you told him you'd gone to meet me."

"Yes, but when we don't return today, he'll know I was lying."

He studied her intently. "And why did you?"

She lifted a shoulder and walked to a bookcase to peruse the spines of the books. Or at least pretend to. "I didn't want my father to be angry with you. I was— am—still hopeful we will work together."

"Your father will be furious with me if we don't marry, and since we aren't going to, it's fair to say his ire is unavoidable," Gideon said wryly.

She dashed a quick look in his direction. "Perhaps."

"He's made it clear he expects us to wed. I can't imagine a scenario in which our failure to do so doesn't enrage him."

"Enrage is a strong word. I will simply have to convince him we do not suit." She moved along the bookshelf and sent another glance at Stratton. "He will be gravely disappointed, but I will point out that there are other descendants."

Stratton took a few steps toward her, drawing her to stop and watch him. "That is truly all that matters to him—that you marry a descendant."

She heard the disdain in his voice and doubted he would ever understand. "I told you before. My father is from another time. He's wanted to arrange my marriage for as long as I can remember. If I can allow him that privilege while finding a husband I can admire, if not love, then it will have worked out perfectly."

"Life is not that tidy." He turned from her and

stalked toward the door. "I'll go and get the horses and bring them around front."

"Wait. We aren't quite finished." When he turned to face her, she continued. "We'll need to stay somewhere in Glastonbury tonight."

"Yes, we'll arrive late."

"There's a small inn on the southwest edge of town—The Golden Stag."

He arched his brow at her in question. "If you know of it, do the proprietors know of you?"

She shook her head. "I've never stayed there. I've only ridden by, but I remember it because the sign is beautifully painted." He nodded, then began to turn again, but she stopped him, saying, "Stratton, do not try to leave me behind again."

His shoulders stiffened. "Don't make me feel cornered again."

She realized that was important to him for some reason. No one liked to feel trapped, but she sensed it was more than that. "We're in this together," she said softly. "I like sharing this journey with someone, especially someone as invested as I am."

He didn't relax at all. In fact, his features seemed to harden. He took a few steps toward her, his eyes dark. "We are not in this together. The treasures belong with the Order, not your father."

"My father is the Order. He keeps them safe on the Order's behalf."

Stratton snorted. "Regardless, they shouldn't all be in one place."

She narrowed her eyes at him again. "Then why did you give him two of them?"

Scowling, he looked away from her. "Do you even know how to be quiet?"

"Apparently, only when you kiss me."

His gaze snapped to hers, and suddenly, the large room felt as close and intimate as the closet-sized library they'd been in upstairs. She took a step toward him and then another. He didn't move, his eyes holding hers. And then he blinked.

"I'll get the horses." He turned and strode from the library as if the flames of hell licked at his boots.

Daphne stared at the empty space where he'd stood. What an idiotic thing to say! Why had she brought up that kiss? Because being in his presence made her want to do it again?

That was absurd. And yet it was true.

He'd made it abundantly clear he had no interest in her beyond *having* to take her to Brue Cottage. She knew he'd abandon her at the earliest possible moment. Which meant she had to make herself indispensible if she wanted to find that cloak.

Or maybe she wouldn't need him. Maybe she'd learn the cloak's location from the woman at Brue Cottage, and she could keep it from him. She didn't really want to do that. She agreed the treasures belonged with the Order, for safety's sake, but she also recognized that the items had belonged to his ancestor. Of course he'd want to find them. To hold them. To feel that connection.

A shiver danced across her shoulders. Oh, to feel that bond with something concrete from the past...

"Miss Foliot?"

Daphne blinked and looked toward the doorway. Lady Stratton stood at the threshold and swept inside as soon as she made eye contact with Daphne.

Dipping into a curtsey, Daphne murmured a greeting. "I apologize for storming in earlier."

The countess arched a brow. "Did you storm?"

"I came unannounced."

"I understand why. Septon told me about your research with Morgan le Fay. And you seek the cloak?"

"I do."

"It belongs to my family, my son—rightfully. I know the Order wants to keep it safe, but truly, if Gideon wishes to take it along with the other treasures, it would be within his rights."

"Can he claim to own something that wasn't ever his or wasn't given directly to him?" Daphne asked.

Lady Stratton's lips curved into a half smile. "And how do we know they weren't?"

"Is there something you want to share?" Daphne asked, torn between finding the woman irritating and intriguing.

"The legacy of Arthur and his knights is strong in my family. Before we knew we were descended from a knight, my family has long treasured the stories. My family hired de Valery to document the tales."

"Those are treasures in themselves," Daphne said.

"Nothing is more of a treasure to me than my son. Despite whatever you may have heard about him, he has a warm heart and a gentle soul."

Gentle? He was stoic and guarded. But yes, Daphne had glimpsed warmth and humor, and those were the things that had attracted her. "I'm afraid I haven't heard much about him. I don't pay any heed to gossip."

The countess looked surprised and pleased. "How wonderfully refreshing. Well, let me tell you the truth so that you can completely ignore everything else you might hear. Gideon's father was a debauched reprobate. He was rumored to have killed his first wife, which I never believed. He was capable of many cruelties, but I don't think murder was one of them. He preferred to humiliate those he wanted to hurt, but mostly he just liked to drink to excess and engage in lewd activities." Color rose in her cheeks, but she didn't turn from Daphne. "He did his best to pass his proclivities on to Gideon, and he was successful—for a while. But then Gideon met Rose, and everything changed. She was the sweetest young woman." Her expression turned sad.

Daphne's gut clenched. "Who was Rose?"

The countess blinked, her dark lashes fluttering like grass in a summer breeze. "Rose was his wife. Did you not know he was married?"

The revelation stung. Why hadn't he told her? Was that why he'd run? "No, I did not." She wanted to ask a hundred questions but didn't dare.

"He doesn't talk about it, at least not that I've seen. Losing her was incredibly painful."

Daphne summoned the courage to ask one question. "May I ask what happened to her?"

"It was a riding accident. Her death was awful enough, but Gideon learned she'd been carrying his babe." The countess finally looked away, but just for a moment, her throat working as she swallowed.

Daphne's heart twisted. Stratton's restrained manner made sense to her now. She also understood why he wouldn't want to marry. Again. Why hadn't he told her about Rose? Daphne thought she maybe understood that too.

"I know you were expecting to marry him," Lady Stratton said. "Please know that my son needs love. More than anything, he needs love. Please don't marry him if you don't love him."

How could she love him? There hadn't been time for

that emotion to take hold. And yet, she'd seen the potential for it to develop. Or perhaps she'd been listening to her father spin tales of her marrying a descendant for so long that she'd conjured a romantic union in her head, regardless of the gentleman.

She suddenly felt a bit sick about the whole thing. There was one more thing she understood: why he'd left Ashridge Court. Daphne stepped toward the countess. "I don't love your son, Lady Stratton, but I care for him. He doesn't wish to marry me, and I won't allow him to be forced into it. We will find the cloak together and deliver it safely to the Order." And then what?

At that moment, she had no idea.

Chapter Nine

"WE ALREADY SERVED dinner," the innkeeper's wife said, her dull blue eyes regarding Daphne with a mixture of skepticism and fear.

They'd decided Daphne should wear a veil to avoid being recognized in Glastonbury. It had proven a good idea since their inn of choice on the outskirts of town—The Golden Stag—had been full. They were now at The Bell and Goat, the fifth place they'd tried and likely their last option. They were exhausted, the moon was obscured by clouds, and it was late.

"But you do have a room?" Gideon repeated, transferring the bag, which carried the food they had left after pausing to eat a few hours earlier, to his other hand.

"We do, but what's wrong with 'er?" the woman asked, again looking toward Daphne.

"Nothing," Daphne said in a rather sunny tone that he had to give her credit for. "I had an accident as a child, and it left my face rather disfigured. Hideous, actually. Would you like to see?" She grasped the bottom of the veil, and Gideon wondered what the hell she was about. There was no nasty scar.

The innkeeper's wife raised her hands and turned her head as if Daphne were a beast who might attack. "No, no! Keep yerself covered. Aye, we have a room."

Gideon swallowed a laugh. "Good. We don't require dinner, just a pair of beds."

The woman shook her head, and a gray-brown

strand of hair came loose from her haphazard bun. "Don't have a pair. Just one room left on the second floor, and it's got one bed. If ye don't want to sleep with yer *sister*, I could give ye some extra blankets for the floor." The way she said sister seemed to insinuate she didn't believe they were siblings as he'd introduced them.

"Whatever you have is fine. I already paid your husband when he took the horses." Gideon had been loath to leave them with the man until satisfying himself the innkeeper knew horseflesh and would tend them carefully after their journey. It had become clear the innkeeper loved horses and spent a great deal of his time with the beasts and left the management of the inn to his wife. After meeting Mrs. Downey, Gideon could understand why. It wasn't that she was unpleasant to look at—which she was and which made her fear of Daphne's "scar" rather ironic—but her general appearance of shabbiness and gruff demeanor.

"The extra blankets would be welcome." Gideon prayed they would be free of fleas and filth. He glanced around the small keeping room and was relieved to see it appeared tidy, if not spectacularly clean. One table in the corner was cluttered with dishes, but he suspected that was her meal and they'd arrived as she'd finished. The floor could use a good sweeping, but that was perhaps the way it always looked at this time of day.

"I'll fetch 'em," Mrs. Downey said. She pinched her nose and squeezed the bridge, then sniffed. The sound was loud and grating, and Gideon fought the urge to clear his throat in response. "I'll let ye show yerselves up. Just two rooms on the second floor—yours is on the left at the top of the stairs. Mine's the one on the right, so don't get lost." She pivoted slightly away from them and bellowed, "Bess!"

A girl of maybe twenty came running from the back, wiping her hands on her apron. "Yes, mum!"

"Get some blankets and take 'em up to the second floor. And get a fire goin'!"

The girl nodded and took herself off.

"Er, thank you," Gideon said. He put his hand at the base of Daphne's spine and guided her toward the stairs. They climbed to the first floor in silence. At the landing, she turned and whispered, "The bed better be clean."

He hoped the same. "Just go."

She continued on and at the next landing turned to the left. The ceiling was low, and Gideon had to bend his head. Daphne opened the door to their room and hesitated on the threshold. A single sconce lit the landing and spilled a meager amount of light into the dark chamber.

Noise from the stairs drew Gideon to turn. It was Bess with an armful of blankets. She rushed by him and stopped short before running into Daphne. "Beg yer pardon, mum." She dipped a curtsey.

Daphne plastered herself against the doorframe to allow her to past. Though Gideon couldn't see her face, he could imagine her expression—something that said, *What is going on in this inn?*

After depositing the blankets on the bed, Bess used flint to start the fire in the hearth, which was opposite the door. Gideon rushed to help her build it into a decent fire, setting the bag on the floor near the wall. She shot a nervous glance in his direction and murmured her gratitude as her face flooded with color.

Once the fire was going, she lit a spill that she took from the mantel and ignited two candles that were also on the mantel. Gideon stood and, as his head nearly grazed the ceiling, realized this was the only place in the room where he could stand at his full height. The roof pitched down at the other ends, and at its lowest point, the height of the room was maybe five and a half feet. It was a petite room, sized perfectly for Daphne.

Bess turned to face them, looking first at Gideon but quickly averting her gaze as her face once again turned bright pink. She then tried to focus her attention on Daphne, only to widen her eyes slightly in distress— had she heard Daphne talking about her disfigurement? Or perhaps Mrs. Downey had told her before she'd come up. Whatever the reason, her gaze dove to the floorboards. "Shall I make up a bed for ye on the floor?" she asked.

"That won't be necessary," Gideon said.

She nodded once. "Privy's out back. Breakfast is early, but not too early. Mrs. Downey doesn't like to be disturbed, so I do ask that ye be quiet like." She shuffled her foot. "But then I s'pose sleeping is fairly quiet…" Her voice trailed off, and Gideon had to hide a smile at the girl's exuberance.

He moved toward her and withdrew a shilling from his pocket, which he pressed into her hand. "Thank you, Bess. We'll be quiet."

She looked up at him and this time smiled along with her blush. "Thank ye, my lord." She looked horrified. "I don't know why I called ye that. Ye just seem so…lordly," she finished lamely.

"I am not a lord." He wondered if she somehow knew who he was, but how could she? He'd never been to this part of Glastonbury, and he'd introduced himself and Daphne as Mr. and Miss Morgan.

"Ye will be to me," she whispered. Then she turned

and scurried from the room, closing the door *quietly* behind her.

Daphne whipped the veil from her face and looked about the room. "I am so glad to have that off." She settled her gaze on him with an amused glint in her eye and a small smile teasing her lips. "Bess is going to dream about you tonight. And maybe all the nights in the future."

He grunted in response as he picked up one of the candles from the mantel and walked toward the bed, bending his head as he went.

"How does it look?" Daphne asked, removing her hat and looking about before settling her gaze on a pair of hooks on the wall near the door. She went and hung her hat on one of them.

"Like a bed." He set the candle on the nightstand.

"You've been rather short all day." She picked up the saddlebag and took it to the small, rickety table on the other side of the room.

"Really? I feel quite tall." He stood at the shortest part of the room as he investigated the bedding.

Daphne's laughter filled the room for a brief moment before she clapped a hand over her mouth. "I forgot to be quiet," she whispered loudly.

"I doubt Mrs. Downey is up here yet," Gideon said since it looked as though she still had chores to do downstairs. But what did Gideon know? Perhaps she left it all to poor Bess and had already gone to bed. "No sign of fleas, and the bedclothes look clean enough."

"Enough? That doesn't sound encouraging. But I daresay we don't have much choice at this hour."

"We have no choice—this was our fifth attempt at lodging, if you were counting."

"I wasn't, actually, but I'm glad to know you pay attention to such detail." She loosened the cravat of her riding costume. "Do you want anything to eat or drink?"

"No, I think we should sleep. We do need to be up early." He arched a brow at her. "Aren't you exhausted?"

"Strangely, no. I am filled with anticipation for tomorrow." Her eyes gleamed in the dim, flickering light from the fire and two candles. She walked to the opposite side of the bed and turned back the coverlet. "Oh, this is just fine." She ran her hand over the sheet. "If a bit scratchy."

"Good. I'll sleep over there." He pointed to the other side of the room and went to pick up the blankets.

"You don't have to," she said. "The bed is big enough. We can always roll one of the blankets and put it between us—for propriety's sake."

"I think propriety has already been breached."

She pursed her lips—so pink and succulent. "Then we'll put it between us to keep us from temptation."

He was suddenly incredibly tempted. Whether from her words or his fixation on her mouth, he didn't know and it didn't matter. "No."

"Oh, don't be a martyr," she said with a sigh. "It was a very long day, and you're tired. I promise I won't touch you."

Was that a danger? He had to bite his tongue to keep from asking if she wanted to. Ever since she'd mentioned kissing him again earlier—had that just been today?—he'd found himself coming up with situations in which that might happen. Sleeping with her in a bed was one sure way.

It would be so easy to revert to the old Gideon. To flirt with her, to take whatever she would give him and let the consequences be damned. But he'd worked hard to leave that man behind. Besides, she deserved better.

"Stratton, don't you trust me?"

He couldn't tell if it was a taunt or a genuine question. Either way, he didn't like it. Trust had nothing to do with it. It was about honor and respect. "I respect you too much to overstep, and sharing your bed would certainly overstep."

She exhaled. "You're quite chivalrous, but then I should have expected nothing less from a descendant of Gareth. He was one of the kindest, most chivalrous of Arthur's men."

"I know." It was yet another reason Gideon strove to live up to that standard. He took the blankets and went across the room, where he built a makeshift pallet on the other side of the fireplace.

He removed his coat and hung it next to her hat, but decided he should wait to continue disrobing until she got into bed. He sat in one of the wooden chairs at the table and immediately worried it might collapse beneath him.

She brought him a pillow and set it on the pallet. "If you're uncomfortable or you get cold, you can join me in the bed. It will be fine, really." She smiled at him encouragingly, as if she were trying to coax him to canter for the first time.

He recalled that memory of his father with a burst of warmth. For all his faults, there had been plenty of moments during which he'd displayed great affection for Gideon. It wasn't until the last few years that Gideon had come to realize what a prick he'd been to pretty much everyone but him. He wondered if

Daphne had the same blindness where her father was concerned. If so, Gideon wasn't sure he wanted to open her eyes, not because she shouldn't see, but because how could it be his place to make her do so?

Gideon stood and blew out the candle on the mantel. "We should get to sleep."

With a nod, she turned and removed her coat. Taking her hat from the hook, she hung her coat, then put the hat on top of it. She went to the corner near the bed, and he realized she was going to disrobe.

Hell.

He turned the chair away from her and tried to ignore the sound of rustling fabric. When he heard the bed creak, he turned slightly. The candle next to the bed went out, and he decided it was safe to remove his boots, cravat, and waistcoat. He'd sleep in the rest.

If he could sleep.

As soon as he crawled onto the pallet, he was acutely aware of the hardness of the floor, as well as the frigidity. The proximity of the fire was a slight help, but he couldn't help looking longingly at the bed.

Only because it would be warm and comfortable—at least more comfortable than this. Not because of her.

Tired as he was, it was still some time before he drifted off. And it was long after he heard her breathing grow even.

Time ceased to make sense, however, for when the scream awakened him, he shot off the pallet, and it took him a moment to realize where he was—and who had made that sound. Rushing toward the bed, he knocked his head against the ceiling and swore.

She thrashed in the bedclothes, tearing the bed asunder. He leaned down—more than he already was—and gently shook her. "Daphne, wake up. You're having a nightmare."

It took a long moment, but her eyes finally flew open. She screamed again.

Then her hands wrapped around his biceps and squeezed. Christ, she was strong.

"Daphne, it's me. Gideon. You're safe."

Her eyes were wild, her lips parted. She'd taken her hair down so that a long braid hung over her shoulder, but dark strands had come loose and brushed against her face. He stroked them back with one hand while he cupped her shoulder with the other. "Shhh, you're safe."

She seemed to calm, her grip on his arms loosening and her color returning. But then a pounding on the door startled her again. She dug her fingers into his sleeves, and her face went white again.

"What the bloody 'ell is going on in there?"

Gideon gritted his teeth and threw a caustic look at the door. He returned a sympathetic gaze to Daphne. "I'll be right back. It's just the idiot innkeeper's wife."

"Did I make noise?" she whispered, looking frightened.

"Don't worry about it." Without thinking, he brushed his lips across her forehead, then went to the door. Opening it a bare inch, he forced a pained smile for the woman who stood outside with her hands on her hips. Her gray-brown hair stuck out in all directions, having almost completely tumbled from whatever style she'd hoped to attain the day before.

"Ye woke me up," the woman grumbled. "Why's she screamin'?"

"She had a nightmare, I'm afraid," Gideon said. Inspiration struck. "She was attacked by a dog as a child—that nasty scar—and sometimes the memories wake her at night."

Mrs. Downey's eyes widened, and she jerked back. "Lor, what a terrible thing. Yer poor sister."

"She'll be quiet the rest of the night," he said. "Thank you for inquiring after us." He closed the door before she could say another word.

He heard her retreating footsteps as he turned to go back to Daphne.

She sat up, her face still pale. "A dog?"

"You started it with the accident story." He shrugged. "It made sense."

"It did indeed," she murmured. "But you told her I'll be quiet the rest of the night." Her gaze was dark with worry.

"This will continue?" he asked.

She winced. "It might." She ran her thumb and finger down her braid. "Honestly, I don't usually go back to sleep after it happens because I don't want to have the dream again."

He sat on the edge of the bed. "What dream?"

She looked down and plucked at a loose thread on the coverlet, which was pulled up to her waist. "Of being alone."

Being alone had made her scream? "Why does that frighten you?" He kept his voice low, not because of Mrs. Downey, but because the moment seemed to call for quiet.

She inhaled rather unevenly and then let the breath out haltingly. "It's the same dream I've had since I was a child. My mother took a trip to Cornwall when I was nine and never came home. I went looking for her once and got lost in the woods overnight." She slowly lifted her gaze to his.

The stark fear in her eyes chilled him to the bone.

"That had to be terrifying." He thought of how he'd felt after his mother had left. He'd also been nine. But he'd known his mother wasn't coming back—she'd sat him down and tearfully told him that she'd see him in the summer. What was worse: knowing your mother was abandoning you or learning your mother would never return? "What happened to your mother?" he asked.

"No one knows. She simply disappeared."

That was definitely worse. Gideon still had his mother. "I'm so sorry, Daphne."

"Sometimes I think she's still out there, waiting to be found. I think of her alone. And then I think of her dying alone." She shuddered and looked away.

Gideon couldn't stand it another moment. He put his arms around her and moved closer, pulling her against his chest. "Terrifying doesn't begin to describe it."

She tucked her head beneath his chin, and he gently stroked her back.

After a few moments, he asked, "What was she like?"

"Beautiful. Which sounds superficial, but her face is so clear in my mind, even after all this time. She had the softest smile and the kindest green eyes. She always made me feel so loved and so safe."

"It sounds as though her beauty was more than on the outside."

She pulled back slightly and looked up at him. "Yes."

They stared at each other a moment, and he traced his thumb from the center of her chin to the side of her mouth. "I might describe your smile the same way."

Her lips rounded just briefly. "Oh."

He dropped his hand from her face and inched backward. "We should go back to sleep. Will you be all right?"

"I don't know if I'll be able to sleep. When I was younger, my father used to watch over me after I had a nightmare."

Gideon struggled to reconcile that with the man he knew. In the end, he couldn't do it, but he was glad to hear Foliot wasn't entirely horrid. "I'll watch over you."

"Here?" Her gaze drifted over the bed.

He shouldn't. But she looked so damn hopeful. And the truth was that he felt a need to protect her. Thinking of her alone in a forest all night coupled with the loss of her mother turned him inside out. It was no wonder she had nightmares.

"If you want me to." He already knew the answer. She'd invited him to join her earlier, and now it was beyond that—she needed him to stay.

"Yes, please. If you won't be too uncomfortable."

He stood up and circled the bed, then climbed beneath the covers. A shiver promptly jolted his frame.

"Cold sheets?" she asked with a small smile.

"Frightfully." He grinned at her in return. "Go to sleep, Daphne."

She lay down and burrowed beneath the coverlet. "Good night, Gideon."

She turned to her side, presenting her back to him. It was a long time before he slept, and his last thought was that she was the only woman besides his mother and wife and Cate to call him Gideon.

AS THEY TURNED down the lane toward Brue Cottage, Daphne looked toward Gideon, who was riding to her left. The veil was a nuisance, but it allowed her to stare at him as much as she wanted.

And she wanted.

She'd found him attractive and chivalrous before, but after he'd rescued her from the darkness last night, she was ready to recommend him for sainthood.

Perhaps that was excessive. Knighthood, then. Definitely knighthood.

He's already an earl, silly.

Her father had been absolutely giddy to wed her to a descendant who was also an earl.

Her father.

She tried not to think of him. He would be furious when she told him she didn't want to marry Gideon. The truth was, she *would* marry him. She liked him. Actually, she was rather smitten with him. Not that she planned to tell *him* that.

The lane terminated at the house, a pretty Tudor with a gabled roof and dozens of mullioned windows grouped together throughout the façade. As they rode up to the house, no one came to meet them.

She peeled the veil back from her face and swept it over her shoulder. "What should we do with our horses?"

Gideon glanced about. "I'll tie them to that tree over there." He dismounted, then helped her do the same. She tried to ignore the spark of heat that flared from where he clasped her waist.

Once she was on the ground, he tended to the horses while she went to the door. She waited for him to return before knocking, but she didn't have to. The door opened just as he arrived at her side.

A very small woman blinked up at them, her dark eyes large in her petite round face. She was older than both of them, but not yet middle-aged. "Good morning." She sounded hesitant, cautious.

Gideon stepped forward, but Daphne spoke first. "Good morning. My name is Daphne Guilford, and this is my associate, Gideon Kersey."

They'd decided to use their real names. Well, somewhat real. She was using her mother's name, which she used when she traveled, and they'd decided not to refer to Gideon by his title. They didn't want anyone at Brue Cottage to have preconceptions about why they were there. The name Foliot was likely too well known to them, and Stratton may have been as well.

"We've come to speak with you about the writer Elidyr." They'd also decided to start with that and planned to use Rhys Bowen's manuscript as a point of discussion.

The woman's mouth twisted into a slight frown. "I'll ask my mistress if she wants to see you."

She closed the door in their faces, surprising Daphne. She blinked at the wood, then turned her head toward Gideon. "How odd."

His mouth quirked into a brief smile. "A bit."

The door opened again to reveal a different woman. This one was taller, with dark, upswept hair and sharp gray eyes that reminded Daphne of a bird of prey. She wore a gown that was at least a decade out of style but that flattered her slender frame. Overall, there was something familiar about her, but Daphne couldn't quite determine what.

She looked at Daphne. "What did you say your name was?"

"Daphne Guilford."

A deep frown creased the woman's face, making her

look older than she was, which Daphne guessed to be maybe thirty. Like Gideon. Daphne glanced toward him, wondering how old he actually was.

The woman squinted at Daphne. "Not Daphne Foliot?" She blew out a breath and started to turn.

Daphne exchanged a look with Gideon, then stepped forward. "Wait! I am Daphne Foliot."

The woman pivoted back toward her and narrowed her eyes. "Why did you lie?"

Undaunted by the woman's odd behavior, Daphne countered with "How did you know I was Daphne Foliot?"

"I've seen you before—from a distance. I know you're interested in Morgana. If you were Miss Foliot, I wanted to invite you in."

Daphne grinned. "Splendid!"

The woman frowned again. "But you lied."

Wincing, Daphne rushed to say, "Only because I was afraid the name Foliot might actually hinder me. I had no idea it would impress you."

A dark brow climbed the woman's forehead. "It takes a great deal to impress me, Miss Foliot. I am *curious* about you, and I will let you know if you reach the stage of making an impression." She abruptly turned her attention to Gideon. "And you are?"

Gideon inclined his head toward Daphne. "Her associate."

"Bodyguard, perhaps? I'd say footman, but you seem too well-bred for that. Probably for a bodyguard too. Is there a chance you're in love?" She looked between them.

"No," they said in unison.

"Shame. I love love." She exhaled. "Come in, then." She turned from the door and bustled through the entry hall.

Daphne realized the tiny woman was holding the door open. She closed it behind them as they moved inside.

"Go on," she urged, gesturing for them to follow the other woman, whose name they had yet to learn.

Daphne hurried to catch up to the woman and did so as she entered a large room that overlooked the lawn behind the house. In the distance, the blue of the River Brue snaked through the green.

The room was a combination library and sitting room, reminiscent of Rhys Bowen's library, but far more cluttered. There were books on shelves, on tables, on chairs. A map was spread over a settee. At least three teacups sat around the room, and they weren't decoration.

The woman went to the settee and swept the map from the cushion, folding it quickly and tossing it atop a nearby table. Then she took what had been the only vacant seat—an overstuffed floral armchair with a large blue patch on the cushion.

Gideon motioned for Daphne to sit, then deposited himself beside her on the settee. He removed his hat and set it on the cushion beside him, noticing Daphne did the same with hers. "You have us at a bit of a disadvantage," he said. "We don't know who you are."

She laughed, a deep, resonant sound. "You came to visit me, and yet you don't know who I am. How quaint."

"We came to visit Brue Cottage," Gideon said matter-of-factly. "In fact, we'd hoped to meet a woman who must be older than you."

She leaned forward. "How old? There are a half dozen of us living here." She paused and glanced toward the ceiling. "No, seven. Yes, there are seven of us now." She smiled briefly. "I forgot that Marianne joined us last month."

Daphne blinked, thinking their hostess was rather...eccentric. She glanced toward Gideon. "How old?"

"At least eighty."

Their hostess gave a solemn nod. "That was my grandmother. Oh, I'm Gwyneth. I'm named after her, so if you came looking for Gwyneth Nash-Hughes, I am she. So you needn't be disappointed." Her mouth spread in a wide smile.

"Nash?" Gideon asked. "That is my mother's name."

Miss—Mrs?—Nash-Hughes cocked her head to the side. "Is it? Was Lord Richard Nash your relation?"

"My grandfather."

Miss Nash-Hughes's eyes widened and then sparkled as she smiled once more. "I thought you looked familiar."

"And I thought *you* looked familiar." Daphne was utterly confused.

"Yes, because I look like *him*." Miss Nash-Hughes waved her hand toward Gideon. "Because we're related."

"We are?" Gideon looked and sounded as shocked as Daphne felt. He stared at their hostess, and Daphne did the same. Then she stared at Gideon, who sat to her left. She suddenly saw why Miss Nash-Hughes seemed familiar. She and Gideon looked as though they could be siblings.

"Oh yes. We are descended from the same person— Sir Gareth."

Gideon gaped at her. "Extraordinary." The single word was heavy with awe.

Miss Nash-Hughes directed her attention to Daphne. "We are also related to Morgana, but we'll talk about that in a moment." She looked back to Gideon, and Daphne felt dismissed. "You must call me Gwyneth. Do you mind if I address you as Gideon?"

"No."

"He's actually the Earl of Stratton," Daphne muttered.

Gwyneth didn't seem to hear her. Or she was ignoring her. "Did you come to see the Beckery Texts?"

"We did," he said, and Daphne was glad to hear him use the word "we." "I'll be honest with you, because I feel that I must. I am looking for Arthur's cloak."

"Normally, I would throw you out at this point. Everyone comes here looking for the texts and either the cloak or one of the other treasures." Gwyneth rolled her eyes. "But you actually have a reason to do so. They belong to you."

"Do they not also belong to you?" Daphne asked.

Gwyneth managed to send her a brief glance. "Somewhat, but they are supposed to pass along the male line. Except for the heart. What wasn't buried with Gareth, that is." She held up her hand. "I am getting ahead of myself. Let me start at the beginning."

She opened her mouth to continue but then froze for a moment. It was as if she'd forgotten what she was going to say. "I should have offered you refreshment," she said. "I can summon tea or cakes or something else if you're *really* hungry."

"No," they answered in unison again. Daphne was eager to hear the woman's tale, and apparently, Gideon was too.

"Thank you," Gideon added with a smile. "Please

continue."

Without hesitation, Gwyneth plunged forward. "Brue Cottage is the location of an ancient circle of women—healers who practice the old ways."

"Magic?" Daphne asked and wished she hadn't as soon as Gwyneth sent her a perturbed stare. "Sorry," she muttered and dropped her gaze to her lap.

"No, *I'm* sorry," Gwyneth said. "I am not always adept when it comes to social situations. I don't wish to be brusque. I am just so thrilled to have my cousin here." She beamed at Gideon before turning her gaze back to Daphne, and this time, it was decidedly warmer. "I am happy to see you too—and I want to talk to you about Morgana. It's just, well, we're *related*." She shot a grin toward Gideon, who smiled in return. In fact, it was the most boyish, relaxed expression Daphne had ever seen on his face.

"To answer your question," Gwyneth continued, "yes, magic. In a manner of speaking. We are spiritual and connected to the earth in ways most people can never imagine. And that's all I shall say about that. Morgana was one of us, raised in our order. She was sent to Cornwall to study with another group of healers, and that is where she met a young Arthur. They formed a bond but parted. They didn't meet again until her nephews were sent to fight for him. Her sister, Morgause, was worried all her sons would die, and she asked Morgana to go and bless them."

Daphne was absolutely rapt and ended up echoing Gideon. "Extraordinary."

"From then on, she stayed with Arthur as his healer. Mostly. She came back here on occasion. It was all documented by Elidyr." She gestured toward the bookshelves. "I'll fetch the Beckery Texts in a moment so you may read them. Or you can take them with you." She looked at Gideon as she said this.

He gaped at her. "You'd let me take them?"

"They're yours. They tell our family's history, and I do not have any children, nor do I expect to. They should go to someone in our lineage, and that is you."

"I don't have any children either." His voice sounded dark and tight, as if it were constricted with pain. Daphne thought of the child he'd lost and suspected it was.

"But you might," Gwyneth said. "In fact, I am all but certain you will. Just as certain as I am that I am barren."

"How can you know that for sure?" Daphne asked, thinking it must be magic.

Gwyneth fixed her with a flat stare. "When you make an effort to get with child and always come up empty, you know for sure."

Heat rose up Daphne's neck, and she could only think to nod in response. She'd planned to ask how she could be certain that Gideon *would* have children, but decided she didn't want to ask any more questions of that nature.

"It's a shame since we have always taken care to preserve our lineage, but others in our order will do so."

"Order?" Gideon asked, his attention clearly piqued.

Gwyneth chuckled. "Not *that* Order, and yes, I'm aware of that nonsense organization. My grandmother thought we might unify with them—she was quite taken with that Pritchard fellow. But he got too greedy and didn't respect our ways, so she severed the connection."

So that was what had happened. Daphne glanced

toward Gideon and wondered how much of this he would share with Septon.

"Now let me tell you about the treasures." Gwyneth's eyes lit, and her enthusiasm was palpable. "As you know, there are thirteen, and as you likely know, they were given to Gareth by Arthur and the other knights when he married. In truth, the cloak was given to him much later, when Arthur no longer had need of it, but this fact is generally lost along with so many others."

Daphne wanted to know what that meant but didn't dare interrupt.

"Gareth kept them safe from those who would seek to take them and use them for their own devious plans. He vowed to take them to his grave, and he did. Except for the sword and the cloak, which he gave to his son, and the heart, which he gave to his daughter. Those items have been passed down generation to generation until they were hidden. I have heard rumors that they were found. And I don't mean that hideous fake heart that's in the Ashmolean Museum." She made a face.

"Yes, the sword was found several weeks ago and the heart more recently."

She lifted her hand to her chest and widened her eyes as she leaned forward. "You've seen them?"

"They were in my possession," Gideon said.

Gwyneth frowned. "*Were?* Where are they now?"

"Safe for the time being." Gideon apparently didn't plan to tell her where they were, and Daphne saw no need to do so either. She didn't think Gwyneth would appreciate Gideon giving them to anyone. "Once I have the cloak, I will retrieve them."

"Did you use them?" Gwyneth asked, her voice

taking on a breathless quality.

"I used the sword."

"And it flames?" At his nod, she sat back and lowered her hand to her lap, beaming in wonder. "Marvelous."

"The other ten treasures are with Gareth?" Gideon asked.

"Yes." Gwyneth narrowed her eyes shrewdly at Gideon. "I can anticipate your next question, and the answer is no. I do not know where that is. That is the final mystery. The eternal secret. Please don't go looking for him."

"Even to return the heart, sword, and cloak?" Gideon asked softly.

Gwyneth startled in surprise, her eyes widening and her jaw dropping for a brief moment. "You would do that?"

"I *intend* to do that."

"You don't want them for yourself?" She sounded rather befuddled. "That would be your right."

"Perhaps, but it is my duty to keep them safe from those who would misuse them. And to keep everyone safe from the harm they could cause." Gideon's pledge was so noble and so honest, Daphne couldn't help but want him to succeed. Which meant *not* giving the cloak to her father.

Gwyneth leaned back against her chair with a sly smile. "You are the Worthy." She said the word as if it were a title, with great reverence. "The prophecy foretold you would come, but we didn't know when."

Daphne couldn't help but stare at Gideon, at the look of sheer astonishment that drained most of the color from his face. And then Gwyneth stole the rest of it by saying, "What if I told you the cloak has been in your possession all along?"

Chapter Ten

GIDEON'S ENTIRE BODY trembled with awe and anticipation and a thousand other emotions. The Worthy—what did that mean? *He* had the cloak?

He fought to regain his composure. "I would know if I had the cloak, and I do not."

"Do you have a chest containing items from the Nash family?" Gwyneth asked.

"Yes, but there isn't a cloak inside it." He went over the contents of the chest in his mind, his heart thumping. Definitely no cloak. The overwhelming joy he'd felt a moment ago was utterly destroyed by a terrible sense of loss.

She sat forward in her chair, more animated than she'd been yet. "There has to be. It's been there for centuries. The chest has been replaced a time or two, but the contents should be there."

"Someone may have stolen it," Daphne said, wincing apologetically in Gideon's direction.

Of course someone had stolen it. But who? The chest had been in his family's possession and its presence kept secret from most everyone—including him. "I didn't even realize the chest existed until very recently."

"That is not surprising. Generally, it is passed on when it must be—and not a moment sooner. I take it your grandfather just died?"

"No, he died two years ago."

Gwyneth sucked in a breath. "And you're only now

learning of it? That is not how that was meant to be handled." She scowled and then exhaled, forcing her features to relax. "It may have gone missing in that interim. Do you know where it's been?"

With Rhys, and Gideon would wager his life Rhys would never steal something, let alone from him. "Yes, and it's been protected and safe. I'm certain of it."

She pouted briefly in disappointment. "Ah, well, what is past is past. Do you have the chest with you now?"

Gideon shook his head. "I don't."

She didn't seem surprised, nor was she upset. "You will go get it and bring it to me."

"How will that help matters if the cloak isn't there?" Gideon couldn't begin to imagine.

"I should like to see what *is* in the chest. We may be able to determine what happened to the cloak."

"Is the chest…like the treasures?" Daphne asked.

"You mean enchanted." Gwyneth looked up at the ceiling for a moment as if she were weighing how to answer. She lowered her gaze to Daphne with a succinct "Yes."

Gideon was suddenly desperate to fetch the chest. He stood. "We'll go immediately. It's two days away. You could come with us," he said to Gwyneth.

She shook her head vigorously. "No, no. I don't leave Glastonbury. You'll have to bring it back here."

How…frustrating. But he wouldn't be angry, not when she'd shared so much. He could scarcely believe he'd found someone he could call family. That feeling of being alone that he and Daphne had talked about last night had permeated his soul for so long. Knowing he had an extended family and a purpose as Gareth's descendant filled him with joy.

Daphne rose from the settee. "I don't suppose you have any writings by Morgana?"

Light danced in Gwyneth's eyes. She jumped up from her chair and flew to the bookshelves. Holding up her hand, she fluttered her fingertips along several spines before removing a book. She spun to a long worktable, much like Rhys Bowen's but even larger, which stood near the center of the room.

She set the book down and gently opened the cover, then peered over at them. "Aren't you going to come look at it?"

Daphne scrambled to join her, and Gideon followed. "What is it?" Daphne asked reverently.

"A few recipes for tonics and other things. But they are believed to be in her hand." Gwyneth gestured to the ancient vellum on which was scrawled a barely legible list of ingredients. The ink was quite faded on the loose pages, which were simply tucked into the book.

"How do you know it's her?" Daphne breathed, her gaze glued to the wonder before her.

Gideon was thrilled for her—to see something written by a woman you'd long studied had to be incredibly exciting. And satisfying. "She's who you thought she was," he said.

Daphne glanced up at him, her eyes vivid with emotion. "Yes."

"Turn the page," Gwyneth said. "Just be careful."

Hesitantly, Daphne gently flipped the vellum. There was another list of ingredients. Gwyneth encouraged her to keep going. A third list. And then on the fourth page, something different: a letter written to Morgause and signed, *Your loving sister, Morgana.*

"That's how we know," Gwyneth said softly.

"Actual proof she was real." When Daphne lifted her head, her eyes were damp with unshed tears.

"Yes, but you can't say so, I'm afraid." Gwyneth exhaled sympathetically. "To confirm Morgana's existence—or Arthur's, for that matter—is to expose Brue Cottage to scrutiny and unscrupulousness. People always try to steal from us, and attempt to sneak in to learn what they can, like Pritchard. The only reason I'm sharing this with you is because I know how hard you've worked to prove Morgana isn't the manipulative sorceress the stupid French wrote her to be. And because he's family." She gestured toward Gideon, then abruptly turned and went back to the bookshelf. When she returned, she carried three books.

"These are the Beckery Texts." She stood aside and gestured for Gideon to come and look at them.

He couldn't possibly read them now. He was too anxious to go to Hollyhaven to fetch the chest. "Will you keep them for me?" he asked her. "I'll be back as soon as I can with the chest."

"They should go into the chest." She clasped her hands at her waist and nodded. "This is a sound plan."

"We should go," Daphne said, looking at the Morgana documents wistfully.

Gwyneth moved toward Daphne and pinned her with a dubious stare. "Are you sure you aren't in love with Gideon? If you were together, I might decide to let you have one of the recipes. You won't be able to definitively prove it was Morgana's, but the age is accurate and you could say it *likely* is. Plus, there is proof that she's a healer in the Beckery Texts."

Septon's Beckery manuscript already proved it, but Gideon didn't point that out. His cousin, while lovely, was a bit mercurial, and he feared she would demand he return it. Or give it to Gideon. In fact, perhaps Gideon would ask the Order for it.

"I'm certain we aren't in love," Daphne said, in answer to Gwyneth's question and glancing toward him. "Though I hold him in very high esteem."

Their eyes met, and Gideon realized he felt the same about her. He'd been angry that she'd tried to trick him into marriage, but acknowledged she had, in her mind, good reason. She was trying to please the only family she had left. He could understand why that connection was so important to her.

"Let's see where things are when you return," Gwyneth said with a chuckle. "Are you certain I can't feed you something before you go?"

"No, we only recently broke our fast," Gideon said. He stepped toward her and took her hands in his. "You have been most hospitable. And you've given me more than I could ever have hoped for."

She threw her arms around him and hugged him tightly. "You have done the same. I shall look forward to your return."

When they parted, she patted his shoulders before dropping her hands. Then she bellowed, "Margaret!"

The tiny woman came into the room but didn't seem to be in a hurry.

"Will you please show our guests out?" Gwyneth asked. "Fetch their headwear from the settee."

Daphne turned to Gwyneth and curtsied. "Thank you for sharing your knowledge with us. This has been one of the best mornings of my entire life."

Gwyneth gave her a bright smile. "I'm so glad."

With a final nod, Gideon turned and guided Daphne from the library, his hand at her back.

Margaret led them back to the entry and handed

them their hats before opening the door. The morning—for it was still morning despite how event filled this day already seemed—was bright, with high clouds scuffing across the sky.

Gideon bowed to Margaret, and Daphne curtsied again before stepping outside, where she swept her hat onto her head. She strode toward the horses, and Gideon followed, clapping his hat low over his brow.

He untied the animals and helped Daphne into her seat. "How I loathe this veil," she said. "I'm leaving it off until we reach Glastonbury. Is there any chance we can skirt the town?"

He climbed onto his horse. "Only if you want to ride even closer to Ashridge Court."

She exhaled. "No. We can spend tonight in Keynsham at my cottage."

"Won't someone be waiting there for us?" Gideon asked. He wiped a hand over his chin and frowned at her. "We haven't discussed what comes next."

"Because we had no idea what we'd find here." She shook her head, her expression one of amazement. "I still can't quite believe it all…"

"Everything we hoped." Almost—he still didn't know where Gareth's tomb was located, but he'd puzzle that out too. First, he'd get the chest and find the damn cloak. How he wished they could ride straight through the night to Hollyhaven. He could if it wasn't for her… In fact, why was he even taking her? He didn't need her at all any longer.

"My father will wonder where I am," she said, interrupting his internal debate. "He would have expected us to return yesterday. We should stop in Glastonbury so I can dispatch a note to Ashridge Court."

"Saying what?" Gideon shook his head. "It doesn't matter. You don't need to dispatch a note. You need to return home."

She narrowed her eyes. "You're going to find the cloak without me?"

Their time together had come to an end. "I can't let you give it to your father."

"I don't plan to."

He'd already started to turn his horse toward the lane, but he stopped and blinked at her. "You don't?" When she shook her head, he asked, "What changed your mind?"

"Gwyneth was right. It—and the other treasures—are your heritage. They belong to you. And to her. The Order can want to keep them safe, but it isn't their responsibility. Or their right."

"Your father will not agree with you," he said darkly.

"I know."

The path Gideon was on didn't include her. "Daphne, it would be best for you to return home and forget about the cloak—and about me."

"Probably, but I don't want to. I would like to see this through." She straightened, looking him earnestly in the eye. "Once you have the cloak and have found Gareth's burial site, you can be rid of me."

He doubted he'd ever be rid of her entirely. He hated thinking of her going back to Ashridge Court, to her father—because she felt alone. And because Foliot was a murderous lunatic. How could he send her back there?

Gideon studied her. "If you wrote to your father, what would you say to buy us time?" Did it really matter? She'd supposedly ridden to meet him as he returned from Keynsham. She was as good as ruined.

Never mind that he'd *actually* been alone with her—including in a bed—for the past day.

She lifted a shoulder. "I could tell him that we already wed?"

He didn't like that she was so cavalier with her reputation. "And then what happens when people learn we were never married? You would likely be ruined."

"As we've already discussed, I have no plans to join Society nor do I care what people think of me."

"I used to feel that way," he said quietly. "Then you reach a point where you realize it matters, that it affects those around you." He thought of Rose and how some ridiculed her for marrying a man like him. He also thought of the pitying stares directed his way and the whispered comments he heard bits and pieces of after his mother left. *"Oh, that poor boy. To have two profligate parents…"*

"And who would it affect?" she asked. "My father?"

Because she was alone. She didn't have a mother or a half brother or a half brother's father who would stand in as your father or a newfound cousin who was overjoyed to claim you as kin.

But she did have her father. And really, wasn't that worse than being alone?

"Daphne, if you have no plans for a future in Society or to marry someone who would be horrified by your behavior, particularly pretending to be married to me, I will consent to being your fake husband."

She grinned. "Excellent. Let us be on our way to Glastonbury, and I will stop at a coaching inn to post a letter to Ashridge Court."

"As you wish." He pinched the edge of his hat, and she steered her horse down the lane.

Glastonbury was a short ride—barely a quarter hour

when they cantered for part of it. He led them toward a coaching inn where they'd tried to find lodging the night before. However, before they reached the gate, three horsemen rode straight for them. They were forced to pull their horses to a halt.

Alarm flared through Gideon, tensing his muscles and speeding his heart. He looked over at Daphne, but she'd pulled the veil over her face when they'd reached town.

"Stratton!" one of the men called, and Gideon instantly recognized the symbol stitched at the bottom edge of their coats on the front right side: a small gold cup with a stem—a grail. These were Foliot's men.

Two of them put their hands on pistols strapped to their sides but didn't draw them. They were in the middle of a semi-busy street. Gideon glanced about, wondering if he could evade them.

Daphne pushed up her veil. "What is this about?"

The one who'd yelled Gideon's name rode close to Daphne and cast a threatening look toward Gideon. "Your father was most distraught when you didn't return yesterday."

"I sent a note ahead," she said. "We had a problem with a horse and were forced to delay our journey."

She was really quite good at coming up with a believable lie quickly. At least it seemed believable to him. Whether it fooled her father's men, Gideon couldn't tell.

"We'll escort you to Ashridge Court," the man, who appeared to be the leader of the group, said, sending dark, suspicious looks toward Gideon.

"That won't be necessary," Daphne said brightly. "Lord Stratton and I were wed early this morning, and now we plan to take a wedding trip."

The man's jaw dropped, and another man rode up beside him and muttered, "Foliot won't like that," loud enough for Gideon to hear.

"You'll need to come with us," the leader said.

Daphne shook her head. "Please convey our apologies to my father. I know he will be disappointed to have missed the ceremony, but we simply couldn't wait." She cast a loving look toward Gideon, her smile positively beatific. If she decided scholarly pursuits and treasure hunting didn't suit her, she could certainly make a life on the stage.

"We have strict instruction to bring you back to Ashridge Court." The man frowned at Gideon. "Willing or not."

Hell, there wasn't going to be a simple or easy way out of this. Gideon grasped the reins of his horse, ready to flee if necessary, and sent a sharp look toward Daphne. He inclined his head slightly, trying to silently communicate that they might need to run.

He squared his shoulders and addressed the leader. "Lady Stratton and I are eager to be on our way. Her father's wishes, while important to us, are not our primary concern. Again, please convey our apologies to Foliot, and let him know we will see him soon. Come, Daphne."

Perhaps they'd just let them go…

But of course, they wouldn't. The leader rode directly into Gideon's path. "You must come with us."

"Oh my," Daphne said rather loudly, drawing everyone's attention. "I'm afraid I don't feel well." She slumped to the side, causing her horse to prance sideways. And then it reared with a loud whinny.

Gideon's heart stopped for a moment. He kept control of his mount, lest it react to the other horse's distress. Two of the men's horses did react. One reared, and the rider lost his seat. The other bolted. Only the leader remained. It was now or never.

Before Gideon could shout for Daphne to go, she whipped past him, her body bent low as she kicked the horse into a gallop. It wasn't terribly safe, given the traffic around them, but it was necessary. And damn, she was good.

Gideon took off after her and worked to come abreast of her mount. He looked back and saw the leader was following them.

"We should split up," she shouted. "Up ahead, you go right and I'll go left. Meet me at The Black Sheep in Coxley. If I don't show up within the hour, go on without me—you must complete your quest. Don't follow me!"

Before he could dispute her plan, she veered left. Gideon knew the man would follow her—and he wasn't wrong. After he turned right, Gideon looked back and saw the man hesitate for the barest moment before steering his horse in Daphne's wake.

He should go after her. What would the man do when he caught her? Force her to return to Ashridge Court? And then what would Foliot do? Particularly when he learned she'd lied about getting married. It would be easy enough to verify.

You must complete your quest. Don't follow me!

Her words pealed in his head and ultimately kept him from turning his horse around. She'd told him what to do—what he needed to do. And yet...

Hell and the devil.

THE VEIL WHIPPED at Daphne's face as she rode for the outer edge of town. If she'd been on an open road, instead of having to navigate intermittent traffic and turn corners, she might be able to outrun him. But she wasn't on an open road, and she could hear the thunder of the horse's hooves behind her.

Daphne turned her head and saw just how close her pursuer was. She was never going to make it.

Defeat curdled her gut as he yelled, "Stop! My horse can outrun yours!"

Gripping the reins, she slowed her horse, murmuring words of gratitude and encouragement. She and the horse were breathing heavily when they came to a stop. They'd left the denser buildings behind and were at the start of a lane that looped around to the main road north. She'd been so close.

The guard stopped beside her and grabbed the reins of her mount. "Silly chit," he growled. "Why did you run?"

She arched her brow at him in disdain. "Because I don't want to return to Ashridge Court. Isn't it obvious?" She rolled her eyes and let out a grunt of dismay. Better he caught her than Gideon, however. Now he would be free to return to Hollyhaven and fetch the chest. Perhaps she'd be able to get away and meet him at Brue Cottage…

"Too bad," the man said, scowling at her. "That's where we're going—back to your father."

He was not going to be happy that she'd lied to him. She could say that Gideon had promised to marry her so that her father's anger would be directed at him, but she wouldn't do that. She'd instigated this mess when she'd led her father to believe that she was in love with

Gideon and he'd consequently announced their betrothal.

No, her father was to blame. For all of it.

She exhaled and took a deep breath as her heart rate slowed. The guard held on to her reins and started his horse into a slow walk.

She knew there were people who disliked her father, who found him unscrupulous and harsh. But he'd always told her to ignore them, for they were jealous, vindictive people who didn't like to see her father's wealth or his ascension in the Order. They also wished they could be descended from King Arthur himself as he was.

Daphne had meant to query Gwyneth about that, but there had been so much going on during their interview that she hadn't had a chance. When they returned, Daphne would ask if she could verify that lineage. She didn't doubt her father, but it would be wonderful to have proof. Even if she couldn't share it.

A sound cut into Daphne's thoughts just before her reins went slack. She looked over at her father's man and saw him collapse to the side, sliding from his horse to the ground. His horse whinnied in distress and took off. The man didn't fall off completely for several yards, but when he finally hit the ground, the horse didn't stop. If anything, it went faster down the lane.

What had just happened? She turned at the sound of another set of hooves.

Gideon raced toward her and pulled his horse to a stop when he reached her. "Are you all right?"

"What did you do?" She glanced toward the fallen man up ahead.

"I hit him with a rock." He shrugged. "What else was I supposed to do?"

"You were supposed to meet me at The Black Sheep."

"It doesn't look like you were going to make it," he said wryly as he walked his horse toward the man lying on the ground.

Daphne walked her horse beside his. "You don't know that. I had an hour to get there."

He sent her a pained look. "Are we really going to debate this?"

"You weren't supposed to follow me."

"I'm not supposed to do many things, yet I've always done whatever I damn well please." They'd arrived at the unconscious man, and Gideon quickly dismounted. He bent down and checked the body.

"Is he alive?" Daphne was afraid to know the answer.

"Quite." Gideon climbed back onto his horse and started walking again.

She kept up with him. "We're going to just leave him there?"

He glanced toward her. "That seems the best plan, don't you agree?"

Yes, but it still felt a bit cruel. "Will he be all right?"

"He'll be as good as new. With a bump on his head." Gideon pointed to the back of his skull.

"I can't believe you hit him with a rock. You've excellent aim."

"Thank you."

"You really shouldn't have come back." But she was so glad he did.

Even if a small voice in the back of her mind was telling her she should return to Ashridge Court in order to preserve what was left of her reputation. She didn't want to abandon their quest.

Their quest.

Was it really theirs? Gideon didn't need her at all. She looked over at him and wondered why he'd come back for her, especially when she'd told him not to.

Then she realized he wasn't leading them out of town. In fact, they were turning onto Benedict Street.

"Where are we going?"

"Just ahead." He walked his horse a bit faster, and she moved to catch up.

The tower of St. Benedict's Church came into view, and she suffered a moment of panic. "If we go by the church, we may run into my father's men. What if they go back to the church to confirm our wedding? The one that never happened."

"Perhaps, but I plan to sneak in through another entrance." He led them off the road and dismounted near a tree.

She stared at him. "What are you doing?" When he didn't answer, she assumed he had a plan to bribe the vicar to say he'd married them.

"I don't think the vicar will go along with your plan."

"I think he will," Gideon said, helping her down. "That's his job."

She gaped at him while he tied the horses. Then he took her hand and walked the short distance to the church, where he skirted the building and, as intended, found a back entrance.

Pulling at his hand, she stopped when they were inside, forcing him to turn around. "The vicar will never agree to this."

Gideon turned and blinked at her. "Why? It's not yet noon."

"Noon?"

"I realize it's irregular to purchase the license and

conduct the ceremony without waiting a week, but I have plenty of coin and I'm an earl. Or at least I will be when Parliament confirms my inheritance."

She couldn't have heard him right. "I beg your pardon?"

"I said, it's irregular that—"

"I know what you said." She shook her head. "I'm just trying to understand what you mean. Are you marrying me?"

"Yes."

Her jaw dropped. "Why?"

He tipped his head to the side and contemplated her as if she'd sprouted another nose. "It seems the smartest plan at this juncture, and it was the original plan, after all."

"But you don't want to marry me. Or anyone else."

"This will buy us time to find the cloak, and it will protect your reputation. After the ceremony, you can write a note to your father, as we'd planned earlier, and the vicar can even bloody sign it." Gideon turned and started toward the nave. "Now, where can we find the vicar?"

And they would be married.

Daphne grabbed his forearm, wrapping her fingers around his sleeve. "Gideon, you don't have to do this. I should probably return to Ashridge Court. You don't need me."

He turned to face her once more. "No, I don't need you," he said softly. "But as you told me once—or maybe it was a dozen times—we're in this together."

Her heart swelled, and for a moment, she couldn't speak past the knot in her throat. So she nodded.

"Besides, you have an annulment plan." He winked at her and turned toward the nave again.

As he started forward, she hurried to walk beside him. 'I don't actually have a plan."

He glanced down at her with a half smile. "I trust you. So far, you've proven rather adept at coming up with believable lies."

His cavalier attitude was somehow charming and yet concerning. What if they couldn't secure an annulment? She clasped his forearm again and drew him to stop.

Once more, he turned toward her. He exhaled and looked at her patiently.

"We are sticking to the original plan," she said. "This is a marriage in name only."

"Yes." He answered quickly enough that she wished he'd hesitated just a *little*. "Now, can we please find the vicar? We're running out of time."

They couldn't marry after noon.

She steered him in another direction toward the vicar's office. "This way."

A short time later, she was the Countess of Stratton—at least for now—wife of a descendant of Gareth. Her father would be ecstatic.

She, on the other hand, was astounded. And maybe just the slightest bit happy.

Chapter Eleven

RIDING UP THE lane to Hollyhaven, Gideon imagined what Rhys and Margery might say about his new bride. He and Daphne had decided they would tell them the truth, and Gideon was fairly certain they'd be unhappy that he'd married under such circumstances. That was because they had married for love—as both their children had.

He stole a quick look at Daphne. She'd changed her riding habit entirely when they'd stopped at her cottage in Keynsham to pick up clothing and other items for the journey. Gideon had met her great-aunt Ellie, who'd been delighted to learn that her beloved great-niece had wed an earl. She'd tried to persuade them to stay, but they'd demurred. Neither wanted to risk running into her father's men in case they came looking for her. Just because they were married didn't mean her father wouldn't try to bring her back to Ashridge Court.

Gone was the veil hiding her face, leaving her stunning profile exposed for his hungry gaze.

Hungry?

Yes, he desired her. That much he would admit. And was afraid of.

Last night, they'd stayed at an inn, and he'd slept on the floor again. This time, he'd remained there because she hadn't, thankfully, suffered another nightmare.

A groom met them outside the house to take their horses to the stable. Gideon thanked him and guided

Daphne to the door.

"I'm a bit nervous," she whispered. "Last time I was here, I gave them a fake name."

"They'll understand," Gideon said. "They're incredibly kind."

"They seemed that way. When I was here before, I was struck by how close they all were as a family. It was rather endearing."

Was that a note of envy in her voice? Or was he thinking of how he used to feel when he would see Rhys and Margery—and Penn and Cate—in the summer? They'd always treated him like family, but he'd still felt like he didn't belong. Perhaps because his father had worked hard to remind him of that when he returned to Stratton Hall. *"Remember, Gideon, you are my son. Nothing else matters."*

The door opened, and it was Margery who greeted them. "Gideon! And Mrs. Guilford." Her voice carried a note of curiosity. "What a surprise! Come in." She ushered them into the library, where Rhys was standing near his worktable.

"Gideon, it's good to see you so soon. Mrs. Guilford." Rhys said her name with a bit of a question, as Margery had done.

If they were surprised to see him in the presence of their recent guest, Gideon was surely about to shock them completely. "Allow me to present my wife, Daphne Foliot Kersey." It wasn't precisely the right way to introduce her, but he thought it best to just put her name out there so Rhys and Margery would know who she was.

Their reaction was immediate. Their eyes widened, but it was Rhys who spoke. "As in Timothy Foliot's daughter?"

"Yes," Daphne answered. She curtsied to them. "Gideon and I married just yesterday."

Rhys blinked at him, seeming utterly bewildered. However, Margery spoke this time. "Congratulations to both of you. We should drink a toast."

"You should know this is a temporary marriage—in name only," Gideon said. "We plan to seek an annulment."

Rhys and Margery exchanged looks, their brows creased. "Why did you get married at all, then?" Rhys asked.

"Foliot expected us to," Gideon said. He waved a hand and exhaled some of the tension from his shoulders. "It's rather complicated. We are on a quest to find the cloak together, and it was simplest for us to marry. For the time being."

"Annulments aren't easy," Rhys said, clearly concerned.

"No, but we have a plan." They still didn't, but if he lost the earldom, he could cite fraud as the reason for the annulment. He hadn't shared that with Daphne because he didn't want to tell her about his illegitimacy, not when Penn was trying so hard to keep from being the earl. Furthermore, he hadn't wanted to tell her about the vicar and his proof since the man was currently being held hostage by her father.

Unless Septon's men had rescued him by now. Gideon hoped so for the man's sake.

"First, however," Gideon continued, "we must find the cloak. And that's why we've returned."

"It isn't here," Rhys said. "Is there a clue in my library somewhere?"

"In a manner of speaking."

"Let's sit," Margery said. "You must be tired after

your journey." She led them to the seating area, where she took a chair near the settee and Rhys took another. That left the settee for Daphne and Gideon.

"Speaking of your journey, where did you come from?" Rhys asked.

"Glastonbury. Before that, we visited Septon. He plans to marry my mother." That fell out of Gideon's mouth before he'd even decided to say it.

"Margery gave him a supportive smile. "Are you happy about it?"

Gideon arched a shoulder. "I suppose. It will be strange."

Rhys blew out a breath. "And a relief. I take it Septon was helpful in your quest? Why did he direct you back here?"

"He didn't." Gideon looked from Rhys to Margery and back again. "He directed us to Brue Cottage."

Margery glanced at Rhys, who, like her, didn't react to that name. "Where is Brue Cottage?"

"Near the River Brue, I imagine," Rhys said, earning a sardonic stare from his wife. He blew her a kiss, then returned his attention to Gideon. "*What* is Brue Cottage?"

"It is home to an ancient order of healers," Gideon said. "Morgana was one of their rank."

"Morgan le Fay?" Margery looked toward Daphne. "That had to have been thrilling for you to visit such a place."

Daphne's face lit. "It was." She exchanged a look with Gideon, silently asking if she could elaborate. He nodded in response. "Elidyr was a monk at the nearby Beckery Chapel, and he wrote a series of manuscripts."

"The Beckery Texts," Rhys whispered. "I've heard rumors of those for some time. I had no idea they were real. Did you get to see them?"

"No, but we will when we return," Gideon said.

"They belong to him," Daphne added. "As a descendant of Gareth, they're his stories, and Gwyneth wants him to have them."

"I plan to bring them here," Gideon said. "Along with one the Order possesses. I just have to talk them into giving it to me first. You should study them. They belong in your library. There is no finer scholar in Britain."

Rhys blinked, then fixed Gideon with a proud stare. "Thank you. I would be honored to have them for as long as you permit."

"Who is Gwyneth?" Margery asked.

"The leader—I think?" Daphne looked at Gideon, who again nodded in response. "The leader of the order at present."

Margery coughed. "They call themselves an order?" She was perhaps the least supportive of the Order of the Round Table. The Order—and not Camelot—had attacked her and Rhys during their own quest to decipher the coded de Valery manuscript.

"She scoffed at the Order of the Round Table," Gideon said. "You would like her, Margery."

Margery grinned. "I look forward to meeting her. If I may."

"So what in particular brings you back here?" Rhys asked.

"The chest from my grandfather that you gave me when I was here last," Gideon said. "Daphne didn't tell you Gwyneth's full name—Gwyneth Nash-Hughes."

Rhys's brows lifted in surprise. "You're related?"

"At some point along the line. We are both descended from Gareth."

"And indirectly from Morgan, since she was Gareth's aunt." Daphne's tone was a mix of admiration, pride, and perhaps a bit of envy.

"How extraordinary," Rhys said.

"I am fairly certain that's what Daphne and I both said," Gideon quipped. "The chest has been in our family since that time."

Rhys frowned. "Not that chest, surely. It's far too new to be from the sixth century."

"She said it had been replaced a time or two," Daphne said.

"She also said the cloak was inside, but it is not." Gideon pressed his lips together, suddenly quite anxious to see the chest again. He realized it was hidden in the secret room behind Rhys's bookshelf, and he wouldn't want to open that in front of Daphne. "If you could have the chest fetched, I'd like to look at it later." He hoped Rhys understood.

"And we'll need to take it back to Brue Cottage so Gwyneth can help us determine what happened to the cloak."

"How can she do that?" Margery asked.

"She didn't say, but their order clearly possesses knowledge I can't begin to understand." Gideon wondered if their talents were learned or innate. Since they were related, was there a chance he was like them?

"Well then, I'll be most anxious to hear that story." She stood, prompting her husband and Gideon to do the same, and turned toward Daphne. "Come, Lady Stratton. You probably want to retire for a bit before dinner. We'll investigate the chest afterward."

Daphne stood. "Please, call me Daphne." She spoke to Margery but looked to Rhys too.

Margery moved her gaze from Daphne to Gideon.

"Do you want separate rooms?"

"Yes," he said, noting that Daphne didn't answer. He hoped she wouldn't have another nightmare.

Daphne found Gideon's gaze. "I'll see you at dinner."

He inclined his head, and the women left. Margery closed the door behind her.

"My wife is incredibly astute," Rhys said. "You know, I would marry her all over again if I could." He turned and strode to the bookshelf, and this time, Gideon saw him pull on a book—likely a fake book— which sprang the secret door open.

Gideon hesitated, and Rhys beckoned him forward. "Come in."

Following Rhys into the small room, which truly was the size of a closet, Gideon took in the contents—a single, slender bookshelf, a larger chest, and the smaller Nash chest. Overall, the chamber was even smaller than Septon's secret library.

"This is where I'll keep the Beckery Texts," Rhys said. "So you know they will be safe."

"Thank you."

Rhys gestured toward the chest. "Do you want to grab that?"

Gideon hefted the box and carried it out into the library, where he set it atop the worktable. His fingers fairly itched to open it up, but he was also absurdly nervous. "I know it isn't in there," he said, perhaps unnecessarily.

"Do you want to check?"

Of course he did. Gideon opened the lid and removed every last thing until all that remained was the purple velvet lining. He pressed against the fabric, but it was just the velvet and the box. Frustrated, he swore an oath as he dropped into a chair at the table.

"May I?" Rhys asked, coming to stand beside Gideon's chair. At Gideon's nod, he felt around the box and investigated the items sitting around it. "I suppose we should look for a clue. Saying the cloak is in the box could mean the path to the cloak is in the box." He gave Gideon a wry glance. "That is often how these things work."

Gideon glanced toward one of the books he'd removed. "The de Valery text already contained a code, but that was to find the Anarawd text. It seems unlikely there would be another in that book."

"Unlikely, but not impossible." Rhys's brow creased. "There's also the Anarawd text, but I don't think that would contain clues as to the location of the cloak. The cloak was hidden much later."

"So maybe it is in the de Valery manuscript?" Gideon asked, his frustration turning to eager curiosity.

Rhys stroked his chin. "Maybe. What is the third book?"

Gideon looked up at him. "You haven't looked?" The chest had been in his possession for a while.

"I didn't." Rhys pulled up a chair and sat down beside him. "These don't belong to me. I merely kept them safe for you."

"You are perhaps the most honorable man I know." Indeed, Gideon wasn't sure such honor still existed.

Rhys clapped him lightly on the shoulder. "If you think so, then I must be doing something right." He smiled, then fetched two pairs of gloves from his desk. "Let's investigate this book."

After donning the gloves, Gideon laid his palm across the dark blue cover, as if the text could impart some knowledge without him even opening the tome.

Or if it would maybe tingle in his touch like the treasures did. It did not.

He opened the book and was immediately struck by the stunning illumination of the first page.

The Knights of the Round Table

"The condition is absolutely splendid," Rhys whispered with great reverence.

"How old is it?" Gideon wasn't an expert like Rhys, but he suspected it was at least four hundred years old.

"I have a suspicion." He glanced over at Gideon. "May I turn to the last page?"

"Of course."

Rhys pulled on his gloves and carefully closed the book, then turned it over. He opened the back cover and then flipped to the final page.

The slight sound of his breath drawing in sharply was followed by a smile curling his lips and a light of excitement dancing in his eyes. He lightly touched the corner of the page where a small smudge marred the vellum.

Gideon knew enough to recognize that it wasn't a smudge. "Is that what I think it is?"

Rhys grinned. "De Valery's mark. He made a third manuscript. And since the Nash family charged him with making the others with a hidden code that would reveal the location of the Anarawd text, we must consider this manuscript also serves a purpose."

Gideon's heart pounded in his ears. "To find the cloak?"

"Perhaps. We must take our time investigating this book. I hope you aren't in a hurry."

"I am, but only because I'm anxious to retrieve the heart and the sword from Foliot. The longer he has them, the longer I worry."

"What are you doing with his daughter?" Rhys shook his head. "I'm sorry. Perhaps it isn't my business, but I didn't expect you to marry again—at least not any time soon and certainly not to the daughter of a man as despicable as Foliot."

"She doesn't see him that way," Gideon said a bit defensively. "Much the way I didn't see my father the way everyone else did."

"I see. But your eyes were opened eventually." Rhys's mouth formed a grim line. "She should understand what kind of man her father really is."

"And I'm certain she will someday." Likely soon. "I'm just not certain I'm the one who should tell her."

"You're her husband. I would argue there is no one better."

"Her *temporary* husband." Gideon felt the need to point that out.

"Yes, you plan to get an annulment. As I said, that will be difficult."

"Not under the argument of fraud. We didn't disclose my prior marriage or provide proof of Rose's death. Plus, I led her to believe I am the Earl of Stratton."

Rhys's brows darted up his forehead as his eyes widened briefly. "You expect Penn to inherit the title."

"It seems likely." Gideon could mention Septon's plan to obtain the proof and liberate the vicar, but until that actually happened, Gideon saw no benefit in bringing it up. There was no need to raise Penn's hopes, and Rhys would surely tell him about it.

Rhys looked at him intently. "You don't seem upset."

If he dwelled on it, he would be, Gideon supposed. "I've plenty else to think about right now. Anyway, I can't control what happens there. Furthermore, I am *not* the earl—Penn is."

Rhys winced. "He desperately wants to avoid that."

"I know," Gideon said quietly. "And if there's a way I can help him, I will."

"Not for you, but for him." Rhys's eyes took on a glint of admiration. "You have far more honor than you think."

That reminded Gideon of what Gwyneth had said. "Do you know what 'the Worthy' means?"

Rhys's brows drew together. "Gareth is sometimes referred to as Gareth the Worthy."

So it was another piece of his heritage, then. "Gwyneth called me that—the Worthy."

"Because you're a descendant?"

"Well, she's a descendant too," Gideon said. "I suppose because I told her I plan to take the heart, the sword, and the cloak to Gareth's tomb to reunite them with the other treasures and keep them hidden forever."

"Did she tell you where that is?"

"She said she didn't know." Gideon wasn't entirely certain he believed her, but he was even more certain that if she did, he wouldn't persuade her to tell him if she didn't want to.

"I would believe her," Rhys said. "If she seemed to support your endeavor—and it sounds as if she did— then she would have no reason to keep the location from you." He closed the book once more and flipped it over again. "I think you and I have a book to read."

Gideon grinned, eager to share this with Rhys. "We do indeed. I think you should fetch the glass."

"The one that revealed de Valery's code? Yes, I think I should." He quickly stood and went to the secret room to obtain the glass. Returning with the item, he sat back down. "Do you plan to share all this, along with whatever we find, with your wife?"

Gideon tried not to wince. "Could you just refer to her as Daphne?" In his mind, his wife was Rose.

"Of course."

Gideon wasn't sure how much he would share. He didn't think she would tell her father the location of the burial, but how could he be certain? Could he really trust her? Should he?

Rhys handed him the glass. "You do the honors. The discovery should be yours."

"My pleasure." Gideon took the glass and opened the book.

AS THE SECOND course arrived on the table, Daphne glanced longingly at the door. Margery had told her at the start that Gideon and Rhys would not be joining them. Instead, they were eating—or not—as they combed through the chest in Rhys's library.

Daphne couldn't help but feel left out, just as she knew the chest wasn't hers to investigate. The fact that she was even here and that Gideon had married her was still more than she could quite comprehend. He could have ridden away from her in Glastonbury— she'd told him to—but instead, he'd come after her. And then made her his wife. Even if it was only temporary, he'd welcomed her along on this journey to find the cloak and reunite the treasures.

That was the core of her unease. They hadn't discussed the reuniting part, and she suspected it would involve betraying her father. She hoped it didn't, but that would require her to convince her father that the treasures belonged with Gareth. Surely her father would see the benefit in doing that.

"I used to do that," Margery said, drawing Daphne from her thoughts.

"Do what?" Daphne glanced toward her hostess, who sat at one end of the table to Daphne's left, and speared a green bean on her plate.

"Watch for Rhys. When we were first married, I would sit here waiting for him to finish in his library. He gets horribly engrossed in what he's doing." She sipped her wine. "I gave up and started taking dinner in there. You may have noticed there's a small table in the library, away from his precious workspace."

Now Daphne wondered why they weren't dining in there right now. Because they hadn't been invited. Or at least, *she* hadn't been invited. Perhaps Margery had.

"They'll join us when they're finished. Or frustrated." Margery grinned. "Or both." She gave her attention to her plate for a few minutes.

Daphne ate two more beans and another bite of duck, then decided she was finished. Her insides were a bit of a jumble with all that had happened the past few days. She wondered about her father's reaction to the note she'd sent. She'd apologized for the wound his man had suffered and had explained that she and Gideon had simply wanted to be alone. She'd written the letter much the same way she'd behaved at Ashridge Court—as if she were terribly in love with Gideon. That ought to please her father enough to lessen any of his anger.

In truth, it wasn't hard to pretend to have a tendre for Gideon. He was everything she might want in a husband—intelligent, brave, honorable, and caring. That his presence made her heart hammer and his touch caused her skin to tingle was simply an embellishment on an already wonderful package.

Had his wife felt the same way? Surely she had. Daphne wondered at the reason for their marriage, assuming it had taken a far more traditional course than theirs.

Margery pulled Daphne from her thoughts once more. "I met Rhys when I brought him a medieval manuscript to evaluate. I had hoped to sell it to him. My aunts and I were in need of funds."

"And did you? Sell it to him?" Daphne asked.

"No." She laughed. "As soon as I found out it might lead to treasure, I kept it for myself."

Daphne smiled, glad for the distraction from her thoughts. "What sort of treasure?"

"It ended up being just an old manuscript, but it was incredibly valuable to my husband. And to me because it brought us together."

Was she referring to the Anarawd text? Daphne was dying to ask but didn't. She truly felt as if she were on the periphery at Hollyhaven. But then she often felt alone and had since her mother had disappeared.

"Just as this quest has brought you and Gideon together," Margery said softly.

Daphne felt heat climbing her neck and prayed it wouldn't extend to her face. "Yes, but our union isn't like that."

"Yet, but I find things have a way of changing when you least expect them to."

"Gideon has made it quite clear he is not interested in having another wife." Daphne cringed as soon as she said it. She was irritated at being left out. "I shouldn't have said that."

Margery put down her utensils and picked up her wineglass. "It's not anything I don't already know. What has he told you about Rose?"

Daphne also abandoned her fork. "Not much. I don't wish to pry."

"Did you know he had a scandalous reputation before he married her?" Margery asked.

"His mother mentioned something to that effect."

"Oh, you met Lady Stratton?" Margery sipped her wine and set it back on the table. "How was that?"

"Fine, I suppose. She clearly loves her son." Seeing that love had made Daphne miss her own mother in a way she hadn't in years.

"I ask because Gideon is usually rather tense around her and especially with Septon."

Daphne hadn't sensed that, but then her time at Septon House had been rather short. Still, she suspected she knew the reason. "Because she left Gideon when he was a boy."

Margery nodded. "He told you about that?"

"Briefly, but I could see that it still pains him."

"I'm sure it always will," Margery said. "We always tried to make sure they saw each other at least once a year. Gideon would come here in the summer and we would take him to Westerly Cross—his grandfather's estate—to visit his mother. That stopped when he was about fourteen, I think. By then he was incredibly angry with her, likely as a result of listening to his father spew poison about her. He was a horrible human being." She shuddered.

"Unfortunately, Gideon spent several years behaving in his image," Margery continued. "Thankfully, he veered from that path and decided to marry. He wanted to improve his reputation and bring dignity back to the earldom he would inherit someday."

Enthralled with Margery's story, Daphne pivoted to face her. "That's when he met his wife?"

"Some people who knew his father and wanted to help Gideon rise above him went out of their way to introduce him to marriageable young ladies. He was invited to a series of house parties—he was quite busy that summer and fall." Margery inclined her head toward the butler, who removed their dishes. "He spent the Christmas holiday with us and met Rose at a gathering in Monmouth. She was precisely the kind of wife he was looking for: sweet-natured, kind, and sharply intelligent. And she fell quite madly in love with Gideon."

Daphne's heart twisted. Margery didn't say that Gideon had done the same, but it was implied. Rose had been everything he wanted. And Daphne was confident Rose's father hadn't tried to arrange their marriage.

"Gideon was heartbroken when she died," Margery said sadly. "To make matters worse were the rumors that he'd caused her death." Margery's eyes darkened with anger. "Such nasty, malicious gossip. People are so cruel."

How could anyone think Gideon would do such a thing?

"That's awful," Daphne said. "And that is why I don't go to London or even Bath. I don't care for gossip or balls or any of that nonsense."

Margery smiled. "It's a shame you and Gideon don't plan to stay married. You and I would get on quite well. I've never cared for those things either. And my daughter, Cate, has no patience for foolish people.

When she takes her place as the Countess of Norris next Season, I daresay she'll conquer London as easily as she does everything else."

Hearing her mother's pride was another knife in Daphne's heart.

Oh, she didn't want to be melancholy! She was being a ninnyhammer. "I'm sure she will," Daphne agreed. "Though I barely met her, she left quite an impression on me."

Margery laughed softly. "That's my Cate. But know the feeling was mutual. She was very taken with your scholarly pursuits. The two of you must get together. I'm sure you have much to share."

Daphne thought so too. "I will look forward to that."

A movement in the doorway drew them both to turn their heads. Gideon and Rhys came into the dining room, both looking rumpled and tired. Gideon's cravat was askew and his hair was disheveled, as if he'd run his hands through it repeatedly. However, instead of appearing sloppy, he was devilishly handsome.

Margery smiled at them. "Just in time for port and trifle."

"We can definitely use the port," Rhys said, pressing a quick kiss to his wife's cheek and then taking his chair at the other end of the table. "I'm afraid we have nothing to show for our efforts."

Gideon sat opposite Daphne, his dark mood palpable in the stern set of his jaw and the pleat marring his forehead between his brows.

"Not even a clue about the cloak?" Daphne asked.

"Not that we could find." Rhys thanked the butler for bringing the port, and they soon all had glasses.

"Well, it's a good thing we're returning to Brue Cottage," Daphne said. "Gwyneth should be able to help us."

"I can only hope," Gideon muttered. But he didn't sound very hopeful.

Daphne knew what it was like to struggle to be optimistic in the face of frustration. She'd run into more walls in her search for Morgan than she had doors. "Just think of all we learned at our first visit, and how much more we have yet to learn."

"Daphne's right," Margery said. "When will you return to Brue Cottage?"

"Tomorrow." Gideon glanced toward Daphne, who nodded in agreement. "First thing."

Daphne had to admit she wished they could stay at Hollyhaven a little longer. The family environment, even with just Rhys and Margery, was so inviting.

The butler served the trifle, and Gideon looked over at Margery. "Did you serve this for me?"

"Of course. It's your favorite."

Yes, family. Daphne ached for it.

"Do you remember the first time you had it?" Margery asked, her hazel eyes sparkling in the candlelight.

"The first summer I came here," Gideon said, spooning a bite of trifle toward his mouth. "I demanded it when I returned to Stratton Hall, and my father instructed the cook learn to make it. He did not want me liking *anything* better at Hollyhaven." He devoured the spoonful of trifle, and, after he swallowed, added, "Cook did a passable job, but it was never as good as Mrs. Thomas's." He sent a look toward Thomas, the butler, who inclined his head with an appreciative twinkle in his eye.

"What else did you do here?" Daphne asked.

"Penn and I played games and rode horses," Gideon

said. "Those are among my fondest memories."

Rhys chuckled. "And Cate trailed you, begging to be included."

Gideon winced. "We were not very welcoming."

"Older siblings rarely are," Margery said. "You also spent time in Rhys's library. He made sure you could read and write Latin as well as Welsh."

"*Roedd yn athro da.*" Gideon sent Rhys a warm look of gratitude.

Daphne understood Welsh even if she could barely speak it herself. Gideon had said that Rhys was a good teacher. She was reminded of her father and how she understood Welsh only because he'd encouraged it. He'd provided her with the best tutors to educate her in languages, literature, and history. She was far more learned than any other woman she knew. With the exception of Cate, probably.

"You taught your children to be scholars," Daphne said to Rhys.

"I taught them as I was taught," Rhys said before sipping his port. "My father was the foremost expert on medieval literature in all of Britain. He had very high expectations of me."

Margery looked down the table at him as she lifted her glass. "Which Rhys exceeded."

Rhys's lips curved into a small smile. "Perhaps. He cast a very long shadow."

"At least it was something you could be proud to live up to," Gideon said with a hollow laugh.

Daphne blinked at him, thinking his father's influence had impacted so much of his life.

Rhys started to frown, then pressed his lips into a flat line. "You have much to be proud of, Gideon. We are proud of you. You will be an excellent earl."

Margery nodded in agreement and lifted her glass once more. "To the Earl of Stratton and Lady Stratton."

Daphne exchanged a lingering look with Gideon. Drinking a toast to their faux union seemed wrong, but she wasn't about to upset her gracious hostess. Everyone drank, and they finished their trifle.

Rhys announced that he was exhausted from their work and would retire. Margery joined him, leaving Gideon and Daphne alone with their port after Thomas cleared the plates.

The butler left the bottle between them and Gideon picked it up to refill his glass. First, he looked at her in question. She nodded, and he refilled first hers and then his.

"Margery and Rhys are absolutely delightful," Daphne said.

"Yes, they are."

"You seem like a part of their family." She hoped she didn't sound envious. Except she was.

He sipped his port and set his glass on the table, keeping his fingers on the base of the glass. He stared at the dark red liquid. "I guess I am. It's damn puzzling."

"Why? They clearly love you."

"Yes, but sometimes I wonder how that's possible." He shook his head, then took another drink. Before she could work up the courage to dig deeper, he said, "We should discuss the next steps in this quest."

She straightened in her chair, stiffening her spine. "We should."

Gideon ran his fingertip and thumb along the stem of his glass. "Assuming we are able to find the cloak, I will use it to take back the heart and the sword from your father's vault."

She frowned at him. "You don't have to steal them. We'll tell him the treasures must be returned to Gareth. He will like that, I think."

The sharp sudden burst of laughter from Gideon startled her, and she nearly spilled her port. A large drop of the red liquid splashed onto the back of her hand. "Why are you laughing?" She couldn't help but scowl, then brought her hand to her mouth so she could lick the port away.

When she looked across the table, she saw him staring at her mouth. And the laughter had disappeared.

His gaze heated her, but she ignored the sensation. "Why did you laugh?"

He sobered, his eyes darkening as he looked at his glass. "Because your father won't just let me take the treasures back."

"He will when you explain your intent. He only wants to keep them safe."

He ran his hand through his hair, showing her exactly what he'd done to tousle it. "Christ, Daphne, are you really that naïve?"

His words slammed into her with sharp force. "There's no need to be rude."

"Forgive me, I'm tired. There's a side to your father you don't see. He wants the treasures for his own devices."

That was preposterous. Reining her anger, she asked, "And what are those?"

"I'm not entirely certain, but your father is the leader of a faction within the Order that seeks to rid the Order of any nondescendants and to acquire the treasures."

Daphne's pulse kicked up so that her chest was

nearly heaving. "That's absurd. You're mistaken. The Order protects the treasures."

"The Order prefers to leave them be. They will only take them, as they did with the Heart of Llanllwch, when they are concerned they might be stolen. In that instance, they hid it. They didn't lock it away in someone's personal vault."

"Perhaps that's what they plan to do this time too," Daphne said. "My father is an important member of the Order. He wouldn't take the treasures for himself."

He leaned forward over the table, his eyes a dark gray that reminded her of an angry storm cloud. "That's precisely what he's doing. He wants to use them for his own purposes—and I intend to make sure he doesn't."

"But you don't know what those purposes are." She stood abruptly, her anger getting the better of her. "I'm not going to sit here and listen to you defame my father."

Gideon leaned back in his chair and looked up at her. "I know you love him. He's your father. But he's not who you think he is."

She started to shake. "How can you claim to know him better than me?"

"I can't, and I won't. But I know a part of him that you don't. I didn't want to be the one to tell you, but we can't continue on if we aren't aligned. I can't have you telling your father that I intend to take the treasures to Gareth's tomb."

"I wouldn't do that. You're wrong about my father. He doesn't want the treasures for himself."

He speared her with a narrow-eyed stare. "If you're going to tell him I plan to take them, we will part ways tomorrow."

She didn't want that. She wanted to find the cloak.

But why? She'd wanted to find it to impress her father, and if she couldn't tell him, why did she care?

Because she wanted to share the discovery with Gideon. At least she had until he'd prattled nonsense about her father.

"I can see you're conflicted," he said. "Sleep on it, and let me know in the morning." He tossed back the rest of his port, stood, and departed the dining room without a backward glance.

Daphne stared after him, all but certain their precarious alliance had completely collapsed.

Chapter Twelve

GIDEON CAST HIS head back, leaning the base of his skull on the top of the chair as he stared at the library ceiling. Shadows from the flickering lamp at the end of the table danced across the wood. If he squinted, one of them looked like someone wearing a cloak.

He closed his eyes and breathed deeply, his mind wandering back to his conversation with Daphne earlier. He hadn't meant to bring up Camelot or her father's intent, but the time had come. He'd meant what he said: she couldn't come to Brue Cottage if she meant to tell her father. But if she didn't come, he'd have to find another way to take the heart and the sword from Foliot's vault.

Because his current—and only—plan required her.

He could try to don the cloak, assuming he found the bloody thing, take the keys from Foliot, and sneak into the vault, but it would be far easier if he had help. Foliot kept the keys on his person as far as Gideon could tell, so stealing them would prove difficult, even if he couldn't be seen.

So he needed her.

No, you don't, his mind argued. It would be *easier* with her, but he'd do what he must without her if it came to that. And it certainly looked as though it would.

Damn. He liked her. He enjoyed spending time with her. In another lifetime, he might have pursued her…

He opened his eyes and saw another, larger shadow on the ceiling. Jumping from the chair, he was prepared to commit violence.

Daphne gasped in surprise. "My apologies. I'll just leave you to it."

He felt bad for startling her. "What are you doing down here?"

"I was…restless." She stepped forward, her hands clasped at her waist, where a ribbon cinched her coral-pink dressing gown. Her hair was a long, dark rope against her shoulder in a thick braid. "I decided to take a walk down the stairs, and I saw the light in here."

He'd left the door slightly ajar, he realized. He hadn't intended to come in and go through the chest again, but he'd been drawn to the secret room like a magnet, and now here he was with the chest on the table, its contents spread out as they'd been earlier.

"I'm afraid I couldn't resist." He indicated the items on the table.

She came slowly toward him, her face pale in the lamplight.

He turned toward her in concern. "Did you have another nightmare?"

She glanced up at him. "No, but sometimes when I'm in a strange place—like the inn—and I'm unsettled… That's often when they happen."

He'd caused her to be unsettled. "I'm sorry if I upset you. I'd intended to talk with you about that—your father—but I could have done a better job."

"Thank you. It was just—surprising to hear." She edged toward the table. "Is this everything that was in the chest?"

"Yes." He'd read the letter from his grandfather countless times, and there was absolutely nothing about the cloak. "I have to think the cloak has been missing for quite some time." Gideon feared it might be lost forever.

She moved to stand in front of the empty chest. "I wonder if the cloak was already taken to Gareth's tomb."

"I hadn't considered that." Gideon *had* considered what he might do if he couldn't find the cloak. He'd have to get the heart and sword back from Foliot and take them to Gareth—whether he had the cloak or not.

"Can I touch it?" she asked, looking at him tentatively.

"Please."

She ran her hands along the purple velvet. "This is beautiful. I wonder when it was made. And I wonder how many chests there have been—Gwyneth indicated there had been several. What do you suppose happened to the others?"

He wondered the same thing. It was interesting how they often thought of things in the same way. "Perhaps they fell apart from age and use."

"Well, this one is still in excellent condition." She sucked in a breath. "Oh dear, I spoke too soon. This corner has come loose." She held up the edge of the lining and shot him an apologetic glance. "I'm so sorry."

"I'm sure it wasn't your fault." He moved closer to her side and took the fabric from her. "We can fix it." He had no idea how.

She withdrew her hand and inhaled sharply once more. "What did you just do?"

He turned his head toward her. "What?"

"Move your hand."

He lifted the edge of the velvet higher. "Like that?" She was staring at his appendage as if it had sprouted another finger. "What do you see?"

"It's what I don't see," she breathed. "Your hand… I don't see it. I only see the table beyond. It's like you're—"

"Invisible?" Gideon's blood chilled, and time seemed to cease as he looked at his missing hand. She was right. It wasn't there.

"We have to take it out."

"Yes. Bring the light closer." He didn't want to accidentally ruin anything. His hands shook as he began to pry the velvet loose from the box. It didn't take much, and he wondered what had kept it in place to begin with.

Some sort of magic, probably. The same magic that made it look like the simple lining of a box and not a voluminous cloak of invisibility, which it absolutely was.

He pulled it from the chest, surprised at the quantity of fabric.

"Put it on," she whispered.

He tossed it around his shoulders and fastened the clasp at his neck. It fell closed at his front, and he looked down to see…nothing. Or rather, right through himself.

"You're invisible." She blinked at him, her face even paler than when she'd arrived.

"Not quite." He pulled the hood up over his head. The fabric came completely over and pooled around his neck. He could see through it quite perfectly—well enough to see the look of shock on her face.

"Now you are," she said, reaching forward. Her hand connected with his chest. "But I can feel you."

"That's an important thing to know."

"Yes." She lifted her gaze to his, and the shock had warmed into something far brighter—excitement and joy. "This is spectacular."

He pulled the hood from his head and unfastened the clasp. "You try. You're a descendant."

Her eyes widened once more as he whipped the cloak from his shoulders and wrapped it around her.

But she didn't disappear.

She looked down at herself. "I'm still here." She lifted her gaze to his, and he wanted to smooth the wrinkles between her brows.

She wasn't a descendant. Which meant her father wasn't her father, or he'd lied to her. Well, either way, he'd lied to her.

Hell.

Turning, she presented her back to him so that he could take the cloak from her shoulders. He set it over the chair where it just looked like a purple velvet cloak.

"What does that mean?" she whispered as she turned back to face him.

"I don't know." God, he hated that lost look in her eyes. It was the same one she'd had when he'd woken her from that nightmare.

Gideon pulled her against his chest and wrapped his arms around her. She laid her head against him, and he held her tight. Her arms encircled his waist, and she clasped his waistcoat, for he'd long abandoned his coat, a fact he'd forgotten until that moment. For propriety's sake he should have put it back on when she came in.

Propriety? She was his wife.

The word "wife" sent a shock of possession and need through him. Also, a startling desire to protect and care for this woman.

He cupped the side of her face, tracing his thumb along her cheekbone. She lifted her head and looked up at him, her lips parted in potential invitation…

He didn't dare overstep. He'd done that once, but he'd been trying to prove a point. Or something. Damn, he didn't know what he'd done, and he sure as hell didn't know what he was doing now.

So of course he lowered his head and waited for her to push him away. Only she curled her fingers into his back and urged him closer.

That was an invitation.

Their mouths met, and the sensations of need and possession inside him intensified. He slanted his lips over hers and thrust his hand into the hair at her nape. It had been so long since he'd felt like this, as if his body could take flight.

Eager to taste her, he licked along her lip. She opened for him and even met his tongue, tentatively and then with more urgency as her fingers dug into his back and her breasts pressed against his chest.

The layers of her clothing were insignificant, and he could feel her heat like a freshly stoked fire. And that's what he was. He'd lain dormant for years, waiting for this moment when she would kindle him into a burning flame.

Everything about this was a balm to his soul, soothing an ache he'd long ignored. Or forgotten about. Her touch awakened him, and he was both hunter and prey.

She brought one hand from his back and ran her palm up his chest until it rested over his heart. The rhythm increased as his blood pumped through him, building a fervor.

He wanted to feel her too, so he drew his hand forward along her neck, pressing his thumb against her flesh until the steady beat of her heart answered his call. With his other hand, he clasped her waist, holding her tight against him so that they stood hip to hip. Or more accurately, hip to thigh because of their height difference. It was frustrating because his body wanted to fit to hers as they were made to do.

She moaned into his mouth, perhaps echoing his frustration, and he tipped his head the other direction to explore her in a new way. He thrust deep into her mouth, arching her head back.

Her grip grew tighter on his back, and she pushed her hand up to his collarbone and higher until her fingers grazed his neck above his loosened cravat. How he wished he'd tossed that away too.

Desperate for more of her, he moved his hand up her rib cage until he found the soft underside of her breast. He dragged his thumb across the peak and felt it harden through her clothing.

She moaned again, this time breaking the kiss so the low sound filled the air around them. He kissed her cheek, her jaw, her neck, his lips and tongue sliding along her heated flesh as she pushed her breast into his hand.

That she wanted him as much as he wanted her thrilled him. Still, he should go slow…or stop altogether.

Apparently, she'd read his thoughts, because she pulled at his cravat and murmured, "Touch me, Gideon. Please touch me."

Since he was already touching her, he knew what she meant. What she craved. He untied the ribbon at her waist and slipped his hand inside her dressing gown. One thin garment remained between them, but it scarcely hindered him. He could feel her heat and the soft curve of her breast. He cupped her, gently squeezing, then pressed his thumb and forefinger around her nipple.

She gasped. "My legs. I can't…"

He felt her wobble and turned her so that she was in front of one of the chairs. He eased her down and descended with her, dropping to his knees before her.

She put her hands on his shoulders as he continued to fondle her breast. Her eyes were closed, her lips parted as her chest rose and fell with her rapid breaths.

He put his hands on each of her breasts and watched her body respond to his touch. Her nipples rose and her back arched. Her legs parted, just a bit, but enough for him to move between her knees. He pitched his head forward and put his mouth on her through the fabric of her gown.

Her hands clasped his head, her fingers twining in his hair. Her legs opened farther, and he moved closer, holding her breast while he laved the nipple, soaking the linen that separated them.

He'd thought this was enough, but it wasn't. He wanted her bare flesh, silky hot, beneath his mouth. The neckline of the gown was low, but not low enough. He dragged it down, angling it so that it just barely exposed the top of her breast. He pushed her flesh up and caught the nipple in his mouth the second it came free.

God, she tasted like heaven.

She cast her head back with a long, sultry moan that fed his desire. Need pulsed through him, making him hard as stone.

He suckled her harder, drawing on her nipple and then teasing her with light kisses and feather-soft licks. She pulled at his hair, silently begging him to take her in his mouth again.

And then she wasn't silent.

"Gideon, take me upstairs."

It was enough to shatter the bliss that had enveloped him. What the hell was he doing?

He withdrew from her and adjusted her gown so that she was covered. Then he pulled her dressing gown over her chest and retreated from between her thighs.

Her eyes opened, and she blinked at him. "What's wrong?"

"I overstepped. I should not have kissed you." His voice was thick with desire that would go unfulfilled.

She scooted to the edge of her chair, her face lined with confusion. "I wanted you to. I still want you to. This doesn't need to be a marriage in name only."

"I'm afraid it does." He turned from her and grasped the edge of the table to stand.

"Why?"

It was a simple question, and one that probably deserved an answer. Probably? She deserved that and more.

When he faced her again, he saw that she'd retied her gown and her legs were pressed primly together. Her cheeks were still stained pink, and he fought not to think of her breasts with their nipples that were a similar but darker shade.

"I told you I didn't want to marry—I don't want another wife."

"Because of Rose," she said softly.

He averted his gaze toward the window, where the curtains were drawn against the darkness of night. "I haven't been with a woman since she died. I haven't wanted to be."

"But you did tonight."

He heard the uncertainty in her voice and didn't want her to think she was undesirable. He looked at her with a regretful smile. "This isn't about you. Yes, I wanted you." He still wanted her. "But I don't want a wife, nor do I want children."

"How can you say that? You've a title to pass on, and a rich legacy many men would kill for."

She didn't know how true that was, or that her father was one of them. Hell, her father. All this had come about because she'd learned she wasn't a descendant, that her father had lied to her, and Gideon had wanted to comfort her.

Until he'd wanted to satisfy his lust. And hers, apparently.

"Daphne—"

She stood and took his hand between hers. "Just think about what Gwyneth said. That you *will* have children. She probably knows what she's talking about."

He recalled what she'd said, just as she seemed rather fixated on whether he and Daphne were in love. "I think Gwyneth likes to play matchmaker."

And yet he found himself thinking of the other things she'd said, of how she planned to give him the Beckery Texts to pass them to his children. Maybe he did have a duty. If not to the earldom, then to the legacy of Gareth the Worthy...

He gave himself an internal shake. Was he thinking of taking Daphne upstairs to fulfill some obligation he felt? No, he wouldn't do that. When, *and if*, he took Daphne to bed, it would be because he loved her.

Unfortunately, Gideon wasn't sure he knew how to do that.

"Would that be so terrible?" Daphne asked. She exhaled and shook her head. "Forget I said that. I don't wish to dishonor your wishes." She turned to go.

"Daphne, about before…The cloak."

She only turned back halfway so that he could see her profile. "My father lied to me."

"Yes."

"Is he not my father?" She glanced at Gideon but quickly dropped her gaze.

He heard her pain, and it echoed in his heart. "I used to wish my father wasn't my father. When Dyrnwyn flamed in my grasp, I wondered if that meant I had a different father. I couldn't imagine he could be descended from one of the Knights of the Round Table. I think that's because I just wanted it to be true."

"But you aren't a descendant through him," she said.

He shook his head. "No, through my mother. Do you think your father isn't your father?"

"I have no idea." She sounded as lost as she'd looked before. Then she turned her head, and he saw the steel in her gaze. "But I will find out. Good night, Gideon." She moved toward the door.

"Will you be all right?" Gideon asked. "If you have a nightmare, I'll be just across the hall from your room."

"I won't bother you," she said as she reached the threshold.

"I insist. Whatever happens, Daphne, I will always protect you."

But she was already gone.

AFTER TWO GRUELING days of progressively cool and rainy weather, they finally arrived at Brue Cottage. They'd spent last night at an inn, choosing to avoid Daphne's cottage at Keynsham in case her father's men were lurking about. She doubted they would be since she'd sent word that she and Gideon were married, but decided it wasn't worth the risk.

Thoughts of her father made her stomach turn. If Papa had lied to her about being a descendant, what else had he lied to her about? Gideon's assertion that he was the leader of some secret organization within the Order and that he intended to hoard the treasures for himself suddenly seemed possible.

And that broke her heart.

Her father was all she had left in the world, and to think he wasn't the man she'd thought made her question everything. She'd thought of little else during their journey, and she was exhausted.

Gideon came to help her dismount, his hands clasping her waist as he lifted her to the ground. His touch never failed to send a jolt of awareness through her.

When she hadn't been dwelling on her father, she'd been focused on Gideon and the way he made her feel. She could see his turmoil, struggling between the grief he felt for his wife and whatever burgeoning feelings he might have for her. Or maybe she was wrong and there were no feelings. Maybe it was just a physical attraction. And maybe that was why he'd refused her.

For her, it was more. She was all but certain she was in love with him, but she didn't want to think about it. What would be the point?

"Go on inside, and I'll take care of the horses," Gideon said, water dripping from the brim of his hat.

"Hurry," she said. "You need to get inside and dry off."

"The horses have had as rough a journey as we have. I must see to their care." He gave her an encouraging smile. "Go. I'll be fine."

He turned and took the horses toward the stable. Daphne watched him for a moment until an especially large drop of rain managed to evade the brim of her hat and land on her nose.

She rushed to the house and knocked loudly. Thankfully, the door opened quickly, and Margaret ushered her inside.

"You're soaked," she said, rather unnecessarily.

"It's raining," Daphne answered, also rather unnecessarily.

Gwyneth swept into the hall, her dark hair piled high atop her head. Long gold earrings hung from her ears, and she wore a heavy emerald pendant that lay just above the neckline of her dramatic black-and-gold robe.

"Goodness, you look like a drowned cat," Gwyneth said. "Margaret, have a bath drawn immediately."

Margaret rushed off as Gwyneth wrinkled her nose at Daphne. "Let's take your hat and coat off here, shall we?" Gwyneth said.

Daphne removed her hat and wordlessly held it out.

Gwyneth waved her hand down. "Just drop it on the floor, Margaret will fetch it later and dry it out. Do the same with your coat. And your gloves."

Daphne worried her coat was ruined, but she had other riding habits. She peeled her gloves away and didn't bother turning them right side out before letting them fall to the marble floor. With shaking fingers, she began to unfasten her coat. "Gideon is in the stables taking care of the horses."

"Edward will send him up."

Overcome with a series of deep shivers, Daphne looked over at Gwyneth. "Who's Edward?"

"The groom." Gwyneth came forward. "You poor dear, let me." She brushed Daphne's hands away and finished with the coat, then helped remove it from Daphne's quaking body. "Come with me." She took Daphne's frigid hand between her very warm ones and led her into a great hall.

Stairs marched up the right wall, then turned to the left, where they landed on a gallery that overlooked the hall. Gwyneth pulled her up the stairs and along the gallery, then steered her to the right into a sitting room.

But they weren't at their destination yet, apparently, for Gwyneth pulled her into another room that could only be described as a bathing chamber. A fire roared in the hearth on the opposite wall, and Margaret worked with another woman to fill a tub situated rather near the fireplace.

Gwyneth set about helping Daphne completely disrobe. The room wasn't terribly large and, due to the size of the fire, was much warmer than the rest of the house. It was far warmer than she'd been in…well, as long as she could remember, really. She continued to shiver, but not as violently, and soon they lowered her into the steaming tub.

The hot water enveloped her, and she sighed as her body began to finally relax completely. A strong, delicious floral scent curled around her.

"Lean back and close your eyes," Gwyneth said, easing her back against the tub, which was perfectly designed to accommodate precisely the position Gwyneth suggested.

Daphne closed her eyes and gave herself over to the sensations of warmth and comfort. "What is that smell?"

"Jasmine and lavender. The bath tonic will help you

relax. You'll soak for a bit—you need to warm up. We'll be back in a while."

The water worked an incredible magic, soothing Daphne's sore muscles and calming her agitated spirit. She wondered if it would be bad to fall asleep. Surely she could drown...

Whether she slept or not, she didn't know, but she was in a complete state of bliss when she heard a gentle splash. Opening her eyes, she looked down her body at the tub. She hadn't made the noise.

Looking to her right, she saw there was now a screen separating her from the other half of the room. She recalled there had been other tubs in the bath chamber. At least one. Perhaps two.

And someone was in one of them on the other side of that screen.

She didn't have to think too hard to know who it was. The thought of Gideon so close—naked and, well, just *naked*—brought her to full awareness.

Yet she was still incredibly relaxed. Her body felt heavy, but her flesh tingled with...something. She inhaled deeply, and the scents of jasmine and lavender filled her senses.

Another sound from the other side of the screen sent a flutter of arousal through her: he moaned.

What was he doing? *Probably enjoying the bath, silly!*

She'd likely moaned in delight when she'd first climbed into the tub. It had been absolutely heavenly. But then she'd also moaned the other night when he'd touched her and put his mouth on her.

Her breasts, already weighted with delicious lethargy, grew heavier for an altogether different reason. Without thinking, she brought her hand up and cupped herself as he'd done. It wasn't the same, but if she just imagined it was him…

She closed her eyes and squeezed the nipple. A low moan escaped her lips, and she clamped her teeth together, praying he hadn't heard her.

Sensation moved along her heated flesh and pooled in her lower belly. The hunger she'd felt there the other night intensified until she wanted to weep with desire.

Maybe if she touched herself there, it would help. She moved her other hand between her thighs and pressed on her flesh. A burst of pleasure flashed over her, but it was fleeting. The hunger returned tenfold. She pressed again, and again felt a moment's release. Once more, the need increased.

Well, this was bloody frustrating.

She opened her legs and put more of her hand over herself. A whimper slipped past her lips, and her gaze shot toward the screen.

She heard the slosh of water, as if he were leaving the bath. What if he was coming over here? Part of her wanted to stay in the bath and invite him to join her. But the other part of her, the part that was mortified at the thought of him seeing her in such a state, drove her to grip the side of the tub and pull herself out. The air was much cooler, and she dove for a large towel that hung from a hook behind the tub.

But she didn't move quickly enough, and Gideon came around the screen.

"*Daphne.*"

The word was low and dark and so arousing that the need between her legs grew even more acute.

She stood, frozen, her hand on the towel but otherwise completely bare to his perusal. He held a towel around his hips, and aside from that, he was also bare. From the top of his dark head down over the sculpted planes of his chest and abdomen, the former sprinkled with dark hair, to his muscular legs, also dusted with dark hair, below the towel.

She'd always been impressed by his size—he was tall and broad of shoulder—but standing as he was now, she was utterly captivated by him. His height, his strength, his palpable masculinity.

He turned to the side, presenting his profile. "I didn't mean to intrude. I heard a noise and wanted to make sure you were all right."

Heat flushed her face. He'd heard her. She quickly pulled the towel from the hook and wrapped the towel around herself.

"I'm fine." The words were squeaky, as if she were a mouse.

"Good." He didn't move, and she noticed the front of his towel jutted out...

She turned her back to him and tried to think past her embarrassment. Or maybe it was her desire. Whatever it was, she was completely confounded.

Thankfully, they were saved from further discomfort by the arrival of Gwyneth, Margaret, and the third woman.

"You're both out," Gwyneth said. "Lovely. Dinner will be ready shortly. You don't need to dress to the usual degree—we are far less formal at Brue Cottage. Gideon, we don't have a valet, I'm afraid."

"I don't either," he said.

He didn't have a valet? Obviously, he hadn't been traveling with one, but Daphne had assumed he employed one at home. Apparently not. Where was his home exactly? Stratton Hall? Somewhere in London?

Oh, this was good. Things to think about that weren't his naked form.

"Come, Daphne," Gwyneth said, "Margaret will help you get ready."

Daphne didn't require a maid. She also didn't necessarily want to expose herself to Margaret, not when her body still felt flushed and sensitive. "I don't require assistance either, thank you."

Gwyneth shrugged. "She'll at least show you to your room—through there." She pointed to a door that was partially blocked by the screen.

The third woman adjusted the screen, and Margaret went to open the door.

"Gideon, your room is on the other side. In the interest of haste, why don't you just go through Daphne's chamber? There's an adjoining door."

There was? Daphne didn't need to know that. She'd spend the entire night praying he'd come through it.

Daphne walked to the door and looked back at Gideon, who'd returned to his side of the screen, which she could now see. Their gazes connected for a brief moment, and it was as if he'd touched her. A scalding, enticing touch that only made her want more.

Except he hadn't *actually* touched her.

Oh, this was going to be a very long night.

Chapter Thirteen

GIDEON BENT TO scoop up his clothing, but Gwyneth said Nancy, the third woman in the bathing chamber that was full of too many damned women, would gather them up. Not that any of them signified beyond Daphne. He could barely think straight after seeing her nude.

It had been a long time since he'd seen a woman in her natural state, and he felt like a lad of sixteen. His cock throbbed almost painfully, and he was certain they were all aware of it. How could they not be? He'd hoped to use his clothing to mask his obvious arousal.

Instead, he strode toward the doorway but had to stop short because Daphne was at the threshold. He could squeeze by her, but they would certainly touch, and that seemed a very bad idea. Unless he wanted to continue where they'd left off the other night. And while that might sound like a very *good* idea, it was not.

Why is that, exactly?

Gideon was ready to punch that voice in the back of his head.

Because he wasn't going to take advantage of their temporary marriage to satisfy his lust. Though from the way she was looking at him, she perhaps wouldn't agree that he'd be taking advantage. Her gaze kept dipping to his erection, which wasn't helping matters. And dear Lord, now she was licking her lower lip.

"Pardon me," he said, startling her to move into the bedchamber. He stalked through it as quickly as possible and, finding the door on the opposite side, escaped into safety.

He closed the door and collapsed against the wood, his breath coming as fast as if he'd run across the bloody room at full speed.

"Don't dawdle for dinner." The voice—Gwyneth's—coming through the door as if she stood right behind him, and he supposed she did, made him pitch forward in surprise.

Blast, he supposed he didn't have time to take care of his inconvenient arousal just now. Instead, he went to the window and wrestled it open so he could bask in the cool night air.

Once his body was back under his relative control, he found his clothing, which someone had unpacked from his saddlebag and arranged in the armoire. He dressed quickly, then made his way from the chamber. Margaret loitered at the end of the gallery that overlooked the hall. "The dining room is through the great hall." She gestured down toward the stairs. "I'm waiting for Miss Foliot."

Miss Foliot.

"She is Lady Stratton now."

Margaret's eyes widened, and her brows arched high. She gave a single nod. "Felicitations."

"Thank you." He made his way downstairs and into the dining room, which was completely vacant. Why had he needed to hurry?

There was, however, wine on the table. He poured a glass and took a healthy drink, appreciating the warm ruby liquid as it washed down his throat. Perhaps if he drank the lot of it, he'd be able to sleep tonight. If not, he was bound to be tortured knowing Daphne was just a short walk away.

And why not? That was how he'd spent the past two nights. First, at Hollyhaven when she'd been just across the hall and he'd listened desperately, hoping she might have another nightmare and necessitate his care. What kind of beast *was* he?

Then last night at the inn, where they'd had to share a room, but it had thankfully had two beds. Still, he'd been able to hear her disrobe and had remained awake far too long listening to her sleep. Again, hoping she might require his assistance.

All in the name of being able to touch her again. Yes, he was a beast.

The air around him suddenly changed. He turned and saw her standing in the doorway. She was dressed in a simple gown that couldn't have been hers. The wardrobe she'd brought along consisted of two riding habits and two dresses, one suitable for day wear and another for dinner. This was none of those. It was white, with volumes of sheer material that, piled together, made her look like the sweetest, most tempting confection. He supposed the excess was so that it wasn't completely transparent, for just one layer of it would certainly be. It reminded him of the garment she'd worn the first night he'd dreamed of her.

He pictured her nude as she'd been in the bathing chamber, but with the diaphanous material draped across her lush body. Christ, he was going hard again. He should've taken the time to toss himself off. Except he suspected he'd be in the same predicament anyway. His reaction to Daphne was profoundly erotic and growing more so by the minute.

She moved into the room, and the candles from the chandelier above them caught the pearlescent light of a strand of pearls woven into her dark locks, which had been swept into a simple yet artful style.

Seeming to realize he was looking at her hair, she touched it gently. "Nancy is quite good at styling hair. She insisted."

"You look lovely." It was a gross understatement, but he didn't think there were words to sufficiently describe her beauty or the devastating effect it had on him.

"Thank you. You look splendid too." Her gaze dipped over him, again seeming to hesitate the slightest bit in the region of his groin.

He pivoted and took another drink of wine before offering to pour some for her.

"Yes, please," she answered.

Glad to have something to do, Gideon set his glass on the table and poured one for her. He moved to give it to her and tensed, praying their hands wouldn't touch while also wishing just as fervently that they would.

"You're *married*?"

Startled by Gwyneth's sudden arrival, they both turned toward the door and neither grasped the glass of wine. It tumbled to the carpet splashing ruby claret across the blue-and-red pattern.

"Oh my goodness, I am so clumsy," Daphne said.

Gideon bent to pick up the glass. "It was my fault."

Gwyneth waved her hand. "Leave it. Margaret will take care of it."

Gideon set the empty glass on the table.

"Now, tell me why you let me put you in separate rooms if you are husband and wife." Gwyneth moved to the table and poured wine into the third remaining glass and handed it to Daphne. Then she took the glass they'd dropped, refilled it, and promptly took a drink.

She really was an odd woman. But endearing at the

same time.

"It's not a real marriage," Daphne said. "My father wanted us to marry, and we wanted to complete this quest together, so it seemed the most expedient…course."

Gwyneth looked from Daphne to Gideon and back to Daphne, then back to Gideon. "That makes absolutely no sense."

"It's temporary," Gideon said, hating that word more than he ever thought possible. When he thought of never seeing Daphne again, his chest constricted and he fought to draw a deep breath. "We plan to seek an annulment." He hated that word even more.

Gwyneth's brows drew together, and she stared at them with a thoroughly bemused expression. "You're both mad. Clearly the forces of nature have pushed you together—as you should be. I will hope that you regain your senses. And when you do, you'll thank me for putting you in adjoining rooms." She smiled and took another sip of wine.

"Now, let us eat." Gwyneth swept to another door and knocked loudly on the wood. "We don't have a formal staff here, so Margaret will just bring out one large course." She came back to the table and took a chair on one side, leaving Gideon and Daphne to take the two seats opposite. It was obvious Gwyneth wanted them to sit close together.

Anxious to talk about anything but his marriage to Daphne or anything else relating to the two of them, Gideon said, "We found the cloak."

Gwyneth's eyes grew animated, and she leaned forward. "Did you! How wonderful. Where was it?"

"In the chest. I thought it was just the lining."

Her lips spread into a cat's smile. "Things aren't

always what they seem."

No, they weren't, and he'd learned that lesson many times. Hopefully some day he'd remember it.

"Did you know it was the lining?" Daphne asked, sounding rather suspicious. And now Gideon was too. He was also a little annoyed with himself for not thinking of that too.

"I didn't," Gwyneth said. "But I hoped it was still in there somehow—that's why I wanted you to bring it to me. You see, the women of Brue Cottage have always provided the chests to the Nash family. That's how I knew the cloak was inside it."

Gideon had wondered if there'd been some sort of enchantment on the cloak to make it at least somewhat adhere to the chest and appear to be lining.

Margaret came in with a tray, followed by another woman they hadn't yet met who carried a second tray. They set platters and bowls of food around the table but close enough so one of them could reach each item without getting up.

Gwyneth helped herself to pheasant and then passed the tray across to Gideon. He offered a serving to Daphne first.

Setting the pheasant down, Gideon took a bowl of peas from Gwyneth. "Now that we have the cloak, we plan to return it and the heart and sword to Gareth. We just need to find where that is."

"We can discuss that tomorrow," Gwyneth said.

Tomorrow? Why not now? Before he could ask, Gwyneth focused her attention on Daphne. "Tell me, dear, why did your father want you to marry Gideon? Aside from the obvious."

Daphne glanced toward Gideon. "The obvious?"

Gwyneth blinked at her. "He's an earl. And very

attractive."

Gideon looked sideways toward Daphne and saw color rise up her neck and into her ears, turning the tips a fetching shade of pink.

"He wanted me to marry a descendant," Daphne said.

"That's important to him?"

"Yes, he's a member of the Order of the Round Table."

"Well then, of course it is. I'd forgotten for a moment that he was a member." She cut a piece of pheasant and waved her fork in the air. "What a silly organization. I really don't understand their purpose."

Daphne picked up her wineglass. "To protect the Thirteen Treasures and keep proof of Arthur and his knights away from scrutiny."

"Why? People have a right to know their history. And they've gotten it dead wrong for centuries. Arthur wasn't some perfect leader. Just as Morgana wasn't an evil sorceress." She narrowed one eye and nodded toward Daphne, who lifted her glass higher in silent toast.

"If people delve too deeply, they'll find the treasures," Gideon said.

Gwyneth peered at him with an unflinching stare. "As you have?"

Gideon shifted. At first, he'd pursued them with the intent to possess them—or at least to give them to Foliot, who intended to keep them away from those whom he called the zealots within the Order. "I only want to put them where they belong."

"Which is why you are The Worthy. That you found the cloak only confirms what I thought." Gwyneth turned back to Daphne. "So your father wanted you to marry a descendant. He has to be ecstatic that you landed an earl—and a good-looking one at that—who is also descended from Gareth the Worthy. You can't do much better than that. Unless you're a descendant of Arthur himself, but there aren't any more of those, unfortunately."

"There aren't?" Daphne's gaze darkened, and Gideon was close enough to her to feel her stiffen.

Gwyneth shook her head.

Daphne used her knife to viciously cut her pheasant into small pieces.

Gideon realized then that her father had told her he was a descendant of Arthur. He brought his hand to his lap, then reached over and touched her leg gently—and quickly, lest he want to linger.

She glanced at him, and the hurt in her gaze speared into him more sharply than any blade. She turned her head to look at Gwyneth. "My father is rather obsessed with Arthur and the treasures. He's wanted me to marry a descendant as long as I can remember."

"What a happy coincidence that you fell in love with one, then." Gwyneth smiled before she focused on her plate once more.

"I'm not—" Daphne turned her attention to her plate too, but not before her ears turned pink once more.

Was she in love with him? God, he hoped not. He wasn't worth that emotion.

The rest of dinner passed with conversation about the history of Brue Cottage, which had been here in one form or another since the seventh century. Women who were accomplished healers who wished to study with other healers came here. Some could claim a relation to other women who had lived at Brue

Cottage, while others could not. It didn't matter to those in residence. All were welcome—provided they were women.

"If your marriage doesn't last, but I am sure it will," Gwyneth said to Daphne, "you're welcome to return here and live with us. It would be wonderful to have a historian to continue recording our stories. We haven't had one in residence since the middle of last century."

"What a wonderful offer. Thank you." Daphne's lips curved into a smile, and she sat a bit straighter. She deserved to look and feel like that all the time.

When they'd seemed to eat all they could and had finished the bottle of claret, Gwyneth stood. "It is time for my nightly meditation and exercise." She stepped away from the table. "Tomorrow, we will discuss Gareth, and you'll bring the chest to the library."

Gideon nodded. It was currently in his chamber upstairs, having been transferred there with his clothes.

Gwyneth glided toward the doorway, then turned her head to look at them over her shoulder. "Don't be fools—the world is full of far too many of them. Sleep well!"

When they were alone, Gideon stood from the table. "She is committed to playing matchmaker." He pulled Daphne's chair out so that she could rise.

"Yes, quite."

They left the dining room together, and he pondered offering his arm, but then she'd touch him and touching seemed destined for more touching. Which they should probably avoid.

So they walked upstairs side by side in awkward silence, the air crackling between them like an electrical storm. They arrived at his chamber first, and she paused.

"Good night, Gideon."

"Good night, Daphne." Though she'd seemed to cheer up by the end of the dinner, he still sensed a rawness within her. "If you have a nightmare—"

"You're only a door away." She flashed him a smile. "Good night."

Then she turned, and he watched hungrily as the gauzy material of her gown swayed with her hips. How he longed to sweep it all away…

Instead, he walked into his chamber and threw his clothes off in frustrated jerks. Standing nude in the middle of the chamber, he stared at the door separating them. A slender, terrible, hateful door.

His cock was already at half-mast and had been throughout most of dinner. It would take just a few quick strokes to bring himself to the brink and probably only a few more to send him over the edge.

But she was so fucking close, he could practically taste her. Or hear her. He suddenly recalled the seductive whimper she'd released in the bath. Christ, he'd almost come on the spot.

Without thinking, he walked to the door, every fiber of his being pushing him forward. Or maybe it was those damned forces of nature Gwyneth had prattled on about.

He hesitated, his hand on the latch. His body screamed for him to open it, to take what they both wanted. No, to give her a night of ecstasy that would banish the shadows of loneliness that lived in her gaze.

He turned the latch. And then everything went black.

Chapter Fourteen

GIDEON'S BODY FELL backward, his magnificent naked form sprawling atop the carpet. Daphne rushed into his room and knelt beside him. "Gideon?"

His eyes were closed, but he was breathing. Of course she hadn't killed him. But she'd apparently knocked him unconscious with the door.

Or not.

One of his eyes opened and then the other. He raised his hand to his forehead, where an angry red mark slashed across his flesh.

"Are you all right?" she asked, smoothing his dark hair back from the wound. Well, it wasn't really a *wound*.

He narrowed his eyes at her with a look of confusion. "Did you hit me with the door?"

"You must have been standing right on the other side." She glanced down at him, heat flashing through her. "Naked."

He looked at her. "And you are not. Naked."

She wore her dressing robe. "I'm naked beneath this."

The confusion in his gaze sparked into curiosity. "You were coming in here to seduce me?"

She looked over him again, one of her brows riding high on her forehead. "And what were you doing—coming to my room to play chess?"

"Naked chess does sound rather amusing."

"Amusing? I'm not sure I could focus on chess at all." Her gaze drifted downward again. His *nakedness* was most distracting. Especially since his cock was swelling. Every time she looked, it was a bit larger.

"You have a point there," he said, reaching up to pull a pin from her hair.

"Are we flirting?" she asked, feeling suddenly breathless.

"Hmm, I think so." He tugged another pin free and another, tossing them aside as he let lock after lock of her hair down.

"Does this mean you aren't going to send me back to my room?" She held her breath.

"Not unless you ask me to."

She exhaled with relief as desire washed through her. She'd expected him to protest. She'd never imagined he would flirt and seduce. Could you seduce someone who was also intent on seduction?

She hoped she was about to find out.

He pulled the last of the pins free, and her hair fell down, cloaking the sides of her face. He touched her cheek and then stroked her hair back until he cupped the base of her skull, drawing her down to him.

She didn't need much urging. Lowering her mouth to his, she was surprised when he was open for her, his lips and tongue eagerly devouring her the moment they met. His hand dug into her scalp, holding her captive while he kissed her. Thoroughly. Deeply. Sensually.

Breathless, she tore her mouth away to gain some much-needed air. He kissed along her jaw and down her neck as he clasped her waist. "Put your leg over me," he commanded.

She wasn't entirely sure what he meant at first.

"Like I'm a horse, and you're riding astride," he said without stopping his endless barrage of kisses.

She moved over him, until her knees were on either

side of his waist. "Like that?"

He let go of her head and grasped her hips, moving her lower until she felt the length of his shaft between her legs. "No, like *that.*"

She closed her eyes, and lights flashed behind her lids. The sensation of him against her was almost too much to bear. "Gideon, I can't get—"

"You can, and you will. Patience, love." He untied the sash at her waist and parted the sides of her dressing gown, exposing her flesh inch by inch. "Off."

She let it fall down her shoulders and shrugged it from her arms, leaving herself exposed to his hungry gaze. As in the bath earlier, she felt sensitive and weighted with desire, as if it would crush her with its intensity.

He skimmed his hands up from her hips, brushing over her rib cage until he met the undersides of her breasts. He lifted them gently, seeming to test their weight. He gently stroked her flesh, teasing her with light, airy touches that left her aching for more.

"*Gideon.*" The word was a plea. A whimper. A prayer.

He pulled her nipples, softly at first, then with more strength. He closed his thumbs and forefingers over them and tugged, drawing a gasp from her lips. She realized she was pushing down on him, seeking relief for her desperate sex.

She stopped herself and tried to ease back, but he brought one hand down to her waist and held her fast.

"Don't stop," he murmured. "I can feel how wet you are. Do you know what that means, Daphne?"

She shook her head.

"It means you want me. It means you want me inside you. Do you want that?"

She nodded.

"Tell me."

"I want you inside me." In that moment, she would have said anything. To anyone.

"Good."

He moved his hand across her lower abdomen, dipping down until he found the nest of curls that guarded her sex. And he kept going, his fingers stroking over her flesh until he found a spot that made her jerk and cry out.

That was the place she'd pressed in the tub, only it felt much better when he did it. Probably because he bloody well knew what he was doing. And thank God for that.

Using his thumb, he circled her flesh, tormenting her with sweet temptation. She wasn't sure what she wanted, but her hips began to move and she rubbed herself over his shaft. The friction of it along with his thumb was the best thing she'd ever felt in her life.

She closed her eyes and focused on the rhythm of it.

"Yes, Daphne. Move."

Taking his direction, she rotated her hips, back and forth, side to side. Each movement brought a new, spectacular sensation, heightened by the incessant stroke of his thumb.

But soon it wasn't enough. She began to whimper again, her body moving faster as she tried to achieve something she couldn't name.

Suddenly, he bucked up, and before she knew it, he'd swept her off him and into his arms. He carried her to the bed and laid her on the coverlet. Then he climbed up and knelt between her legs, his fingers stroking deftly over her sex.

She moaned, desperate for relief. He slipped one finger inside her, and the penetration swept her right back to where she'd been. No, past it. This was where she wanted to be. He retreated, then slid in deep, filling her and repeating the motion until she cried out. She parted her legs wide and clasped his hips. This was divine, but there had to be more.

The sensation of being filled grew. Was that two fingers? She wasn't watching. In fact, her eyes were closed. She was barely aware of anything except the ecstasy building inside her.

"Let it take you away, Daphne," he urged, his voice dark and seductive. "Give in to it. Do you feel it?"

Her body was rising, sensation soaring within her. She came up to meet his thrusts. Whatever she was looking for rushed upon her, driving her over the edge of desperation into a field of bliss. She cried out, and suddenly, there was more of him.

She felt him between her thighs, his cock sliding into her channel, stretching her flesh. There was a flash of discomfort as she accommodated the intrusion, but there was also a keen sense of anticipation with the promise of pleasure.

Opening her eyes, she met his stormy gaze. He looked as if he were in pain, but she recognized that feeling. A moment ago, before the intense pleasure had swept her away, she'd thought she'd never find satisfaction. But of course it was right there—she had only to trust him.

She more than trusted him. She loved him.

Pulling his head down, she kissed him deeply, wanting to be joined to him in every way possible. He kissed her back, his tongue driving into her mouth as his sex stroked into her body. He coaxed her legs up to curl around his waist, fitting them even more perfectly together.

Then he set a rhythm—pressing into her and sliding out. With each thrust, she held him more tightly, welcoming him into her body in search of another release. If that were even possible.

But it seemed it must be. Ecstasy built within her, and he began to move faster. Her body quivered with desire, pushing her again toward the pinnacle she'd just achieved. But this was a bit different—the feeling of him fully inside her, his body aligned with hers, their limbs entwined. He groaned between kisses and put his hand between them, his thumb teasing her again until she cascaded into the well of pleasure once more.

She fell back against the bed, and he left her. She heard him grunt but didn't open her eyes. She was too spent. Too heavy with joy.

After a few moments, she felt him leave the bed. Now she opened her eyes. "Where are you going?"

"Just tidying up. Get under the covers. Unless you want to go back to your room?" There was a note of uncertainty in his voice.

"I don't." She climbed under the covers and yawned.

He returned, joining her between the cool bedclothes. "I need to warm you up," he said, drawing her close against him.

She kissed his shoulder and burrowed into his chest. "I couldn't possibly be cold in your arms."

He kissed her head. "Then I better not let you go."

She prayed he never would.

THE SKY WAS barely beginning to lighten when Gideon stirred. The warm body beside him roused him fully awake. It had been years since he'd slept with another person—and he'd never thought to do it again.

What the hell had he done?

He looked over at Daphne, her dark auburn hair curling against her back, which was to him. He resisted the urge to press his body alongside hers. He'd done enough last night.

Rolling to his back, he stared at the dark blue canopy stretching over the top of the bed. Was it really that terrible? He'd wanted her, and she'd wanted him. He smiled and rubbed his forehead, which was still a bit tender, thinking of how she'd opened the door into him.

It was only terrible if they annulled the marriage. Then she would be a spoiled woman. At least he'd taken the precaution of leaving her body before spilling his seed.

Hell, she was going to be ruined either way. It was likely common knowledge that they were wed—he had to assume Foliot would bray about it to anyone who cared to listen and even to those who didn't. An annulment would be ruinous to her, even if it was his fault due to fraud.

He turned and leaned up on his elbow, bracing his head on his hand while he looked at her. She was so delicately beautiful. So strong and independent, and yet so vulnerable and alone. It was that last part that ate at him. He didn't want her to be alone.

Or maybe it was that he didn't want to be alone anymore either.

Was there a chance they could have a future together? Could they be happy? He thought of Rhys and Margery and their joyful life together. Now their children seemed to have found the same thing. Gideon also thought of his mother, whom he'd been angry with for so long. At last she might finally have true happiness—and peace.

He'd just never imagined those things for him. His father had persuaded him that he and Gideon weren't meant to be monogamous. They had to marry, of course—for the title—but their wives had to understand their masculine needs. That Gideon had once believed that toxic nonsense made him fairly ill. He supposed the fact that he didn't any longer was proof that he wasn't like his father. And didn't that mean he could be worthy of love?

Worthy. That word had taken on a higher meaning in recent days. He still wasn't sure it was an accurate description of him.

Daphne turned over, her hair falling over her face. She pushed it back, and her eyes fluttered open. Her gaze was mostly a mossy green in the faint morning light that had just begun to spill into the room from the window behind Gideon.

"Good morning," he said.

"Good morning." She smiled shyly. "I trust you slept well."

"Better than in quite some time." That was certainly true. "You?"

"Same." She scooted closer but didn't touch him. "Thank you for letting me stay last night. I hope you don't have any regrets."

"No." He'd had second and third thoughts, but after them—or maybe it was looking into her eyes just now—he realized he'd choose the same action again. And perhaps again. His cock was already stiff.

"Good." She smiled wider and moved even closer. She splayed her hand across his chest and stroked him from the hollow of his throat down across his nipple, making him gasp. "Are you sensitive here like I am?"

"In a different way, probably."

She closed her thumb and forefinger over him and gently pulled. "Different, how?"

Desire shot through him, sending more blood pounding into his cock. "Perhaps not all that different." As she continued her exploration, moving to his other nipple, he croaked, "Daphne, we should perhaps get dressed. Gwyneth will be expecting us soon."

"Hmm, I wonder how this feels." Daphne leaned forward and licked his nipple.

It was a slender line between excessive pleasure and near pain. He wanted to flip her onto her back and sink deep into her body, but she had to be sensitive from last night.

"Gideon?" Her tongue darted across his skin again.

He managed to growl, "Exquisite."

"Truly? It sounds as if you're being drawn and quartered."

"God, I hope that's not what that actually sounds like." Good, maybe if she talked to him about torture, he'd be able to stop thinking about shagging her senseless.

She laughed against him, tickling his flesh. Her hand skimmed down his chest, her fingertips grazing along his abdomen. Then she went lower, and he gasped. She touched his hip, and his cock twitched.

"*Daphne.*"

"Yes?" She kissed his chest and wrapped her hand around his shaft. "Oh, this feels rather splendid. Is it all right that I'm touching you here?"

"It's more than all right." It was bloody spectacular.

"You said you haven't been with a woman…in a long time. What can I do?" She tipped her head back and looked up at him, her gaze liquid heat.

"What you're doing is fine," he ground out.

She slid her fingers along his length. "I have no idea what I'm doing. Surely you can give me a little instruction…" Her hand closed over him, and she moved it up and down his shaft.

"Ah, it feels as if you know precisely what you're doing. I'm not sure I can offer additional instruction." Indeed, her *grasp* of the activity was going to drive him straight into sensual oblivion.

Her mouth traveled a downward path as she used her lips and tongue to spin him into a frenzy of lust. When her head disappeared beneath the covers, he froze, his muscles tensing in anticipation.

"*Daphne.* What are you doing?"

"Something I read about. I may have lied when I said I had no idea. I have *some* idea. I like to research, you know."

Her words, though muffled, enflamed him. The moment her lips touched his flesh, he bucked from the bed. Pushing the covers back, he cradled her head and murmured, "Sorry."

"Don't apologize." The words were muffled again because she had him between her lips. And then she took him into her, and he was absolutely enthralled.

The combination of the sensation of her mouth and tongue stroking over him and of the visual stimulation of what she was doing sent another rush of blood to his cock. She held the base while she worked, behaving as if she'd done this a hundred times. Jealousy spiked through him, and he felt like a hypocritical ass. He wasn't going to think of her past—true or not—or his.

The only thing that mattered was this moment.

Her mouth closed around him, taking him deep, almost into her throat, where the muscles constricted. Shit, he was going to spill himself. It was too late.

"*Daphne.*" He gripped her head with one hand and fisted the bedclothes with the other as he came in her mouth.

Expecting her to pull back, he let go of her and cast his head back as his orgasm swept through him. But she didn't pull back. She continued to lick and suck him until he was utterly spent.

When he finally opened his eyes, she lay down beside him with a rather satisfied smile. Indeed, she looked as if she'd been the one pleasured.

"You liked that," she said, sounding quite proud. As she bloody well should.

"Obviously." He shook his head. "No. Like does not begin to describe my feelings about that." He rolled over her, covering her body with his. She gasped in surprise and curled her arms around his neck. "Your turn." He lowered his head and kissed her. She tasted salty, and he realized he'd never kissed a woman after…that. He'd never wanted to.

He wanted to do that with her and so much more.

Starting with the more. He plundered her mouth, tasting every part of her, and stroked his hand down her collarbone until he found the soft globe of her breast. Dragging his thumb over the taut peak, he cupped her. She dug her fingers into his shoulders in response.

"Gideon! It's time to come downstairs!"

Gwyneth's voice broke through his sexual haze, forcing his head up. He scowled and swore. "We're ignoring her." He bent and licked Daphne's nipple.

She shuddered. "*Gideon.*" His name was an urgent whisper, and he could interpret it many ways. He chose to think she was urging him on.

But she tugged at his hair. "We need to get dressed! Don't you want to talk to her about the de Valery manuscript in the chest? The sooner we find the location of Gareth's final resting place, the sooner we can return the treasures."

And the sooner they could part.

He stilled and sat up. He didn't want to contemplate what came after their quest. He wanted to lock the door and spend eternity in bed with her.

She scrambled to sit up, and he leaned forward to kiss her hard and fast.

Her brow pleated, as if she were rethinking going downstairs. Then she smiled and bounded from the bed. "Let's go."

He watched her pluck her dressing gown from where it lay forgotten on the floor along with her hairpins and then go into her chamber. Reluctantly, he got dressed, each movement feeling as if he was marching toward some inevitable doom.

When he was garbed and combed, he picked up the chest and went into her room. She perched on a padded seat in front of a dressing table and was finishing her hair.

He came up behind her, and she met his reflection. "Ready?" she asked.

He nodded, and she stood, smoothing her gown. As they left her room and made their way downstairs, Gideon had the sense that last night and this morning had been a stolen time and likely couldn't be repeated. They'd leave here and go to Ashridge Court. Who knew what awaited them there?

Gwyneth was waiting for them in the library, seated at the end of the long worktable. Her gaze snapped to the chest in Gideon's arms, and she smiled. Then she lifted her eyes to Gideon's and apologized. "I didn't mean to interrupt a blissful morning. However, I do have a schedule to keep. You're both welcome to stay as long as you like. Now, let me see this chest."

Gideon ignored her comment about their morning and set the chest down in front of her, curious if she would find something they could not. "There's a manuscript written by Edmund de Valery—one we weren't aware of."

She stood and opened the chest. "Sit, both of you."

Gideon and Daphne exchanged a look before they each took the chairs on either side of her.

"I am aware of this de Valery manuscript, but I've never seen it, of course. I haven't ever seen anything in this chest." She removed each item, giving special care to the Anarawd text. Cracking open the cover, she exhaled in wonder. "How magnificent." She turned partially toward Gideon. "I wonder if you might consider allowing me to study these items for a short period of time."

"Of course I would consider it." He trusted her. "I assume they would be safe here."

She looked around the room. "You see what we keep, what we've protected for centuries. It's amazing what women can get away with. Men pay no attention."

Daphne giggled, her eyes sparkling, and Gideon couldn't help but smile.

Gwyneth picked up the de Valery manuscript last and waved for Gideon to scoot the chest back. Then she sat and placed the book on the table in front of her. "These are a collection of fables."

"They're variations on tales in the other de Valery manuscripts. Rhys Bowen and I found them perplexing. They seemed to be embellished versions."

"Yes, that's precisely what they are. The hope was that this book would be copied and those copies circulated and these would become the accepted 'history.'"

"But it hasn't ever seen the light of day," Gideon said. Rhys had certainly never heard of it before.

Gwyneth nodded. "The supposition is that it contains something it shouldn't. That de Valery included information or a...clue that led to...something."

Daphne leaned forward, intent on the book but glancing toward Gwyneth. "Do you have any idea what?"

"No, but let me look," she murmured, opening the cover. She drew in a sharp breath and touched the illumination on the first page.

"Shouldn't you wear gloves?" Gideon asked.

Gwyneth speared him with a condescending stare. "We are very careful, and we are...special. No, I shouldn't be wearing gloves. You, however, probably should."

"I do when I handle the manuscript," he said, feeling admonished.

"Excellent." She beamed at him. Yes, she was most peculiar. And endearing.

She quietly flipped through several pages before looking over at Gideon. "Goodness, this could take me quite some time. Perhaps you should go back upstairs and finish what I interrupted." She moved her gaze to Daphne and smiled benignly.

Daphne's ears turned that adorable shade of pink

again, and Gideon resisted the urge to do as Gwyneth suggested. Instead, he gestured toward the book. "There's an odd story included. It's about St. Gildas."

Gwyneth's gaze snapped to his. "St. Gildas? Where?"

"Toward the back," Gideon said. Gwyneth flipped through the pages until he recognized the page. "There," he said.

She leaned over the tome and read. It was a handful of pages long, with illustrations.

"It just seemed strange to have a story about St. Gildas amongst everything else about the knights and giants and the like."

She frowned at the book, then cast her head back to stare at the ceiling. She'd done that on their last visit too, and he recognized she was thinking.

"St. Gildas was a monk in the late fifth and early sixth centuries. He was born the same year as the Battle of Badon Hill."

"So he was a contemporary of Arthur," Daphne said.

"Yes, though he refers to him by another name. He wrote a rather interesting history of the Britons. He ended up in Brittany as abbot of Rhuys."

"Didn't he spend a great deal of time in Ireland?" Daphne asked, sparking Gideon's continued admiration for her vast array of historical knowledge.

"Yes, he traveled quite extensively, especially for that time. He was born in present-day Scotland. He was quite prominent in early monasticism in Wales—and here. He visited Beckery Chapel, and there's mention of him in the Beckery Texts."

"Why is he in this book?" Gideon asked. He'd begun to think this was vitally important.

"I'm not entirely certain." Gwyneth stood and went to one of the bookshelves to remove a tattered volume that he recognized from their last visit as one of the Beckery Texts. She set it partially in front of Gideon and opened the cover. She was hasty but careful as she thumbed through the pages until she found a rather short entry along with a drawing.

Gideon's heart began to beat faster. He came partway out of his chair as he leaned forward. "Is that an island?"

"Yes. Flat Holm, I believe. Let me just read it…"

It was Latin. Gideon could read it too.

Ynys Echni, which was actually Welsh and meant Flat Holm, was an island in the Severn Sea.

Gideon peered up at Gwyneth. "Is the Severn Sea Bristol Channel?"

"Yes. Flat Holm is between Weston and Lavernock."

Gideon went back to reading. Gildas had lived there as a hermit for several years. And during his stay, he'd presided over a burial. Gideon felt a hand on his right shoulder and looked up to see that Daphne had come to stand next to him.

The most wonderful excitement surged within him. "Read it," he said to her.

He sat back in his chair to allow her better access.

Gwyneth paced away from the table and then came back. She stared down at him. "You think the burial was for Gareth."

Gideon's body thrummed with barely contained enthusiasm. "Don't you?"

Tipping her head to the side, Gwyneth shrugged. "It's possible."

"De Valery put St. Gildas in his book for a reason," Daphne said, pivoting from the book. She'd apparently finished reading. "Gwyneth, you said de Valery included a clue to something."

"*I* didn't say that. But that is what has been presumed. I always reserve my judgment until I can read something for myself."

Gideon sat up in the chair, straightening his spine. "You have to admit the presence of that story doesn't fit."

Gwyneth tapped a finger against her lips. "It is odd."

"If it is a clue," Daphne said, "then it's pointing us to St. Gildas."

Gideon gave Gwyneth a long, hard stare. "You read the story just now. It mentions Gildas spending time at a monastery near Ynys Witrin. Do you know where Ynys Witrin is, or do we need to scour the library looking for it?"

"Ynys Witrin is thought to be an early name for Glastonbury. He could be talking about Beckery Chapel."

"Which takes us to the Beckery Texts," Gideon said, his heart still beating a rapid pace. "Where Gildas is placed at a burial on Flat Holm Island. I think de Valery was telling us where Gareth is buried."

"It's a bit of a leap," Gwyneth said, frustrating Gideon.

Gideon sat back in the chair and rested his hands on his lap. "It's all we have."

Gwyneth bustled back to the de Valery text at the head of the table. "It's not enough. There has to be a way to confirm it."

"And what if there isn't?" Gideon stood. He needed to expend some of the energy pulsing through him. He paced the length of the bookshelf. At the end, he turned back toward the table where Daphne and Gwyneth both watched him. "I'm certain he's there." He just knew it in his bones.

"Then let's go." Daphne's simple belief in him made his chest expand and his heart soar.

"We have to get the Heart of Llanllwch and Dyrnwyn." Gideon's mind was already planning ahead.

Gwyneth braced her hands on the table on either side of the de Valery manuscript. "You're taking a chance. He may not be there."

"It's the best lead we have." Besides, he was certain.

"When do you want to leave?" Daphne asked.

"As soon as we can."

Gwyneth straightened. "You shouldn't go alone, especially after you anger Daphne's father when you take the other treasures." She glanced toward Daphne, whose expression had gone stoic.

Gideon agreed, but Penn was at Oxford, and that was three days from here. "I don't think my—help can arrive in time. He's at Oxford." He'd almost said half brother, but he wouldn't reveal that, not if there was a chance Penn didn't have to be the earl.

Gwyneth's mouth split into a wide grin. "You're in luck. We have pigeons who fly to Oxford."

Both Gideon and Daphne gaped at her. "You do?" Daphne asked.

Nodding, Gwyneth went to her writing desk situated near the windows and came back with a small piece of paper. "Write your message on this." She inclined her head toward a pen and inkwell farther down the worktable.

Gideon moved to draft a note to Penn. As he sat down, he glanced up at her. "How will he get it?"

"There is a small group of us—just three women at present—at Oxford. They conduct research there, and we often correspond about important findings. Sometimes I require information from them, and sometimes they require information from me. We've been using this system for a few centuries now. It works wonderfully."

Amazed, Gideon picked up the pen to write.

"I think I would like to live here," Daphne said wistfully.

"I doubt he'll let you," Gwyneth said, inclining her head toward Gideon.

"It won't be up to him," Daphne said with an edge of hauteur.

"No, but you won't want to either."

Gideon worked to ignore their conversation—both because he wanted to focus on what to say on such a small piece of paper and because he didn't want to think about the future just then.

Once he was satisfied with a succinct message, he scrawled it on the paper and stood to hand it to Gwyneth.

"Who is this for?" Gwyneth asked.

"Penn Bowen." Gideon had asked him to meet at Weston as soon as possible. He calculated that he would arrive in three to four days' time. That should give them ample time to do what they needed at Ashridge Court.

"He's the Assistant Keeper at the Ashmolean. Our women will ensure he gets it." Gwyneth took the paper and went back to her desk, where she wrote on it as well. "I've just put his name on the other side. I'll deliver this to Edward—he manages all our animals, including the pigeons—as soon as we're finished. First, I want to hear your plan to retake the heart and sword."

"It involves the cloak," Gideon said.

"Oh yes! In our haste to look at the de Valery

manuscript, I neglected to study the garment." She went to the chest, where it was still folded in the bottom. Before she reached inside, she looked over at Gideon. "May I?"

"Of course."

Carefully, she withdrew the cloak, and Gideon could already see that its magic worked for her. Where the garment touched her hands, she became invisible.

"Marvelous," she whispered, pulling it around her shoulders. She fastened it around her neck and now looked like a floating head. She looked down, and her brow creased. "It must be rather short on you."

Gideon moved around the table to look at her feet, but of course he saw nothing. "It was just the right length."

Gwyneth laughed. "Morgana thought of everything with her enchantment." She removed the garment and folded it before handing it to Gideon. "This should serve you well. Will you leave the chest and the other items here?"

"That seems safest. I don't think I will need any of the other contents." He couldn't imagine needing the texts, and he'd looked through the loose papers, most of which were genealogical records and other notes regarding family history that didn't pertain to Gareth. He didn't recognize the jewelry, but Rhys hadn't thought that any of it was older than the thirteenth century, meaning it wasn't from Gareth's time.

Gwyneth narrowed one eye at Gideon. "If you do find Gareth's tomb, what do you plan to do?"

"Leave the treasures there."

"So that anyone can come along and find them again?" She shook her head. "You'll need to do a bit more than that if you want to keep them from being found."

"Is there a way to hide them forever?"

"Yes, an enchantment, and since you're a direct descendant of his, I believe you can create it. Give me a few minutes." She'd already started to move away from them. "Prepare your things, and I shall meet you in the hall." She turned from them, and though they hadn't discussed their plan for Ashridge Court, Gideon knew they'd been dismissed.

He guided Daphne from the library and back up the stairs toward their chambers.

"She thinks you can do magic," Daphne said. "Like Morgan."

"She was apparently my relative," he said, trying to think how he could possibly work magic. And yet he already had, in a way, when he'd used the sword and the cloak.

"My envy is great." She gave him a warm smile. "What is our plan when we arrive at Ashridge Court?" she asked him as they walked along the gallery overlooking the great hall.

"I'm not certain—it depends on your father's reception. Have you any idea what that will be?"

"He'll be happy to see us wed but angry that he was excluded from the ceremony. Honestly, us missing the jousting tournament may have upset him the most."

Her father was bizarre as well as despicable and mad.

He walked her to the door to her chamber and opened it so she could go inside. "And how will you be? Will you confront him about lying to you?"

"I want to—I'm still furious. But that could jeopardize our endeavor. We'll have to endure a celebratory dinner with whatever guests still remain from the festival. How quickly do you want to take the items and leave?"

As quickly as possible, but they had to be careful. "We have to come up with a plan to do that. I need the keys to the vault."

"He keeps them on his person at all times. Unless he's sleeping."

"Do you know where they are, then?"

"In his chamber, right next to his bed. I know that because I went in there one night—many years ago—when I had a nightmare. When he got up to take me back to bed, he put the keys in the pocket of his dressing gown."

Gideon wiped a hand over his face and pulled on his chin as he thought through their options. "I could go in there in the cloak—after he's asleep. Then I'll go down and go into the vault." He muttered a curse. "Except he has guards there at all times."

"I was just going to ask how you'd manage to get in without the guards seeing you. You'd be invisible, but they'd see the keys go into the locks and the doors move. We'll have to distract them. I can do that." She seemed pleased to have a job.

"I'd feel better if you stayed out of this entirely."

She pursed her lips at him in a half frown. "We're in this together. You need me."

It would be easier with her help. "How will you distract the guards?"

"There are two ways to get a man to forget what he's about."

Gideon knew what at least one of them was. "You're not doing the first one."

She grinned. "Your jealousy is quite satisfying. But not that. Food."

Laughter bubbled from Gideon's lips. "Food? You

think you can distract them with food?"

"I think that when I put a sleeping agent in the keg of ale, our task will become quite easy. You'll get the treasures, return the keys to my father, and we'll leave. When he awakens the next day, he won't even realize the treasures are missing—unless he goes to the vault and checks them every morning."

Gideon wouldn't put it past him to do that. "Even if he does, we'll be long gone."

"Precisely." Her expression was smug.

"Where are you going to get a sleeping agent?" he asked.

"Hopefully from Gwyneth. It seems like something she would know how to do."

Gideon swept her into his arms and kissed her soundly. "You're rather brilliant."

She twined her arms around his neck and smiled. "Thank you for saying so."

He kissed her again, this time lingering as long as he dared. Reluctantly, he pulled away. "We'll have to continue that later. I'll meet you downstairs."

As he walked across her chamber to go into his room, she said, "At least we won't have to pretend to behave like a happily married couple for my father."

Did that mean they were a happily married couple? He wasn't sure that was true—at least not yet.

Their plan was good, but things could go wrong, and once they returned the treasures, what would happen then? Gideon still had to find a way to dismantle Camelot. They couldn't be allowed to continue unchecked. People had died.

And though Daphne was angry with her father now, once Gideon destroyed him, he doubted their marriage would be happy at all.

Chapter Fifteen

LARKIN, THE BUTLER at Ashridge Court, a burly man in his middle forties who always looked as if he should be operating a smithy instead of running a household, greeted Daphne and Gideon when they arrived just before noon. "Good morning, Lady Stratton. Your father will be ecstatic to see you. Welcome again, Lord Stratton."

"Thank you, Larkin," Daphne said, wondering if "ecstatic" was truly an accurate way to describe her father's reaction. They would find out shortly. "Please have our things sent to my room."

"Of course." The butler inclined his head.

Daphne moved past him into the entry hall and waited for Gideon to come up beside her before continuing into the great hall. She doubted her father would be present at this time of day, but she braced herself nonetheless. No doubt someone was already delivering the news of her arrival to him.

"Are you all right?" Gideon murmured, placing his hand on her lower back.

His touch was soft and simple, but he might as well have taken her in his arms. Her body responded, swaying toward him. Perhaps it was due to her unsatisfied arousal from that morning. More likely, she would always be drawn to him.

"Yes, just a bit nervous. I expect I will be until we're in Weston." She shook her head gently. "In fact, it might be until we're on Flat Holm and the treasures are safely with Gareth."

Gideon kissed her forehead, and her father appeared at the top of the stairs. He descended quickly and held his arms out when he reached the bottom.

"Daphne!" he boomed. "I am so glad to see you. Come and hug me so that I know you aren't angry with me."

Daphne sent Gideon a look with a very slight shrug, as if to ask why her father would think she was angry, then went to hug her father. "Why would I be angry with you?"

"Because you got married without me." He sniffed and held her tight. "You were always such an independent princess."

She smiled in spite of her anxiety. He hadn't called her that in a very long time. "I'm sorry, Papa. It's my fault. I wanted to be alone with my husband, and I couldn't wait to marry him."

He pulled back and tucked her arm through his. "So you rode out to meet him on his way back from Keynsham and got carried away?"

"I'm afraid so." She sent Gideon a broad, flirtatious smile. On the ride from Brue Cottage, they'd discussed the need to display excessive affection so as not to arouse her father's suspicions about what they were doing. Now that she was back home with her father, doubt infiltrated her brain. What if Gideon was wrong about him and his desire to find the treasures? What if Camelot wanted to protect them? What if there was no Camelot?

Daphne turned her head toward her father. "You're truly not angry?"

He gazed at her with love, and the doubt in her mind grew. "Of course not. All I ever wanted was for you to be happy. I'm a bit disappointed, but I'll get over it. Now, tell me what you've been doing the past several days. Let us repair to the library." He looked over at Gideon in question. "Gideon?"

"Let's." Gideon gave him a benign smile. Couldn't he look a bit more enthusiastic?

She tried to send him a wordless glance that might convey the need to be more animated, but he was already walking through the hall toward the library. Once they arrived, she perched on the settee near her father's favorite chair by the hearth. He sat down there as she expected he would, and Gideon took the seat beside her. He landed very close to her so that their thighs were almost touching. If she adjusted just a bit to the right, she could ensure that happened.

"You look very happy," Papa said. "That pleases me. I realize my arrangement of your union was rather unorthodox in modern times, but I could tell you were right for each other."

Daphne edged closer to Gideon so they were indeed touching. "Yes, Papa, I must ask you why you didn't introduce us before now. You've known Gideon for quite some time." She affected a pout.

Papa laughed. "Forgive me. I wasn't quite ready to give you up. Even now, I'm a bit teary over losing you to him." He looked toward Gideon, and she thought she saw a bead of uncertainty. Did he regret choosing Gideon?

"You will never lose her completely," Gideon said. "She is still your devoted daughter."

Oh, that was well played of him. Daphne looked at him in admiration. No, it wasn't hard to display excessive affection, because she was already in love with him.

"Now tell me where you've been." Papa looked between them, his elbows resting on the arms of his chair.

"We went to see Rhys Bowen," Gideon said. They'd discussed how to answer this question and decided it was better to tell him they had been looking for the cloak. Gideon wanted him to believe he was dedicated to finding the cloak for Camelot.

Papa's dark gaze lit with interest. "Did you learn anything?"

Gideon frowned. "I'm afraid not, and we did spend quite a bit of time looking through his library."

"You're still quite close to him?" Papa asked. He sounded surprised.

Gideon nodded. "Yes. We've known each other for quite some time, and he has a soft spot for me."

"How fortunate for you," Papa murmured. He briefly tapped his finger against the arm of his chair before looking back to Gideon. "What about Septon? You should visit him next." It might have been a suggestion, but there was a weight to it that made Daphne think it was a bit more. She began to sense a tension between them. *Was* her father regretting his choice for her husband? Or was he simply angry that Gideon hadn't married her the way he'd wanted him to?

"We could." Gideon sounded a bit hesitant.

"Won't he be your stepfather soon?" Papa asked. "Surely he will want to help you in your quest to find the cloak. One would think he'd be driven by guilt."

"One would think." Gideon's voice was tight, and Daphne wasn't sure if it was irritation with her father or with Septon. She knew he blamed the man for stealing his mother. And why wouldn't he?

"Well, after you stay here for a few days, I think you should go to Septon House. And send my best, of course." Papa smiled at Daphne. "I have missed you, my girl, as I always do when you are off gallivanting about. Some would say I'm far too lenient, but as I said, you are an independent princess, and who am I to stand in your way?" He chuckled. "Would you ride with me this afternoon?" He glanced toward Gideon. "If you don't mind, I'd like a bit of time with my daughter. I know her time here with me is short, and soon I'll have to visit you at Stratton Hall."

"I don't mind," Gideon said.

Daphne took the opening her father had provided to execute the next step in their plan. "If you'll excuse me, I will go upstairs for a brief respite, then. I'll meet you later, Papa."

She stood, and both men rose to their feet.

Gideon touched her back and kissed her temple. She turned her head and smiled up at him, and again, it wasn't an exaggeration of her feelings. Then she turned to go, but her father stepped forward and bussed her cheek. Speaking of guilt, she felt a pang of the emotion when she considered what they were plotting to do. Right now, she would go up to her father's office while Gideon kept him occupied. It was necessary, but it also felt a bit wrong.

She believed Gideon was telling her the truth—or at least the truth as he believed it. But it was still so difficult for her to accept. Until she remembered that her father had lied to her about being a descendant. Yes, if she could focus on that, it wouldn't be hard to maintain her resolve to accomplish what she and Gideon had planned.

After leaving the library, she went upstairs and made

sure no one was about before going into her father's study in his private apartments. She might not have much time, so she went straight to his desk and the secret drawer she'd found so many years ago.

She'd remembered the drawer as they'd ridden from Brue Cottage. Gideon had wondered if her father possessed a second set of keys to the vault. That had triggered Daphne's memory of a long-ago day when she'd been hiding beneath her father's desk. She'd found a secret drawer, and inside were a set of keys. She was confident they were to the vault. Obtaining them would be easier than trying to steal the ones her father kept with him at all times.

Pushing the chair back, she knelt down next to the desk and stuck her head in the cutout where one's legs would go. She felt along the right side for the button that would release the drawer. It was flush with the rest of the wood and easy to miss… Her fingers grazed the slight edge, and she pressed.

A spring sounded, and the drawer popped out. She found the keys and immediately tucked them in the pocket of her riding skirt. Her fingers had grazed something else in the drawer. Curious, she felt inside, and her hand closed around the edge of a slender book.

She withdrew the ledger—for that was what it looked like—and brought it out from under the desk so she could see it properly. Opening the cover, she sucked in a breath as her heart began to pound.

Written in bold lettering across the top of the first page was the word CAMELOT. In her father's hand. Beneath it was a list of names, but his was not among them. One name, however, stood out immediately: Gideon, Viscount Kersey.

Dread mingled with shock to ice her spine.

Why was his name there? She turned the page, but it was blank. Then she heard a noise outside the study, and panic overtook all else. She slid the book back where she'd found it, because she didn't think she could hide it if someone was indeed coming inside, and snapped the drawer closed.

Standing quickly, she grazed her head on the edge of the desk. She swallowed an oath and walked quietly toward the door, listening intently for someone outside the room. Hearing nothing, she eased the door open and made a hasty departure.

She went directly to her chamber, which wasn't far, and finally let out a full exhalation when she was safely inside. But she didn't feel relieved. She was perplexed and apprehensive.

Why had Gideon's name been on a list of Camelot? She wanted to ask him, but he wasn't here. Their bags had been delivered and their clothing unpacked. As discussed with Gideon, she put the keys into his bag for him to find later.

Though she was agitated, she still had more to do. She went to her bag and found the bottle of tonic Gwyneth had gleefully given her before they'd left that morning. Daphne would add it to the ale supply, and everyone who drank ale with dinner—which would be everyone save her and Gideon, who would only pretend to drink it—would be fast asleep within an hour or two.

With everyone unconscious, Gideon would sneak into the vault, steal the treasures, and they would be on their way to a pair of horses Gwyneth would have staged about a mile from the house. They'd plotted that part with Gwyneth before leaving Brue Cottage too.

It wasn't a foolproof plan, but they'd considered

many angles and felt this was as close as they could get. What she hadn't considered was finding Gideon's name on a list entitled Camelot. He'd said it was a rogue faction intent on hoarding the treasures. But surely he wouldn't be a part of such a group. Or had he lied? Or had he lied about what Camelot really was?

Her head suddenly hurt. Maybe she should take some of this tonic so she could stop thinking about this for a while. But no, she had to get the liquid into tonight's keg and then ready herself to go riding with her father.

In the meantime, she'd try to think about what to say to Gideon. She had to ask him about the list. If they had any hope for a future, and she really wasn't sure they did, it couldn't be based on lies.

THE AIR BETWEEN Gideon and Foliot had seemed rather thick since the moment the man had come into the hall, but as soon as Daphne departed the library, it had become practically solid with tension. Oh, Foliot was putting on a good show for Daphne, but Gideon knew what the man was capable of and recognized the flashes of distrust in his gaze.

What Gideon didn't know was if it was simply due to being left out of their wedding or if he was suspicious of Gideon. If it was the latter, their entire plan could be in jeopardy.

"I am deeply sorry we didn't attend the jousting tournament and get married here," Gideon said. "I'm afraid the heart worked a little too well, and Daphne was most insistent."

"So I gather." Foliot sat back down in his chair, and

Gideon dropped onto the settee. "I won't lie—I was rather angry. And I'm still a bit hurt. If you and Daphne are fortunate to have a daughter, you will understand."

A daughter with bright hazel eyes, wavy auburn hair, an inquisitive nature, and a sharp mind... Gideon suddenly wanted that more than anything. For the first time, he thought of a future with children without suffering that horrific pang of having lost one along with his wife. "I think I might already," Gideon said quietly.

"Ah, I think you do." Foliot's gaze softened, and whatever the man's crimes, he clearly loved his daughter. Gideon's insides knotted. "Daphne is my entire world. I know you think other things may be more important to me, but they aren't. *She* is the most important thing. You must make her happy, or it will not end well for you." He said this with a light tone, but there was a steel in his gaze that Gideon recognized as a threat.

Yes, this man might be a monster, but he was also Daphne's father. And Gideon knew precisely what it was like to have a monster for a father. What it was like to idolize that father only to be rudely awakened to his true nature.

Gideon ached for the truths that Daphne would soon face and wished he could protect her from them. It was why he hadn't detailed her father's offenses. Hopefully, he wouldn't have to.

But then what did that mean? Did he think that once he'd returned the treasures to Gareth that Foliot would stop looking for them? Would he give up on Camelot and suddenly become an honest, righteous man?

Why not? Gideon had changed himself. He'd gone

from a wastrel to an earnest husband to a grieving widower to a thief and accomplice to violence. And now he was trying to atone for all of it by returning the treasures and protecting them from the likes of Foliot. Would it be enough?

No. Nothing would ever be enough.

He realized he should say something to reassure Foliot of his commitment to Daphne. "I will endeavor to make Daphne happy and keep her safe. That I can promise you." Gideon didn't know what their future held—if it would include an annulment or not—but he would protect her with his dying breath.

A question stole into his mind, and he spoke it before he could censor himself. "What happened to Daphne's mother?"

Foliot's eyes widened for a bare moment. "She spoke of her? She rarely does anymore."

"She disappeared a long time ago—nearly fifteen years?"

"It troubles me still," Foliot said, his gaze darkening. "She was a scholar, like Daphne. She'd taken a trip to Cornwall to visit Tintagel. Like Daphne's passion for Morgan le Fay, she had a similar obsession for Merlin. She was convinced some of the Thirteen Treasures are guarded by him even now. Once, she got a bit too close to learning something, and the Order asked me to keep her in her place." His voice hardened, and Gideon began to see why Foliot might be at odds with the greater organization. Why he might seek to poison it from within.

Foliot looked away momentarily, his jaw stiff. When he returned his gaze to Gideon's, it was laced with venom. "I believe they killed her."

It was a shocking accusation, and yet Gideon had

heard enough about things the Order had done over the centuries to think it was at least possible. "Do you have evidence?"

Foliot's lip curled. "You sound like one of them. But then I suppose you are."

"As much as you," Gideon said, knowing Foliot's leg bore the same tattoo as his. How Gideon wished he could erase the mark now. Once the treasures were restored to Gareth, he wanted to go back to Stratton Hall and simply be an earl. If that was even possible. He wondered if Septon had managed to free the vicar and steal his proof, but didn't dare raise Foliot's suspicions by mentioning the vicar at all. "I wasn't trying to defend them. You know how I feel about the Order."

"You still despise Septon, then?" Foliot had exploited Gideon's hatred for the man to recruit him to Camelot.

"My feelings regarding Septon have not changed. My father's death makes my mother less of a pariah, I suppose, but the damage was done long ago."

"It was never about your mother," Foliot said softly, his gaze sharp. "This was always about the boy they'd destroyed with their illicit love affair."

The old fury rose up inside Gideon. Foliot was doing it again, stoking Gideon's anger to pit him against the Order because it would serve Foliot's goals. For a while, Gideon had shared those goals, and he needed to ensure Foliot believed he still did. "I'm still committed to Camelot," Gideon said. "However, I might be of more use to you if I knew what you intended to do once you have the treasures in your possession."

Foliot put his hands on the arms of the chair and stared at Gideon, his gaze penetrating. "I have many plans, but they start with removing Septon and the other leaders from the Order."

"How will you remove them?" Gideon suspected he knew, but he wanted to hear the man say it.

"By using the treasures to force them out. They keep their power by controlling information about Arthur and the knights and the Thirteen Treasures. If I have the treasures, I have the power and I can control the Order. Then we can build a true Order that is made up only of descendants, those who are worthy of power."

Gideon had to bite his tongue to keep from asking how that plan could possibly include Foliot since he wasn't a descendant. "You really think you can drive them out?"

"They will go to any lengths to keep the treasures secret. If I threaten to expose them, they'll do as I say. They're nothing if not completely dedicated to their cause."

As was Foliot, but Gideon didn't point that out. Instead, he said what the man wanted to hear. "I shall look forward to the day when we can control the Order. I expect you'll have a prominent place for me. I am Gareth's descendant after all."

Foliot smiled broadly. "Yes, that is precisely why I chose you for Daphne. You will have a most prominent place, right beside me, along with my daughter and your children. We will create a dynasty that will endure."

A dynasty. The man was mad. And he wasn't going to give up on his objectives when the treasures disappeared. He'd continue to look for them—and at what cost?

Gideon wasn't sure, but he'd have to find a way to stop him for good. Just as he was going to have to tell

Daphne the entire truth about her father.

And pray she didn't hate him for doing it.

Chapter Sixteen

THOUGH DAPHNE HAD been married only a handful of days, she felt like a different person now that she was back at Ashridge Court. Or maybe it was that so much had changed. Or, more accurately, had come to light. As she handed her horse off to the groom, she slid a look to her father, who was conversing with the head groom.

They'd had a lovely ride, reminding her of the almost daily rides they'd taken together after her mother had disappeared. He'd been an especially attentive father during that time, and it had helped ease Daphne's pain. She struggled to reconcile that caring man with what Gideon had told her.

Gideon.

Whom was she to trust?

Papa finished with the groom and came to her side. "What a splendid afternoon. I'm so pleased we could spend some time together." He offered her his arm.

She curled her hand around his sleeve, and they started toward the house. "I am too."

The late-afternoon sun was warm on her back after their invigorating ride. They'd ridden over the estate and then up Glastonbury Tor, one of her father's favorite places. One of Daphne's too. Arthurian legend aside, the view was beautiful.

"I know I encouraged you to marry Gideon, but I must admit it's strange to think of you as married," Papa said. "Are you happy with him?"

"Oh yes." She infused her tone with joy. "He's a very caring person. I'm fortunate to have found someone like him. Rather, I am fortunate *you* found someone like him for me." She squeezed her father's arm.

Papa paused and partially turned toward her. "You're certain you're happy? I didn't force you into something you didn't want, did I?"

She furrowed her brow. "Goodness, no. You know me, if I hadn't wanted to marry Gideon, I wouldn't have."

He chuckled softly. "That much is probably true."

The truth was that she'd been a bit infatuated with Gideon since the moment they'd met. It was more than his physical attractiveness. He possessed an air of confidence and quiet consideration that was indescribably captivating. She'd never met a man like him. Now that she thought about it, perhaps the heart *had* worked in some way. Once, she would have said that was preposterous, but she'd seen the cloak make Gideon and Gwyneth invisible. She knew the magic of the treasures was real.

And if Gideon had lied to her about Camelot, perhaps the heart had only allowed her to see his best traits. She wished she'd asked Gwyneth how, exactly, the heart was meant to work.

They started walking toward the house, and she felt the tension in her father's arm. Or maybe that was *her* anxiety. She was so conflicted about what Gideon had revealed to her concerning her father, as well as what she'd found in her father's desk earlier.

Whether due to an inability to keep her emotions buried or to a lifelong trust of the man beside her, she blurted, "Papa, what is Camelot?"

He laughed. "You know what Camelot is, silly girl.

Do you mean where do I think it's located?"

"No, not that Camelot." While she hadn't thought first before asking, she chose her next words carefully. "I came across mention of a secret group called Camelot in a document in the Bowen library. It was a short history of the Order of the Round Table—"

Papa did stop then, and his eyes had narrowed. "Such a thing exists?"

No, but she couldn't say that now. Clearly, she'd imagined the wrong sort of excuse. "Apparently."

"The Order has never allowed a history to be recorded, and such a thing should be obtained and destroyed. We are a secret organization, Daphne."

"Yes, I know that. Would you like me to go back and burn it?"

"No, it would be best if you could bring it to me so that I may give it to the governing body. They will want to know what information is out there, as well as try to determine who violated the rules by exposing our secrets." His brow creased. "This is a very serious matter. I should like to know how Bowen obtained it. He is not a member of the Order. Was Gideon not alarmed by this?"

"I didn't ask him about it." Daphne wished she hadn't said anything, but it was too late now. "It was a short document, with barely any information. Truly, you've told me more about the organization than I learned from reading it."

"Except you asked me about Camelot," he said softly.

"Yes. It mentioned an organization within the Order called Camelot and that its objectives may not be aligned with its parent."

Papa looked past her for a moment, as if he were

trying to collect his thoughts. He smiled at her and then started walking toward the house once more. "I've heard of Camelot, of course. However, their intentions aren't entirely clear. If the Order is a secret society, Camelot is both incredibly secret and deeply mysterious. Many of us in the Order are troubled by their existence, but it's such a shadow group that we just can't be sure of their objectives."

"You are not a member, then?"

He looked at her sharply. "No. Did someone say that I was? I would be quite bothered if someone suspected such a thing, but then people who are in Camelot generally deny its existence." He exhaled. "Sometimes I wonder why I remain in the Order, but when I contemplate leaving, I realize I would miss the camaraderie and connection regarding all things Arthurian." He flashed a faint smile and lifted his shoulder in a slight shrug.

His explanation seemed quite reasonable, and she wondered if Gideon could be mistaken about him. In fact, what if her father had infiltrated Camelot on behalf of the Order? It could also be that her father was lying to her now, just as he had about being a descendant.

They were nearly to the house, and she wanted the truth. She stopped and turned toward him. "Papa, I learned something else. There are no living descendants of King Arthur."

Surprise and some other darker emotion flashed in his eyes before he looked away. "Was that in the document about the Order?"

"Yes." The lies burned her tongue. Were they excusable in the interest of learning the truth? To be honest would be to expose Gwyneth and Brue Cottage, and Daphne wouldn't do that. Her future—the only future she might have—could very well lie within those walls, and even if it didn't, she wouldn't risk the women there. "The document listed the knights from whom the Order's members are descended, and Arthur's line was noted as having died out some time ago."

"That is perhaps true, but it isn't known for certain. There is a possible line, and that is the one from which we are descended. Perhaps I wanted so badly for it to be true that I perpetuated a falsehood." He looked at her with sadness and regret. "You know what being a descendant means to me."

She did. "Is that why you wanted me to marry a descendant? So that if we weren't from Arthur's line, I would at least marry into one of the knight's?"

He took her free hand and squeezed it. "I'm so sorry, Daphne. I can see now how selfish I've been. And old-fashioned." He let out a soft laugh. "I spend too much time in days gone by."

She gave him a reassuring smile and squeezed his hand in return. "I know, Papa."

"You seem to have learned a great deal," he said. "Are you certain you didn't learn anything about the cloak?"

She hesitated the barest moment. She wanted to tell him the truth. She wanted to share the discovery with him. He'd be so overjoyed. But she wouldn't, not until she spoke with Gideon first. "No."

Papa studied her face, as if he suspected she was lying. "Are you certain Gideon didn't? I wonder if I should…" He looked away, troubled.

"What, Papa?"

He winced. "I suspect Gideon may be a member of Camelot. I'd heard rumors, but I liked him so well that

I refused to believe them. And now I find his behavior regarding your marriage so…odd. You say you're happy, but since this is a moment for honesty, I must tell you something of which I am ashamed." He took a breath and continued to hold her hand. "Gideon brought the Heart of Llanllwch to me, and I suggested he use it to help you fall in love with him. I thought it would help facilitate your marriage. I knew you would get there on your own, but now I wonder if I haven't pushed you into a union with a man whose secrets could threaten the Order. And maybe even you."

He looked so upset, so *sorry* that Daphne hugged him. "Oh, Papa." After a moment, she pulled back and tried to give him an encouraging smile even as her insides were in utter turmoil. "It will all work out."

"I don't know that I share your optimism. What if Gideon finds the cloak and keeps it for Camelot? The rumors are that they want to obtain the Thirteen Treasures and part from the Order."

Daphne had loved two men in her life—her father and Gideon. And both were now asserting that the other had lied. Whom was she to trust? The man who made her body tremble with desire and her heart nearly burst with love? Or the man she'd known her entire life who had likely made some bad decisions motivated by selfishness and a need to belong to something bigger than himself? She understood wanting that connection. She'd been searching for it her entire life.

And she'd thought she'd finally found it with Gideon. However, when she compared the amount of time she'd spent with him versus the man opposite her, she wondered if she'd been duped. If Gideon was a member of Camelot and wanted to obtain the treasures for himself… *Wait.* He wanted to take them to Gareth.

He didn't want to keep them.

Except the other ten treasures were supposedly in Gareth's tomb. What if he wanted to go there so he could take them too? What did he need her for, then?

To take the heart and sword from her father's vault.

And the plan was already in motion. Gideon likely already had the keys she'd left for him, and the tonic had been administered to tonight's keg. It was too late for her to stop it unless she exposed the scheme.

She felt as if she were tied in knots. She didn't know whom to trust. Anger and frustration combined with sadness, and she just wanted to run back to Brue Cottage and cry on Gwyneth's shoulder.

"Daphne?" Papa asked softly, drawing her from the tumult of her emotions. "Is there something you know about the Thirteen Treasures?"

She blinked at him. He'd mentioned the treasures, and she'd gone quiet. Of course he would think that. She could tell him now… "I don't. And Gideon doesn't have the cloak." This lie nearly made her choke. If he was telling her the truth and Gideon had used her, she wasn't sure what she would do. She'd never felt so alone.

Papa cupped her face. "If you decide you don't wish to be married to Gideon any longer, there is a way out."

Oh God, he wasn't suggesting something despicable, was he?

Papa dropped his hands, his gaze caressing her with kindness and empathy. "I have learned he is not the heir to the earldom of Stratton. He has an older half brother who will inherit. The half brother's existence was kept secret until their father died. There is proof of his birth, and a vicar will present it to the House of

Lords. Gideon married you under fraudulent circumstances. You have ample basis for annulment if you'd prefer to end the marriage."

Daphne felt as if the world had turned sideways. Even a cloud moved over the sun, darkening the sky and making the air suddenly colder. She shivered. She'd been the one to suggest annulment, and Gideon had said it would be difficult, but then he'd married her anyway. When she thought of the way he'd kissed and touched her, of last night at Brue Cottage... She felt so insignificant that if a breeze picked up, it would surely blow her away.

"I...don't know." It was all she could manage to say.

"The heart may have a hold on you, Daphne. I am so sorry. If I could go back and change what I did, I would do so. I can't begin to express my regret and sorrow. This is all my fault." His voice broke, and a tear floated in his eye.

It was at least partially his fault. But it was also hers. Because she'd fallen in love with Gideon and was completely vulnerable to whatever he might have planned.

"I need to go." She turned and fled, walking away from the house and the stable so she could think by herself for a while. She didn't know what she was going to do. Someone she loved was lying to her, and she didn't have much time to decide which one it was.

GIDEON HAD ALREADY dressed for dinner. For the hundredth time, he felt for the keys tucked into an interior pocket in his waistcoat. Then his gaze went to the bed, where the cloak was hidden beneath his pillow. As soon as everyone was asleep, he would dash up here to fetch it and then head to the vault. Hopefully, everything would go as planned.

He hadn't seen Daphne since she'd left the library earlier, but assumed she'd taken care of everything she'd needed to. Where was she? Surely she and her father had finished their ride some time ago.

The door opened, and she came inside, still wearing her riding habit. Her face was a bit flushed, and light creases marred her brow. She didn't quite meet his gaze.

He went to greet her. "I've been wondering where you were."

"I went for a walk. I'm afraid I'll need to hurry to prepare for dinner. Just give me a few minutes. My maid, Jolley, will be up momentarily." A quick smile lifted her lips, and he felt a moment's relief.

She disappeared into the dressing chamber, and a few moments later, he heard Jolley enter through the door that connected with the servants' corridor. Gideon paced, then sat, then got up and paced again. He went over the plan in his head, and then he fixated on why Daphne might have been upset. The obvious answer was that she'd had to spend a good deal of time with her father. After everything Gideon had told her about him, and the manner in which they'd plotted to deceive him, it was likely she was feeling conflicted.

Gideon wished her father wasn't such a blackhearted scoundrel.

It seemed an interminable amount of time before she emerged from the dressing chamber. But it had been worth the wait. She wore an evening gown of deep gold embellished with purple embroidery. "You truly look like a princess," he said. Though their marriage had been arranged, he believed he would have chosen her—if he'd been able to get to the point where he'd wanted to marry again.

He realized he *was* at that point. He didn't want an annulment. He wanted to see where their future might lead.

"Thank you." Her gazed drifted over him. "You look very handsome." She sounded reserved. Nervous almost.

He stepped toward her, wanting to alleviate any lingering effects from the time she'd spent with her father. "How was your ride with your father?"

"It was nice. It reminded me of when we used to ride when I was younger."

He took her hand—she hadn't donned gloves and neither had he. "I'm glad you were able to enjoy a pleasant afternoon." It might be the last one they shared.

She pulled away from him and turned toward her dresser. "I need to fetch my gloves."

He frowned. Something was very wrong. "Daphne, is there something the matter? Did your father upset you?"

She opened a drawer and withdrew a pair of long white gloves. When she turned back to face him, her eyes sparked with a touch of heat. "When I went to get the keys from my father's desk, I found a ledger marked 'Camelot.' In it was a list of names. Yours was among them."

Bloody hell.

"Are you a member of Camelot?" Her voice held a bare tremor, and Gideon worked to keep from flinching.

He should have told her when he'd told her about her father. "Yes. Your father recruited me."

"My father's name was not on the list."

"If it's your father's list, that would make sense," he said, feeling defensive but also wholly regretful for having kept the truth from her. But he'd had good reason—he hadn't expected their relationship to last. He hadn't thought he'd want it to.

"My father says he is not in Camelot. However, he says you likely are."

Anger unfurled in his chest. "I just admitted it." Unlike her cowardly father, who would continue to lie to her. "Your father is lying. He's the head of Camelot."

"How can he be if Camelot is made up of descendants? Isn't that what you told me? How can my father lead a group of which he can't even be a member?"

Gideon's ire didn't fade, but her argument wasn't bad. "I don't know how he gained access. He fooled everyone, apparently."

"So I'm a fool," she said softly, looking away from him.

"*No.*" He stepped toward her, but she took a step back. He swallowed and worked to rein in his emotions. "You're not a fool. You love your father. This has to be incredibly difficult. I remember how I felt when I learned my father had hurt my mother, that he'd flaunted his women in front of her and done countless despicable things."

Her gaze flicked toward him, and he caught a bare flash of sympathy. "So we are both cursed with horrible fathers?"

"It seems that way." His throat tightened. He felt as

though he was losing her. Her father had been the most important person in her life forever. Why would she take Gideon's word over his?

"Why didn't you tell me?" She didn't look at him, and her voice sounded so small.

He wanted nothing more than to take her in his arms and soothe her pain. Which he had caused. Christ, he was as awful as he'd ever been. "I've done things I'm not proud of, Daphne. I should have told you. But to reveal all of it..." She wouldn't like him anymore. She'd pursue an annulment as quickly as she could.

And he wouldn't blame her. But right now, he needed her to see their plan through to the end. "We don't have much time. We need to get to dinner. Is the plan in place?" Or was she so upset with him that she hadn't put the tonic in the ale? Worse, had she told her father everything?

She nodded. "Yes." Then she looked at him, and there was a surprising ferocity in her gaze. "I committed to this plan, Gideon. I committed to you. I expect honesty."

"And you shall have it," he swore. There were so many things he wanted to say to her, that he *must* say to her, but now wasn't the time. He didn't want the stress of tonight hanging over them. He wanted to be alone with her without fear of interruption, and then he would bare his soul.

Then he expected she would leave. That would be the smart thing to do. He cocked up everything he touched. He ought to make Penn be the earl, because he'd likely fuck that up too.

Another wave of anguish crashed over him. He should tell her about that. And he would. He *had* committed fraud—it wasn't just a convenient excuse—

and she was entitled to know. Yes, he'd give her the means to leave. It was the least he could do.

"Daphne, I'm asking you to trust me tonight. When we're away, I will tell you everything—and then you can decide if I'm worthy."

There was that word again. It had crept out of the recesses of his mind and fallen from his lips. The thing he was expected to be and yet was certain he couldn't.

She didn't speak, but he could see that her mind was churning. Her gaze was dark with uncertainty, her face pale.

"Can you trust me?" he asked.

"I told you I committed to the plan," she said. Taking a deep breath, she began to pull on her gloves.

It wasn't really an answer, and Gideon realized he was going to have to do what he asked of her—he would trust her. There was nothing else he could do. Besides that, he wanted to. He *needed* to.

He fetched his gloves from the table near the door and pulled them on. His hands weren't shaking, but there was a low thrum vibrating through him. Excitement, anticipation, anxiety, fear. He turned to wait for her.

Also hope.

She walked to his side and looked up at him. Her gaze had cleared, and there was a businesslike seriousness to her expression. "Let us conduct our deception. Remember, don't drink the ale."

Her use of the word deception told him how she felt about it. But she'd tainted the ale and was apparently prepared to see the plan through. Meaning she wouldn't have told her father.

He hadn't lost her yet, but the danger was real. He'd do everything in his power to hold on tight.

Chapter Seventeen

FOLLOWING A SLIGHTLY subdued dinner since most of the guests from the medieval festival had left, those remaining gathered for port and sherry in the drawing room that adjoined the great hall. A few had drunk ale at dinner, and Gideon could already see the effects of the sleeping tonic starting to work. Several of them hid yawns behind their hands.

Gideon hoped the guards had imbibed plenty of the ale in their dining hall belowstairs. Just as he hoped Daphne had managed to ensure that the guards stationed outside and in the vault received their portions before they'd gone on duty.

She stood on the other side of the room with another woman, both sipping sherry. Daphne had also drunk two glasses of wine at dinner, and he wondered if there was a particular reason she was drinking more than normal. Such as being upset with him. Or preparing to deceive him by telling her father their plan.

He was being paranoid. Or not. He'd asked her to betray her father. And he wasn't sure he'd blame her if she couldn't.

After a while, several people excused themselves, leaving just a small group. To ensure that everyone had retired, especially Foliot, Gideon and Daphne would be the last to go up.

Gideon made small talk with one of the remaining gentlemen, but he soon started yawning as well. Then he excused himself, and a few minutes later, it was just

Gideon, Daphne, and Foliot.

Foliot yawned, and Gideon wondered if he'd any ale. He hadn't been seated close enough to Foliot—something else that had made him wary since Daphne had sat on her father's right—to see.

"I suppose it's a bit of an early night, then," Foliot said. "Just as well, as I find I'm fatigued." He kissed Daphne's cheek. "Good night, dear." Then he inclined his head toward Gideon. "Gideon."

"Good night," Gideon said.

As soon as he left, Daphne turned to Gideon. "Shall we go up?"

"Yes." Gideon moved to touch her but decided not to.

They made their way upstairs in silence and, as soon as they got to their room, moved to change their clothing. Relief surged through Gideon. Apparently, she still meant to follow through with the plan.

Gideon didn't change his waistcoat, so the keys to the vault remained secure. When he was dressed in his riding clothes, he fetched the cloak from beneath his pillow. He reached for the bedside table, where he'd stashed a pistol that afternoon. He'd managed to steal one from Foliot's guardhouse where the weaponry used by his guards was stored. The pistol was primed, but Gideon hoped he wouldn't have to use it. He tucked it into his coat as Daphne emerged from the dressing chamber.

Garbed in a fetching dark purple riding ensemble, she was breathtakingly lovely. But then it didn't matter what she wore or if she wore nothing at all—she was incomparable.

"I'm going now," Gideon said, drawing the cloak around his shoulders.

She nodded. "I'll wait here until I'm sure you've gained access." They'd already planned that if for some reason the guard outside was still awake, Gideon would return immediately and they'd either come up with a plan to lure him away or Gideon would try to knock him unconscious. He preferred to find the man asleep. Things would be so much easier that way.

It seemed as though Gideon should say something else, but he couldn't find the words to breach the tension between them. He would—tomorrow when they were away from here.

He pulled the hood up over his head. "Can you see me?"

"No."

He turned and went to the door, and as he opened it, she said, "Be safe."

She cared for him. Or she expected something bad was about to happen.

God, he'd be happy to have this night behind him.

He hurried down the stairs, slowing his pace as he neared the bottom. Two maids were in the great hall, cleaning. He kept his steps soft as he cut across the hall to the tapestry that covered the alcove leading to the vault. They didn't so much as look in his direction.

A mix of excitement and apprehension propelled him to move faster. He held his breath as he gently lifted the edge of the tapestry and slipped behind it. The guard was slumped on the floor in the corner. Gideon exhaled with relief as jubilation coursed through him.

He reached into his waistcoat and pulled out the keys. It took a few tries to match them with the right locks, but he was soon inside the vault. Opening the door slowly, he put his hand on his pistol in case the interior guard wasn't asleep. After he'd surveyed the room and seen the second guard sprawled on the floor, Gideon's shoulders relaxed.

After closing the door securely behind him, Gideon went to the chest and found the key that fit its lock. The lid creaked as he opened it. There, lying inside where he'd left them, were the Heart of Llanllwch and Dyrnwyn.

He picked up the heart and thought of Daphne. If he wished right now that she loved him, could he be sure that she'd stay by his side? He slid the stone into his coat pocket and drove the thought from his mind lest he cause something he couldn't undo.

Next, he hefted the sword, still in its scabbard, and felt the familiar vibration. Pulling back the cloak, he slipped the weapon through a belt he'd donned beneath his coat. He let the cloak fall, rendering him invisible once more.

He closed the chest and locked it, then looked around the room. There were many treasures here— old manuscripts, Roman coins and artifacts, ancient pottery and jewelry, and weapons of iron and stone.

But Gideon had what he needed. It was time to go meet Daphne to deliver the keys, and she would return them to her father's study.

Anticipating their easy escape, he hurried from the room and locked the door completely, making it appear as if it hadn't ever been disturbed. If Foliot didn't know the treasures were missing, it would hopefully give Gideon and Daphne time to travel far away from Ashridge Court. The guards likely wouldn't want to tell their employer they'd fallen asleep at their posts. And Daphne had written a note explaining that she and Gideon were going to London to answer his writ of summons.

With a final look at the snoring guard, Gideon made his way to another alcove, this one behind the stairs. The great hall was now, thankfully, empty, but he reminded himself that no one could see him.

Daphne was there waiting as planned. He lowered the hood and handed her the keys, murmuring, "I have them."

She nodded. "I'll be right back." She hesitated. "I wish that cloak worked for me so I could wear it upstairs."

He didn't want her to be nervous. Or afraid. "Do you want me to return the keys?"

"No, you don't know how to trigger the drawer. And if you were seen opening doors, it would be a problem. I can explain my presence."

He looked down at her costume. "In a riding habit at midnight?"

She frowned. "We didn't think of that, did we? I'll be quick."

"You could also stop and don a dressing gown." He should have thought of that earlier.

She shook her head. "I don't want to take the time. I just want this to be over."

He understood that. "I feel the same." He wanted to kiss her—for luck as much as to comfort her and to show he cared.

But she turned and dashed toward the stairs.

Gideon paced impatiently, mentally following her path. As the minutes dragged, his apprehension mounted. What if her father was in his study? What if he'd discovered her there?

"You found the cloak." Foliot's voice hit Gideon like an arrow.

Gideon turned to see Daphne's father emerging from

a hidden door in the alcove and swore under his breath.

Foliot studied Gideon, his gaze trying to detect what he couldn't see below Gideon's head. "It's astonishing. The heart and the sword are incredible, but this… This is unparalleled." He lifted his eyes to deliver a pointed stare at Gideon. "So you plan to steal them all from the Order."

"They don't belong to the Order," Gideon said, putting one hand on the hilt of Dyrnwyn and the other on his pistol.

Foliot's lip curled. "You're a thief regardless of who you're taking them from."

"Papa."

Gideon turned his head to see Daphne standing just outside the alcove.

Foliot took a step forward. "Daphne, I've caught your husband stealing from me, but then I should have expected it. This is the second time he's stolen Dyrnwyn from someone—the first being Cate Bowen."

Daphne looked toward Gideon, her lips parting in surprise. "Is that true?"

Something else he should have told her—and planned to. "Yes. I took it from her for your father. Ask him."

"That's not true," Foliot said calmly. "Daphne, I'm afraid you can't trust anything this man says." He looked at her sadly. "I understand why you felt you must help him. I'm so sorry. The heart has ruined everything." He turned his attention to Gideon. "You have it with you, the heart? Release Daphne from its spell at least."

Wait, did Foliot think that Daphne was only helping Gideon because of the heart? That would have been an interesting deduction *if* Gideon had actually used it.

Was it possible it had partially worked? What if nothing between them had been real—at least on her part? What he felt had been absolutely true. As real as the dread gathering in his gut.

Gideon had been about to protest, to tell Foliot that he hadn't used the heart. Instead, he pulled it from his pocket and met her gaze, saying, "I don't want Daphne to love me."

It was a lie. He *did* want her love. More than anything. The despair in his belly threatened to tear him in two.

"Very good, thank you." Foliot pulled a pistol from his coat and pointed it at Gideon. "Now give it to me, along with the sword and the cloak."

Gideon drew his own pistol and unsheathed Dyrnwyn. "I can't do that."

Daphne stepped forward. "Please, both of you, put your weapons away." The anguish in her voice was torture for Gideon.

"Be careful, Daphne!" Foliot waved her back. "He's a killer in addition to a thief. He shot Cate's maid in pursuit of the sword and had her husband's brother killed."

His lies were unconscionable. Gideon nearly shot him on the spot. "Stop putting your crimes on me. I did neither of those things."

"The men who were with you are here and will confirm it." His gaze was ice-cold, and Gideon knew Foliot's men would do whatever he said.

Gideon looked to Daphne. "I know he's your father, and you love him, but he's not the man you want him to be."

Her eyes were dark with sadness and disappointment. "I'm not sure you're the man I wanted you to be either."

The knife in his chest twisted. "I told you I wasn't." His voice nearly broke. "I'm sorry, Daphne."

"Hand her the treasures, Gideon." Foliot cocked his pistol.

Gideon had no idea what Daphne meant to do, but he wanted to have faith in her. So he did. "I'm going to leave. Daphne, I hope you will come with me."

Foliot lifted the gun an inch, pointing it at Gideon's heart. "Don't make me shoot you."

"Papa, *don't.*"

Gideon saw her move, and fear ripped through him. He raised Dyrnwyn, and its light filled the alcove. Foliot gasped. It was enough for Gideon to use the sword to knock the pistol from his hands. It fired as it hit the floor, and Gideon swung his gaze to Daphne to make sure she was all right.

Foliot lunged forward, but Gideon slashed the sword and drove him back.

Daphne grabbed her father's arm. "Papa, please. He'll kill you."

Gideon froze for a moment, staring at her. She believed him—she believed Gideon was a killer. "I wouldn't," he croaked. But the evidence seemed to the contrary given his movements and the fact that the sword was flaming brighter than it ever had.

"Papa, let him go," she said, tears streaming down her face. "He's taking the treasures to Gareth. We'll find him."

And with that, Gideon at last knew her intent. Whether she'd been going to help him and had just changed her mind or she'd planned to betray him all along didn't matter. The path had led them there. She'd chosen her father.

Gideon turned and fled.

DAPHNE SPUN INTO her father and hugged him tightly. He hesitated, but his arms came around her, and he patted her back.

She cried harder. "Papa, I'm so sorry. I can't believe I *loved* him."

"It's all right, my girl. I'll find him, and he's the one who will be sorry."

Pulling back, Daphne wiped her eyes. "I think the spell from the heart is broken."

"It appears to be, and thank God for that. I never should have done any of this between you and Gideon." Papa's lip curled. "I suspected that he betrayed me once, and I was a fool for believing he hadn't."

No, Daphne was the fool. She'd never seen her father for the man he was. How could he look at her with such concern—and love, or at least what he thought love was supposed to be—after lying to her so effortlessly?

From being a descendant to not being in Camelot to accusing Gideon of horrible crimes, he'd done everything in his power to control everyone around him. He'd even tried to manipulate her into marrying Gideon. No, he hadn't just tried. He'd been successful.

Her heart split in two when she thought of the anguish in Gideon's eyes. He thought she'd chosen her father. Which was what she'd wanted him to believe. Because it was what she needed her father to believe. If Gideon was to achieve his objective, Daphne had to outmaneuver her father.

"We must go after him," Papa said.

Daphne nodded and sniffed. "For the treasures."

"Yes, we mustn't let him hide them, but it sounds as if you may know where he's going—where Gareth's tomb is located." Papa's gaze was both hopeful and shrewd.

"I do," she said with determination. "It's on Bardsey Island." The island off the northern coast of Wales was perhaps the final resting place of Merlin. Some stories indicated the Thirteen Treasures lay with him.

Papa frowned. "But that's where Merlin is likely buried. Gareth wouldn't be there too, would he?"

"That's what Gideon believes." Daphne worked to sound as firm and convincing as possible. "I wish I could tell you why, but he didn't always share everything with me." Gideon was right about her—she was perhaps a little too accomplished at fabricating lies. Perhaps she'd learned the skill from her father without even realizing it. She suddenly felt very ill.

"That is quite a distance," Papa said stroking his chin. "Is he going alone?"

"He thought we were going together."

"We shall rouse my men to go in pursuit. Would you like to accompany them?"

Them… Didn't he plan to go? "I think I'd prefer to return to Keynsham."

Papa patted her shoulder. "My poor girl. You must feel terribly betrayed."

That much was true. But the pain she felt came from her father. Mostly. She wished Gideon hadn't kept things from her, though she supposed she understood why he had. She was the daughter of his enemy. Why *would* he expose himself to her? He'd started to, but she knew he'd resisted that too.

"I'm also exhausted," she said, which was also true. "I just want to go home. To Hawthorn Cottage."

"Very well. I'll summon Argus to accompany you."

Hell, she didn't want Argus to accompany her, because she wasn't going to Keynsham! "That isn't necessary, Papa. Take him with you to Bardsey." *Yes, take everyone.*

"I'm not going." Of course he wasn't. He rarely left Ashridge Court.

"Why not? This is so important to you. You could obtain all Thirteen Treasures at once." She really needed him to go. "Would you pass up the chance to see Gareth's tomb?"

"That is rather tempting, but Bardsey is awfully far. And what if Gideon lied to you and has gone somewhere else? No, I'll stay here as I usually do. My men are quite capable, and Davis will lead them well."

Davis was a Welsh gentleman who'd tried to court Daphne a few years ago. He was attractive and charming, but there'd been something unsavory about him, and Daphne had discouraged his attention. When he'd persisted, her father had informed him that she would marry a descendant. That had put an end to his advances. Still, Daphne had never cared for him, and he was among her father's most trusted men.

Daphne tried once more to persuade her father to go. "I hope you don't regret not going."

"I hope *you* don't," he countered. "Now we must rouse these guards, if we can. I went for a late-night stroll and found several of them sleeping. When I was unable to wake them, I knew something was amiss. Have you any idea what Gideon did to them?"

"I don't," she lied once more.

His gaze lingered on her, and he sighed. "Pity. Well, we'll get them up and send them on their way at first light."

"I'll help you, Papa," she said, feeling as though she must. She didn't think he was suspicious of her, but wanted to be overly careful. "Then I shall go. I hope you understand my need for solitude."

"Of course, dear."

It took several hours and copious amounts of cold water to wake all the men. As they prepared for their journey to Bardsey, Daphne readied herself to leave. So far, she hadn't devised a strategy to get rid of Argus so that she could go where she really planned: Weston.

The men departed as the first hint of day began to lighten the sky. Daphne and Argus set out on horseback as dawn broke, heading north to Keynsham. When they were on the other side of Glastonbury, Daphne slowed her horse from a trot and walked to the side of the road.

Argus joined her. "Is something amiss, my lady?"

Hearing him call her my lady was a bit jarring. She'd tried to think of a reason to part ways with him, but she was apparently out of convenient lies. Or perhaps she was weary of telling them once she'd realized how like her father she was. Instead, she was going to tell Argus the truth. He'd been with her for nearly two years, and she hoped she'd garnered at least a modicum of loyalty. And also hoped she hadn't ruined that when she'd left Ashridge Court without him to pursue Gideon the first time.

"Argus, I'm not going to Hawthorn Cottage."

His brows rose beneath the brim of his hat. "Where are you going?"

"I'd rather not say."

"I'll accompany you wherever you'd like."

He would? Was it really that easy? She'd expected him to insist she go to Keynsham—or return to Ashridge Court. "That's very kind of you, but I don't need a companion."

He frowned. "I'm afraid I can't let you go alone. You left without me recently, and aside from your father's anger that I allowed you to leave—"

"You didn't," she rushed to say. "I left without telling you."

"Your father didn't see it that way. In any case, you shouldn't be traveling alone."

He sounded like Gideon, and, like Gideon, she suspected he wasn't going to let her brush his concern aside. What would happen if he came with her? They'd arrive in Weston later today, and then she'd be with Gideon—if he'd have her.

She fixed Argus with a steely stare. "Can I trust you?"

"I've always tried to be dependable and trustworthy. I put your safety above my own."

"Will you also put my husband's safety above your own?"

He blinked at her. "Where are you going?"

"Please answer the question, Argus."

He nodded. "If you ask me to, yes."

"I am asking you to." She paused and waited for him to nod again. "Thank you. We're riding to Weston—we must turn west at the road ahead. And we must ride quickly."

If Gideon had followed their plan, he would have rested at Meare, which was just west of Glastonbury, until morning. Then he would have set out for Weston, which was just twenty miles away, where they would await Penn and arrange for passage to Flat Holm as soon as possible.

However, she worried that Gideon would try to go alone after what had happened at Ashridge Court. He'd be anxious to return the treasures to Gareth.

"We'll move as quickly as possible," Argus vowed.

They set off once again, and Daphne's anxiety shifted from how she would evade Argus to how she would convince Gideon that she hadn't betrayed him.

Chapter Eighteen

GIDEON PAID FOR two nights at the Drunken Mermaid, a smaller inn away from the busy center of Weston. The captain who would take him to Flat Holm the day after tomorrow had recommended it.

The day after bloody tomorrow.

Climbing the stairs to his room on the first floor, Gideon cursed the weather for what had to be the dozenth time. The captain had said the winds were too high to get to Flat Holm today and would likely be tomorrow too. Gideon had considered finding a small boat that he could row himself, but the passage was difficult for smaller vessels, and it was much more likely for him to become stranded, as had happened to others in recent years.

This way, you can wait for Penn, he reminded himself.

While that was true, it also gave Foliot a chance to catch up with him and ruin the entire plan. That was the primary reason he'd chosen the Drunken Mermaid—it was small, in a somewhat questionable area, and the innkeeper had been amenable to bribery. He would keep Gideon's presence as secret as possible.

Hopefully, Foliot wouldn't find him, and hopefully, he wouldn't be able to find a boat that would take him to Flat Holm. It had taken Gideon several hours to locate a willing captain, and he prayed Foliot would be unsuccessful.

Would Daphne come with him?

Pain tore through Gideon. He'd tried so hard to keep

her from his mind, but it was a nearly impossible task. The vision of her standing beside her father telling him what Gideon intended to do pierced him like the sharpest blade.

He'd thought to be doing this with her. She'd said they were in it together. Now it felt hollow. He was still committed to returning the treasures, but the joy of doing so was greatly diminished.

In fact, joy seemed all but unattainable. He looked forward to the bottle of brandy the innkeeper had promised to bring up shortly.

He unlocked and opened the door to his room and exhaled. It was small but well-appointed with a large four-poster bed, a good-sized fireplace that would easily heat the room, a tall dresser, and a table with a pair of chairs.

Gideon deposited his saddlebag on the end of the bed and went to the wide single window. He pushed aside the blue linen curtains to look out at the harbor and beyond. The Bristol Channel was dark and choppy today, and rain had begun to fall. He couldn't see Flat Holm but knew it was out there. No, *he* was out there. Gareth.

Turning, Gideon went to unpack his bag, which held the heart and the cloak, which he left in the bag, along with a few extra items of clothing he'd packed separately at Brue Cottage. As he stored his clothing in the dresser, more images of Daphne rose in his mind: her glorious body, her tantalizing smile, her mouth exploring him with sweet abandon. That seemed so long ago instead of just yesterday morning.

Next, he worked to start a fire, which he'd told the innkeeper he would do, and soon had a warm blaze. The room had been a bit cool, but Gideon had barely noticed, numb as he was.

A rap on the door drew his attention. Now he could spend the rest of the day and night as sotted as the namesake of the inn.

He opened the door, and the innkeeper handed him a bottle and a glass. "Here's your brandy. Some chit came looking for you. I sent her on her way."

It had to have been Daphne. His pulse quickened. "Was she alone?"

"No, she had a man with her—seemed like a servant. He stood a bit behind her and didn't interfere."

It didn't sound like Foliot, but Gideon had to be sure. "What did he look like?"

"Tall fellow, wide as a doorframe across the shoulders." The innkeeper shook his head. "I wouldn't want to tangle with him."

Definitely not Foliot. "Thank you." Gideon took the brandy and the glass, and the innkeeper closed the door and left.

Setting the bottle and glass on the table, Gideon moved to the window to see if she might still be on the street below. His gaze moved up and down the lane. There—she was on a horse and the large man the innkeeper had described rode another beside her. The rain had increased, and Gideon could see they were drenched.

Despite her betrayal, his heart ached. He wanted to bring her inside to dry and warm her. To hold her close and never let her go.

They walked their horses to the side of the lane, before another inn. The groom dismounted, then helped her. Gideon told himself to turn away, to stop the torture of wanting what he couldn't have.

He started to pivot, but froze when he saw a

movement. A man grabbed her groom, and a second went for Daphne. Gideon didn't hesitate before tearing from the room and bounding down the stairs. He was out in the rain-soaked street in a trice, racing toward her.

She shrieked as the miscreant held her fast. Her groom was engaged in fisticuffs with the other one. Gideon grabbed the man holding Daphne and tossed him aside. The man sprawled into the street.

Daphne blinked at Gideon. "Where did you—"

Gideon didn't hear the rest of her question because the man he'd thrown gripped Gideon's leg and tried to pull him down. Gideon kicked at him and then reached down to pick him up by his dirty cravat.

Growling, Gideon hit the man and sent him sprawling once more. Then he pulled Dyrnwyn, which was still strapped to his waist, from its scabbard. The sword flamed pale blue, and Daphne's assailant raised his hands in front of his face.

"Don't hurt me!" he cried.

"Go!" Gideon threatened, moving toward him with the sword. The man scrambled to his feet and slipped as he tried to run away. Gideon turned to the other man, but he and Daphne's groom had stopped fighting and were staring at the sword.

Gideon took a menacing step toward the other criminal. "You'd better run."

The man did exactly that, taking off down the street after his companion.

Daphne moved closer to him. "Gideon, people are staring."

There weren't many about, but they were, in fact, staring. Gideon quickly sheathed the sword, then he took Daphne by the arm and guided her back toward the Drunken Mermaid. Her groom followed.

Once they were inside, he let her go. Then he pierced the groom with a nasty stare. "You're supposed to protect her."

"I was," he said defensively. "I nearly had the other man subdued. They only wanted coin."

Gideon turned to Daphne. "Why didn't you just give it to them?"

"Because I need it," she said, wiping her hand over her face and grimacing at the contact of her wet glove.

Gideon went to the window at the front of the common room and looked outside. "Where's your father?"

"At Ashridge Court."

Of course the coward had stayed home. He always did. Gideon snorted as he turned around to face her. "He surely sent more than him." Gideon gestured toward her groom.

"This is Argus, my personal manservant. Argus, this is my husband, Lord Stratton." She conducted the introduction as if they hadn't parted under the most terrible of circumstances. And as if their marriage was perfectly ordinary. "My father sent far more than Argus. To Bardsey Island."

To…where? Gideon blinked at her. "Why?"

She stood there sopping wet, water dripping from her hat onto the floor. "Because that's where I told him you went." She paused before adding, "He sent Argus to accompany me to Keynsham."

Gideon stared at her as his brain tried to comprehend what she was saying. "You are not in Keynsham."

"No, I'm not." Her gaze held his, and in that moment, he knew everything he needed to: she hadn't chosen her father. She'd chosen him.

He stepped forward and swept her sodden hat from her head, knocking it to the floor. Then he cupped her face. "I love you."

Her lips curved up. "I love you too."

Gideon kissed her, uncaring that Argus was standing right behind her. Hell, the entire town of Weston could be lined up to watch and he wouldn't give a fig. She was here with him, and that was all that mattered.

Except, perhaps, for her shivering.

"Come upstairs. You need to get warm."

"Yes, please." She glanced back toward her manservant. "What about Argus?"

Though Gideon was thrilled to see her, he wasn't sure he could trust the man. He slid a look toward Argus and whispered, "Does he work for you or your father?"

"My father, but he is loyal to me. I didn't tell him we weren't going to Keynsham until we'd left Glastonbury. He wasn't able to tell anyone."

"And he won't send word?"

"I can hear you," Argus said. His voice was deep and raspy. "No, I won't send word. While it's true I work for Foliot, I've looked after Lady Stratton long enough that her safety is of paramount importance to me." He took a step toward Gideon. "Can I trust her with you? Foliot has described you to me as a thief and a killer."

Daphne stepped between them, her frame still quivering with cold. "I trust Gideon with my life, so you can do the same." She turned to Gideon. "Can we go upstairs now?"

Gideon put his arm around her, heedless of her wet clothing. "Yes. Argus, the innkeeper is about. See if he has a room for you and have Daphne's bag sent up."

"I don't have a bag," she said, wincing. "I was supposed to be riding home."

"We'd best get to drying your clothes, then." Gideon inclined his head toward Argus and picked up Daphne's hat from the floor. Then he guided her up the stairs. "Left at the landing. We're at the end of the hall."

Small puddles formed where she walked. As soon as she stepped into the chamber, Gideon closed the door and strode to set her hat on the hearth. She joined him there, holding her hands out as she tried to remove her gloves.

Gideon took over, stripping the garments from her fingers and dropping them next to her hat. Then he untied her cravat and tossed it atop the other items. She tried to unbutton her coat, but he pushed her hands away and completed the task for her.

After the coat, he unlaced her skirt and let it fall to the floor. Her shirt came next, then he knelt to remove her boots. Those he carefully set before the fire, thinking they would take quite some time to dry out. It was perhaps a good thing they couldn't go anywhere tomorrow.

He stood and helped her remove her petticoat and corset. She stood before him in a dry chemise, but she was still shivering with cold. "Let me get the coverlet from the bed."

"Can you remove my stockings?" she asked between chattering teeth. "They're very wet."

"Of course." He'd forgot the bloody things. Grabbing a chair from the table, he dragged it in front of the fire. He knelt before her once more and realized his coat was rather damp from his time outside. Unbuttoning it, he shrugged it from his shoulders and set it on the floor. He also removed Dyrnwyn from his waist and propped it in the corner.

Returning his attention to Daphne, he pushed up her chemise. His breath tangled in his lungs. He'd undressed her so quickly and with a keen attention to making her warmer, that he hadn't fallen prey to the allure of her body.

Until now.

Pushing up the chemise, he bared her knees and settled the linen atop her thighs. He loosened the garters and slipped each one, along with the stocking, from her legs. Now *he* was trembling, but not from cold. There were so many things he wanted to do to her. To show her.

He stood and hurried to the bed, dragging the coverlet from it and bringing it to wrap around her in the chair. She sat forward and stood so that she could arrange the fabric about her body. Then she collapsed once more, and Gideon set to laying her clothing out so that it would dry. He draped her skirt over the back of the other chair and positioned it near the fire.

He laid everything out except the petticoat. That should go over the chair too. But she was in the other chair. As he stood there dithering about what to do with the garment, she stood up.

"Put the petticoat here," she said. "I'll go to the bed." Had her voice grown husky?

"You should stay by the fire where it's warmest."

She turned and looked at him over her shoulder. "The bed will be warm." Her lids drooped over her eyes in a seductive fashion.

Gideon reached for her, his body flushing with desire. He worked to keep his arousal at bay. "We have much to discuss."

She nodded, her gaze dropping to the floor. "Yes. I hope you can forgive me." She looked back up, her hazel eyes connecting with his. "I only pretended to take my father's side so you could get away."

"I know that now." But in that moment... He'd been devastated. "There's nothing to forgive." His voice was dark and raw.

She gave him a shy look. "Did you mean what you said downstairs?"

"That I love you?" She nodded. "Yes."

"Show me. Please." She curled her arms around his neck. Gideon lifted her and carried her to the bed, laying her back as she spread the coverlet beneath her.

Gideon swallowed. Though she still wore the chemise, the shape of her body was visible beneath the white linen. She was a gift he was certain he didn't deserve.

"Daphne, I'm not sure I'm worthy. Some of the things your father said... I did steal the sword from Cate. And I led a group of men that shot her maid when I wasn't with them."

She pushed herself up and knelt before him, cupping his face. He hadn't shaved since Brue Cottage the previous morning, and her fingers rasped against the whiskers. "Gideon, you are not a bad person. I can think of no man more worthy for me than you."

She leaned forward and pressed her lips to his. He didn't know if she meant it to be a sweet joining, but he grabbed her to him and kissed her as if he were a starved man. Which was true. He was absolutely ravenous for her.

She clutched at his shoulders as he drove his tongue deep into her mouth. She angled her head and began to pluck at his cravat, tearing the silk away with a few easy flicks. Then her fingers began unbuttoning his waistcoat as he pulled the pins from her hair. He tried to toss them on the table beside the bed, but he had no idea if they hit his target.

Once his waistcoat was open, he shrugged it from his shoulders, then whipped his shirt over his head, momentarily breaking their kiss. But it was quickly resumed, their lips and tongues meeting with fierce passion.

She wanted him to show her he loved her? He knew precisely how.

He trailed his mouth from her lips to her jaw and then down along her neck. She cast her head back, and he gently guided her to lie on the bed. He bent with her, licking and sucking her flesh, at one point leaving a dark pink mark at the top of her breast that quickly began to fade.

She gasped as he worked, her fingers tangling in his hair. He paid special attention to her breasts, which he adored. She was so sensitive, and he loved to make her moan and writhe. And he knew he could intensify her sensations.

He kissed between her breasts and dragged his tongue down her abdomen, swirling it around her navel before descending farther. Skimming his hand across her hip, he found her sex, stroking his finger along her wet folds. He could smell her arousal and couldn't wait to taste it.

Parting her dark red curls, he teased her clitoris, making her hips come up off the bed as she groaned. Then he replaced his fingers with his mouth, licking her sex.

"Gideon!" She dug her hands into his scalp.

He looked up her body to see her watching him, her

eyes slitted. "Didn't your research reveal this act?"

"Yes. But I—" She opened her eyes wider. "I don't know. It feels so strange."

He used his thumb to tease her flesh. "Strange good or strange bad?"

"Strange…good. I suppose it's just new and different."

"Like when I put my finger in you the first time." He followed his words with the motion, stroking his finger into her wet sheath. "That was strange good?"

"That was strange *divine*." She closed her eyes and cast her head back with a sound that was part sigh and part gasp and entirely seductive.

"When I'm finished, you can try to think of a word to describe this." He parted her and dipped his tongue inside her. He braced his hands on her inner thighs and held her while he ravaged her with his mouth, licking and sucking as she cried out again and again.

She moved with him, her muscles tensing. He guided her legs over his shoulders and cupped the back of one thigh. Suckling her clitoris, he pushed a finger into her, driving in and out to send her to the edge of release. She clenched around him, and he used two fingers, triggering her orgasm.

She tightened and cried out his name. He buried his tongue inside her and worked her flesh with his fingers until her body relaxed beneath him.

He stood back and bent to pull off his boots. His stockings and breeches quickly followed, as did his smallclothes. He went to join her on the bed and found her looking up at him, her cheeks flushed and her eyes a bit glazed.

"That certainly *felt* like you loved me."

Gideon couldn't help but laugh. "Daphne, you are

incomparable."

She held her arms out to him, and he lay down beside her, drawing her into his arms. "As much as I enjoyed that—and I did *immensely*—I want to feel you against me." She kissed him, her tongue sliding along his.

He rolled her to her back and settled between her legs. "Like this?" he asked between kisses.

She wrapped her legs around his hips. "Yes. But more. I want all of you." She brought her hand up and smoothed his hair back from his face. "Gideon, I don't care about your past or the man you used to be. I only know the man you are now and the future we can have together. I want that. I want *you*."

Overcome with emotion, Gideon kissed her again, his mouth devouring hers as if he could take her very essence into himself. That was what he wanted—to be joined with her. Now and forever.

Unsealing his mouth from hers, he gripped his cock and guided himself into her sex. When he'd slid as far as he could go, he stroked her clitoris, drawing a low, soft moan from her lips. He took that into himself too, kissing her again, more softly this time as he mimicked the rocking of his body into hers.

Gradually, he increased the rhythm, making longer, faster strokes. She caressed his back, skimming her fingers over his muscles and down to his backside. She gripped his hips, urging him faster, and moved her legs up, opening herself to him even more.

Desperate for release, he increased their speed, slamming into her as his pleasure built. His orgasm was so close. He wanted her with him.

He bent his head and kissed her cheek, then her ear. "Come with me," he rasped, driving into her as his body began to release.

She wrapped her arms around his back and held him close, her body rising to meet his. Blood rushed to his cock as he came, her muscles clenching around him. He pumped into her until he was spent, his body collapsing onto hers as he fought to catch his breath.

She cradled him against her, kissing his cheek, his neck, his shoulder. Some minutes later, he rolled to his back, and she snuggled against his side.

"That was different," she said. "You...finished inside me. You didn't do that at Brue Cottage."

"No. I was trying to prevent a baby." He hadn't even thought about it this time.

She pushed up onto her elbow and looked down at him, her hair draping across her shoulder and tickling his. "I don't want you to do that."

"Good, because I didn't." He turned his head to look at her. "But maybe I should have. I don't know how to be a parent. I've had terrible examples."

"If we had a contest for whose father is worse, I am confident I would win."

Her tone had held a wry note, but tears pooled in her eyes. He drew her against him, stroking her back and kissing her forehead. "Don't cry, Daphne. There is no contest. They're both horrid. And I'm going to do my best to not be like them."

She looked up at him, her gaze fierce. "You couldn't ever." She glanced away for a moment. "Could we not talk about them just now?"

He didn't particularly want to discuss them at any time, but he supposed they must—at least her father and how they would deal with him after they restored the treasures to Gareth.

Gideon kissed her temple and ran her silken dark

copper hair through his fingers. "We don't have to talk about anything."

"We should probably discuss the plan to return the treasures."

"Actually, we have plenty of time for that. As luck would have it, the weather is not conducive for the crossing." He hadn't thought it was lucky, but his opinion had completely changed. "The wind is too high today and will likely be again tomorrow. I've retained a captain to take me—us—over day after tomorrow."

"So we have the rest of today and tomorrow to…?"

"Wait for your clothes to dry." He reached for the edge of the coverlet and worked it from under them, pulling it over their bodies to keep her warm.

"Is that all?" She pouted up at him.

"I am fairly certain we can come up with other activities." He gave her a devilish grin and pinned her to her back once more, eliciting a gasp from her lips.

She narrowed her eyes at him in seductive promise. "I was hoping you would say that."

Chapter Nineteen

"WHEN ARE WE leaving on the morrow?" Argus asked after they'd finished dinner in the common room the following evening. He'd pledged to come with them and provide whatever assistance he could, for which Gideon had said he was grateful.

"Not until midafternoon," Gideon answered. "I'd hoped to leave in the morning, but the captain wanted to be sure the wind had passed."

The day had been miserable, with the rain coming down sideways at one point. It had been the perfect day to spend indoors with one's husband. Daphne couldn't stop sneaking looks at him or finding a reason to brush his arm. She'd even reached under the table and stroked his thigh. That had earned her a heated look filled with promise.

"I'll be ready," Argus said.

They bid good night to Argus, and Daphne preceded Gideon up the stairs. He'd brought a bottle of port for them to sip in front of the fire.

Gideon unlocked the door, and they stepped into the room. He'd barely closed it before she turned and pressed herself against him, quickly untying his cravat and exposing his throat. Grabbing both ends of the silk, she pulled his head down so she could kiss him.

After a long, thorough exploration, she released him. "I've been waiting some time to do that."

His mouth curled into a heart-stopping smile. "Should we forgo the port?"

"I'll have a small glass." She took the bottle and glasses from him and went to the table to pour. "You stir the fire."

He went to the hearth and stoked the flame, and a moment later, she brought him a glass. He tapped it to hers. "To tomorrow."

"To tomorrow." She sipped her port. "I do hope Penn makes it in time." She sat in one of the chairs, which they'd left angled before the hearth.

"I do too, but I don't think we can wait if he doesn't," Gideon said, sitting beside her and taking her hand in his.

"We could. It's not as if my father is on his way here."

"I will feel better—no, I will feel *right*—when the treasures are where they belong." He glanced toward his saddlebag beside the bed where the cloak and heart resided. The sword leaned against the corner. "We will watch carefully for his arrival." Argus was going to position himself at the road on which they expected Penn to arrive in order to direct him to the boat.

"Will he come alone?" She'd wondered if his wife would join him but hadn't asked Gideon before now.

"I don't know. He would certainly have brought his assistant—Egg. But he's otherwise engaged." He frowned, his forehead creasing into deep lines. "Or perhaps not."

"Why do you look so concerned?"

"We haven't discussed the earldom, and we should." He let go of her hand and turned toward her. He took a drink of port, perhaps for fortification. "Penn is my half brother. His mother left our father when she was carrying Penn. My father had no idea there was a child. Everyone thought she had died. Indeed, the rumor was that he'd killed her."

"Wasn't that also a rumor about you...and your wife?" she asked.

"Like father, like son, apparently." His tone was wry, but she knew the gossip had to have hurt him.

"You are not like your father."

He gave her a sardonic look. "We can debate that later. To continue the story, Penn's mother delivered the child in the parish in which she grew up. The vicar recorded Penn's birth and promised to reveal it whenever she asked or upon the death of our father. Penn's mother became ill when Penn was around nine or ten, I think. She took him to Rhys to foster and told him the truth of Penn's sire. But she swore Rhys to secrecy, and Penn never knew the real identity of his father until several weeks ago."

Daphne couldn't imagine learning such a thing after so much time. "How did he take that?"

Gideon pressed his lips into a grim frown. "Not well. Penn is a scholar like his father—Rhys, I mean—and an adventurer. He was not raised to be an earl, nor does he have any desire to be. In fact, he'd prefer to avoid being the earl even more than I'd like to have the title."

"That seems like an easy problem to fix, then."

"Yes, but it's not. As soon as we learned about Stratton being Penn's father, Penn dispatched Egg to search for the vicar to stop him from sharing his proof and revealing Penn as the earl. But the vicar went missing on his way to London." Gideon looked away from her. "The next part is why I didn't tell you about any of this."

When his gaze met hers again, there was empathy and regret. "Your father kidnapped the vicar and has been keeping him somewhere on the estate at Ashridge Court. He promised to destroy the proof of Penn's birth if I married you."

Daphne stood, her legs shaking with anger, and she clutched the glass in her hand. "I wish you'd told me."

He stood with her and took her glass, putting them both on the table. "I didn't want to be the one to destroy the love you had for your father. I'm so sorry, Daphne. I know how that feels—to look up to someone and love them so much only to learn they're not the person you thought they were."

She fought to find her voice. "Because of your father?"

He nodded. "Two very despicable men. And in your case, something beautiful came from it."

She turned to him and took his hands in hers. "Stop denigrating yourself. I'm not going to allow it anymore. You are incredibly beautiful to me." She tipped her head to the side. "Perhaps beautiful isn't the right word. Ruggedly handsome." She brushed her hand along his beard, which he still hadn't shaved. "You take my breath away, actually."

He brushed his lips over hers. "As you do mine."

She blinked up at him. "And how did you take the news about Penn?" she asked softly, thinking it must have been devastating to learn he wasn't the heir as he'd thought he was *and* that he was illegitimate.

"Also not well." The edge of his mouth ticked up into a half smile. "My father raised me to be the Earl of Stratton. That's all I ever expected to be—a debauched lord who drained every drop of pleasure he could from life."

"You aren't a debauched lord."

"I very easily could have been, if not for Rose." He

exhaled. "That's not entirely true. I'd begun to see my father for what he was, and I didn't want our family's reputation forever stained. I sought to find a well-respected young lady to make my wife."

Daphne summoned the courage to ask about her. "Margery said you met her in Monmouth."

He nodded. "She was shy, but also witty. I could tell right away she was a jewel just waiting to shine."

Daphne's heart twisted. "I can see you loved her."

His features darkened. "I grew to, but I didn't realize it until she was gone. That emotion was completely foreign to me." His gray gaze met hers. "Until you. And this...this is much different from what I felt for Rose. What I feel for you is like a...storm on a summer day. It's calm and beautiful, and then it rages with power and a different kind of beauty.

"When I lost Rose, I fell into despair, but when I thought I lost you at Ashridge Court, I wasn't sure I would continue on after I returned the treasures. Without that purpose and without you—"

She stood on her toes and kissed him hard and fast. "You have me. We have each other."

"I was going to say that I'd considered staying on Flat Holm and becoming a hermit."

She arched a brow at him and tried not to laugh. "Like St. Gildas?"

"Without the sainthood, probably."

Now she did laugh. "Lucky for you, I am here and we have a lifetime ahead of us after we return the treasures to Gareth."

He didn't smile with her. "And what of your father? He's not going to be happy that you betrayed him or that we hid the treasures. I doubt he'll rest until he finds them again."

She walked to the chair and sank into it in defeat. "You're probably right. I have no idea what to do." She looked up at him, feeling helpless. Her father was obsessed, and he'd never rest knowing his daughter knew the location of the Thirteen Treasures.

Gideon sat beside her and took her face in his hands. "I promise you we'll find a way to live without him interfering in our lives."

Daphne didn't know how, but she believed he would try. "I don't want to think about him anymore tonight." She left her chair and hiked up her skirt as she climbed onto his lap, straddling him. He'd shown her how to ride him in bed last night, and she'd enjoyed the power the position had given her.

She pressed down on him, feeling his thickening shaft between her legs. "I think we're wearing too many clothes."

"I think we might break this chair if you try to shag me on it."

She laughed again, so glad for his humor. "Shall we try to find out?"

He shook his head and stood, carrying her up with him. "I have a better idea." He took her to the bed and set her on her feet beside it. "Whoever gets undressed first gets to be on top."

He'd barely finished speaking before she began unbuttoning her cloak. "No fair," she said. "Your cravat was already untied."

"Allow me to rectify that." He reached for her cravat, and untied the knot, then slid it from her neck. Instead of tossing it aside, he looked at it and raised a brow, then laid it on the bed.

She shrugged out of her coat and asked, "Why did you do that?"

He lifted a shoulder. "Might come in handy later. As a blindfold. Or a...restraint."

Heat flooded her body and gathered in her sex. She began to move faster.

"Would you have a preference?" he asked seductively.

"Whatever you think I might like." She sounded breathless and eager. "Never mind. I like everything you do to me."

He leaned forward and drew her earlobe into his mouth, sucking her flesh until she gasped. Raising his mouth, he whispered, "Good thing I have a cravat too."

THE FOLLOWING MORNING dawned gray but calm; however, the captain refused to leave until their scheduled departure time. Frustrated, Gideon returned to the inn where he and Daphne made sure they were prepared. The heart and cloak were in a bag with a long strap that Gideon could wear diagonally around his torso from shoulder to hip. And of course, he would carry Dyrnwyn on his belt.

Daphne surveyed him. "You almost look like a pirate with that beard."

He'd tried to shave that morning, but Daphne had asked him to wait until they were finished with their quest. She'd said he looked dashing. He'd countered that she liked the feel of it in certain places. She'd blushed and said yes, provided he was *careful*.

"I'll take that as a compliment," Gideon said. "Let us be on our way."

"Do you have the blessing Gwyneth gave you?" Daphne asked.

Gideon's eyes widened. It was the thing she'd gone to fetch before they'd left Brue Cottage. "I can't believe it, but I forgot about it." He went to his saddlebag and rummaged around before finding the folded parchment. Turning back to Daphne, he tucked it into his coat. "I'm so glad you remembered."

She smiled at him. "Now we're ready."

They left the inn on foot, and Daphne repeated her hope that Penn would arrive before they departed for Flat Holm. Either way, Argus would join them at the appointed time.

The captain was ready when they arrived at the boat. Jago was a burly man with thick sideburns and a gold tooth. He could have passed for a pirate—or more likely a smuggler—and Gideon wondered if he'd been one at some point during the war with France. He had no plans to ask.

Jago squinted at them. "I thought ye said there were four of ye, maybe five."

"I said there were three for certain and perhaps as many as five," Gideon replied.

"Still only two of ye."

"The third will be along presently."

"We don't have time to waste. You can only stay a few hours on the island before we have to return."

Gideon looked up the street and saw Argus riding toward them. Behind him were…five more horses? As they neared, Gideon recognized Penn and Amelia.

"Is that…Cate and Lord Norris?" Daphne asked.

"I believe it is." Gideon recognized the earl's excellent riding form. The man had clearly spent a good portion of his adult life on a horse. Bringing up the rear was Penn's assistant, Egg.

They arrived at the dock and dismounted. Penn came toward him, and they embraced warmly. "I understand congratulations are in order." Penn turned to Daphne and bowed. "Welcome to the family, Lady Stratton."

"I get to hug her first!" Cate rushed forward and wrapped her arms around Daphne. "I'm so glad you married Gideon. I knew we were meant to be friends, but now we can be so much more." She stood back and beamed.

"I didn't ask you to stop for reinforcements," Gideon said to Penn.

Penn grinned. "No, but they were on the way. If you think Cate would have let us live if we'd left her out of this, you don't know her very well."

"I know her well enough to acknowledge you have the right of it." Gideon took Cate's hand. "My apologies for not summoning you and Norris—we only had a way to contact Oxford." His gaze flicked to Norris, who likely still despised him, which Gideon wholly deserved.

"By pigeon, I heard," Cate said. "I'm looking forward to hearing more about that."

"I can't wait to tell you all about it," Daphne said, her eyes alight.

"We are glad to be here," Norris said. "What you're doing is quite noble."

Gideon appreciated the man's support more than he could say. "Thank you."

"Are we going to bloody Flat Holm Island or not?" Jago asked, disrupting the reunion.

Gideon turned to the captain. "We're going. But we need to stable the horses. Give them ten minutes."

Jago shrugged. "That's ten minutes of time ye're

losing on the island. And the price is the same."

"That's fine," Gideon said. They arranged for Norris, Egg, and Argus to take the horses to the Drunken Mermaid.

As they boarded the boat, Jago counted them. "That's five, then."

"Plus the three who are coming back," Gideon said.

"That's more than five. Ye keep acting as if I can't count. Eight's a tight fit. The price just went up."

Gideon thrust a pouch of coin at the man. "This should be more than enough."

"Aye, it should. Remember, if ye take too long, I'll leave ye there overnight, and if the weather's bad tomorrow, ye may be stuck there for a while. One gent was out there for a week. Found some old graves, though." Jago hadn't mentioned that part before.

"Do you know where?" Gideon asked.

Jago shrugged. "I think they're marked now, but I can't say for sure. It's not a very big island."

Gideon exchanged a look with Daphne and with Penn. "Do you think those could be part of Gareth's burial site?"

"It's hard to say," Penn said with a shrug. "I daresay we'll find out soon."

"Should we split up when we get there?" Daphne asked. "We could cover more ground, since time is apparently short."

"If one team finds it, how do we notify the other?" Penn shook his head. "No, I think we have to stay together.

Gideon agreed. Norris, Egg, and Argus returned, and at last they set out across the channel.

The boat was long, with a crew of four oarsmen, including Jago.

"So you have the cloak?" Cate asked with excitement. "Can we see it before you put it in the tomb?"

Gideon suspected they'd all want to see it before he hid it forever. "Yes, I'm happy to demonstrate it for you." And then he would hide it away forever. "I wonder what the tomb will be like."

"It could be a mound," Penn said. "In which case, I suggest we bury these three treasures as deeply as possible within the mound."

"Or it could just be a burial," Cate said. "My fear is that we won't be able to find it."

They fell silent, perhaps deep in thought as the boat cut through the water. The island came into view, and Gideon could see that it was fairly small. Perhaps it wouldn't be too difficult to find Gareth after all.

"There are a few places to land," Jago said. "I'm going to the closest one on the southeast side."

Gideon's pulse began to speed up as they neared the island. He rested his hand on the hilt of Dyrnwyn and felt the familiar hum.

Jago landed the boat. Penn and Norris disembarked first and helped everyone onto the beach. "Ye've got about two and a half hours," Jago said. "We'll leave without ye if we must."

"Understood." Gideon led the group toward a path that wound up the hillside. The breeze was steady, and the cries of gulls filled the air.

The climb up the path took nearly a quarter hour, and Gideon worried they wouldn't have enough time to complete their search. Perhaps they *should* split up.

However, he didn't have a chance to raise the issue, because the moment he crested the hill, the sound of several pistols cocking jolted him to a stop. Standing before him, flanked by at least a dozen men, was Timothy bloody Foliot.

Chapter Twenty

❦

DAPHNE GRIPPED GIDEON'S hand and squeezed with everything she had. The wind whipped her skirt and tried to take her hat from her head. She couldn't believe her father was here. He had to have followed her. Defeat crushed her chest.

"I'm surprised to see you so far from Ashridge Court," Gideon said, his voice dark.

Lifting a shoulder, Daphne's father seemed quite relaxed. "Sometimes you have to personally see to things, such as when your daughter misleads you and you have to follow her. Welcome to Flat Holm." He grinned and spread his arms out as if they were going to have some sort of celebratory reunion. Daphne's stomach turned.

"How did you find us?" she asked.

Papa pouted at her and took a step forward. "Well, it was no thanks to you, of course. Bardsey Island, indeed. It was clear to me that Gideon had somehow enchanted you—either with the heart or something else." He slid a distasteful look toward Gideon. "You don't really love him," Papa said to her.

Daphne moved closer to her husband. "I do, Papa. I love him more than anything, and it's not because of the Heart of Llanllwch or anything else aside from the man he is. I love his intellect, his kindness, and his honor."

Gideon squeezed her hand back, and she clung to the faith that they would find their way out of this mess—

all of them.

Papa narrowed his eyes at Gideon. "I'm not convinced. Your husband has proven himself to be a blackguard time and again."

Daphne lunged toward him, but Gideon held her back. "Just stop with the lies! You're the blackguard. You had Lord Norris's brother killed, and you kidnapped a vicar to manipulate Gideon to marry me. You're despicable."

Sadness flashed in her father's eyes, but it was quickly replaced with a dark rage. Daphne knew she was seeing the real man. Had he always been that way, or had he somehow become corrupted while she'd failed to notice?

"We'll see if you still think so when we're finished," Papa said coldly.

"Finished doing what exactly?" Penn asked. He'd come to stand on Daphne's other side.

Papa turned a bland smile toward Penn. "We finally meet. You've been a thorn in my side for quite some time, always reaching an artifact or finding a clue before I can. Until Davis and Vincent took the dagger from you. Quite easily, I might add." He flicked a glance toward two of his men who'd stepped forward.

Daphne recognized one as the odious Davis, whom she'd spurned. The other was a large, rather ruthless-looking fellow she vaguely recognized from Ashridge Court. His gaze focused on Penn's wife who had moved to his side. Penn put his arm around her.

"Pleasure to see you again," Vincent said, leering at Amelia. "I believe we have unfinished business." Daphne recalled Gideon telling her yesterday that when Penn had found the dagger, Amelia had tried to steal it from him. She'd actually shot at him and Egg. She and

Gideon had shared many things yesterday. That felt like a lifetime ago.

"Look at her again, and I'll pull your entrails through your nose." Penn's voice carried a deadly ice that matched the cold fury in his gaze.

Vincent laughed, and Davis joined him. Daphne felt Gideon tense. "You were protective of her then too, but we got the dagger anyway," Davis said.

"Until we got it back," Penn taunted.

Scowling, Davis took a step toward Penn.

"Later," Papa said. "Our primary task must be finding Gareth's final resting place. We arrived yesterday, though it was blessed difficult with the weather, and thoroughly searched the island. Unfortunately, we haven't found anything." He fixed Gideon with an expectant stare. "Now that you're here, you can direct us where to go."

"I haven't the vaguest notion." Gideon's response held an edge of triumph as well as defiance.

Papa's face fell. "That's exceedingly disappointing. I suppose we'll have to start digging all over the island. We could be here for days. Maybe even weeks."

"Our boat is waiting for us," Daphne said.

"I can easily pay him to leave," her father said with a careless wave. "He's quite amenable to money. How do you think I learned you'd hired him to bring you here?"

"Prick," Gideon breathed. More loudly, he added, "We're not going to help you."

"Indeed? I think you can be persuaded." Papa inclined his head, and Vincent strode forward to grab Amelia from Penn's side. Penn surged toward the man, but Vincent pointed his pistol at Amelia while Davis directed his weapon between Penn's eyes. "You may want to ask your brother to stand down," Papa said to

Gideon.

"I'm going to kill you," Penn said through his teeth. It wasn't clear if he meant Davis or Vincent or Daphne's father. Probably all of them.

"With my help." Norris had stepped forward, his formidable height and form causing at least one of the retainers to move back.

"Finley, take their pistols before they try something foolish," Davis said.

A lanky fellow with a sharp nose went around and took pistols from all the men. He paused at Argus and looked back toward Davis. "Him too?"

"Argus, come here," Daphne's father said. "Have you also turned against me?"

"You charged me with keeping Lady Stratton safe, and that is what I have done."

Papa cocked his head to the side and exhaled. "For now, yes, him too." Papa gestured for Argus to retreat. Finley took his weapons—a pistol and a long knife, which he knew to ask for.

"Check the women too," Vincent said. He grinned at Amelia. "This one at least knows how to shoot."

"I don't have a pistol," she spat.

Vincent laughed. "I don't believe you. Lift your skirts and show us, or I'll do it for you."

"Touch her, and it's the last thing you'll use your hand for," Penn said.

"Just shut up already," Davis said. "Or I *will* shoot you."

"Not in the head, if you don't mind," Papa said as Amelia lifted her skirt and pulled forth a small pistol, which she angrily thrust at Vincent. "Penn is wickedly good at finding things," Papa continued. "My wager's on him locating this tomb." He turned his attention to

Gideon. "The treasures, please. Starting with the sword." His gaze dipped to the weapon at Gideon's waist.

Gideon's hand had been on the hilt, but in the face of more than a dozen pistols, he apparently hadn't wanted to draw it. That, and Daphne had been clutching his sword hand.

After giving her hand another squeeze, Gideon took the scabbard from his belt. With reluctance she could feel, he handed the sword to her father. "You're actually going to touch it?" he asked with sarcastic heat. "You refrained before because touching the treasures would have revealed you aren't a descendant. We all know that now."

Papa glared at him. "You know nothing. I *am* a descendant, regardless of what nonsense you heard and put in my Daphne's head."

"Then take the sword from the scabbard. Let's watch it flame." Gideon's lips spread in a feral smile. "I'd be happy to threaten you with mortal danger to provoke its power."

But her father wouldn't be goaded. His gaze turned frigid. "I presume the heart and the cloak are in the bag around your middle?"

Gideon whisked it over his head and threw it at her father's feet. "This is temporary. I'll be taking those back for Gareth shortly."

Papa winced and handed the sword to the man nearest him. "Carry this. It's heavy."

"It will be for everyone but me," Gideon said. "Only a descendant can easily carry it."

"He's right." This came from Cate. "Let him take it."

The wind gusted, surprising everyone, and Penn lunged at Davis. Vincent pressed his pistol to Amelia's temple. "Don't make me shoot the pretty. That's not in my plans, and you'll make me angry if you foil my plans again."

Penn retreated, but Davis shoved him to the ground. "Stay there."

Penn lay on his back, his blue eyes spitting fire and the promise of violence. "Vincent, before this day is out, you're going to be dead."

Vincent howled with laughter. "Doubtful. You may be, however."

"Enough," Papa said. "We must get to work. Penn, make yourself useful, and I'll see Vincent leaves your wife alone. Though, I'm quite furious with the both of you for costing me Forrest."

Papa was referring to Amelia's former husband, whom Gideon had also told her about yesterday. He'd worked for Daphne's father and had been tasked with taking the Heart of Llanllwch from Amelia and Penn, but he'd died trying.

Gideon had been right about Camelot and about Daphne's father—they were evil. Her mind scrambled as to how they were going to escape this. She didn't think her father would hurt her. It seemed he believed she was still under a spell. Could she somehow pretend to break it again? She wasn't sure he'd believe her a second time, especially since it seemed he hadn't believed her the first time.

How was it that she'd been able to convince him she loved Gideon when they'd first met at Ashridge Court but not that she hated him? Because her father believed what he wanted to, which was for her to be loyal to him. It was the only way he could reason that out in his mind. He was, she realized, mad.

"Let us walk around the island and assess the

landscape," Penn said, exchanging a look with Gideon.

"I suppose that's a place to start," Papa said with resignation. "Davis, assign everyone to a captor. Except Daphne. She'll come with me." He bent to pick up the bag with the heart and cloak.

Davis looked profoundly disappointed but went about assigning at least one guard to everyone in their party. There were fourteen of them, plus her father, so they had enough to assign two to each of the men.

Norris went to help Penn stand while Gideon turned to Daphne and brushed a kiss against her temple. "I won't be far behind," he said. "I'm not going to let anything happen to you."

She nodded and went haltingly to stand with her father. Deciding to try to go along with his madness, she asked, "Do you really think I'm still under a spell?"

"Of course you are, dear. Why else would you be helping that man instead of me?"

Because you're insane?

Her father scowled at the guard who was trying—and failing—to carry the sword. He kept having to put it down. "Bloody well give it to Gideon, then." Papa whirled on Gideon. "Try to take it from the scabbard, and we'll shoot Penn. Or his wife. Or both."

With an expression of relief, the guard handed the sword to Gideon, who easily took it up and reattached it to his belt. He put his hand on the hilt and gave a dark look that dared anyone to tell him not to.

A few moments later, they started along the path, and her father explained that it rounded the island. It didn't take them long to walk to the opposite end of Flat Holm. It was rather flat with long grasses and large shrubs, and short, stubby trees. Likely the wind didn't allow anything to grow very tall.

"Stop."

The single word from Gideon drew Daphne and her father to turn to where he stood just behind them, flanked by two of her father's guards.

"What is it?" Papa asked, his voice full of anticipation.

"I think we're close." Gideon looked around. "But there's nothing here."

Papa stared at him with deep intensity. "Why do you think we're close?"

"The sword is vibrating." He fixed her father with a steely stare. "It…communicates with me."

Papa's brows dipped low as he eyed Gideon with suspicion. "You think it's trying to tell you the tomb is close? How would it know?"

"How the hell does it flame when I wield it? How does the cloak render me invisible? If I knew how any of it worked, I could make more treasures."

Her father's eyes lit. "You could?"

Daphne could practically see his mind turning with ideas, and she was afraid of where they might lead. "Papa, he doesn't know how."

"That doesn't mean he can't learn." Papa smiled. "Something for us to explore! And a reason to keep you alive, although until you plant your seed in my daughter and ensure the continuation of Gareth's line, you are incredibly valuable to me."

Horrified, Daphne gaped at her father. "That was your intent?"

Papa took her hand. "You will be mother to a future king! Just think of it. We'll have the treasures and a child worthy of the throne. Camelot will be reborn!"

He was beyond mad. Daphne feared he was irretrievably gone in the head. Her chest ached, and her throat burned.

"We have to find the treasures first," Gideon said. "The tomb is close. The sword's vibration has grown increasingly stronger as we moved in this direction." He kept walking, moving off the path and through the grass to look out over the water. This side of the island had tall rock faces that extended into the sea so that there was a literal edge one could fall from.

Gideon turned, the horizon at his back. "It's here. The sword is fairly humming. It knows it's almost where it belongs."

"Well, it's not staying here," Papa said sharply, joining Gideon at the edge of the cliff, but leaving several feet between them. Still, it would be easy for Gideon to simply push him over... Was she really thinking of killing her father?

Daphne shook her head and blinked away tears. How had it all come to this?

Papa turned and looked at Davis. "There were caves in the rocks, weren't there, when we took the boat around the island?"

Davis nodded. "A few." He strode to the cliff's edge and looked over. "Down there."

"That may be it," Papa said. "Gideon, Daphne, and I will go look."

Gideon shook his head. "Not Daphne. She stays up here. I'll go with you. And Penn. He should come in case we need his...expertise." Gideon looked to his brother, who nodded with an air of malicious anticipation.

Papa chuckled. "Penn's not going anywhere near that cave. Come, let's find a path. Or make one."

Daphne went to join them and looked over the edge of the island. The rock face was almost entirely vertical.

There were a few places to perhaps walk, but it looked treacherous, particularly with the wind. "Papa, that looks awfully dangerous."

He gave her an encouraging nod. "It will be fine, my dear."

"No." Gideon stepped toward her father. "She's not going."

Papa inclined his head toward Davis, and everything happened very quickly.

Vincent gripped Amelia tightly. Davis hit Penn in the head with the butt of his pistol, sending Penn to his knees. Another of the men dragged Cate to the cliff and held her at the very edge by the arm, his intent to let her go quite clear.

Norris howled and lunged toward her, heedless of the men at his sides. A pistol fired, and Norris reeled, clutching his hip.

Cate cried out, and Gideon pulled Dyrnwyn loose. The blade shimmered with pale blue flame, and he held it toward her father. Gideon was close enough that he could easily kill her father, and Daphne wasn't sure she could stop him. Or if she would.

"Tell them to stop," Gideon growled. "Or you die."

"They'll just kill you all," Papa responded, his voice deep with certainty. "Besides, you won't kill me. Not with Daphne watching. She would never forgive you."

"I thought you said she was under my spell. If that's the case, I could do anything, and she'd still be in my thrall."

Daphne felt as if her entire body were pulled taut, just waiting to shatter at the slightest movement.

The man holding Cate pushed her over the edge so that if he let go, she'd tumble to the rocks below.

"Gideon!" The plea came from Norris, whose hip

was turning red with blood.

Anguish lined Gideon's face. He sheathed Dyrnwyn and bared his teeth at her father. "We're going to the cave now. If anything happens to anyone up here, I will kill you without a second thought, and I don't give a damn who sees it." He didn't spare a glance for Daphne. She could sense the fury radiating from his body.

"You first," her father said, gesturing to a place where the rock face was more sloped than straight.

Gideon looked to Penn and Norris and then to Cate, who was now safely away from the edge of the cliff. Then he took Daphne's hand, and they walked to the top of the path. But it wasn't really a path. Just the only way that might take them to the cave. If they were careful.

The slope was steep and the way narrow. The rocks were also slick. "Hold anything you can, including me," Gideon said, letting go of her hand as he made his way down.

"I'll go next," Papa said, earning another scowl from Gideon. "I'll make sure you don't fall, my girl." Papa gave her a loving smile that made her want to vomit.

Daphne followed them down, and it was several long, arduous minutes before they saw an opening. It required a long step over a wide void to get there, however. Daphne held her breath as she watched Gideon grip the rock and swing his leg onto the lip of the opening. His foot slipped, and Daphne shrieked.

But he didn't fall. He clutched at the rock, and his foot found purchase. Then he disappeared into the opening. Her father followed but went more slowly.

A moment later, Gideon stuck his head out of the cave and reached for Daphne. "Give me your hand and put your other hand on the rock. I won't let you fall."

Her legs were nowhere near as long as Gideon's. Fear paralyzed her for a moment.

"You can do it, Daphne," Gideon urged softly.

She took a deep breath. And a huge leap of faith.

Gideon clasped her hand and held her tightly. She never would have made it on her own—he all but dragged her into the cave. As soon as she put both feet on the rock floor, she threw her arms around him.

The cock of her father's pistol sounded, echoing behind him. "Now you may drop Dyrnwyn," he said to Gideon, aiming the pistol at his heart. "As I said, I don't wish to kill you, but I will if it becomes necessary. I'll find another descendant."

"We may need the sword for light," Gideon said, and Daphne was impressed with his ingenuity. He was also right—the cave was bound to be as black as a moonless night.

Papa narrowed his eyes. "You raise a valid point. But if you come after me again, I won't hesitate to shoot you. Now, let's see what we can find, shall we?" Papa said with glee, motioning for them to precede him to the back of the cave.

Daphne took Gideon's hand, and they stepped into the darkness.

Chapter Twenty-one

GIDEON PULLED DYRNWYN from the scabbard, and the light seemed bluer and brighter than it ever had before, even at Ashridge Court a few days before. Was that because it was so close to the other treasures?

It was all Gideon could do to keep from plunging the blade directly into Foliot's cold, black heart. But when he thought of killing Daphne's father in front of her, his gut churned and he just couldn't do it.

Still, they had to find a way to keep him from obtaining the treasures.

The cave went back quite far, curving to the left. Then suddenly they were in a large chamber. In the center was a raised platform on which sat a stone sarcophagus.

"It's him," Foliot breathed.

Gideon's anger dissipated for a moment as he felt a surge of connection to whatever was in the tomb—he knew Gareth was here.

Foliot moved past the sarcophagus. "The treasures! Bring the light!"

Gideon followed him, glancing at Daphne as they walked. At the back of the cave stood a chariot. It looked like drawings he'd seen of Roman vehicles—two wheels with a shaft and a yoke. The wood gleamed with a luster that belied its age.

Foliot touched the carriage. "This would take you anywhere you needed to go faster than is currently possible. We could likely get to London from here in a day. Can you imagine?"

Daphne went to a table on which sat several treasures. The basket of plenty that would replenish food at will and a horn that granted the drinker whatever beverage they desired.

"Then there's this," Foliot said, gesturing to the halter hanging over the side of the carriage of the chariot. "This halter would summon any horse to your side."

Gideon joined Daphne at the table. He touched the knife that would cut anything, whether at a feast or in battle, along with the whetstone on which blades sharpened by a brave man would kill their victims. However, blades sharpened by a coward would do nothing. Gideon slid a glance at Foliot, thinking the whetstone would do nothing for him. Just as the cauldron would also likely do nothing. Only meat put in by a brave man would cook.

The final items on the table were the crock and dish, which worked much like the horn, providing whatever food a person would want.

Gideon looked about. "Where is the chessboard?"

The thirteenth treasure was an enchanted chessboard that would act as opponent to whoever played it. Alone as he'd been, Gideon had once thought it might be a good thing to have. Now, he only wanted to play chess—hopefully the naked variety—with Daphne.

"Here," Foliot said from behind them. Another small table sat in the corner of the cave, the chessboard atop it. He turned and looked at Gideon. "Aren't you tempted to use one of the treasures?"

"Not particularly." He was, however, tempted to study them, especially with Penn and Cate. But that wasn't his quest—he would leave the treasures with

Gareth, as they were meant to be.

Foliot directed his attention to the chessboard. "You're a fool."

Daphne pulled Gideon close to her and picked up the horn. "You can summon any drink," she whispered. "You could wish for ale with the sleeping tonic."

He kissed her cheek. "You really are the most brilliant woman." Gideon looked over at Foliot. How would they take him from the cave if he was asleep?

"How will we get these out?" Foliot's query filled the cave as he regarded the chariot. "This one in particular will be a problem. I wonder if the cave continues on and comes out somewhere." He walked to the smaller opening in the rock behind the chariot.

"Foliot, we can't get the chariot out," Gideon said. "You'll need to leave it behind."

Foliot joined them at the table. "We aren't leaving any of it behind." His gaze gleamed as he studied the treasures before him.

"I changed my mind," Gideon said, picking up the horn. He wished for ale laced with enough sleeping tonic to make the drinker sleep for a day. "Would you care for some ale?" He offered Foliot the horn.

Foliot took it and looked inside, his eyes lighting. "Wonderful!" He lifted it to his lips, then frowned. "What is it?"

"Just ale," Gideon said.

Frowning, Foliot set it down and backed away. "Then why didn't you drink it?"

"I was being polite by offering it to you first. I'll drink it." Gideon picked up the horn and ignored the alarm lighting Daphne's eyes. Before the liquid reached his lips, he wished for it to be replaced with regular ale.

As he drank, he prayed the horn was working as he directed. When he finished, he wished for the sleeping tonic to be added once more, then handed the horn to Foliot with a smile. "Delicious."

Foliot took the vessel but didn't lift it to his mouth. His gaze was dark and suspicious, and Gideon feared the man was coming to the conclusion that it was necessary to kill Gideon after all.

"You're persuading me as to the benefit of these treasures," Gideon said, hoping to break through the man's lunacy.

"How can I know you actually drank any of this?" Foliot asked. His paranoia was evident in the thin tenor of his question and the wild light in his eyes. "You've demonstrated over and over that you can't be trusted. Even though you're a descendant, your usefulness has come to an end. I must eliminate those who fail to support my objectives." He flicked a sad look toward Daphne. "Your mother did that—she learned I wasn't a descendant and threatened to tell the Order. As if they would have listened to her. Still, I couldn't risk her spreading lies."

Daphne's jaw dropped open, and her eyes were wide with shock and a myriad of other dark emotions. Gideon's heart ached for her and the pain her father had mercilessly thrust upon her.

"You killed my mother?" She sounded so small and scared and wounded. In that moment, Gideon truly wanted to kill Foliot.

"I'm sorry, Daphne." Foliot lifted his pistol, and Gideon's pulse sped. He raised Dyrnwyn in response. But before he could strike, Daphne lunged forward with the knife and drove it straight into her father's heart.

Gideon gasped.

Foliot's eyes widened. "My girl?"

Tears streamed down Daphne's face. "I'm sorry, Papa. You're mad. You're…evil. I can't let you hurt anyone else. And not Gideon—I love him."

Foliot fell to the floor, his hand coming up to the knife protruding from his chest. "When you awaken from the spell, you'll be devastated." He looked to Gideon. "What have you done to us?"

Blood gurgled from Foliot's mouth as he collapsed backward. He twitched once and then stilled, his eyes staring, unseeing, at the roof of the cave.

Gideon turned to Daphne and wasn't sure what to do. Shock etched her features, and despair curled her body forward as she clapped her hand over her mouth.

"Daphne." He couldn't find any words that would ease this moment.

Her shoulders shook, and she turned to look at him, lowering her hand. "I had to do that." The words held no emotion. "He killed my mother. He was going to kill you."

"Yes, he was." Gideon had felt the truth of it in the sword. Whenever he was threatened, it vibrated strongly, but even more so when the risk was imminent and powerful. "I'm so sorry, Daphne."

She fell forward, and he caught her sobbing form. He dropped the sword to the floor and gathered her close, stroking her back and hair and murmuring words of love and comfort.

Abruptly, she pulled back. "We need to hurry. Norris is hurt."

"Yes, and we need to get back for the boat. If it's not too late."

"Papa came on a boat. We can use that one if we

must."

Gideon nodded. "But first, the treasures." And then they'd have to deal with Foliot's men. Gideon turned to Foliot and exhaled. "Daphne, look away."

He didn't turn his head to make sure she did as he asked—it was her choice. Gideon bent and pulled the knife from Foliot's chest. Blood pooled over his coat, and Gideon wiped the blade over the man's midsection to clean it. He set the weapon on the table, then went back to Foliot, opening the bag and removing the Heart of Llanllwch and the cloak.

Standing, he considered putting them on the table, but they seemed more important than what was there. Instead, he went to the sarcophagus and stood on the platform beneath it so he could see the top of the lid. A large cross was carved into the stone on the upper portion. Gideon placed the heart in the center of it, then he draped the cloak over the lower half of the sarcophagus.

He turned and removed the scabbard from his belt. Then he went and picked up Dyrnwyn and sheathed it. He clasped Daphne's hand and led her back to the sarcophagus. Letting her go, he set the sword on top in the center.

"You really mean to just leave them all here?" she asked, her voice small and soft.

"I have to," Gideon said. "They are remarkable, but it's my duty to keep them hidden. I felt it from the moment I first wielded Dyrnwyn, and meeting Gwyneth convinced me completely. Speaking of Gwyneth, there is one more thing I must do." He took Gwyneth's parchment from his coat pocket and read the Old Welsh enchantment she'd given him before they'd left Brue Cottage:

*Bless this place and the treasures within. May
Gareth rest here forever undisturbed.*

He refolded the paper and, on a whim, placed it atop
the casket between the heart and the top of the sword.
He said a silent prayer for his ancestor, and then started
when a rock fell from the ceiling. The ground began to
shake, and terror gripped his heart.

He grabbed Daphne's hand. "We need to go!"

She pulled on him turning toward the back of the
cave. "What about my father?"

"We can't worry about him now. The cave is
collapsing!" Gideon tugged her toward the opening,
hoping he could remember the way since they were
now running in the darkness with rocks tumbling
around them.

Dust rose in the air, and he coughed as he fought to
propel them forward. After what seemed a frightening
eternity, he glimpsed light ahead. It grew brighter, and
he went faster. The opening of the cave shrank as rocks
fell and covered the entrance.

Pulling Daphne in front of him, he nudged her to the
edge of the cave. "You have to move quickly. I'll be
right behind you. Grab the rock like you did last time."

She shook her head. "My legs aren't long enough to
bridge the gap. You have to go first."

She was right, dammit. He squeezed past her and
clasped the jut of rock, then swung himself to the path.
He reached back and shouted, "Take my hand."

A rock fell, hitting his wrist. Pain shot up his arm,
but he put his hand back for her to clasp. "Daphne!
Hurry!"

She scrambled from the cave, raising her arm and

trying to find the outcropping amidst the falling debris. She wasn't moving swiftly enough. The rocks beneath her feet began to split. Gideon's heart stopped—she wasn't going to make it.

He grabbed hold of whatever rock he could find and prayed it wouldn't come loose. Throwing his arm out, he clasped her wrist and pulled with everything he had.

Her feet swung free, and she shrieked. Gideon brought her against him. "Hold on!"

She threw her arm around his neck and climbed onto his back. He worked to get them more securely onto the path that wasn't really a path. He clambered up along the rocks as dust and pebbles and larger pieces cascaded around them. It was as if the world was falling apart.

At last they neared the top. Suddenly, there was a hand reaching for them. "Give me your hand!"

It was Penn.

"Take Daphne!" Gideon yelled. "Daphne, grab hold of Penn."

Penn extended his hand and clasped Daphne, pulling her from Gideon's back and bringing her to safety atop the cliff's edge. Gideon reached for the ground, but the rock beneath him gave way, and he slipped.

"Gideon! I'm coming!" Penn threw himself down and reached over the side. "Take my hand!"

Gideon stretched his arm, the one that wasn't throbbing from the falling rock that had struck his wrist, and just barely managed to touch Penn's fingers. He couldn't get the purchase he needed to go that extra inch.

Penn compensated, however, reaching farther and grasping Gideon securely. "I've got you now, and I'm not letting go."

Gideon met Penn's deep-blue gaze and saw a depth of emotion: bravery, desperation, love. How had he ever felt alone?

Gideon used his other hand to push himself up, wincing as pain lanced through his wrist. Penn pulled him up and over the cliff's edge, but they didn't linger on the ground.

"Where's everyone else?" Gideon asked, looking around as Daphne rushed to his side and put her arms around his waist. He held her tight for a brief moment, looking over her head at Penn.

"When the ground started to shake, these two tried to take Amelia and Cate with them to their boat." Penn's gaze drifted to two bodies on the ground—Davis and Vincent.

"But you didn't let them."

Penn shook his head. "While we dealt with them, the rest ran off. Come on, we need to hurry." He paused. "Where's Foliot?"

Gideon shook his head but said nothing. Penn gave a slight nod, his mouth set in a grim line and his gaze acknowledging what Gideon was trying to communicate.

They started to run along the path, and Gideon took hold of Daphne's hand once more. Halfway to the other side of the island, the earth stilled. They stopped and looked around.

"It's over," Gideon said. He squeezed Daphne's hand.

"Can we go back?" she asked. "To get my father?"

Gideon hated the sadness and regret in her voice. "I don't think we can. The words Gwyneth gave me— they're a spell that will hide the cave and everything inside it forever."

"So if we did go back, what would we see?" Penn asked.

"Probably nothing?" Gideon guessed. "We could go look, but we'll be stuck on the island for certain."

"We shouldn't risk it. You did what you set out to do—the treasures are safe and where they are meant to be," Penn said with a hint of resignation.

"I'm sorry you didn't get to see them," Gideon said. "Truly." He wished this had all happened so differently. And it might have if not for Foliot. He looked at Daphne, whose shoulders still drooped. Sadness lined her face, and Gideon hated Foliot anew for what he'd made her do.

"Let's get to the beach," Penn urged. "Argus and Egg helped Norris to the boat with Amelia and Cate."

"How is he?" Daphne asked, sounding small and terrified at Gideon's side as they hurried along the path.

"Disagreeable," Penn said. "We've kept something on the wound, and the bleeding seems to have slowed. It looks like the lead may have just nicked him."

"Thank God," Gideon said as they neared the path that led down to the boat.

They ran to the beach, and Jago scowled at them from the boat. "Ye owe me more money now since we had to wait." He looked around, his gaze wary. "At least that earthquake stopped."

Gideon had reached his limit. He stalked onto the boat and right up to Jago until their chests touched. Gideon had several inches on the man, and glared down into his shocked eyes. "Since you took extra money from the man who tried to kill us, I'm going to call it even. *Let's go.*"

Daphne moved past him and went to sit next to Cate, who was holding Norris's hand and generally fussing over him. Gideon collapsed beside Daphne, the stress of the day pouring out of him. He began to shake.

"Gideon, are you all right?" Cate asked in concern.

"When I think of how close I came to losing all of you…" He looked around at the faces of the people he loved, and his breath twisted until he gasped.

Daphne took his hand and pressed herself to his side. "It's all my fault."

Everyone snapped their gazes to her, but it was Cate who spoke first. "Don't be ridiculous." She flinched. "Sorry, you aren't being ridiculous. But it wasn't in any way your fault. You aren't to be blamed for your father's crimes."

"He was horrible. I had no idea what he was capable of. What he actually *did*." Her shoulders began to tremble, and Gideon knew she was reliving what had happened in the cave, particularly the revelation about her mother. He gathered her close and held her tight to his side.

"What happened down there?" Penn asked from Gideon's left, where he sat next to Amelia. "Did something trigger the earthquake, or was that just a stroke of luck?"

"It wasn't lucky for us," Gideon said. "We barely escaped the cave. Foliot was still inside."

Cate lifted her hand to her mouth and looked at Daphne in sympathy. "Oh dear. I'm so sorry, Daphne."

"He was already dead," she said, her voice suddenly flat. "I had to stab him to protect Gideon."

Amelia reached over and touched Daphne's hand. "Any of us would have done the same."

Gideon sought to redirect the conversation. He stroked Daphne's back while he spoke. "I put the treasures on Gareth's sarcophagus."

"He *was* there?" Penn asked, and Gideon could hear the longing in his voice. How he would have loved to see the tomb.

Again, Gideon regretted Penn not being able to study the treasures. "Far back in the cave, there was a room. He was on a platform, in a stone sarcophagus. A simple cross was engraved on the top. I set the heart on the cross, draped the cloak at his feet, and placed Dyrnwyn in between."

"Then he read a blessing," Daphne said softly. "It was some sort of enchantment, and I think it started the earthquake to destroy the cave so that it can't be found again."

Gideon had wondered the same thing—because of who had given him the words to read. He would ask Gwyneth when he saw her next, but already knew in his heart that he'd done what he needed to protect Gareth and the treasures for all time.

"What blessing?" Penn asked.

Flashing a brief smile at his brother, Gideon said, "We have much to tell you."

Penn put his arm around his wife and grinned. "And I can't wait to hear it."

THEY RETURNED TO the Drunken Mermaid, filling the place to the brim. Egg and Argus had to take lodging in the stables.

Penn and Egg had immediately located a surgeon, who'd come to stitch Norris up. He'd had a great deal of brandy since then and was fighting to keep his eyes open as they sat in the common room following dinner.

Daphne felt utterly numb. She wasn't sure what was harder to believe, that her father had been such a villain or that she'd killed him. Gideon had reminded her multiple times that her father had been mad. Daphne couldn't stop asking herself why she'd never seen it.

Because he'd been adept at hiding it from her, which meant he hadn't been *that* insane. He'd been manipulative and malevolent. He'd also been caring and supportive, but in retrospect, he'd been guided almost entirely by his own ends. What sort of father suggested a man maneuver his daughter into marriage? He'd done precisely that when he'd counseled Gideon to use the Heart of Lllanllwch.

She was having a very hard time reconciling the father she'd known and loved with the blackguard who'd committed so many crimes, including trying to kill her husband. Perhaps the hardest thing to accept was that she'd do it again—kill her father—to save Gideon.

She leaned over to Gideon and whispered, "I'm going to retire." She just couldn't spend another moment with these people who had risked themselves to help her and Gideon.

Gideon nodded, then took her hand and pressed a kiss to the back.

"Wait, where are you going?" Cate asked, her brow creasing. "You can't go yet."

Daphne worked to summon a weak smile. "I'm exhausted."

"I was shot." Norris's drunken pronouncement drew chuckles from the assembly, including Daphne, who was glad to have a bit of humor. Norris tried to focus on Daphne. "I suspect you feel guilty, but you can't. No one here blames you. The only person I blame is him." He jabbed his thumb toward Gideon. "Or at least I did for a while. He's brought himself up to snuff."

"More than," Penn said, giving Gideon a warm, heartfelt stare.

"I was deserving of blame," Gideon said before turning his attention to Daphne. "You are not."

"I know this is a terrible time," Cate said to Daphne. "But if you go upstairs, you won't have us to cheer you up. We're a family. That's what we do." She smiled broadly, and then Norris's head slumped over on her shoulder.

Cate exhaled loudly. "Oh dear, I suppose we must pour Elijah into bed. Egg, will you help me?"

Argus stood. "We'll manage him, my lady." He and Egg, a somewhat crotchety little man who also managed to be endearing, particularly in the way he cared for Penn and Amelia, roused Norris enough to muscle him to the bedchamber located on the ground level. It was a small room, but they thought it best for Norris to avoid the stairs.

Cate came over to Daphne and bent to hug her. Daphne rose and met her halfway, welcoming her embrace.

"I'm so glad to have you in our family," Cate said, smiling. "Everything's going to be all right—you'll see." She trailed after the trio of men into the chamber she occupied with Norris.

Daphne sat back down, and Penn filled their glasses—sherry for the ladies and brandy for him and Gideon. Argus and Egg returned and immediately excused themselves to head to the stables.

"Are you sure Elijah should travel tomorrow?" Amelia asked. She sat close beside Penn, across the table from Daphne and Gideon.

"He was adamant," Penn said. "Right now, he outranks all of us. Until Gideon secures his title."

"*If* I secure it," Gideon said. "Foliot never said what happened to the vicar and his proof."

Penn's eyes narrowed with determination. "Which is why we're riding for Ashridge Court first thing."

Daphne had thought about this the last few hours, now that she fully knew her sire. "I would be willing to wager that my father took the proof from the vicar the moment he kidnapped him. He would have kept it, of course, but it's either in his vault or somewhere else." She looked at Penn. "We'll find it, and you can do with it what you will."

"I hope you're right," Penn said. "Gideon is the rightful earl. I wouldn't have the faintest idea how to run Stratton Hall, nor do I want to learn." He shuddered and kissed Amelia's temple.

"He can't very well work at the Ashmolean and travel all over Britain if he has to care for an estate," Amelia said.

"*We* can't travel all over Britain," Penn clarified, looking at his wife with love. "I have a partner now."

How lovely that sounded. Daphne cast a sideways look at Gideon. Were they partners? She'd said they were in this together, but "this" was over now. They'd completed Gideon's mission. They loved each other— of that she was certain—but they hadn't discussed even one day of the future that lay before them.

Amelia yawned, and Penn finished his brandy. "Time for us to retire too. We'll see you in the morning."

Gideon tipped the rest of his brandy back, then set

his empty glass on the table. "Drink up, Lady Stratton."

Daphne sipped her sherry but didn't finish it. She turned to him and searched his gaze. "I don't need to remain Lady Stratton."

His brow knitted. "I don't want an annulment, do you? Besides, it looks as though my plan to use fraud as a basis for it won't work. Penn is going to move heaven and earth to keep that vicar quiet. He wanted to leave tonight, but Amelia talked sense into him."

"No, I don't want an annulment. But Gideon, I don't know where to go from here." Her heart felt so hollow and yet full at the same time. When she looked at her husband and felt the support of his family around her, she glimpsed a future she wanted so very badly.

"Then it's a good thing I do." He winked at her as he stood from the table. Then he swept her into his arms and carried her upstairs.

Daphne couldn't help but smile. "Where are we going?"

"To bed, of course." He bounded up the stairs and bore her into their room, where a pleasant fire crackled. Gideon set her down and shook out his wrist before turning toward the door and closing it.

"Your arm must hurt," Daphne said. She'd made sure the surgeon had looked at it after tending to Norris. It wasn't broken, but it was swollen.

"Yes, but not too much to carry my wife, who weighs next to nothing. It's also quite capable of undressing said wife." He came toward her with seductive intent.

She held up her hand. "Gideon, wait. How can you still love me after what I did today?"

He closed the distance between them and took her in his arms. "I will love you every day no matter what you do."

"How can you say that? I took another person's life… My father—"

He brought her against his chest. "Shh. I've done plenty of things I regret, and I didn't have half the reason you did. I know it's going to take time, but you mustn't blame yourself."

"That's the problem," Daphne said, pulling back to look up into his beloved face. "I'm incredibly sad, but I don't regret what I did. I would do it again to save you." She reached up and cupped his cheek. "Perhaps you should shave in the morning." He laughed softly, and she rushed on. "I've never felt a connection to anyone the way I feel with you. I didn't realize what I'd been missing or, really, what I'd been searching for. You've given me a family. A home."

"And you've given those things to me. Whatever else your father did, he brought us together. For that, I will be eternally grateful."

She hadn't thought of that. Suddenly she felt a flash of peace. "Thank you." She stood on her toes and kissed him.

And then he did what he'd promised and took her to bed.

Epilogue

One Week Later

"SO MANY MEN here… It's so *odd*." Gwyneth shook her head at the congregation of people in the library at Brue Cottage.

Gideon took a tally. Besides him, there was Penn, Elijah—who was doing very well, particularly since coming under Gwyneth's care—Rhys, and Septon. "We appreciate your hospitality."

Indeed, Gideon was still a bit surprised she'd opened Brue Cottage to them. Three days ago, he'd brought Elijah here so that Gwyneth could tend his wound, which had started to fester. She'd taken them in immediately and set about working her magic, perhaps literally, on Elijah. Today, it was as if he'd never been shot.

"Rhys seems to be enjoying the Beckery Texts," Gwyneth said, eyeing the worktable where Rhys was poring over the ancient manuscript. Septon was at his side, equally rapt over a second manuscript, while Penn studied the third.

Gideon chuckled. "They all are."

"Do you have an appropriate place to keep them at Stratton Hall?" she asked.

"There's a locked library there where my father kept his meager collection of valuable antiquities. It will suit. However, I plan to allow Rhys to keep the texts for as long as he likes."

"That's very generous of you," she noted. "What of the Nash chest?"

"That is coming with us to Stratton Hall."

The question of the earldom had been settled. Upon arriving at Ashridge Court, they were surprised to find Septon there. His men had finally rescued the vicar, who reported that Foliot had indeed taken his ledger. When he'd asked for it back, Daphne had told him, regretfully, that it had been destroyed. Then she and Gideon had found it in her father's vault and given it to Penn, who'd gleefully burned it to ash in the massive fireplace in the great hall.

"But you'll have to hold on to the chest a bit longer because Daphne and I must first go to London."

"Ah yes, you have an earldom to claim." Gwyneth cocked her head. "Such an auspicious title you have— Gideon the Worthy, Earl of Stratton."

"Also Viscount Kersey. Which I will share with my son, who will use the title as a courtesy." His gaze strayed to Daphne where she sat at the end of the worktable with Cate, looking at Morgan's writings.

"Come, I want to speak with Daphne," Gwyneth said, starting to turn.

"Just a moment," Gideon said, halting her movement. "Tell me what happened at the cave." He'd already described the tomb to her and how the enchantment had seemed to start an earthquake, but hadn't wanted to ask about whether the treasures—and Gareth—were hidden forever.

She gave him a mildly perplexed look. "I wasn't there. How can I tell you what happened?"

"What I mean is, what happened to the treasures? Can someone go and dig through the rubble to find them?"

"Ah, I see. I don't know for certain of course, but I believe when you said the enchantment, you triggered the collapse as well as a spell that will hide the treasures—and Gareth—forever."

"Not even the Worthy can find them again?" he asked, thinking that maybe, just maybe, he might try to find them with Penn and Cate someday. They would love to see them.

She arched a shoulder. "Who knows? But I would caution you against seeking them again, unless you are certain your objectives are pure. And even then, you may wish to leave them buried. You saw what they did to Foliot." She cast a look toward Daphne. Then Gwyneth abruptly turned and strode toward the table, her bright turquoise skirts billowing about her ankles. Gideon followed her.

"Daphne, I want you to have one of those recipes," Gwyneth said. "You won't be able to say it was authored by Morgan, but it will support the Elidyr text that calls her by name."

Daphne blinked up at her. "You mean the one Septon brought?" He'd presented the original, which he'd somehow obtained from the Order, to Gwyneth when he'd arrived earlier.

"Yes. I want you to have that too. That way, you can prove Morgana's existence—and the credit of the discovery shall be yours."

Joy spread over Daphne's face, and Gideon stifled the urge to hug Gwyneth. Instead, he leaned toward her and whispered, "Thank you."

"She deserves that," Gwyneth said, turning to the bookshelves. "I have other things to give you. You'll need something more than that and your chest to start a decent library if you want to compete with Rhys or

Septon."

Gideon laughed. "I don't think I could."

Septon stood from the table. "I'd like to give you some things too. As a wedding gift." He smiled at Gideon and then Daphne.

"And what shall I give you in return?" Gideon asked. His mother and Septon planned to marry after Gideon and Daphne finished their business in London.

Septon looked toward Gideon's mother, who sat across the room with Margery, Amelia, and Elijah, who was relaxing with his feet up. "You've already given me too much," Septon said, his eyes glazing with tears.

The great love Septon had for Gideon's mother was palpable, and when Gideon looked at Daphne, he knew he'd do anything to have her at his side. Perhaps he'd found it within himself to forgive Septon after all.

Much later, after a long dinner during which daring tales and raucous laughter were shared, followed by more storytelling in the library, Gideon guided Daphne into their bedchamber—the very one in which they'd first consummated their union.

As soon as the door closed, she began to strip his clothes away, and he did the same for her. Within minutes, they tumbled to the bed, and Daphne pushed herself on top of him.

He lay on his back and arched a brow as she kissed his chest and worked her way down his body. She didn't pause long at his cock, which made him rise up on an elbow to see what she was about.

She knelt between his legs and traced her finger over the tattoo on his calf. "Will you stay in the Order?"

He propped himself up on an elbow and looked down at her. "No. I wish I could remove that."

She skimmed her hand up his leg, over his knee, and

along his thigh. "Perhaps you could change it into something else."

That was an excellent idea. "I hadn't considered that. Earlier, I asked Septon what the Order would do now that the treasures are hidden forever."

Daphne's hand stilled, which was good because it allowed Gideon to think more clearly, but bad because he'd rather lose his mind to her for the next while. "Are they?" she asked.

"That's what Gwyneth believes. The enchantment will ensure no one can find them." He hesitated before revealing the rest. He wouldn't keep secrets from her. "*I* could find them—probably. But I won't."

She looked up at him. "Not even to share them with Penn and Cate?"

"It's tempting, but no, I think it's best they remain hidden."

Her gaze warmed with emotion. "I think that's very astute—and brave. What did Septon say about the Order?" she asked.

"That there are other objects to protect—namely Excalibur." He shook his head. "I want nothing to do with that or anything else the Order sticks its nose in."

"Can you leave the Order once you've joined?" she asked.

"Septon says I will always be welcome, particularly since I'm a descendant."

"You're Gideon the Worthy," she said with a dazzling smile that made his heart somersault.

"He tried to persuade me to join the governing council. Can you imagine?"

"Yes, I *can* imagine. Of course they would want the man who extinguished this iteration of Camelot to join their highest ranks."

"I hope it's extinguished," Gideon said. The men who'd worked for her father hadn't returned to Ashridge Court, and the few who'd been left behind to guard the estate had eagerly transferred their fealty to Daphne. She hadn't wanted it and had removed them from their posts immediately. "I'm not sure how we can confirm they're gone, because we don't know who else in the Order was following your father."

"Actually, we do. My father's ledger—the one that led me to learn you were once in Camelot. There are a dozen or so other names."

"Excellent. We shall turn that over to Septon immediately and allow him to deal with it." Septon had said the Order would seek to expel anyone who'd followed Foliot. "It won't be our problem any longer." Gideon had made sure Septon understood that. His dealings with the Order, with anything to do with their bloody objectives, were completely over.

"I'm glad." She resumed the movement of her hand along his thigh.

His cock twitched with desire, and he held his breath, waiting for her to wrap her hand around him. When she didn't and instead left the bed, he couldn't help but gape after her. "Where are you going?"

"Just looking for something…" She bent down, and he stared hungrily at the delectable curve of her backside.

When she righted herself, she turned and sauntered toward the bed with a wicked smile.

"Whatever you have planned will have to wait," he growled. "After that display, I've a need to put you on your knees like the other night."

She shivered, her nipples tightening. Holding up his cravat, she said, "I was just going to blindfold you. But we can do that another time." She held her hand out to drop the silk, but he gently clasped her wrist.

"Don't let me interrupt your plans. There's plenty of time for both our fantasies."

She leaned down and kissed him, her lips and tongue exploring him passionately before she drew back. "We have plenty of time for *all* our fantasies. Thank you for making mine come true."

Gideon cupped her head and pulled her down for another kiss. "Thank you for helping me find some again. I love you."

"I love you." Her lips curled into a smile as their mouths met, and it was as if joy were something Gideon could touch and hold in his hand. It was, he realized. She was joy and love and home and family. She was everything.

And he would never let her go.

Thank You

Thank you so much for reading *Captivating the Scoundrel*. I hope you enjoyed it! If you haven't read the other books in the series featuring Cate (Romancing the Earl, book 2), Penn (Lord of Fortune, book 3), and their parents (Lady of Desire, book 1), you won't want to miss their quests for treasure and love as they face off against the Order of the Round Table.

Would you like to know when my next book is available? Sign up for my reader club at http://www.darcyburke.com/readerclub and follow me on social media:

Facebook: http://facebook.com/DarcyBurkeFans
Twitter at @darcyburke
Instagram at darcyburkeauthor
Pinterest at darcyburkewrite

Let's keep in touch! I have two fun Facebook groups:

Darcy's Duchesses for historical readers
Burke's Book Lovers for contemporary readers

I'm also a member of the Jewels of Historical Romance. I hope you'll visit our Facebook group, the Jewels Salon. Read on for links to our Fabulous Firsts collections, two six book anthologies featuring starters for our most beloved series—each set is just 99c!

I hope you'll consider leaving a review at your favorite online vendor or networking site!

Be sure to check out my other historical series, The Untouchables and Secrets and Scandals.

If you like contemporary romance, I hope you'll check out my Ribbon Ridge series available from Avon Impulse, and the continuation of Ribbon Ridge in So Hot.

I appreciate my readers so much. Thank you, thank you, *thank you*.

xoxox,

Darcy

Books by Darcy Burke

Historical Romance

Legendary Rogues

Lady of Desire
Romancing the Earl
Lord of Fortune
Captivating the Scoundrel

The Untouchables

The Forbidden Duke
The Duke of Daring
The Duke of Deception
The Duke of Desire
The Duke of Defiance
The Duke of Danger
The Duke of Ice
The Duke of Ruin
The Duke of Lies
The Duke of Seduction
The Duke of Kisses
The Duke of Distraction

Secrets and Scandals

Her Wicked Ways
His Wicked Heart
To Seduce a Scoundrel
To Love a Thief (a novella)
Never Love a Scoundrel
Scoundrel Ever After

Contemporary Romance
Ribbon Ridge

Where the Heart Is (a prequel novella)
Only in My Dreams
Yours to Hold
When Love Happens
The Idea of You
When We Kiss
You're Still the One

Ribbon Ridge: So Hot

So Good
So Right
So Wrong

Author's Note

I chose to set this story in and near Wales both because of the subject matter and because my grandmother, Selma Rita King Finney was born in Cardiff in 1916. I still have family there and was fortunate enough to visit several years ago. It's a beautiful land with charming people, and while the Welsh language is difficult to pronounce, I find it lovely—probably because I can still hear my great-uncle Alec singing it.

The thirteen treasures of Britain are mythical objects that appear in various legends. They have been used in countless stories and in many ways (Harry Potter's Deathly Hallows are somewhat based on them). I adapted them for the Legendary Rogues series and added the Heart of Llanllwch for purely narrative purposes.

The Order of the Round Table is a completely fictional group, but is based on the myriad secret societies that have existed for centuries. The circle of women healers based at Brue Cottage is also fictional, however Beckery Chapel was real and was the earliest monastic life in Great Britain. They made a fascinating discovery of human remains there from the fifth or early sixth century—Arthur's supposed time. Legend says King Arthur may have visited and so in my story, he did.

Edmund de Valery, Anarawd, and Elidyr are fictional characters as are the documents they produced. St. Gildas, however, was real and he did live as a hermit on

Flat Holm. As for Flat Holm, it is home to a lighthouse, farmhouse, pub, and gift shop and not much else. The note about a man being trapped there is true. That happened just before this story in 1815. Gareth was one of Arthur's knights, but the extension, "the Worthy" is entirely my imagination.

Of course there is no proof that King Arthur, his knights, the Round Table or any of Arthurian legend is real. I'd like to think it's a little bit history, with a dash of embellishment, and a lot of great storytelling.

A note about marriage licenses in this era: a common license was easy to procure within one of the party's parishes provide they could afford to purchase it. If they could not afford it, the banns would be read in church for three consecutive Sundays. The point of licenses and banns was to ensure parties were able to wed—that they were of age and there were no impediments, such as other spouses. Without the handy internet to look up records, you can imagine how easy it might be for people to commit bigamy. In this story, Daphne and Gideon are wed in her parish so he would have been able to purchase a common license for them to wed. However, that license would have required them to wait seven days, which was time this story didn't have to spare. So, with a little bribery, flashing Gideon's "earl card," and some story magic, they wed immediately (and without having to prove Gideon's wife was truly dead).

Praise for Darcy Burke's

Legendary Rogues Series

LADY of DESIRE

"A fast-paced mixture of adventure and romance, very much in the mould of *Romancing the Stone* or *Indiana Jones*."

-All About Romance

"...gave me such a book hangover! ...addictive...one of the most entertaining stories I've read this year!"

-Adria's Romance Reviews

ROMANCING the EARL

"Once again Darcy Burke takes an interesting story and...turns it into magic. An exceptionally well-written book."

-Bodice Rippers, Femme Fatale, and Fantasy

"...A fast paced story that was exciting and interesting. This is a definite must add to your book lists!"

-Kilts and Swords

LORD of FORTUNE

"I don't think I know enough superlatives to describe this book! It is wonderfully, magically delicious. It sucked me in from the very first sentence and didn't turn me loose—not even at the end ..."

-Flippin Pages

"If you love a deep, passionate romance with a bit of mystery, then this is the book for you!"

-Teatime and Books

Secrets & Scandals Series

HER WICKED WAYS

"A bad girl heroine steals both the show and a highwayman's heart in Darcy Burke's deliciously wicked debut."

—Courtney Milan, *NYT* Bestselling Author

HIS WICKED HEART

"Intense and intriguing. Cinderella meets *Fight Club* in a historical romance packed with passion, action and secrets."

—Anna Campbell, *Seven Nights in a Rogue's Bed*

TO SEDUCE A SCOUNDREL

"Darcy Burke pulls no punches with this sexy, romantic page-turner. Sevrin and Philippa's story grabs you from the first scene and doesn't let go. To Seduce a Scoundrel is simply delicious!"

—Tessa Dare, *NYT* Bestselling Author

TO LOVE A THIEF

"With refreshing circumstances surrounding both the hero and the heroine, a nice little mystery, and a touch of heat, this novella was a perfect way to pass the day."

—The Romanceaholic

NEVER LOVE A SCOUNDREL

"A nice mix of intrigue and passion...wonderfully complex characters, with flaws and quirks that will draw you in and steal your heart."

—BookTrib

SCOUNDREL EVER AFTER

"There is something so delicious about a bad boy, no matter what era he is from, and Ethan was definitely delicious."

-A Lust for Reading

The Untouchables Series

THE FORBIDDEN DUKE

"I LOVED this story!!" 5 Stars

-Historical Romance Lover

"This is a wonderful read and I can't wait to see what comes next in this amazing series..." 5 Stars

-Teatime and Books

THE DUKE of DARING

"An unconventional beauty set on life as a spinster meets the one man who might change her mind, only to find his painful past makes it impossible to love. A wonderfully emotional journey from attraction, to friendship, to a love that conquers all."

-Bronwen Evans, USA Today Bestselling Author

THE DUKE of DECEPTION

"...an enjoyable, well-paced story ... Ned and Aquilla are an engaging, well-matched couple – strong, caring and compassionate; and ...it's easy to believe that they will continue to be happy together long after the book is ended."

-All About Romance

"This is my favorite so far in the series! They had chemistry from the moment they met...their passion leaps off the pages."

-Sassy Book Lover

THE DUKE of DESIRE

"Masterfully written with great characterization...with a flourish toward characters, secrets, and romance... Must read addition to "The Untouchables" series!"

-My Book Addiction and More

"If you are looking for a truly endearing story about two people who take the path least travelled to find the other, with a side of 'YAH THAT'S HOT!' then this book is absolutely for you!"

-The Reading Cafe

THE DUKE of DEFIANCE

"This story was so beautifully written, and it hooked me from page one. I couldn't put the book down and just had to read it in one sitting even though it meant reading into the wee hours of the morning."

-Buried Under Romance

"I loved the Duke of Defiance! This is the kind of book you hate when it is over and I had to make myself stop reading just so I wouldn't have to leave the fun of Knighton's (aka Bran) and Joanna's story!"

-Behind Closed Doors Book Review

THE DUKE of DANGER

"The sparks fly between them right from the start... the HEA is certainly very hard-won, and well-deserved."

-All About Romance

"Another book hangover by Darcy! Every time I pick a favorite in this series, she tops it. The ending was perfect and made me want more."

-Sassy Book Lover

THE DUKE of ICE

"Each book gets better and better, and this novel was no exception. I think this one may be my fave yet! 5 out 5 for this reader!"

-Front Porch Romance

"An incredibly emotional story...I dare anyone to stop reading once the second half gets under way because this is intense!"

-Buried Under Romance

THE DUKE of RUIN

"This is a fast paced novel that held me until the last page."

-Guilty Pleasures Book Reviews

" ...everything I could ask for in a historical romance... impossible to stop reading."

-The Bookish Sisters

THE DUKE of LIES

"THE DUKE OF LIES is a work of genius! The characters are wonderfully complex, engaging; there is much mystery, and so many, many lies from so many people; I couldn't wait to see it all uncovered."

-Buried Under Romance

"..the epitome of romantic [with]...a bit of danger/action. The main characters are mature, fierce, passionate, and full of surprises. If you are a hopeless romantic and you love reading stories that'll leave you feeling like you're walking on clouds then you need to read this book or maybe even this entire series."

-The Bookish Sisters

Ribbon Ridge Series

A contemporary family saga featuring the Archer family of sextuplets who return to their small Oregon wine country town to confront tragedy and find love...

The "multilayered plot keeps readers invested in the story line, and the explicit sensuality adds to the excitement that will have readers craving the next Ribbon Ridge offering."
    -Library Journal Starred Review on YOURS TO HOLD

"Darcy Burke writes a uniquely touching and heart-warming series about the love, pain, and joys of family as well as the love that feeds your soul when you meet "the one."
                            -The Many Faces of Romance

I can't tell you how much I love this series. Each book gets better and better.

                            -Romancing the Readers

"Darcy Burke's Ribbon Ridge series is one of my all-time favorites. Fall in love with the Archer family, I know I did."
                            -Forever Book Lover

Ribbon Ridge: So Hot

SO GOOD

" ...worth the read with its well-written words, beautiful descriptions, and likeable characters...they are flirty, sexy and a match made in wine heaven."

-Harlequin Junkie Top Pick

"I absolutely love the characters in this book and the families. I honestly could not put it down and finished it in a day."

-Chin Up Mom

SO RIGHT

"This is another great story by Darcy Burke. Painting pictures with her words that make you want to sit and stare at them for hours. I love the banter between the characters and the general sense of fun and friendliness."

-The Ardent Reader

" ...the romance is emotional; the characters are spirited and passionate... "

-The Reading Café

SO WRONG

"As usual, Ms. Burke brings you fun characters and witty banter in this sweet hometown series. I loved the dance between Crystal and Jamie as they fought their attraction."

-The Many Faces of Romance

"I really love both this series and the Ribbon Ridge series from Darcy Burke. She has this way of taking your heart and ripping it right out of your chest one second and then the next you are laughing at something the characters are doing."

-Romancing the Readers

About the Author

Darcy Burke is the USA Today Bestselling Author of hot, action-packed historical and sexy, emotional contemporary romance. Darcy wrote her first book at age 11, a happily ever after about a swan addicted to magic and the female swan who loved him, with exceedingly poor illustrations.

A native Oregonian, Darcy lives on the edge of wine country with her guitar-strumming husband, their two hilarious kids who seem to have inherited the writing gene. They're a crazy cat family with two Bengal cats, a small, fame-seeking cat named after a fruit, and an older rescue Maine Coon who is the master of chill and five a.m. serenading. In her "spare" time Darcy is a serial volunteer enrolled in a 12-step program where one learns to say "no," but she keeps having to start over. Her happy places are Disneyland and Labor Day weekend at the Gorge. Visit Darcy online at http://www.darcyburke.com and sign up for her newsletter, follow her on Twitter at http://twitter.com/darcyburke, or like her Facebook page, http://www.facebook.com/darcyburkefans.